LORD OF THE NIGHT

The Hive World Equixus is a place of darkness and ice. Bereft of the sun, huddled in the corridors of their anthill-home, its citizens cower and pray to their God-Emperor for blessings and mercies...

Amidst the squalor Interrogator Mita Ashyn struggles to prove herself worthy of her master, employing her psychic talents in the name of the Holy Inquisition despite the revulsion and suspicion of those around her...

And, skulking in the shadows, something new has come to Equixus: an ancient force fuelled by dark purposes and bleak intentions. Before its unholy rampage is over the city will tremble at the feel of its claws, the empires of the Underhive will rise against their overlords, and in the endless darkness a battle will be fought to determine once and for all who is the Lord of the Night...

Also by Simon Spurrier

FIRE WARRIOR

More storming action from the grim darkness of Warhammer 40,000

• GAUNT'S GHOSTS •

The Founding

FIRST AND ONLY by Dan Abnett
GHOSTMAKER by Dan Abnett
NECROPOLIS by Dan Abnett

The Saint

HONOUR GUARD by Dan Abnett
THE GUNS OF TANITH by Dan Abnett
STRAIGHT SILVER by Dan Abnett
SABBAT MARTYR by Dan Abnett

The Lost

TRAITOR GENERAL by Dan Abnett

• SPACE WOLF •

SPACE WOLF by William King
RAGNAR'S CLAW by William King
GREY HUNTER by William King
WOLFBLADE by William King

• CIAPHAS CAIN •

FOR THE EMPEROR by Sandy Mitchell
CAVES OF ICE by Sandy Mitchell
THE TRAITOR'S HAND by Sandy Mitchell

• THE SOUL DRINKERS •

SOUL DRINKER by Ben Counter
THE BLEEDING CHALICE by Ben Counter
CRIMSON TEARS by Ben Counter

A WARHAMMER 40,000 NOVEL

LORD OF THE NIGHT

Simon Spurrier

A BLACK LIBRARY PUBLICATION

First published in Great Britain in 2005 by
BL Publishing,
Games Workshop Ltd.,
Willow Road, Nottingham,
NG7 2WS, UK.

10 9 8 7 6 5 4 3 2

Cover illustration by Scott Johnson.

A CIP record for this book is available from the British Library.

ISBN 13: 978-1-84416-157-7
ISBN 10: 1-84416-157-9

Distributed in the US by Simon & Schuster
1230 Avenue of the Americas, New York, NY 10020, US.

IT IS THE 41st millennium. For more than a hundred centuries the Emperor has sat immobile on the Golden Throne of Earth. He is the master of mankind by the will of the gods, and master of a million worlds by the might of his inexhaustible armies. He is a rotting carcass writhing invisibly with power from the Dark Age of Technology. He is the Carrion Lord of the Imperium for whom a thousand souls are sacrificed every day, so that he may never truly die.

YET EVEN IN his deathless state, the Emperor continues his eternal vigilance. Mighty battlefleets cross the daemon-infested miasma of the warp, the only route between distant stars, their way lit by the Astronomican, the psychic manifestation of the Emperor's will. Vast armies give battle in his name on uncounted worlds. Greatest amongst his soldiers are the Adeptus Astartes, the Space Marines, bio-engineered super-warriors. Their comrades in arms are legion: the Imperial Guard and countless planetary defence forces, the ever-vigilant Inquisition and the tech-priests of the Adeptus Mechanicus to name only a few. But for all their multitudes, they are barely enough to hold off the ever-present threat from aliens, heretics, mutants – and worse.

TO BE A man in such times is to be one amongst untold billions. It is to live in the cruellest and most bloody regime imaginable. These are the tales of those times. Forget the power of technology and science, for so much has been forgotten, never to be re-learned. Forget the promise of progress and understanding, for in the grim dark future there is only war. There is no peace amongst the stars, only an eternity of carnage and slaughter, and the laughter of thirsting gods.

PART ONE:
PREY

'In human terms, the pursuit requires a most singular talent for empathy. It has long been my observation that the greatest of hunters are those who understand how it feels to be hunted...'

–Lord Devisies Beloch, allegedly the
'SkinRipper' of Pilotr Planus, speaking at
an Inquisitorial tribunal prior to execution.

ZSO SAHAAL

IT WAS NOT a gentle awakening.

In the dark, in the spine of the great shattered vessel that had delivered him, the hunter surfaced from his slumber with a hiss. He gagged on dust-dry lungs, pulled a rattling breath through parched lips, tipped back his head, and screamed.

He had been human, once. Even now, through a haze of time and trauma, he recalled how it had been to awake as a mere man: senses flickering to life, memories accreting, dreams receding like echoes. And all of it without panic, without horror; a shadow-gallery of clumsy, flawed processes for clumsy, flawed creatures.

Not so now. Here in the dark, in the smoke and filth and dirtied snow, such gentle comforts seemed an alien indulgence.

The hunter tore his way to alertness with a feral shriek, and his first thought was this:

It has gone.

Someone has taken it.

The hull was cracked.

Blasted apart where tectonic forces had played along its seams, its frescoed surfaces lay lacerated; ragged edges gathering forests of icicles. Beyond the fissures the night swarmed with snow: thick eddies undulating like the surface of an inverted ocean. Lightning flickered in the distance, shooting long shadows across the huge vessel's broken corridors.

The hunter scrambled from the crippled hull without pause, casting out his senses, seeking movement. To his nocturnal eyes the ship was an empty city: a landscape of broken towers and plateaux brimming with snow, cocooned by a curtain of ice

Locating the thieves required little effort. Picking their cautious way along the ship's surface, each inelegant footstep was a thunder-strike in his ears. Protected from the weather by shaggy overcoats, eyes made beady and black by crude snow-goggles, they seemed to the hunter reminiscent of ancient primates: grizzled ape-things investigating a hulk from the stars. He, then, was a demigod hunting monkeys.

The fools. The *thieves*.

They had *taken* it.

They were hurrying, he saw. Perhaps they'd heard his waking scream; perhaps they recognised they were not alone on the ship carcass they'd plundered. Their terror was gratifying, and as he stalked them the hunter ululated once more: a whoop of mingled anger and excitement. He soared across the uneven sprawl of the forward decks with disdainful ease, spring-locked feet barely touching the pitted hull, and swooped to find cover in the shadows of a collapsed buttress. From there, shielded, he could watch his prey, slipping and stumbling, reacting with comical horror to the wind-borne screech.

There were twelve. Ten carried weapons: spindly rifles with torches slung underneath; puddles of light that picked their way down the craft's broken flanks.

The hunter needed no torch.

The remaining two, he saw, carried the group's prize: a sheet of shrapnel forming an improvised stretcher, piled high with plunder. Useless gewgaws, mostly, handfuls of intestinal cabling, chunks of technology ripped from rune-daubed panels. He was too distant to make out the blocky shape he'd been seeking amongst the haul – that sacred item whose theft he would sooner die than permit – but it was certainly there, in amongst the loot. He could *feel* it...

He scuttled vertically like some great spider, rising along the filigree of a command tower, blue-black limbs impelled by silent streams of heated air; oozing from his back in shimmering ribbons. A single bound – legs pulled up close to his chest, arms outstretched – and he sailed above his oblivious quarry, landing upon the barrel of a crippled cannon, its segments arching in rib-like curves above the broken deck. Settling, glutted with the exhilaration of flight, he hunched on all fours and threw back his head to howl once again, a gargoyle wreathed in snow and night.

To the preythings, the clumsy thieves with their guns and lights, the cry must have seemed to have come from everywhere at once; a voice on the cusp of the snowstorm.

Their careful progress collapsed.

Several dropped their weapons and started to run, voices swallowed by the wind. Slipping on icy metal, they went bolting and crying into the dark, scattering across the endless contours of the vast wreckage.

The hunter smiled, enjoying their disarray. Deep within ornate greaves and spine-tipped segments of armour his muscles bunched and flexed, legs propelling him out into the swirling void, ancient technology holding him aloft.

He took the first two – stragglers – as they stumbled along the crest of a propulsion exhaust, hooking his talons through the first's shoulders. Pinned against the splintered metal of a vertical plate, eyes bulging, the thief barely had time to moan before a casual flick removed head from body, arterial paste bright against the ruffled white of his furs.

The second man cast a curious glance over his shoulder and tripped; gagging at the shape picked out in his torchlight. Hunched over his first victim's body, the hunter cocked his head like an eagle, baleful eyes glowing, and scissored his claws together.

'E-emperor...' the thief gurgled, feet skidding on the icy hull, gun tumbling from his grip. 'Emperor preserve...'

The hunter was on him without appearing to move: long blades punching through the man's arms, pinioning him like a butterfly to a page. And slowly, revelling in his captive's panicked moans, the hunter brought his face down and whispered through the settling snow, voice cracked and distorted by voxcaster static.

'Scream for me.'

The others were simple, after that.

Haunted by their comrade's dying shrieks, any vestiges of an orderly retreat were extinguished. Fighting to flee whatever nightmare stalked them, they barely noticed that they were separating out, losing their way. He picked them off one by one with impunity – these panicking fools, these nothing-men – eagerly acquainting them with the force of his anger.

They had *stolen* it. Stolen from *him*.

He cut them and gloried in their screams. He prolonged their punishments with musical control: a chorus of shrieks to further horrify their comrades. Some he toyed with, slashing sinews and joints; others he ripped apart, snatching up their heads in razor claws and pitching them at the survivors, knocking them down like players in some grisly sport. He was a whirlwind of vengeance, a dervish-fury that cut through the scum with the contempt their theft deserved.

Unseen, unheard, he sculpted their fears and stoked their imaginations. With no idea what monster was amongst them their minds conjured possibilities more horrific than even *he* could hope to inflict.

And then only three remained – those that had kept their senses about them – and he clawed his way along the outcroppings of a shattered bulkhead to watch them from above, to decide how they would die.

Two were the litter carriers, he saw, still struggling to bear their plunder. The third – a larger figure with a malformed bulge on his shoulders – guided them, his gun trained on their backs, supplanting their fear with the far more immediate threat of extinction. A large electoo – a spiral dissected by a stylised bolt of lightning – shimmered at the centre of his forehead: a crude symbol of authority.

A leader, then. Some avarice-riddled fool, more intent on preserving the fortune he'd looted than on preserving his own life. The hunter hissed to himself, happy to oblige.

He cast his nocturnal gaze through the morass of broken hullplates and smoking wreckage, sighting along the path his prey were taking, pondering the possibilities of an ambush. And then panic assailed him.

From here the full extent of the massive vessel's calamitous impact was clear to see. At its beak-like prow, now blunted and smoothed to a sheen by the heat of its descent, it had clawed a scarred wedge of rock from the ground; an ethereal fist lashing at the earth. And there, hidden by curtains of dirty smoke at the edge of the crater, waited a transport. Old and decrepit-looking, for sure, striated with rusty lesions and labelled, bewilderingly, '*TEQO*' in patchy glopaint, it was sleekly built nonetheless. If the thieves could reach it they would escape beyond even the hunter's ability to pursue.

Fighting nascent anxiety, digging talons into the buckled metal of his perch, the hunter howled into the shadows and leapt again. His leaps carried him in graceful arcs from roost to roost, gripping verticals and platforms for instants before relaunching, clawing his way along the spires and toppled towers of the ruined craft. For a moment the storm intensified, thick flurries masking the prey's clumsy progress, and the hunter worked his way through the squall with reckless abandon: body flattened, gracile armour cutting the air, jump pack spluttering. When at last the whiteout cleared he sought a vantage point, racing along the promontory of a collapsed sensor turret, and glared out towards the transport.

They were almost there. Clambering down from the edge of the prow, the thieves stood scant metres from their salvation, lifting their loot-stretcher with renewed vigour. The hunchbacked leader outpaced the two carriers and scrambled up the crater wall, swinging himself into the waiting vehicle's cockpit to start its engine. Even through the storm the hunter could hear the machine's growl, could taste the stink of its fuel. He launched himself one final time, overexerted muscles triggering cunning devices within his armour, pumping a slick of combat-stimms into his blood. He shivered with the rush of adrenaline that followed, watching the ground streak past below: a forest of crippled decks giving way to deep, endless grey. Snow by night.

The litter-bearers reached the crater-edge and hefted their burden onto their backs, steeling themselves for the awkward climb. The first hooked a glove into the broken rock and turned, nodding at his comrade, then scowled with a grunt of surprise as something tugged at his arm…

…which was no longer there.

Blood geysered across virgin snow and the stretcher collapsed to the floor, stolen treasures tumbling across the frost. Behind the man, steam rising from leering grille-ventilator, the hunter hissed and brandished the severed arm. He relished the growing fear, exulting in the horror written across these two fools' faces. The merest shrug and the first's heart was punctured, ribs incised like butter. The other ran; blindly, stupidly, away from the crater edge and into heavy snow, stumbling on a drift. The hunter hopped, vulture-like, onto his back, claws plucking at his flesh, and placed a taloned foot upon his head.

There was something pleasantly percussive in the crackling that followed.

Above him, beyond the caldera of the crash site, the transport pulled away. The hunter tensed to pursue – the stimm boiling in his blood; crying out for more carnage, more terminal justice for the insult of the theft – but paused to reconsider. The haul of stolen goods had been reclaimed – scattered across the snow between its bearers' bodies – and he could not simply leave it where it lay on the flimsy promise of one last kill.

Breathing heavily, trying his best to regain calmness in spite of the stimm, he turned to the discarded loot and began to search. The claws of his fists – sabre-like protrusions that dripped whorls of vibrant scarlet across the snow – retracted into patterned grooves with a silken rasp, pulling back to reveal gloved fingers beneath. On his knees, flicking aside the crumpled items of useless technology that had caught the thieves' eyes, he rummaged first in the weapons crates, fingering ornate bolters and shell clips, tapping at grenades, scavenging through packaging with increasing frustration. His search intensified: overturning crates, emptying priceless baubles and ancient technologies across the ice, breath accelerating with each moment.

The suspicion stole over him by degrees – a protracted wave of horror and shame – and he suppressed it over and over, pushing it down into his guts.

He couldn't fool himself forever.

'No!' he roared, claws snickering from their sockets like lightning, slicing through crates and gunmetal barrels, weaving a flickering storm across snow and earth. 'It's not here! It's not *here*!'

The quickening effects of the stimm lasted half an hour, and when his rages and screams were all spent, when the bodies of the men he'd killed could be diced no further, when his claws steamed with bloody red vapour, when finally his mind cleared of the drughaze and began – at last – to awaken fully, only *then* did he think of the thieves' leader. The one that he had allowed to escape. The hunchback.

Or perhaps not a hunchback at all. Perhaps a man carrying a package securely beneath his furs, strapped across his broad shoulders.

Cheated, the hunter slumped to the snow and breathed icy air. Recollections filtered into him, delayed consciousness worked its bitter way through the dying embers of the rage, and piece by piece he accumulated the fragments of who he was. This second stirring, this fattening package of personality and past, stole over him in quiet degrees: a far more *human* awakening than the first.

His name was Zso Sahaal, the Talonmaster, the heir to the Corona Nox, and he had rescinded his humanity a long time before.

MEMORIES ASSAILED HIM: fragmentary and nonsensical. He gripped them as they rushed by, struggling to remember.

There had been a death.

That was how it began: an assassination and a power vacuum.

He remembered the promise that had been made to him: the legacy he was granted, the sacred vows he swore. He'd accepted a holy duty without hesitation, and at the moment of his ascension had stretched out a willing hand to receive it.

The Corona Nox had been his. Briefly.

There had been complications. There had been interventions. *Alien* interventions.

He remembered, through the riot of chattering bolters and screaming voices, in the rush of a psychic storm, the xenos. He remembered the pain and the confusion. He remembered the burning enemy, that brittle fiend, bright helm arched and antlered, staff banishing every shadow to extinction.

He remembered fleeing. He remembered the trap. He remembered the fissure in the fabric of nothing, sucking him down, swallowing him whole.

He had been caged within a timeless prison, and without hope of escape he had emptied his mind and slept. He'd stumbled through endless dreams, grappled with nightmares, and–

–and had awoken to discover the Corona gone.

The leader, yes. The so-called hunchback. *He* had taken it.

AN HOUR LATER, Zso Sahaal stood at the edge of the wreckage and regarded his vessel, the *Umbrea Insidior*, with a wistful eye.

The last time he'd admired her exterior had been from the cramped cockpit of a shuttle, rising towards her from the surface of Tsagualsa, on the eve of his final mission. Even then, gnawed at by impatience, he'd paused to admire her savage form. Artfully decorated in banks of ebony and blue, picked-through with bronze, her towers and minarets endowed upon her an almost ornate fragility.

It was, of course, an illusion.

Vulture-beaked and weapon-pocked, her generariums hulked from her stern like the head of a mallet, cannons decorating the hammer's grip with all the organic tenacity of barnacles upon a whale. Here and there her changing fortunes were transcribed in scars and healed abrasions; all the arts of the Adeptus Mechanicus focused upon improvement, strength, power. More obvious still were the revisions to her structure made by her latest masters: blades and icons arching from her pitted hull, intricate designs dappling her iron snout, stylised arcs of gauss lightning painted in harsh whorls across the darkness of her intricate surfaces.

She had been a strike cruiser, once. Fast and vicious, a fitting chariot for the mission he'd boarded her to fulfil. A vessel worthy of his captaincy.

And now?

Now she was a broken hag. Crooked ribs slumped from fractured expanses. Crevices gaped like whip-wounds where conflicting pressures had buckled and pierced her hull. Her great spine was broken, crumpled across half a kilometre of steaming waste. Her beak had been thrust with such violence into the earth that her flanks had snapped, reactors sagging then pitching up and outwards, shearing vicious rents before detonating; their colossal energies vaporising what little substance had survived the atmosphere's passage.

Sahaal could barely imagine the calamitous impact. Were it not for the evidence of his own eyes – this pitiful thing smeared like metal paste across the ice – he would have doubted that such a vessel as the *Umbrea Insidior* could be brought so low.

Oh, how the mighty are fallen... Where had he heard that before?

It hardly mattered, now. There were more important things to consider. Priorities.

Pursuits.

There were no other survivors – of that he was certain. His inspection of the central corridors revealed nothing but dry bones and ancient fabrics: all that remained of the vassals that had crewed this once-proud ship. Now all as dead as she, and for a good deal longer. Sifting through storerooms, kicking aside mournful skulls, Sahaal began to wonder just how long had passed since his imprisonment began. Had his servants withered and grown old as he slept, as ageless as gold? Had they fallen to dust and ash around him, mayflies around a statue, or had they perhaps taken their own lives, forgoing the tedium of confinement for a swift, bloody release?

Again, he diverted his wondering mind. There would be time for speculation later, once his prize was reclaimed.

In the end his salvage was little better than had been the thieves'. Into a crate he upended as many ammunition clips as he could find, laying an ornate bolter reverentially on top. The looters had missed it when they'd raided the shattered remains of the armoury; never thinking to prise away the mangled sides of the strongbox at the armoury's core, where he had placed it.

It was named *Mordax Tenebrae* – the Dark's Bite. It had been hand crafted on Nostromo Quintus and was, in any material sense, priceless. As Sahaal ran an eye across its familiar stock, its elaborately decorated chambers and skull-mouthed barrel, he found himself wishing that they *had* found it, that they'd stolen *it* in exchange for the one item that he could *not* abide to lose – the very item that had been taken.

It was an impressive weapon, certainly, and he'd maintained it with the respect its magnificence demanded. It had been a gift from his master, and such was his devotion that had it been a knife or a book or a lump of rock, he would have cherished it with an equal fervour. But still, but still…

Like any gun, like any crude projectile-vomiting apparatus, he thought it a clumsy tool: a thing of noise and desperation, of smoke and flame. For all its complexity, for all the care and artistry lavished upon it, it would never rival the purity of a blade.

It would never be as vital to him as the Corona Nox.

Into the crate it went, and along with a scattering of what random munitions and grenades he could find, and a rack of fuelcells for his armour, he took just one last item: a heavy rectangular package, stolen from the wreck's remaining generarium, glowing with a pestilent green tinge. This he loaded carefully between layers of foam, acknowledging that sometimes the precision of a blade would never be enough.

The crate hissed as he depressed its sealing rune, and as he gripped its iron handle he reflected that in another time such an ignoble thing as carrying luggage would have been unthinkable; the remit of the numberless slaves that tended to his every desire.

How the mighty are fallen... A simple phrase, whispering through his mind for a second time, like the ghost of an echo. He realised with a start that it was his master's voice he'd remembered, and with crystal clarity recalled the time, the circumstance, the sentiment.

It had been on Tsagualsa. On Tsagualsa, before the killer came. Gazing into the night, brows beetling together, ancient eyes clouded, Sahaal's lord had turned to him and smiled, and said those words, and in his voice Sahaal could taste his disposition.

Troubled. Bitter. Betrayed. *Haunted.*

'We shall be mighty yet,' Sahaal promised, words lost to the driving snow, fist clenched against his heart.

Lifting the crate to his side, he set his sights upon the faint shadows of the transporter's tracks, took one last glance at the *Umbrea Insidior*, and leapt into the night.

MITA ASHYN

IT WAS LESS an awakening than a rebirth.

Always it was like this, after the trance. Always she allowed the subtle skeins of perception and concept to break free from her focus, shifting her mind state from some inner vantage to the mundane outer realities, the province of conventional sense and thought.

She returned to her corporeal self like an eagle resuming its eyrie, breathing honeyed incense and enjoying the slow trickle of physical sensation. It felt like blood flowing through starved arteries.

In the Scholastia Psykana she'd learnt to call this the *pater donum*: the brief flush of warmth and contentment that followed a scrying trance, like a reward from the Emperor's own hand. She allowed it to work its way along each limb, curling her toes and arching her back.

Relish it, the adept-tutors had taught. Enjoy it whilst it lasts. It was, after all, the single facet of telepathy that justified the term 'gift' where all others equated more accurately to the symptoms of a curse.

The *pater donum* would not last. It would be gone in an instant, and at that unhappy moment all the fierce memories of the trance would crash inwards to drown her.

She opened her eyes, focused on the single guttering candle at the centre of the scrying-ring, and allowed the sludge of recollection to break through.

Her first thought was this:

Something has fallen from heaven.

THE MEDITATION CELL was a simple affair.

Four rockcrete walls arched overhead, sloping together to form a crude dome with a needle of bronze at its core: a conduction point for the astral body. Gone were the scriptures picked out in gold and opal across each wall, gone were the stylised star charts and mantras patterning the seer-dome, gone were the great twisting shelves of chittering incense drones. Such comforts she'd left behind on the fortress-world Safaur-Inquis, and this spartan cube was as far removed from the decadence she'd come to expect as it could be. She supposed she should be grateful for anything at all, given the indifference her new master had showed her, but still... there were limits.

A withered servitor – once human, long since lobotomised, dissected, infested with logic engines and clattering components – poked a stunted limb against her shoulder, its one rheumy eye fluttering spastically. It tried to talk, but the rune-etched staples through its lips and jaw allowed little more than a moist clucking; a long strand of drool wobbling from its chin.

On Safaur, her trance-awakenings had been tended by gentle servants: smooth-skinned subordinates with tongues neatly removed and ownership studs across each eye, hurrying to mop her sweat and massage her shoulders, lovingly recording on scented parchment whatever insights the meditation bestowed. On Safaur her trance-suite flocked with locust-like automata: emeralds for eyes and rubies for jaws, coloured streamers of psychoactive pheromones falling like musk from their tails. On Safaur a dozen cogitators existed solely to interpret her visions. On Safaur the majesty of her quarters was matched only by the view from her central garret, and between assignments she spent hours gazing across the acid shores of the sulphur seas. On the Inquisitorial fortress-world of Safaur-Inquis, her masters wielded their influence with artistry and opulence.

Her present circumstance was therefore somewhat galling.

Here, a one-armed man/machine with a techstylus and a snot-clogged nose was the best the governor's chamberlain could provide. It poked her again, marking her naked skin with a moronic stripe of ink before leaning away, eye rolling. Above it a faulty servodrone corkscrewed erratically across the ceiling, oozing incense. It bashed against the wall with depressing regularity, and she found herself unconsciously counting along – *tap-tap-tap* – like the beating of a plastic heart.

Anything to distract her from the memories.

But no, the warm pleasure of the *pater donum* had passed, the details of this dull little chamber had ceased to offer any but the most rudimentary of diversions, and the growing pressure behind her eyes couldn't be contained indefinitely. Sighing, she pulled a simple robe across her shoulders, clenched her jaw, snuffed out the candle and focused on the details of the trance, still burning bright in her mind.

'Record.' she commanded, waving a hand. The servitor straightened, stylus poised on the fluttering surface of an augur-slate, clucking its readiness.

'There follows the account,' she began formally, ignoring the whispering of the servitor's joints, 'of the *furor arcanum* undertaken in the Emperor's name on this day – date it – by I, interrogator primus of the retinue of Inquisitor Kaustus, on Imperial hive-world Equixus. In service of the most blessed Inquisition and in fealty to his Holiness the Emperor of Man, I attest upon my immortal soul to the provenance of this account, and swear upon its veracity – may my lord else strike me down.' She drew a breath, shivering at the cold. 'Blessings be upon His Throne and dominion. *Ave imperator.*'

She watched as the servitor scrawled the dedication with a mechanical twitch, scrolling the data-slate onto a clean line. She took a moment to compose herself, pursed her lips, then continued.

'For the third time – refer to prior reports – the trance began with the sensation of... altitude.' She closed her eyes and remembered the cold, the dizzying sensation of an abyssal nothingness gaping on every side, ice forming on her skin. She immersed herself in the memory and continued to speak, applying the recall techniques she'd been taught since an early age. 'I... I felt as though I was standing at a great height,' she said, 'and all around me the ground rushed away like the sides of a mountain. Except... a mountain made of metal. I couldn't see anything – there was too much snow – but I knew that if I stepped too far in any direction I'd fall. I'd fall and never stop falling, all the way down to a... a deep darkness, where no light ever shines. I couldn't see it, but... I knew it was there. I could feel it.

'There was a moment of nausea – though…' She half smiled, childishly proud,'… though today, for the first time, I did not vomit.

'It seemed to me, then, that something was drawing near, pushing through the snow, and though I was scared I stood my ground…' She chewed a lip, brows dipping. 'Perhaps I feared the drop more than I feared the approaching presence, I… I don't know. During previous trances I've awoken at this point and my efforts to divine further details have been frustrated. Today I… persisted. I'm certain I caught a glimpse of the… the *presence* in the snow, which has eluded me until now.

'It seemed to be myself.'

She glanced up, aware of how ridiculous the sentiment sounded. If the servitor was even capable of such judgement it gave no indication of it, awaiting her next words with the same dumb focus as before. She tried to relax, reminding herself that the interpretations of the *furor arcanum* were never straightforward, and that the libraries of the Scholastia Psykana were filled with validated predictions that had arisen from the most preposterous of trance-visions.

Still she hesitated, disturbed by the vividness of the dream.

'It was me, but… but I looked different. My hair was cut short and I wore rags, and… there was blood on my face. One of… oh, *Throne*… one of my arms was gone. Bleeding like a fountain… I was trying to say something but the wind was too strong and I… I couldn't hear, and that's when I saw… I…

'I was being carried. In the air, like… flying. I tried to see what was holding me but it was covered by the snow and there was… there was a shadow over its face.'

She was vaguely aware of a tear slipping down her cheek, and distantly – surreally – wondered why it was there. What did it mean?

The words came in a jumble now, refusing to stop, and she felt herself caught up in the same fearful horror as during the trance itself, tumbling and screaming and freezing, all at once.

'I looked into it… the shadow, I mean… and it was like I was falling, straight through the snow towards the ground, and… and something was chasing me, burning me from behind my eyes… Emperor preserve me, it was a pregnant hag – the size of a city – rushing down from the stars… a-and… and she hit the snow and… *ohhh…* her bones broke and her belly split and…

'…and darkness crawled out from her womb.'

She forced open her eyes long enough to check that the servitor had recorded every word. It watched her without comment or movement, fully prepared to wait forever for her next command.

Sighing, Interrogator Mita Ashyn of the Ordo Xenos allowed herself the indulgence of slipping into a deep, exhausted faint.

'AH, INTERROGATOR.'

'My lord.' Mita bowed formally, keeping her eyes lowered. She hadn't yet grown accustomed to her new master's idiosyncrasies, but had learned quickly that his legendary temper was deployed far more readily amongst those who failed to show the proper obeisance. Given that he insisted upon wearing a mirror-helm with only the narrowest of eyeslits, it was perhaps unfortunate that any interested glance towards his surreal headgear was mistaken for disrespect, which of course invited the full force of his wrath.

Inquisitor Kaustus was not a man to cross lightly.

Mita considered herself relatively safe, just as long as she occupied her view with the tails of his chequered robes and the heavy soles of his armoured feet, rather than his feather-mantled shoulders and reflective mask.

'Stop that,' he snapped, proving her wrong, his voice curiously soft for such an imposing figure. 'I won't have my acolytes bowing and scraping like common peasants. I'm your master, girl, not your Emperor.'

'Apologies, my lord.' She straightened and adjusted her gaze vertically, oozing penitence. Perhaps *chest height* would be more appropriate.

Behind her, a couple of the innumerable cowled figures that comprised Kaustus's retinue sniggered lightly, amused at her mistake. She forced down the overwhelming desire to break their heads and forced herself to calm. As the newest member of the entourage she'd quickly learned that rank counted for exactly nothing: technically her command was second only to the inquisitor's, but it seemed respect was earned – not demanded – amongst this colourful crowd. As long as Kaustus continued to humiliate her in front of them their respect would continue to be in short supply.

'I've read the account of your vision,' the inquisitor said, voice dripping scorn, waving a spindly datapad across her view. 'You *fainted*.'

'It was... unusually vivid, my lord.'

'I don't care how vivid it was, girl. I'll not tolerate my servants passing out at the drop of hat.'

'It won't happen again, my lord.'

'No. It will not.' The datapad dipped upwards – the inquisitor's gaze roving across its spidery text. 'Your account makes for... *interesting* reading,' he said. 'What does it all mean?'

'I don't know, my lord. There are no cogitators here to deciph–'

'I didn't ask what some Emperor-damned *machine* would make of it, girl! I asked what *you* think.'

She swallowed, resisting the urge to meet his gaze. Here, in the splendour of his guest suite at the heart of the governor's palace, he was as terrible and magnificent a figure as the legends made claim.

'Well?'

'I... I think something is coming, my lord. Coming here, I mean.'

'"Something". Is that the best you can do?'

She bristled, fists clenching at her sides, struggling to keep the bitterness from her voice. 'Something from the stars, then. Something massive. S-something dark.'

For a moment there was silence. Dust motes circulated through the hard beam of a hovering illuminator, and at the periphery of her vision Mita could see the retinue shuffling its collective feet. Had her words struck a chord?

Kaustus shattered both the silence and her hopes with one deft exclamation.

'Emperor's blood!' he boomed, voice heavy with sarcasm, 'such *detail*! How did I ever cope without a witch at my side?'

Predictably the room exploded, acolytes and cowled disciples venting their sycophantic amusement in gales of laughter. Willing herself not to blush – unsuccessfully – Mita supposed she couldn't blame them. In shared cruelty lay acceptance, a bitter lesson she'd been slow to grasp.

For an instant she found herself hating them. Hating *him*, even; reviling her own master like some undisciplined child... But such thoughts were the gatestones at the head of a dangerous path, and her entire life had been spent studying to ward off such heretical temptations. She willed herself to relax, bore the humiliation with good grace–

–and dug her fingernails so far into the flesh of her palms that blood oozed between her knuckles.

'Enough.'

Kaustus silenced the laughter, tossing aside the data-pad like some broken toy, its ability to entertain spent. An abrupt silence gripped the room and he watched the crowd with narrowed eyes, colossal shoulders squared.

'A mission.'

To Mita, bathed unwillingly in a tumult of psychic emissions, the phrase was like an icy wind. She tasted the hungry anticipation of the retinue; all forced amusements forgotten, minds focused and sharp. She gave them their dues: fools they might be, but they were obedient with it.

'Investigation and salvage.' Kaustus cocked his head towards his staff, barking commands. 'Three teams, three transports. Division pattern delta. Now.'

The entourage divided like a machine, three groups forming in short order. Without the benefit of individual familiarity, Mita could nonetheless detect the more obvious distributions of resource: in each group there hulked the cowled form of a combat servitor; in each a medic fussed with triage apparatus and checked chemical proboscis; in each a hooded priest stepped from figure to figure, administering blessings and prayers.

Kaustus had been collecting disciples his entire life, amassing a crew to shame even the most luminary of fellow inquisitors. With a single command the capabilities and specialisms of the whole had been spliced evenly and instantly, without comment or question or flaw. Even to Mita, still smarting from their scorn, it was a display of impressive efficiency.

She struck what she hoped was an authoritative pose – uncomfortably aware that she alone had failed to fall in. If Kaustus had expected her involvement he gave no sign of it, nodding briskly at each group.

'We rendezvous at gate Epsilon-Six in three hours,' he barked. 'Cold-weather gear, night-sight, fully armed. *Dismissed.*'

The retinue filed from the suite without a word, and Mita reflected that for all their variety, for all the many characters and histories contained within the group, they operated with parade-ground efficiency to match even the most elite of the Imperial guard's storm troopers.

She realised with a start that she was the last to leave, and that Kaustus was staring at her, gloved fingers toying elegantly with the cruciform 'I' medallion around his neck. 'Interrogator,' he said, features unreadable. 'You appear to still be here...'

'My lord,' she swallowed, hunting for a diplomatic method of delivering her enquiries, settling eventually for a lame: 'What are we to investigate?'

The anticipated rebuke for her insolence never came. She imagined the man's lips curling behind the mask: the grin of a cat entertained by its struggling prey.

'That's just it, interrogator,' he cooed. 'You already know.'

She frowned. 'My lord?'

'How did you put it? "Something from the heavens... Something massive... Something dark"?'

'I... I'm sorry, my lord, I don't u–'

'You were right. Albeit somewhat *late.*'

'Late?'

'A vessel – a *large* vessel – crash-landed in the ice wastes two hours ago. Given that we were already here, it would seem remiss to not aid in the investigation.'

'But... but...'

'It's not *coming*, interrogator. It's already arrived. Dismissed.'

She marched out in an unthinking haze, and as she stamped towards her dingy cell to prepare, an ugly foreboding twisted in her guts. Her waking revelation returned to her and she winced against the pain.

Something has fallen from heaven.

THROUGH NIGHT-VISION binox – baroque coils of cabling and lenses enveloping her eyes like a hungry kiss – the hive was a flaming steeple.

Peering over her shoulder, shivering despite thick furs, Mita regarded the city-world as the convoy left it behind, swallowed by the horizon like a melting stalagmite. That there were larger hives on worlds less remote couldn't detract from its magnificence: the city's vastness snagged at her eyes, sucking on her attention. Two hundred million souls, crushed together like termites, eking out their blind lives in the belly of a spine-tipped beast.

Most would never see the sky.

It punctured the air like a gnarled knuckle. Cloud-clad and encased in frost, it was an inverted icicle, its uneven surfaces eroded by time and weather, pitted by industry and accented by turrets and spires. Where once the tempests of Equixus had raged undisturbed, now they found themselves incised, gashed apart by this upstart architecture. It drew a thick blood of lightning, auroras boiling into the night, and the splendour of its crackling crown strobe-lit the bleak wastes for kilometres around.

On this, the planet's unlit face – tumbling in perfect synchronicity with the orbital year – it was always dark, and always cold. Against the gloom, factories belched fiery waste and loading bays vented nebulae of ionic pollution. From the upper tiers, above the drudgery of plebeian life, windows bled galaxies of spilled light. In Mita's eyes, with her binox devouring every luminous pinprick, the hive stood against the darkness like a monolith-god, an effigy thick with fire.

More pronounced still was the brightness in the chambers of her mind: in those unseen tendrils of psychic thought that swarmed about her like the arms of an anemone, she could taste the life of the city. Two hundred million souls, each one a guttering candle of psychic light. Each one as fragile as it was bright.

She turned away, briefly dazzled, and focused instead upon the small convoy. There were four transports – converted Salamanders with widened tracks and pintle flashlights – racing across the ice at an alarming speed. Three contained the Inquisitorial retinue – assorted cloaks fluttering as their mass allowed – whilst in the lead vehicle a squad of the local lawmen, the Preafectus Vindictaire, set their helmeted heads against the wind and glared back towards the others, no doubt deriding the interference of outsiders. Officially the Preafectus was an independent body, administrated by the galaxy-spanning Adeptus Arbites, but a certain amount of diplomatic compromise to Imperial officials was customary. Mita suspected that the inquisitor's involvement had been far from sanctioned by the lawmen, though it would be a brave man indeed who denied an offer of assistance from Kaustus.

The man himself shared her portion of the rear vehicle, gazing out from a raised gantry with face and mind equally as shrouded. The Inquisition trained its operatives to shield their minds from psykers with enviable aplomb, and where the other members of the retinue blazed in her sixth sense like lanterns, *his* radiance was shuttered and barred. He stood with arms crossed, as unperturbed by the cold as if still within his suite, and only his fingers – kneading together – belied the impression that he was a statue: some decorous idol draped in fine cloth. She realised without surprise that she still knew all but nothing about him. In the short time she'd spent in his service the one obvious conclusion she'd drawn was this: The legends were wrong.

Inquisitor Kaustus came complete with a reputation as glowing as the nocturnal hive at his back, and exploited it shrewdly. That he had undertaken great deeds, that he had crushed alien heresies throughout the Ultima Segmentum, she did not doubt. But that he had done so with nobility and honour – with *heroism,* no less, as the myths claimed – was harder to digest. Ruthlessness and heroism did not, in her experience, sit well together.

Mita had begun her tenure as an Inquisitorial explicator direct from the Scholastia Psykana on Escastel Sanctus. Selected by her masters, deemed strong enough to resist corruption without recourse to the crippling Soul Binding ceremony required of lesser psykers, she remembered the shadowy recruitment rituals with uncomfortable clarity. Naked and hairless, the young chosen had shivered in subterranean caverns; servitors gliding amongst them, testing, prodding, twitching. She remembered the shame, mingled with secret relief, as one by one the other youths were borne away by the vapid machines, selected from afar by their new masters. They would be scattered amongst the Munitorum offices, she knew, or perhaps deployed by the Administratum, or even – so the whispers went – inducted into the Chapters of the Adeptus Astartes.

No one had warned her there was a fourth possibility.

She was claimed by the Ordo Xenos of the Emperor's divine Inquisition: that most clandestine of societies. She found herself gobbled whole by an organisation with unlimited authority, tasked to stalk the shadows of the Imperium and keep it strong, pure, and holy. Drugged and hooded, she was initiated into a world of secrecy and paranoia at the age of twelve.

At the age of twenty-five she left the fortress-world of Safaur-Inquis to join the retinue of the Inquisitor Petrai Levoix – blessed be her name – and for six years she was... *content.*

In that time she witnessed the scouring of the necron'tyr megaliths on Parson's Moon. She took a hand in the shattering of the *Waaagh-Shalkaz* when she overcame the warlord's puppet-wyrds. She bested the primacii magi of a genestealer insurrection in the Marquand Straits, and broke the mind of the Hruddite Demagogue of the Pleanar campaign. She earned the rank of interrogator at the age of thirty and, in the crucible of the Ylir uprisings, earned a citation from the Congresium Xenos for capturing the song-sword of a slain eldar warlock.

She was making a difference. She was the inquisitor's right hand. She sought – and earned – glory, and the accounts of her deeds ran in fluttering text-ribbons that she twined through her hair. She was *somebody.*

And then a week before her thirty-first birthday her mistress died – stupidly, pointlessly – in a messy crossfire on Erasula IX. And everything changed.

Abruptly she was no one. Abruptly she was less than nothing, and when all the enquiries and refutations were done she found herself reassigned, re-deployed–

–and re-subordinated.

Staring ahead into the driving snow, daring to study her new master's statuesque form in stolen glances, she wondered how long – if ever – it would take her to regain those heady heights of respect. Tasting the ebb and eddy of the retinue's thoughts around her, each one swarming with the desire to impress, to rise to the top, to be *noticed*, she realised with gloomy certainty that it was not going to be easy.

THE CRASH SITE was as chaotic and as desolate as Mita could have imagined. To see a thing so mighty as a spacecraft so utterly ruined was a humbling sight. Already the snow settled across its fractured flukes, only the jutting paraphernalia of its lance arrays and command turrets breaking through the white sheet like the half-submerged bones of a drowned corpse.

For all that it was a mighty thing, its ancient plates and spars were nonetheless imbued with a great sadness – and a great bitterness. If the other members of the retinue shared the empathic shudder she felt as she ran a questing finger across a frosted bulkhead they gave no sign of it, but their search was conducted nonetheless with unusual restraint, like looters invading a mausoleum.

The vindictors barely exchanged a word with their uninvited assistants, clumsily picking their way towards a wound on the vessel's side, powerful torches spilling light as they entered. By contrast the retinue deployed quickly and efficiently, entering jagged orifices on three flanks. As they quested deep inside, like maggots squirming through rotten flesh, they directed terse reports via the shortwave voxcasters each wore. Kaustus received these bursts without comment, wandering across the vessel's surface, content to allow his minions to explore on his behalf.

She fidgeted in his wake, wondering whether she should have taken it upon herself to join the search. Her mind fluttered through awkward quandaries: should she await his command or assert her own authority? Should she seek to impress him with loyalty and obedience, or would a firebrand self-initiative gain his approval? Without any inkling of his temperament or tastes, such actions could easily dictate her success or failure as his highest ranking servant.

Unable to skim his thoughts, denied the view of his facial expressions, she nonetheless had a fair idea that she'd singularly failed in her attempts to impress him thus far.

'Are there survivors?' he asked, fingers kneading together.

'My lord?'

He sighed, hot vapour curling from the dimpled breathing slats of his mask. 'Interrogator, I dislike being answered with questions.'

'But, my lord, I–'

'I was assured by the ordo that your skills would prove invaluable. Are you now suggesting they were incorrect?' He spoke slowly and loudly, voice thick with condescension, and Mita struggled to control her rising hackles.

'N-no my lord, but–'

'Excellent. Then the time has come for you to show me you're here for a reason, don't you think?'

She tried to form an intelligent response, but as ever the options each seemed as lame as each other. She sighed, nodding in defeat. 'Yes.'

'So? Are there any survivors?'

Forcing herself to calm, she closed her eyes to the glowing traceries of the binox view and unfolded her mind, allowing it to seep into the metal of the craft like acid through stone. Immersed in the Empyrean, she tasted the ship's secrets, she learned its ancient name, she swarmed in its chambers, and she drunk its flavours.

SHE FINALLY STOPPED screaming when the inquisitor slapped her, hard, across the cheek.

ZSO SAHAAL

ZSO SAHAAL LEANED out from his sheltered alcove and drew hungry eyes across the structural anarchy around him.

He'd warmed to his new environment quickly – a predator entering fertile hunting grounds – and couldn't resist a secret smile, relishing the darkness. This chequerboard of shadows, this ferrous jungle, this cavity-filled mountain: here he was indomitable.

Unable to pause, fighting urgency and excitement, he quit his nook and bounded across a plungeshaft, dodging chains and cables: a shadow moving through shadows. Rising across vertical gantries, claw-over-claw, he pushed off with his hooked feet to hop between silent elevators, hanging like gibbeted bodies. Voices filtered from passages to either side and he paused, mimicking the ragged fabric of the wall. In a world of such haphazard architecture one more uneven shape, midnight-coloured and indistinct, was unlikely to draw attention. He unsheathed a claw, shivering at its silky emergence, and waited, every muscle tensed.

Thus poised, with every sense racing and alert, his mind found itself free to wander. It seeped into his memory like oil into a sponge, musing upon how he had found himself here: stalking this ancient labyrinth like a panther in the night.

THE PREVIOUS DAY, leaving the *Umbrea Insidior* countless kilometres behind him, he had watched the city appear by degrees on the horizon. For all its enormity he hadn't paused to admire it, or even to catch his breath – bounding ever onwards, tracing what faint evidence of the thief's passing remained.

At one point a phalanx of vehicles streaked nearby, engines broadcasting their approach long before the snow-haze gave them up. Cautious of confrontation, Sahaal merely pushed himself into the snow and watched them pass, ebony eyes tracking them through scarlet eyeslits. He assumed they must be heading for the crash site, and wondered vaguely what manner of personnel had been dispatched, and by whom. He decided eventually that he didn't care: there were a host of such minor questions to be answered, but nothing must divert him from the Corona.

He'd hastened towards the city, finally losing what vestiges of the thief's tracks remained. Staving off anxiety, he told himself the tracks no longer mattered: the scum's destination could hardly be doubted.

The city was, simply, *vast*.

At its uncertain base, where scarred ridges of stone and snow segued with serried ranks of ferrocrete and steel, he'd come to a deep fissure in the earth. Into the cavity iron foundations coiled down into the dark like the rusted roots of a titanic tree, colonised on every expanse by the grinding structures of industry. The rent billowed its fumes like the breath of a devil; a toothless mouth into the scarred ground.

Above it, where the frosted rock sprouted the lowest towers and tiers like mould, a multitude of heavy-doored gates had greeted his eyes: loading bays and vehicle access points, a hundred and one ways to cross from the arctic waste to the cloying darkness within. And every last one was closed, sealed against the cold.

Sahaal had considered his options. That he must enter the hive was without question, but where to begin? Where to hunt the thief? On the cusp of this vast edifice, hunkering amongst the pipes and cogs of its dermis, he found himself assailed by hopelessness. To find one man within all *this*... He might as well search a desert for a single grain of sand, or a galaxy for a single star.

But, no. No, he could not allow himself the luxury of doubt. He must be focused. He must be driven.

He must be *ruthless*.

He'd slipped into the foundation-crevice like a knife between ribs, swallowed by the dark.

AND NOW, A day later – a day of exploring, of haunting the wastes below the city itself, of stalking this endless parade of corridors and tunnels and pits – was he any closer to his prize?

No.

There was no logic to this underhive realm. Where above tiers crested tiers, joined by tapestry-strewn stairwells and columns of elevators, flanked by devotional statues and preachers' pulpits, here there was madness.

Ancient stairways led to nowhere. Tunnels twisted through knotted girders and plastic waste, collecting chemical sludge. Visceral cables spewed from haphazard partitions, coiling away ever upwards into the city. Collapsed tunnels were rebored or circumvented, uphive-sluices opened to vomit acid upon duct-strewn channels, and elevator shafts full of snowmelt rippled and splashed where slime-scaled *things* coiled in the deep. The weight of the hive settled across pillars and posts like an ever-present promise; like a clock counting out the hours until the fall of the sky.

And the people... Cowering in ghettos around scarce resources, these were the hopeless, the useless, the dispossessed. Divided amongst the petty empires of criminal gangs, scavenging in the dark to feast on fungus and beetle-meat – these were not people. They were animals. *Rats*.

In that first day, as he'd slipped through the undercity's heart like a wraith, Sahaal had felt himself sickened. If this was the reward for devotion to the Emperor, he had chosen his side shrewdly.

He returned his mind to the present, focusing all his attention upon the *step-step-step* of his imminently-arriving prey, and unclenched his right hand. At its tip the gauntlet's hooked claws flexed, mirroring the internal movement: a second set of fingers, power-bladed and bloody-red, slaved to the movements of the first. These too had been a gift from his master, whose generosity was as unpredictable and spectacular as his moods. Sahaal had received them as gratefully as he had his bolter, but had wielded them with far greater relish: finding in them weapons worthy of the precision and purity he craved.

He had named them the *Unguis Raptus* – the Raptor's claws – and in so doing had coined the name of his command company. Before even the Great War his Raptors became justly feared, and in the name of first the Emperor, and then his master alone, they had brought swift death from above to their foes.

If his master had known where the gauntlets were constructed, or by whom, he had never revealed it. They were as much a part of Sahaal now as were his eyes or his tongue.

Or his hate.

Two men exited the tunnel beside him. Dressed in jackets and ferro-salvage pads, they spoke softly and trod with the nervous gait of lifelong underhivers. In these troglodytic caverns caution was as natural as breathing.

It did them little good.

The first was dead before his brain could even register a threat, twin skewers punching out of shadow and into his face, slipping like icicles through the pulp of his eyes. Sahaal shook away the corpse like waste from a shovel, sliding from his alcove to reveal himself to the second. Slowly. *Silently.*

The memory of his master's voice, leading his Legion in lecture-prayer, rustled like pouring sand, flooding his mind:

'Show them what you can do,' it trilled, as soft and cold as dead flesh. *'Steal their hope, like a shadow steals the light. Then show them what you are. The tool never changes, my sons. The weapon is always the same. Fear. Fear is the weapon.'*

In the corridor, standing in the bloody mess of his fallen friend, the second man looked into the face of a nightmare and falteringly, chokingly, began to scream.

'I have questions,' Sahaal said, reaching out for him.

THE MAN KNEW nothing, of course. None of them did.

By the end of the second day there had been twelve. Seven men, four women, one child.

It never ceased to amaze Sahaal how varied were their responses. Some – most – had screamed from the outset. When he came upon them, when he flexed his claws and hissed, when he worked their terror like an artist with a brush, smothering gouache horror on subtle blends of oil-smear dread; in those incandescent moments his heart soared with the righteousness of his work, and they threw back their little heads and – *mostly* – they screamed.

Some, though, were silent. Staring with mute animal-shock; dark eyes bulging, lips twitching, faces bright. In those cases Sahaal took them in his claws and carried them away, slipping down through layers of debris to secret, sheltered places where they could recover their voices at leisure.

Then the screaming could begin.

And then he could ask his questions.

One of the women – deluded, perhaps – dropped to her knees and began to pray; some mumbled litany to the Emperor. Angered by her piety, Sahaal sliced away her fingers one by one, enjoying the change in her demeanour. Holy fools, it would seem, could scream as well as sing.

One of the men tried to fight him. Briefly.

The child… the child had cried for his mother. He'd screamed and blubbed and wailed, though when Sahaal leaned down to fix him with a helmed gaze the tears stopped abruptly, surprising him, and the youth's hand flickered with the bright shape of a switchblade, lunging from below. It seemed that innocence had little business in the underhive.

(The blade had snapped. So had Sahaal's patience.)

And yes, now perhaps he could reflect upon the responses to his work. He could skulk here in the ruins of this derelict factory, on the cusp of a deserted settlement, its floors long since collapsed into the abyss, and consider his palette of fear like a painter scheming to mix new colours.

But always, *always* such distractions were tempered by hate, by focused rage, and by the spectral possibility of failure.

What, he asked himself, had he learnt from his murderous forays? What had he discovered from all his many questions, all his many descriptions?

Nothing. Nothing of the Corona Nox, at least.

He'd gone to pains to illustrate the spiral electoo sported by his quarry – carving it lovingly on each victim's skin – but not one had recognised it. He'd described the thieves' shaggy furs, their crude goggles, even the unknown word – *TEQO* – daubed on their transport; though it was familiar to none. Sahaal did not for a moment consider that his victims might have been withholding: one by one their defences cracked, their sanity shattered, but their ignorance remained intact.

No, he'd learned nothing of the Corona. His revelation had concerned something entirely less pleasing.

Since awaking on this nocturnal world something had eaten at him, gnawing at his psyche. When he took his twelfth victim – a bearded man with copper fletches across his brows and rags draping his wiry form – Sahaal's curiosity had finally overcome him. He'd gritted his teeth, hooked one elegant claw into the wretch's arm, played the bladed edge along the cusp of exposed bone, and asked the question that haunted him.

'What year is this?'

Despite the pain, despite even the terror that had gripped him since first he was attacked, the man had paused with a look of almost comical incredulity.

'W-w-what?'

'The year!' he roared, rippling the waters of the sludge-lake to which he'd brought his captive. He raised the claws of his gauntlet above the man's groin, poised to clench. It was a crude form of threat, but he *had* to know. 'What *year*, worm!'

'Nine-eight-six!' the man wailed, all thoughts of bemusement obliterated. 'Nine-eight-six!'

Sahaal growled, absorbing this unwelcome information. An absence of six centuries was far greater than he'd feared. Adrift upon the trance in the *Umbrea Insidior*, he had been resolutely unable to estimate how long he had spent in silent incarceration. Time moved differently in the warp, and a day's slumber in its coiling belly could easily affect a month's passage in crude reality.

Six hundred years was beyond his most fearful approximation. In a fit of pique he began to bring down his claw, venting his anger on his captive.

And then an ugly afterthought arose, and he paused to form words in the plebeian Low Gothic tongue, so appropriately favoured by the underhive filth. 'The thirty-second millennium? Yes? Answer me!'

For a fraction of a second, the man's lips curled in a dumbfounded, confused smile.

'Wh–'

Sahaal flexed the claws.

'No! No! N-no! F-forty-first!' the words rushed out like an avalanche, jumbled and formless. 'Forty-first millennium, year nine-eight-six! Forty-first! Sweet Emperor's blood, forty-*first*!'

The bottom fell from Sahaal's mind.

He killed the man quickly, too distracted to even relish the moment.

He returned to the factory he'd adopted as his lair.

He scuttled in the dark and brooded. He vented his anger on the shattered masonry of the ancient building, and when the violence overcame him he peeled off one mighty shoulder-guard and began slowly, precisely, cutting grooves into the exposed flesh of his arm.

It didn't help.

One hundred centuries had passed.

IT WAS THE bodies that brought answers, finally.

He had taken them, all twelve, from where they died: dismembered and brutalised, hung high from stanchions in public places and busy roads, emptying their thickening fluids upon the debris below. This was not savagery on his part, nor some crude announcement of territory – but as vital a part of his master's doctrine as was the attack itself.

'Kill a thousand men,' the lesson had run, his master's solemn voice echoing through the warship *Vastitas Victris*, *'and let no man bear witness. What have you achieved? Who will ever know? Who will ever fear you? Who will ever respect or obey you?*

'But kill a single man, and let the world see. Hang him high. Cut him deep. Bleed him dry. And then... Disappear.

'Now. Who will ever know? Everyone. Who will ever fear you? Why, everyone! Who will ever respect you, who will ever obey you? Everyone!

'These humans, their imaginations are strong. Kill a thousand men and they will hate you. Kill a million men and they will queue to face you. But kill a single man and they will see monsters and devils in every shadow. Kill a dozen men and they will scream and wail in the night, and they shall feel not hatred, but fear.

'This is the way of obedience, my sons. They are panicky, gossiping beasts, these humans. It serves us to allow them to be so.'

On the third day, when he had crept through the ductcrawls beneath the local settlements and listened to the villagers' fearful rumours, when two separate posses had ridden out from Spitcreek with furtive eyes and crude weapons to catch the killer, when his fits and rages had exhausted him, there came cautious footfalls into his lair. He watched the invader from above, irritated that his sanctuary should be defiled by such clumsy, thoughtless steps.

The man was dressed strangely, even to Sahaal's eye, sporting a robe of white and red grids. Not some flimsy ragsheet, this, but expensively tailored and elaborately decorated, hung with gold and crystal pendants. Small cables looped delicately through the stitches at the sleeves and collar, and where his flesh showed – pallid and puffy – the wires burrowed into the man's skin, unbroken lines like capillaries. More startling still was his face – what little remained of it – with its near-total coverage by augmetic devices, steel-sheet plating and bristling, spiny sensors. Both eyes were gone, replaced in messy cavities by mismatching bionics, a thick layer of pus and infection marking their boundaries. A duct coiled over his shoulder like unruly hair, and the soft lines of his lips were broken by ragged scars, as if his mouth had once been sealed shut then broken open. Rebreather tubes writhed, hooked into sockets on his chin and neck, like train tracks bisecting his face. Dermis-circuitry patterned his throat, vanishing into the folds of his robes which, on closer inspection, concealed also the hard edges and uncertain outlines of more mechanical devices.

His movements were jerky but precise – like a grounded canary – and Sahaal judged him more machine than man. He would have remained hidden, content to let this unthinking drone remain ignorant of his presence, but for a single detail:

Brandished in one metal-knuckled hand, the man waved before him a sheet of parchment bearing a bold, ink-blotted image, catching at Sahaal's attention and sending adrenaline pounding through his body: a single unbroken spiral, dissected by a jagged stripe. The thief's electoo.

He worked his silent way down towards the intruder without pause, considering his best course of action, fighting excitement. Despite the robe and decoration, the interloper bore all the signs of being little more than some vacuous servitor, obeying whatever simple commands its master had provided. It was therefore with little sense of threat, and a great glut of hope, that Sahaal installed himself in a shadowed recess to watch.

'I know you are there,' the man said, startling him, voice as lifeless as the lens-eyes that regarded him, focused despite the dark. 'I sensed movement before even I entered this place.' The figure twitched its head. 'Your stealth is commendable. *Het-het-het-het...*'

It took Sahaal a moment to realise that the man's harsh chirruping was his mechanical excuse for laughter, and he bunched his muscles in the shadows, temper ignited. This was hardly the behaviour of a mere servitor.

The man squinted up at him, brows twitching around metal studs. 'I cannot see you well,' he said, lips brandishing their ghoulish smile. 'What are you?'

'I am your death,' Sahaal said, patience expiring, and pounced.

The man was heavier than he had anticipated – his mechanical portions more extensive even than they appeared – but he went down with satisfying ease. Sahaal bowled him to the floor with a single bound, claws pushing hard through flesh and cable, pinning him. The diagram fluttered from his hand, the connections of his shoulder severed.

The man did not scream.

'You will tell me what you know of the thief,' Sahaal growled, voxcaster blending his smooth syntax with dangerous, reptilian tones. 'The filth with the spiral on his skin. Who is he? Where is he?'

The man smiled. With half-metre claws pinioning him to the ground, with razor edges playing across bone and muscle, with a thick paste of blood and servo-oil soaking into his decorous robes, he *smiled.*

Sahaal twisted the knives.

'Het-het-het-het…'

Sahaal fought the urge to cut out his tongue.

'My name is Pahvulti,' the man said uninvited, shivering with amusement, eye lenses revolving. 'I think we shall be friends.'

Sahaal almost killed him then, infuriated by the scum's audacity. He jerked a claw free and lashed at his face, ripping across cables and skin. A rebreather tube snickered apart with a hiss and the lens of his left eye shattered, its sutured edges bleeding from fresh sores. Sahaal stopped short – fractionally – of a killing blow, and it required all his effort to force down the rage in his mind.

'The *thief*!' he bellowed. 'Or you die in pain!'

'I doubt that,' the man said, calm to the point of insanity, 'on two counts. First… I don't believe you foolish enough to kill the one person who recognises the symbol you've been slicing onto all your victims. And second, *het-het-het,* I don't *feel* pain. I regard it as an inconvenience I'm better off without.'

Sahaal all but screamed. Did the fool not know how easily he could be crushed? Did he not know what manner of man – what manner of *warrior* – he directed his insolence towards?

As if reading his thoughts, the worm's one remaining eye twitched across Sahaal's armour, taking in every detail of his colossal form. 'I daresay that painlessness is something to which you can relate,' he grinned. 'Space Marines are notoriously robust.'

LATER, IN A place so silent that every spoken word was returned to its speaker's ears in a spectrum of glassy echoes, Sahaal folded his arms and fought for calm.

The man-machine Pahvulti had been crucified. With jagged splints of debris forced between the bones of his arms and a tight cord securing his neck to the slumped pillar Sahaal had chosen as his anchor, he should by rights seem a pitiful thing: stripped naked of his robes, bound with chains and barbed cables, slashed and bleeding in a dozen places.

Alas, his situation did not appear to have dented his enthusiasm, nor silenced his laughter.

'...and at one time, *het-het-het,* I might have prayed to the Omnissiah,' he cackled, 'but no longer, no, no. Not Pahvulti. They tried to turn me, you see? They said the *puritens* had rejected my flesh. *Het-het-het.* Rejected! No! It made me strong! It made me *wise*!'

'Be silent, confound you!' Sahaal's temper was by now comprehensively frayed.

'Are you not interested, Space Marine, in how your new friend came to find you? Are you not interested in my *knowledge*?'

'Call me a Space Marine once more, worm, and I'll cut out your tongue and choke you on it.'

'*Het-het-het,* no, no... Not my tongue. Not while I know what I know.'

'The spiral electoo? Who wears it? His name!'

'Het-het-het...'

Sahaal hissed his anger through the grille of his helm and hooked a claw into what little meat remained of his captive's belly. It was a hopeless gesture – the man had demonstrated nothing but contempt for the notion of torture – but at the very least the moist noises of slicing helped to calm Sahaal's mood.

Never before had a mere human occupied a position of such influence over him. Pahvulti refused to divulge what he knew until Sahaal vowed to spare him, and to offer him such an oath would shatter every code Sahaal believed, tear to shreds every ounce of his dignity and sully every corner of his authority. Under other circumstances he would have laughed at the very suggestion.

Nor could he merely make, then *break*, the oath: Pahvulti had made it clear that he would deliver his information only from afar, well beyond Sahaal's punitive grasp.

For the twentieth time since bringing his captive to this dark, deep well, Sahaal cursed Pahvulti's name, cursed the ill fortune that had gifted him with such leverage, and cursed the warpshit filth that had stolen the Corona Nox and placed him in this situation in the first place.

Zso Sahaal was not accustomed to fear or uncertainty. His natural response to each was to grow *angry*, and in his increasingly violent gashes at Pahvulti's guts, some small portion of his venom was assuaged.

Until–

'Het-het-het... not that it bothers me, Space Marine, but you should be aware...' Pahvulti made a show of grinning, '...that impervious to pain I might be, but invulnerable I am not. Continue to cut me and I am eighty-seven-point-six per cent certain that I shall

perish.' His remaining lens-eye twinkled. 'Just thought you should know. *Het-het-het.*'

He was a calculus logi, or at least *had* been. Over the previous hours Sahaal had been treated to the man's life story at least three times – a repetition which was not helping his mood.

Pahvulti had begun as a human savant-computer of the Adeptus Mechanicus – whose brittle thoughts had aided administrations and diplomats, tacticians and explorators all across the sector. On the day of his fiftieth birthday he was presented with the highest accolade reserved for his kind: the *puritens* lobotomy. This ritualised surgery removed from his scarred brain what little trace of humanity remained, amputated his subconscious, and burned away his pain.

It should have made him pure, mechanical, perfect. It should have brought him closer to his god, and sheltered his weak biology from the predations of temptation. To say that it failed would be a quite spectacular understatement.

His body rejected the implants. He awoke shriven of his pain and his dreams, but excised utterly from the obsessive faith he'd held before. He awoke a greedy, flawed bastard with the mind of a computer, and when his priest-masters ordered that he report for dismantlement, he laughed down his thrice-blessed comm-line and fled.

And now?

Now he was the self styled 'cognis mercator' of the Equixus hive: an information broker whose lattice of influence and spymongering extended to all points. He served the gangmasters with mercenary neutrality, sold his rumours to upcity analysts, hired himself to navy officials to direct pressganging and grew fat and rich in the certain knowledge that he was too valuable, too *vital,* for any fool to kill.

He alone had collated information on all twelve of Sahaal's slayings. He alone noted the spiral scars cut into each corpse. He alone recognised the power, the *lethality,* of the killer on the loose. He alone had compiled maps and behavioural patterns, identifying the point central to each murder. He alone had found Sahaal's lair.

And he alone was bold enough to come *looking* for him, seeking influence and opportunity over whatever force of destruction had entered his territory.

And he alone was fortunate enough to be in a position to achieve both.

Sahaal cursed his name again, flexed his claws impotently, and prepared to cut him free.

MITA ASHYN

THE KNOCKING AT her cell door, which she had been expecting, came in the evening of the third day. The cowled acolyte responsible sniggered as she read the summons he delivered.

Her master demanded an audience.

Having failed utterly to distinguish herself at the crash site of the *Umbrea Insidior* – its name being the only detail she remembered from her trance and subsequent blackout – she expected the summons to herald a formal discharge. The Inquisition was ruthless in defending its obscurity, and if that required ineffectual personnel to be cerebrally cleansed or, worse, *culled*, then so be it.

She had spent the intervening days meditating – neither scrying nor dreaming, but basking in the Emperor's light – and when the summons arrived she had prepared herself for death, or at least lobotomisation, as best she could.

Kaustus received her alone – that was the first of her surprises; she'd assumed the retinue would turn out in force to witness the spectacle of its newest member being cast aside.

'Interrogator,' Kaustus greeted her, not looking up. He sat at a simple desk in the centre of his suite, engrossed in a bundle of parchments and auspex pads, and delicately laid down his writing stylus as she dipped her head in return.

'My lord.'

The second shock, and one for which she was utterly unprepared, was that he had removed his mask. His face was unremarkable – somewhat gaunt, perhaps, bordering on the aquiline – and his hair, tied in a tall black tower that crested his head like a topknot, could hardly be described as outlandish amongst the clashing fashions of the upper hive. But it was his teeth that stood out. Two of them, at any rate.

Inquisitor Kaustus had tusks.

'Orkish,' he said, without prompt.

Mita realised she'd been staring and lowered her eyes, brows furrowing in uncertainty. He hadn't even looked up.

'For three days I stalked the bastard through the tar pits on Phyrra. We'd freed his slaves, wiped out his warband, crippled his fleet and filled his green flesh with more lead than a target range, but the brute wouldn't give in. Warlords are like that. Proud. *Stubborn*.'

Mita fidgeted, wondering if this was some perverse treat the inquisitor reserved for the condemned: a story from his own lips, a glimpse of his secret features, then a bullet between the eyes. If Kaustus noted her tension, he gave little sign.

'We caught up with him on the edge of a volcano,' he continued, turning a page of parchment before him, 'and after he'd hacked his way through my men I fought that piece of xeno filth for two hours. The way I saw it, if he'd killed me he would have taken my head as a trophy.' He twanged a tusk with a gloved finger, finally looking up with a smirk. 'This seemed an appropriate measure.'

Mita wondered if she should comment. As ever, the inquisitor sent her confidence crashing around her, robbing her of any certainty. A wrong word, a misplaced facial expression: in a man as unreadable as this, such things could be disastrous.

On the other hand, if she was here to die anyway...

'I imagine, my lord,' she said carefully, 'they come in useful.'

He nodded, smiling at her boldness.

'Indeed they do. To the ork, symbols of status are vital. I've seen the vermin retreat rather than face a human with tusks greater than their own. I've seen them turn on their own lords when their enemy's fangs are taller or sharper than his. A simple thing, but so very effective.'

Mita's resignation to her fate lent her a dangerous bravery. *Go out fighting,* she thought.

'Though I imagine they make eating difficult.'

There was a cold, uncomfortable silence. Kaustus's eyes burnt a hole through her.

And then he began to laugh.

'It depends,' he said, when the chuckles subsided, 'what it is you're trying to eat.'

'Am I to be discharged?' Mita said, tiring of the niceties. If she was here to die she'd rather skip the preamble.

For the first time she felt as though she had Kaustus's full attention, and she met his gaze openly. He steepled his fingers.

'No,' he said, finally, 'though the idea was... considered.'

Something like relief, mixed with a perverse portion of disappointment, filtered through Mita's mind.

'You gave us the name of the vessel, interrogator,' Kaustus said, 'which is in itself a revealing detail. That you were so... affected... speaks volumes.'

'B-but I could not answer your question, my lord. I could not tell if there were survivors...'

He waved a vague hand. 'Oh, the retinue handled that. There were none.' He fiddled with the pendant around his neck. 'Such remains as they found were ancient things, long since passed beyond the Emperor's light.'

'Then... how did the ship come to arrive here?'

Kaustus worked his jaw, tusks circulating below his eyes. 'My logi have hypothesised it was lost in the warp,' he said, dismissively, 'and has only recently exited.' He fixed her with a glare, all traces of congeniality gone. 'In any case, it's beyond our remit. We are here to investigate xenophile cults, if you remember, not to ponder upon the complexities of the warp. The retinue found nothing untoward in the wreck. Let that be an end to it.'

Mita recalled the psychic terror incumbent within every joist of the vessel's structure, stabbing at her mind like fire. There was something dark to it, she knew, some echo of past horrors that clung to its hull like an aura.

Despite the discomfort she said nothing to Kaustus, aware that his newfound tolerance could end at any moment, and suppressed her internal shudder.

'I have informed the Adeptus Mechanicus of its arrival.' Kaustus grunted, returning his attention to the paperwork. 'I dare say they'll send salvage crews. It matters little.'

'Yes, my lord.' Inside, she screamed: *No, my lord! Something has arrived!*

'Which brings me to my point.' Kaustus lifted a parchment, narrowing his eyes. 'It seems this dreary world is fated to present me with as many distractions as it *can*.' He shook his head, black hair teetering above his scalp. 'I have decided to give you a commission, interrogator.'

Mita's heart stopped. 'My lord?'

'My investigation is bearing fruit. The governor has opened his records and I suspect the presence of a xenophile enclave in the midhive. I wish to concentrate my resources on locating and purging it.'

'O-of course.'

'Of course. So when I received yet *another* damnable request for assistance, this time from the vindictors, of all people – *and* after all the fuss they made when we joined their little crash site excursion – I naturally thought of you.'

Mita wasn't sure whether this was a compliment or an insult, so she nodded discreetly and stayed quiet.

'It seems their commander has a problem in the underhive. Quite what he expects *me* to do about it I don't know, but I'll be damned if I waste another second on the inconsequential internal affairs of this world.'

Mita had a bad feeling about where this was going. 'You'd like me to assist him in your stead...' she said, filled with gloomy resignation, inwardly appalled at the ignominy of such a mission. The *underhive*, warp dammit!

Kaustus regarded her with a grin, needle-like tusks bisecting his face.

'Congratulations, interrogator.'

* * *

A SHORT WHILE later, when the indignity of the commission was beginning to sink in, when her master had provided her with all the documents of authority that she needed, and when she was dismissed with no more than a 'that will be all,' she paused at the exit to Kaustus's suite and cleared her throat.

'*Yes*, interrogator?' Kaustus sighed.

'My lord, you... you said the name of the vessel had been... "revealing"...?'

'And?'

'I... I just wondered... in what way, my lord.'

He narrowed his eyes. 'Curiosity is a dangerous thing, interrogator.'

She nodded, dipping in a supplicatory half-bow, and made to leave.

'Interrogator?' His voice caught her on the threshold of the doorway.

'My lord?'

'The *Umbrea Insidior* disappeared from Imperial records ten thousand years ago. At the end of the Horus Heresy.'

She almost choked, astonished to even hear the name of that most ruinous of times – when fully half of the Emperor's Space Marine Legions had fallen from his light – let alone to have come so close to one of its relics. Little wonder, she realised, that she had felt such a concentration of despair and violence in its crumpled beams.

'Good*bye*, interrogator.'

CUSPSEAL WAS AS low within the hive as one could travel within the broadly defined 'civilised' sectors. It dominated six full tiers, extended in five kilometres in each direction and had a population – depending upon where one chose to imagine its borders – of somewhere between six and ten million citizens. As with all such industrial loci it wasn't so much a city as a borough of the hive itself, segueing horizontally and upwards with such other townships, settlements and factories as had germinated nearby.

The one border that Cuspseal *could* define was its base.

Below its adamantium foundations was the underhive, and there any such abstraction as 'civilisation' – in short supply even in these supposedly urbane zones – could effectively be ignored.

If the underhive was a madhouse, Cuspseal was its padded walls.

Little wonder that the vindictor precinct owed more in its architecture to some medieval fortress than to the industrial anarchy surrounding it. A perfect cube, it bristled with obvious and massive ordnance, much of it trained on the largest of the cavernous openings into the underworld that dotted the Cuspseal's boundaries: a portal its builders had shrewdly positioned it beside. Tramlines and suspended walkways ringed it on every side, rising in metallic layers that thronged with heavily-cloaked workers.

It had taken Mita three hours to descend this far from the upper spire, riding a succession of increasingly decrepit elevators reserved for authorised personnel. Such was the reality of hive life: the sequential tiers represented not only a geographical strata but a division of status – the princely affluence of the upper tiers supported itself on a gallery of decreasing wealth. At its base the hive was a pit of destitution.

Arriving in the centre of Cuspseal's noxious sprawl hot and irritated by the constant checking of papers, Mita was not in the mood to suffer further indignity.

'This,' she snapped, when finally Commander Orodai entered the anteroom in which she'd been waiting, shadowed by a pair of vindictor sergeants and an aide, 'is intolerable.'

Orodai had the look of a man who had resigned himself to receiving an earbattering. 'Yes,' he said wearily. 'I'm sure it is.'

He was an old man, if indeed his face accurately reflected his age. Where others in his position might have opted for rejuve treatments or augmetic components, his features betrayed the sort of leathered erosion rarely glimpsed in high-ranking personnel. As a member of the Adeptus Arbitus, and therefore operating entirely exclusively of the hive's administration, his command was arguably second only – if not equal – to that of the governor himself. For all that, he was a small man in bland clothing, whose psychic emissions betrayed no sense of self-importance. Mita's overriding impression from his warp-presence was of an impressive dedication to his vocation. Still, decorum must be observed.

'I've been waiting two hours!' she barked, stabbing at the air with a finger. 'The inquisitor will hear of this!'

Orodai arched an eyebrow. 'I dare say he hears of everything else.' He offered her a bundle of parchments, which she snatched with bad grace. 'In any case, it couldn't be helped. Your documents required confirmation and your companion was... unhelpful.'

Ah yes, she thought, *my companion...*

'Your men called him an *ogryn*.'

'And?'

'And that wasn't a good idea.'

'No?'

'No. Last time he met an ogryn it kept calling him "Tiny".'

Orodai had the look of a man clutching at straws. 'And that was a problem?'

'Not really. It stopped when he pulled off its arms. I demand that you release him.'

Orodai's expression contrived to suggest that she was in no position to be making 'demands,' but he nodded thoughtfully and gestured to the aide. The man scurried away, oozing reluctance. Mita could well imagine why.

'Under normal circumstances we wouldn't allow his... *kind* in the city,' Orodai said, stroking his grey beard. 'Though perhaps circumstances are not "normal".'

'You forget,' Mita retorted, 'that it was *you* who invited the Inquisition's assista–'

'Actually, we invited the inquisitor's assistance, not that of his lackey and her pet, but let's not split hairs.'

Mita's outraged rebuff was spectacularly postponed.

The door parted with its hinges and her companion entered.

Loudly.

HIS NAME WAS Cog, and he was human – broadly speaking. Whatever feral world had sired him had been isolated for millennia, denied the purifying light of the Emperor's influence, and its sparse population had stagnated in a downward spiral of inbreeding and corruption.

Still human, if only *just*.

Cog and his kin had grown massive. Shunning the need for higher thought, rapid evolution had seen their skins grow thick, their brows brachiate, their chests barrel. Over long centuries of clambering through forests their arms had elongated and formed secondary elbows, their legs had shortened and their hands had grown massive.

Kaustus had found Cog in the slaughterpits of Tourelli Planis, where he was goaded by his captives with energised spears and electroflails, forced to grapple a succession of beasts and automata for the crowd's amusement. His hands had been taken from him, replaced with crude bionics. Watching the giant enter the ring with a tribal prayersong to the Emperor, Kaustus had been impressed with his piety as well as his physique, and had purchased him from the slavers for a princely sum.

Given her own barely-tolerated mutation, since joining Kaustus, Mita had found in Cog an unlikely ally. She knew he regarded her with a simple devotion based on lust, and tolerated his clumsy advances with good grace despite never acceding to them. If stringing-along a gentle giant was all it took to secure his personal loyalty, she judged it a fair price to pay.

Cog had been her natural choice of companion for this degrading foray into the plebeian morass of the hive's lower tiers, and his puppy-like pleasure at her invitation had been touching. He'd remained at her side ever since, as silent as a statue, until the vindictors of Cuspseal had decided his obvious corruption was a step too far and had him tranquilised. Cog was dragged away in chains, Mita's protests were ignored, and her sympathy for whichever poor devil was eventually chosen to release him had been growing ever since.

Cog didn't lose his temper often. But when he *did*...

THE DOOR, SET firmly in a ferrocrete bracket, crumpled like a dead leaf. Cog followed it through with his head dipped and his shoulders hunched, roaring like a hive-tram. The vindictor sergeants reacted as if electrified, staggering away, fumbling for power mauls. A third voice added to their panicky exclamations, and it took Mita a moment to spot Orodai's unlucky aide, clutched in the giant's mechanical hand like a fleshy club.

Cog's beetle-black eyes squinted, seeking the best target, brows collecting in moronic indecision. One of the sergeants settled the matter by thumbing the activator of his maul and shouting 'Stand down, brute!' – an attempt at machismo derailed when Cog contemptuously swatted him with the aide's body. Both men tumbled in a confusion of limbs and squeals towards the wall, which vented a layer of mortar dust at their impact. The second sergeant whimpered.

Commander Orodai, by contrast, had reacted with admirable composure, directing his impatient eye at Mita. To her psychic senses he exuded little fear; only an air of irritation at what he clearly considered to be a waste of his time.

Across the room, Cog picked up the second vindictor, plucked off his helmet like the lid from a tube of paint, and crumpled it into a ball between thumb and forefinger. The man – stupidly, in Mita's view – took a ridiculous attempt at a punch to Cog's face, an attack which earned him a rib-splintering bearhug and a casual toss over the giant's shoulder.

Cog turned his attention to Orodai and advanced, metal fingers twitching. A long cord of spittle dangled from his lower lip.

'I think that will do, interrogator,' the commander said, regarding Mita calmly. 'You've made your point.'

She smiled, nodded with *faux* graciousness, and turned to the advancing monster.

'Cog,' she said. 'I'm fine.' She eked out a small portion of her consciousness and coiled herself around Cog's simple mind, soothing its jagged edges.

'H-hurt you?' Cog said, blinking rapidly. 'Hurted Mita?'

'No,' she said, voice reassuring. 'Look. You see? Not a hair. Now *calm*.'

Cog nodded, accepting her words with child-like trust. He thrust his massive hands into the pockets of his robe and appeared to switch off, like a machine devoid of fuel.

Mita turned to Orodai with a smirk.

'Now,' she said, mollified. 'Perhaps you'd care to explain why *you* requested *our* help?'

Orodai's eyes narrowed, twinkling.

'Perhaps it would be best,' he said, and this time it was he who smirked, 'if you see for yourself.'

SERGEANT VARITENS DID not like mutants. Sergeant Varitens did not like psykers. Sergeant Varitens did not like disobedience or poverty or aristocracy or crime. He did not like the underhive, or the upper spire, or indeed the middle tiers.

As far as Mita could tell, skating delicately across the surface of his mind, Sergeant Varitens did not appear to like much at all.

(Sergeant Varitens did not like the Inquisition.)

(Sergeant Varitens did not like women.)

He and Mita were getting along just *famously*.

'And what is this zone called?'

'Lady, it's the warp's-arse *underhive*. We don't call it anything.'

'But… these settlements… They must have names. What do the people call th–'

'Look.' Varitens turned away from the Salamander's cab, sighing through the mike of his voxcaster. 'You want to stop and ask some of these filth what they call places, or where the local sights are, or which unfortunate bastard they just ate for dinner, you be my guest. Only don't come running to us when you look down and some godless *mutie* has his teeth in your leg.'

They travelled in silence after that.

The underhive had not been what Mita had expected. Trawling across its debris-flows and pitted causeways in the vindictors' Salamander, she found herself admiring the diversity, as if there were some secret beauty – some hidden order – lurking in the decay. Here, salvaged waste was gold. She found herself impressed by the colour and vivacity of the sights, as if life had recoiled from the squalor of its environment in a storm of clashing hues and decorations. Gaudy totems leaned from the shadows, bright graffiti announced a dozen changes of territory: each gang name crossed through by its latest conqueror. Underhivers variously raced for cover or came out to watch as the vindictors passed; shady characters with hands reaching for – but never openly wielding – whatever weaponry they hid within heavy cloaks. Here there was vibrancy in the dark – like the perfect scarlet of a deep sea tubeworm – and Mita struggled to despise it as profoundly as Sergeant Varitens so clearly did.

Commander Orodai had assigned the sergeant as her tour-guide. She suspected he'd done so out of spite.

'Tell me, sergeant,' she said, tiring of the silence, 'what manner of crime warrants the attention of the Emperor's glorious Inquisition? *And* down here in this most...' she parroted his emotionless voice, '*wretched* of places, to boot?'

Varitens regarded her for a moment, face concealed within the featureless orb of his visor.

'Murder.'

She blinked. 'We're investigating a murder?'

'More than one. Five confirmed, probably more. We're taking you to the most recent discovery.'

She shook her head. This assignment was growing more and more ridiculous by the instant.

'Sergeant, it's my understanding that there are several hundred unexplained deaths every day. I imagine the figure is far higher in the underhive.'

'You imagine right, lady.'

'Then I'm afraid I don't understand. Why pay such close attention to *this* one?'

The Salamander turned a corner and began to throttle down, and Mita became aware that her companions were preparing themselves to disembark, hefting mauls and autoguns professionally.

Varitens pointed to a side tunnel, bored from a drift of mangled steel, and cocked his head.

'Through there. You'll understand.'

SHE HAD BEEN a missionary, judging by what little of her clothing remained: a white robe with a hemp cord and a reliquary cache slung across her shoulder, embroidered with golden scriptures.

She had come to this deep, dark place to spread the Emperor's light: as brave and selfless a being as one could ever hope to find. Her reward hardly seemed fair.

The robe was shredded.

The hemp cord creaked around her neck as she twisted above the ground.

The reliquary lay shattered at her feet and the fragments of bone from within – the knuckles of some long-dead saint, perhaps – were ground to dust.

'Emperor preserve us...' Mita hissed, stepping into the tunnel.

The woman had not died here – that much was clear. Whatever violence had ended her life would certainly have spilled out across the murder scene: splattering walls and ceilings, pooling in thick puddles underfoot. This was less a scene of frenzy than an exhibit, a calling-card: neat, tidy, *arranged*.

Her hands were gone. Her eyes had been put out. One foot hung by a single scrap of gristle; the blow that had parted it with such razor ease stopping short – deliberately – of amputation. Her viscera had been evacuated, hanging in translucent loops from the incision across her belly.

And all across her, along every part of her worm-white body, lazy lines had been drawn: fluid ripples and scarlet whorls like the eddies of some mantra-wheel, spinning through holy water. At first Mita had mistaken the lines for red ink, scrawled across the body's skin. She was wrong. Each line was a cut, administered so delicately, so *perfectly*, that not a drop of blood had oozed clear to spoil the effect.

This was not psychosis. This was *art*.

And the artist had not shied from signing his work.

Above the body, carved on the rocky surfaces of the borehole in a clipped, tidy hand, an engraved legend picked at the light of Mita's illuminator and drew her eye.

Adeo mori servus Imperator Fictus
Ave Dominus Nox

She felt her gorge rise and turned away, forcing down bile in her throat. Sergeant Varitens, standing behind her with hands on hips, mistook her disgust for miscomprehension, nodding towards the text and clearing his throat.

'It says–'

'Thank you, sergeant,' she hissed, fighting for dignity as well as air. 'I'm quite capable of reading High Gothic.'

She turned again towards the words, and they seemed to writhe in her eyes with a malevolent life of their own. For an instant she felt the stab of shocking, familiar pain – awash with ancient violence and ageless bitterness – and in that moment knew, without any doubt, from where the murderer had come.

A great darkness, descending from the sky.

Something had survived the descent of the *Umbrea Insidior*...

'*Adeo mori servus Imperator Fictus*,' she said out loud, forming each word clear and strong. 'So die the slaves of the False Emperor.'

She could feel the vindictors staring at her, fidgeting. Even Cog watched her with troubled bemusement, struggling to understand the words.

'*Ave Dominus Nox*. Hail to the Lord of the Night.'

ZSO SAHAAL

THEY WERE CALLED the Glacier Rats.

Their name was scrawled across parchment in the clipped hand of a servoscribe, belying the information's remarkableness in neat, tedious words, as if to render it as dull as any other record; sealed neatly with an uncrested daub of wax.

They were called the Glacier Rats.

Sahaal ran the name through his mind again and again, as if testing its mettle.

Tasting it.

The information broker Pahvulti had taken his leave from captivity. Walking free, ignoring the wounds patterning his necrotic skin, his swagger had been that of a victor, as if he'd somehow earned Sahaal's respect – or at the very least incurred his debt. He'd instructed Sahaal on where to find, and when, the information he'd promised, he'd dipped his head in sarcastic obeisance, then he'd smiled and waggled his brows.

'This is a business of *credit*,' he'd said, cackling his peculiar laugh – '*het-het-het*' – like a gear skipping a tooth, 'the question costs nothing. The answers are priceless…'

Sahaal struggled with the urge to rip the man to shreds. Allowing him to simply walk away required every ounce of his concentrated pragmatism.

The silent vow that he would have his revenge later was little consolation.

'And yet I have paid nothing,' he'd hissed, oozing away into the shadows, struggling for some scrap of dignity.

He was denied even that.

'No… no, you haven't.' Pahvulti's one remaining eye fluttered, cycling through lenses like some perpetual wink. 'But then… the first one is always free.'

And then he was gone.

They were called the Glacier Rats.

And yes, Pahvulti's answers had arrived where he had promised, lowered from some unknown tier down a disused elevator shaft, and Sahaal's cursory attempt to distinguish its source had failed. The information broker was far too sly to be so easily undone: wherever he had his base, he was free – for now – of retaliation.

And yes, Sahaal had roared with hunger as he learned his enemy's name, flexed his claws, chanted their name again and again, but even so… even so…

He was not accustomed to being indebted.

The Glacier Rats. The thieves were named the Glacier Rats.

They were a raider band, the document said. A clan of pirates unconcerned with the territorial squabbles of hivegangs, collecting then pawning such valuables as they purloined. Their founder had been a native of the ice-world Valhalla, joining then promptly deserting the

Imperial Guard on his first tour of duty, sensing far greater opportunity for wealth in the Equixus hive. His name was Tuahli Teqo, and Sahaal's lips curled in a mirthless smile as he recalled the ugly legend sprawled on the side of the thieves' transport: a tag to honour his memory.

Their current leader, in as much as Pahvulti's spies could keep up with the endlessly changing hierarchies of such clans, was named Nikhae, and was recognisable by the luminous spiral electoo on his forehead.

'Nikhae.'

Sahaal said it out loud, as if to ensure its reality, and waved a single claw through the air, dissecting the very sound of the thief's name.

'Nikhae... Nikhae...'

Yes. Yes, it was him. The false hunchback. The thief. The scum. The *worm*.

He had taken it.

At the rear of the sheaf of pages Pahvulti included a map. Marked in blotched ink, scrawled thick by Pahvulti's own hand, the centre of the page sported a bold, dark 'X'.

Sahaal checked the straps on the blocky package attached to his waist, its faint green glow shimmering across the blades at his fingertips.

The Glacier Rats. They were called the Glacier Rats.

Every last one of them would die.

HERNIATOWN HAD FALLEN from grace.

At its edges the weight of the city had broken its own base and collapsed downwards; whole streets sagging into the abyss. Underhivers kept their distance from Herniatown's bowed arcades, naming it well: its wilted streets were a raw bulge of viscera that had squeezed through the muscle wall above, dipping into inky darkness. Once it had been a part of Cuspseal, but no longer. Nestled at the underhive's anarchic heart, it seemed an invasive probe of order, albeit warped incontrovertibly by its descent.

Herniatown was where the Glacier Rats had made their home.

Sahaal reconnoitred the zone with fanatical care: watching, exploring, never intervening. At three separate junctions – where long-deserted hivehabs met along broad concourses – he'd been forced to stay his arm, as Glacier Rat sentries ambled by.

The time would come, he told himself.

They wore long coats of grey and white; a stylised snowflake – dagger tipped and skull-centred – patterning each lapel. They carried lasguns with the exaggerated care of those who'd purchased their own weaponry, and Sahaal bridled to see such fireworks treated with such reverence. Stalking the shadows of their boundaries, he registered not a single threat, and formulated their demise with predatory ease.

Their band was well named, he decided. They were scum; untutored and untrained, as meaningless as their namesakes. Rats, yes. And he was the owl.

He laid his plans with care, awaited his opportunity from the shadows, and then struck.

A SENTRY – YOUNG eyes flitting across all the wrong shadows – was the first to die.

Pacing at the town's northern entrance, the youth had never considered turning an eye upon the ventilation stacks halfway along the tunnel he was supposedly guarding, and despite his enormity Sahaal arose from the vent's crumpled innards with the silence and grace of a striking snake.

The sentry's throat was cut before he registered another's presence, and in his brief instant of surprise – if indeed he felt anything at all – it must have seemed like the walls themselves had exuded claws. The body slumped, its knees folded, and Sahaal passed into the shadows long before its head struck the uneven floor with a wet slap.

Herniatown opened around him like a sacrifice bearing its heart, inviting a blade between its ribs, and he obliged it with savage pleasure. He killed another three sentries in parallel streets, impatient for violence, dispatching each with the speed and silence of a wraith. He displayed their bodies artfully; faint lights catching at every wet cut, glistening in unbroken sluices of crimson, and paused in each case only to curse the soul of his victims as if keeping a tally of his revenge.

'Warp take you…' he hissed, helm absorbing every sound. 'Warp eat you whole.'

When finally the noises he had waited so long to hear arose he was poised within the inverted dome of what had once been a chapel. He clung to the ceiling with the clamp-claws of his feet, dangling like a bat, and relished every echoing nuance of the Glacier Rats' alarm.

It began with a single cry, flitting across the town like a dream, and then multiplied: first a handful of voices, then a score, each crying out in outrage and anger, demanding reinforcement.

The first body had been found.

Sahaal dropped onto and through the chapel's mosaic floor, gliding along the cracked seams of rock at its base, and hastened to Herniatown's opposite fringe. He used the crawlducts to travel in secret: swatting aside giant roaches and rats as he went, jump pack driving him along like a bullet down a barrel. At the town's southern entrance he hopped from a service hatch and quickly snickered thrumming claws through the meaty joints of the gatekeeper's legs. Scraps of the man's coat twisted aside, blossoming with redness, and his strangled grunt of astonishment warmed Sahaal to his core. The man toppled like a felled tree – more surprised than pained – and thrashed in a deluge of his own blood.

This time Sahaal allowed his victim the privilege of screaming.

Before he left the wailing cripple, arteries belching their vibrant load across tunnel walls, he prised open the man's clenched fist, pushed something hard and round into the cage of his fingers, and nodded his head.

'Don't let go,' he said, tonguing the external address stud of his vox-caster.

Then he was gone.

The man's screams echoed like the howl of a gale, and already the cries of alarm from the north were becoming those of query, groups meeting at intersections, trading orders, pointing fingers, heading south to investigate this new tumult. Sahaal watched them rush about like insects from above, safe within a collapsed attic, and relished their panic. To them it must seem as though their territory were surrounded: imperilled from opposite directions, menaced by unseen attackers.

'Fear and panic,' his master had once said, *'are but two sides of the same die.'*

The sentry's screams weakened and died shortly before the bobbing torches reached the south gate. Sahaal imagined him alone in the dark, clutching with increasingly feeble fingers at the grenade in his hand. Sooner or later his grip would falter and the bomb's priming trigger would release.

The foremost group of guards entered the tunnel an instant before the grenade detonated.

To Sahaal, perched like a gargoyle on high, gazing across the levelled towers of Herniatown, the explosion rose like a luminous bubble from the south; its flickering radiance rising across the entire realm. Shadows and highlights were scrawled across every surface, and when the brightness diminished a gout of oil-black smoke twisted, snake-like, above the southern gatehouse.

'Preysight,' Sahaal whispered, and the bitter machine-spirit of his armour nictitated new lenses across his eyeslits, magnifying his view. Brought into sudden and sharp relief, the smoky pall broke apart where the dead and dying staggered, stumbling with faces blackened and limbs gone. There were far fewer than had entered.

Sahaal watched their pitiable lives dwindle away with unashamed pleasure, then leapt from his alcove into the smoke-thick sky, heading downtown.

As he travelled, he took a care to allow himself to be seen. Just brief glimpses flitting across smoky expanses, whooping as he ghosted past hurrying bands of frightened men. He did so at distant points – here in the east, there near the centre, leaping in great arcs across the town's concrete sky. In the ruins of a *librium* to the west he dropped through a shattered skylight and shrieked at the men below, then vanished, slashing at their faces as he went.

At an intersection in the north he hopped from a crumbling wall onto the back of a transport, claws extending with a silken rasp. Two men were dead before he was even amongst them, heads spinning in the vehicle's wake, and their bodies tumbled beneath its tracks with damp, crackling retorts. The two remaining men opened fire. Sahaal activated the external line of his vox, amplified its volume to a dangerous level–

–and *laughed*.

Across all of Herniatown, in every honeycomb passageway of its crumbling boundaries, in every sheltered corner beneath its sunless sky, frightened men and women paused to listen, shivering in the dark.

When finally Sahaal turned his attention upon the zone's tilted, sagging centre, any sense of order to the Glacier Rats' search had long since passed. A nightmare stalked the shadows of their domain, and as rumours of its appearance spread – midnight blue and clothed in lightning, long of limb and hunched of back, with eyes that glowed like rubies and claws like sabres – pandemonium reigned.

Sahaal basked in the air above it all, and laughed and laughed and laughed.

THE CENTRE HAD been a *colereum*, at one time.

A vast hydroponics dome, bristling with sludge-farmed crops, its inwardly-mirrored surface recalled an insect's eye; iridescent and multifaceted. At one time it had disgorged a thousand tonnes of starchpaste every year, diverted among rust-thick pipes to a million habs. At one time.

It had borne its relocation into the abyss with poor grace.

The crops had died when the collapse occurred, their irrigation channels cut forever. What little water filtered into the underhive was tainted by its descent, and those few hardy weeds that had escaped had grown shaggy and truculent, skins thick with mutant bristles. Only the lamps had survived; globular drones of archaic design with thrumming gravmotors and simple logic-minds. They roved the dome with ultraviolet torches blazing, unconcerned with the absence of vegetation, faltering only when their aeons-old fuel reserves perished.

Sahaal straddled the dome like a beetle, limbs moving with insect confidence, drawing himself up its pregnant camber. At its crest he paused, gazed through its scars at the buildings within, and raised his hand to the bandolier straps of his jump pack, plucking at the grenades that dangled there.

The pirates' base was a sprawl of lodges and canvas tents, centred about a stone-walled tower; a fitting headquarters for a leader. There, Sahaal guessed, he would find his prey. Around it guards sprinted between salvage stores and bivouacs with guns brandished, shouting orders; faces milky in the ultraviolet glow. Vehicle engines ignited in a cascade of throaty roars, tracks grinding as they spun towards the *colereum*'s exit.

'We're under attack, Teqo's blood!' Sahaal heard, filtered amongst the screams. 'Dozens of them! All directions!'

A roar from the east told him the bodies of the three slain guards had been found, adding to the confusion, and to the west the dry sound of lasfire – unmistakable in its breathless crackle – supplied the finishing touch.

The Glacier Rats were shooting at shadows.

Nodding, he sunk needle claws into the pinions of the dome, braced every muscle of his body, and closed his eyes.

'In your name, my master,' he said. 'Always.'

And then he drew a breath.

And then he tossed back his head.

And then he *screamed*.

At its maximum volume, the voxcaster of his ancient helm could burst the veins of a man's skull and turn his teeth to powder. He'd seen men fall paralysed to the floor at the Raptor's shriek, and birds fall stunned from the sky.

In Herniatown, the *colereum*'s mirrored dome exploded.

Dozens of men paused in their panic and glanced up, glimpsed a nightmare figure haloed by ultraviolet, then fell screaming as eyes and mouths filled with splintered glass. Their final sight would haunt the brief remainder of their lives: bathed in a shower of jewelled fragments, a banshee on the crest of a razor-tipped wave.

Then the grenades began to fall, and from each roiling fireball a spume of hooked shrapnel sprayed itself outwards, making mince of flesh.

Sahaal stretched out his claws and exalted in the carnage. He felt for an instant that he could *taste* the fear of his victims, and tilted his body to rise on its whispering thermals, bathing in the horror he had sown, glorying in his own awesomeness, ascending to deity on wings of terror!

But–

But, no. *No*!

Even at the peak of such vicious pleasure he shied away, gnashing his teeth. In base exaltations lay an insidious danger. Focus was the key. Always. Focus and devotion.

In vengeance upon the false Emperor, in the name of my Master.

All else was corrupt and meaningless. He must condition himself to feel pleasure in the execution of his work, pleasure at drawing a step closer to his goals... But never pleasure in the act itself.

The fear, the destruction, the death: these were tools. Weapons. Aspects of the artist's palette. Means to an end.

Never the end itself.

* * *

He went amongst the dying men with restraint, after that – although those who fell in his path might not have known it. Most were injured, able only to stagger aside as he passed, claws bloodied. He gave little thought to stealth now: whether his panicking prey saw who – *what* – was in their midst was now irrelevant. None would survive to speak of it.

In a quiet part of his mind he wondered how he must seem to these half-blind worms, supplicating as he passed by, or else cut their throats with the contempt they deserved.

He must appear a giant. He stood far taller than even their mightiest champions, and that despite the hunched posture his armour had adopted. Striding on heavy boots, autoreactive claws flexing at their tips, greaves that tapered towards horn-like knees pistoning above, he moved through their midst like a vulture; treading with care, the twin ridges of his jump pack recalling furled wings, beak-like helm sloping forwards like a jutting jaw.

And where he stepped through curling fronds of smoke and dust, where he moved without fear through sooty flames and hopped across boiling craters, where shadows moved around him like a living mantle, then it was his eyes alone that these dismal rag-men would recall: blazing red, like embers at the heart of a cooling hearth.

The stone tower was all but deserted when he reached it, its guards lying dead from shrapnel wounds at its door, and he swatted the portal from its hinges with a casual shrug. He inhaled as he entered, praying to the cold spirit of his master that here, at last, he would find the prize and its thief.

In the latter respect at least his prayer was answered.

The attack came from above, the flash-flicker of a muzzle igniting warning runes in his eyeplates. He pounced aside even as the hail of lead landed around him, armour whining in protest. Thick plumes of dust and shattered stone danced, and the staccato rattle of a hellfire gun shook the tower from base to tip. The first inelegant sweep of his attacker's hand raked him with lead, and despite the speed of his reaction knocked messy craters into the filigreed surfaces of his armour.

The impacts did not wound him. In those few lucky places that the attacker found his target he failed even to penetrate Sahaal's carapace, inflicting nothing but petulant surface-scars on the midnight blue shell. This was quite enough of an insult to enrage him nonetheless.

He bounded vertically – rising on the wash of his crested engines – and gashed at the wooden spars of the spiral gantry, splinters and singed beams toppling below him; the rhythmic collapse of each level – *koom-koom-koom-koom* – like the pounding of a fearful heart.

The gunman, lost somewhere in a haze of spinning wood, cried out as his platform dissolved. He skittered broken nails along stone walls, clutching for handholds, and hit the ground with an untidy crunch, leg twisted in fractured angles.

He groaned, struggling against the fuzz of shock.

And then something landed beside him. Something vast, clothed in black and blue. Something with the eyes of a devil, that flexed its claws and hissed like a serpent, that stepped closer and leaned down to inspect him, as a cat might a mouse.

Something that ran a blade, almost tender, across the glowing electoo of the man's forehead.

'Nikhae,' it said.

And finally, hearing his own name from this nightmare's shrouded lips, the man's voice came back to him. His shock parted like thinning smoke, and as the claws reached out to touch him he screamed with the ragged vestiges of his breath.

'Where,' the voice hissed, 'is it?'

ZSO SAHAAL LEFT Herniatown an hour later, thoughts clouded. The package he had taken with him had been left in his wake; placed carefully amongst the scraps of offal – shredded by the force of his fury – that had once been Nikhae. It would claim the lives of any who remained within the town's sagging grid, but where the thought of such wide-scale revenge should gratify him, Sahaal felt only emptiness.

The Corona was gone.

It had been sold.

Traded.

Bartered, like some plebeian *commodity*.

He walked from the town's northern entrance without a care for stealth or destination, in a haze, and when a cloaked figure approached from the darkness to bow before him he barely paused, whipping a thoughtless claw into and through its neck in a single motion. The body collapsed and his feet carried him on, and from the shadows a chorus of gasps arose around him. Finally, begrudgingly, he glanced up from the ground to regard this new circumstance.

There were fifty or more, each draped in black, prostrating themselves in terror and awe. More scum, worthy of his blades...

Sahaal sighed, flicked blood from his claws, and prepared for more slaughter.

'H-hail,' one of them said, her wide eyes avoiding his gaze. 'Hail to the Emperor's angel. Hail to the holy warrior.'

Sahaal stared at her, uncertain. He had expected opposition, terror, pitiful aggression – but not obeisance.

'What do you want?' he hissed, and each of them shivered at the sound of his voice.

'O-only to serve you, my lord,' the woman quailed, extending her right hand in a tall salute. *'Ave Imperator.'*

And then the *Umbrea Insidior*'s promethium reactor-cell, the bulky package he had removed so carefully from its crippled generarium, reached critical mass in the heart of the Glacier Rats' territory and detonated with the force of a thousand grenades.

The underhive shook, the floor quaked like a living thing, and as his new congregation cowered around him, Sahaal basked in the phosphorlight of Hernia-town's ruin.

MITA ASHYN

HEMMED ON ALL sides by drooping adamantium walls, the force of Herniatown's devastation erupted not outwards, but upwards.

Above Herniatown stood Cuspseal.

Mita had returned to the lower tiers from the undercity beneath a stormcloud of suspicion and fear. The psychic resonance of the murdered woman – a spectral shadow that only she had felt – had affected her profoundly, and as Sergeant Varitens stalked off to report to his commander she had hastened to a control room at the precinct's peak, pushing aside servitors and tech-acolytes in her haste to reach the communications consoles.

She was thus ensconced, struggling with the infuriating business of conferring with Inquisitor Kaustus, when the quake hit. It had almost been a relief.

Given that the hivelink – a mass of switchboard feeds crammed amongst ducts city-wide – was prone to broken signals and interferences, and that the control room's bustle was as endless as it was raucous, she had expected Kaustus's quiet tones to be rendered inaudible. As it was, his reaction to Mita's report was easily gauged despite its volume: describing to him the particulars of the murders had been an object lesson in futility, and his voice had dripped with an utter lack of interest. She began to appreciate why Orodai had insisted she see the slaughter for herself. Mere words could not hope to describe it.

'…desecration on a… a savage scale, my lord, and–'

'Savage, you say?' his clipped tones had dripped with scorn. 'And in the underhive, no less? Imagine that.'

She'd fancied she could hear him rolling his eyes.

'My lord, I… I know it must seem… insignificant, and perhaps my regard for it appears ridiculous to you, but–'

'It does not appear ridiculous, girl. It *is* ridiculous. Worse, it is a waste of my time. Murders in the underhive! You're a servant of the Inquisition, not some underling lawman sent to solve every tawdry crime.' He huffed loudly, and Mita had imagined him toying with the tip of one polished tusk. 'You will in future not burden me with every tedious item of detail that y–'

'But my lord, I felt such darkness! It… it hangs like a cloud! A shadow in the warp!'

The link's brass speaker, fashioned in the shape of a gasping fish, fell silent. Mita had stared at it, uncertain. Had he severed the connection?

'M-my lord?'

Kaustus's voice had been cold when at last he spoke.

'You will never interrupt me again. Is that quite clear?'

Her stomach had knotted. 'O-of course, my lord. My apologies.'

'My patience has limits, child. Do not test them.'

'I am sorry, my lord, truly... It's just that...' she'd fumbled for words, the memory of the body twisting her guts, flickering before her. Its naked shape haunted every blink and its empty eyes – hollows that led only to shadow – regarded her mutely from her own mind. Should she say it? Should she voice her suspicions? By the Throne, she'd been so *sure*, but now that she came to it, now that it needed to be spoken, suddenly it sounded ludicrous. Melodramatic. *Too much.*

But the words!

Adeo mori servus Imperator Fictus, Ave Dominus Nox.

The words had filled her with such certainty that she'd all but screamed her fears when she saw them, biting her tongue all the way back to Cuspseal, desperate to tell her master.

She must tell him. She *must.*

In the control room, staring at the voicetube with her stomach churning, she'd taken a breath, composed herself, injected formality into her tone, and said it.

'Inquisitor, it is my belief that the taint is abroad within the hive.'

This time the pause had dragged long and deep, and when he spoke Kaustus's voice was so quiet that she'd strained to hear his words.

'Chaos?' he'd whispered. 'You think the city harbours Chaos?'

She'd choked back a retch at the very word, and had gripped the speakertube as if clinging for dear life.

'Yes, my lord,' she said, committed. 'Or... or something like it, Emperor preserve.'

'Interrogator Ashyn,' Kaustus had said finally, and it seemed to Mita that a strange new element had entered his tone, a hint of ice that had not registered before. 'We are servants of the Ordo Xenos. We have come to this world to unmask the cancer that is xenophilia. *That* is the course we shall pursue.'

'But–'

'You are young, interrogator. Already you have served two masters. You lack continuity. You lack experience. You are unqualified in the ways of Chaos.'

'But... my lord,' she'd struggled with the plug of frustration in her throat. Why could he not *trust* her? What reason could he have for such belligerence? 'My lord, I *feel* it. I sense it. It stalks the shadows...'

'That,' and his voice had allowed no room for argument, no hope of persuasion, 'is not in your power to diagnose. Is that all, interrogator? Or do you have more spurious assertions to make?'

Standing there with mouth agape, a forked pathway had presented itself to her, and she had closed her eyes to explore its shimmering angles. Beyond the guiding techniques of the psi-trance, without even consulting the lesser arcanoi of the Imperial tarot, she knew that such echoes of the future – uninvited and uncontrolled – should be mistrusted. They presented fickle visions of what *might* be, writhing on skeins of chance, and the adept-tutors at the Scholia Psykana had warned their charges to be wary of their deceptions.

Nonetheless, the options had been as vibrant as had she been seated in her meditation cell, and she'd regarded them with the tranquillity of a practiced, competent psyker.

On the one hand she could return to her master's side. She could kow-tow to his desires, disregard her own judgements, suppress the condemnation of his eccentricities and accept his authority. She could trust in his righteousness and serve him with the devotion his rank deserved. In time, she could see, she would gain a portion of his respect.

Or she could believe what her heart told her: a path that ran ragged with uncertainty, violence and blood.

And glory.

'My lord,' she'd said, enslaved to her ambition. 'I would ask your blessing in undertaking a hunt.'

'A hunt.'

'Yes my lord. For the killer.'

The speaker crackled softly, as if astonished by her request.

'Interrogator,' it said eventually. 'Either your brain is addled by the crudity of your surroundings or your insolence is greater even than I had feared. Your request is d–'

And then the connection had broken, the lights flickered, and the world turned on its head.

The way Mita saw it – during the hours of madness that followed the quake – an interrupted refusal was no refusal at all.

IN A METROPOLIS as densely populated as the hive, any upheaval causing fatalities in the mere hundreds could barely be considered calamitous. Nor was Cuspseal's regimented architecture overly disturbed by the subterranean blast: its buttresses and spindled towers continued to stand, its bleak factories barely paused in their ceaseless grind, and its cabled walkways simply swayed before resuming their sprawl. And if here or there a habstack found its view altered, or a chapel leaned from its foundation where before it stood proud, then the teeming masses could be relied upon to shrug and thank the Emperor-on-high that the quake had not been more devastating. The ancientness of this skyless place weighed heavily, and deep in their hearts each hiver felt its fragility keenly. It was a house of cards, a tower of glass, and would require but one carelessly cast stone to crumble.

The floor of Cuspseal had developed a tumour. Where centuries before Herniatown had sagged into the shadows, now it had returned in contempt of those baroque towers built on its spine. It shrugged off the habs and trams and levered itself upright, its ceiling bulging from the Cuspseal foundation like some malign growth. It was here, at the disaster's epicentre, that the loss of life was greatest: hivers tumbling from splintered roads, crushed between pounding slabs. Dust boiled up and out like a living thing, breeding a race of staggering mud-caked zombies. In places the rising hillock split, plumes of molten metal rising from its rents, and there the explosion could vent itself, great tongues of fire licking the bases of gantries above. The stink of flesh wrestled with screams of terror for dominance, and for a brief hour Cuspseal resounded not with the usual factorial tumult, but with the sights and scents of a warzone.

It was perhaps a reflection of hive existence that the city barely paused in its industry at the quake's arrival. In the tier above it, or a single kilometre to either side, there the hive was as oblivious as was Governor Zagrif himself, insulated in the hive's peak. If any aristocrat from Steepletown found his apartments powerless for the instant it took ancient rerouters to correct the blip, or if some high-tier merchantman discovered his flow of mouldpaste interrupted before he could reassign his contracts, then such things could be attributed to the whims of the hiveghosts, or the will of the Emperor, or – at the very least – to just another aspect of the creaking, ineffective workings of hive life.

Cuspseal was all but back to normal within two hours, and the only factor of any note to have changed was the spiralling determination of a single woman to investigate exactly what was going *on* in the underhive.

'You want *what*?'

'You heard me. A squad of twenty men. Fully armed, fully armoured.'

'I see.' Commander Orodai sat back in his chair and steepled his fingers, raising an ironic eyebrow. 'Anything else? A set of wings?'

Mita waved a dismissive hand. She'd been too patronised by far less pleasant individuals to be bothered by Orodai's sarcasm.

'I think the men will suffice, for now. And a vehicle, of course.'

He nodded with false earnestness. 'Naturally.'

Orodai's office was a barren space, windowless, made all the less welcoming by the indistinct rustling of servitors in the shadows beyond his desk. Evidently the commander travelled often between the precincts beneath his control, and only his staff of mindless scribes remained constant.

'Save your sarcasm, commander. Whether it pleases you or not, this request carries the full weight of the Inquisition's authority, an–'

'Ha, yes. And is therefore not a "request" at all. It's a demand, girl, and you'd be better off calling it by name. I haven't time for your niceties.'

'Call it what you want. It's all the same in the end.'

Orodai regarded her beneath heavy brows, as if weighing her character by her looks alone. Judging by the taste of his thoughts, he didn't regard either with fondness.

'Let us pretend,' he said, 'that I give you what you want. What sort of madness are you planning on leading my men into?'

'We go to hunt the killer, commander.' This time it was her turn to cock an eyebrow. 'You remember? The one you invited our aid in capturing?'

'I remember. And I remember inviting aid to *spare* my men the trouble, not to draw them away from more important du–'

'Ah... Then you consider the Inquisition fit only for insignificant pursuits?'

'That's not what I–'

'But you just said as much.' She crossed her arms. 'If I were less charitable, I might consider that assertion to border on the heretical...'

She left the veiled threat dangling, watching him carefully.

He knew he was beaten. And in his thoughts – which of course he believed to be entirely private – he cursed her venomously. Inwardly, Mita joined him, briefly hating herself for steamrollering the objections of such a fundamentally honest man. She assuaged her guilt by reminding herself of the mission's importance. She could brook no concessions, no compromises.

'Fine,' Orodai snapped, hunching forward in his seat. 'Have the damned men. But how you plan to find a single killer amongst a multitude is a trick I'd love to know.'

She half smiled, dipping in a bow of genuine gratitude. 'I have my ways.'

'You'll need them,' he said, unimpressed. 'That quake started below. It's going to be messy down there, girl. Messy and mad.'

OrodaI's predictions were unerringly accurate.

It was as if the subterranean blast had expelled not only fire and ash, but some indiscernible smog of *insanity*. In every settlement around the ruined husk of

Herniatown, across every sumpflow and debris-dune, madness had spilled out from the shadows to reclaim its domain.

Most visible amongst the agents of lunacy were the Purgatists – sinister preachers enmeshed in suits of barbs and bones, lashing at the groaning crowds with hook-tipped whipcords. They prophesied the Emperor's return in a hail of blood and smoke, and attested in crazed tones to his wrath. In the city above Mita had noticed advocates of the movement on street corners and mezzanine junctions: moderates with earnest voices and scarred faces, the marks of quiet zeal and self-flagellation.

Not so in the undercity, where eccentricity bred delusion and piety begot fanaticism.

The Purgatists here yelped and howled, struck at the willing crowd, set alight pyres containing 'mutants' and 'witches', and cast quivering fingers towards where Herniatown had once stood, citing the Emperor's splendid venom as the force that had purged so utterly the Glacier Rat filth.

Passing by the lunatic zealots, Mita couldn't prevent a guilty thought from seeping through her defences: *Is insanity the price of faith?*

The deranged-but-pious were not alone in seizing the prospects presented by the explosion. To the gangs the explosion marked not only a territorial opportunity in the Glacier Rats' wake, but a power vacuum. Total war had come to the underhive.

The crackle of distant gunfire struggled to be heard above the shouts of combatants and the thunder of collapsing buildings, gutted by fire or otherwise undermined. On several occasions gangers themselves, flamboyantly dressed in the colours of their pack, appeared beside the debrisflows to snap off a few optimistic rounds at the vindictors in their trio of Salamanders, before vanishing into their warrens like ghosts. Mita thought it somehow exotic: like jewelled wildlife glimpsed at a forest's edge.

The vindictors, of course, endured these sightings with less sentimentality, taking turns to rise into the Salamanders' open-topped diases, vying to pick off those unfortunates unable to seek cover. Mita endured the noisy distractions poorly, struggling to remain focused.

In less enlightened times a hunter might follow a trail of prints, or spend days pursuing rumours and sightings. To Mita such crudities were unthinkable: the maelstrom of emotion that comprised the psychic environment was as perceptible to her as the scorched earth of its roads or the buckled struts of its walls. The shadow she sought – an oilslick of malign influence and, yes... yes, she was certain, the *taint* – wound its way throughout like a spectral cord. Whether it represented the killer's exact trail or not was irrelevant; its loci were places he had been, its tentacles were the paths of people he had stalked. Without a clue as to who or what the killer was, she nonetheless tracked his flavour; she followed the strings of his emotion, blossoming and nebulising in his wake. He was angry.

Angry, and cold and bitter.

'Right at the junction,' she instructed the Salamander's pilot, eyelids closed, and watched the manoeuvre through a spectrum that employed neither light nor colour.

The trail had led them on a merry dance already, and she dimly suspected the Preafects thought she was inventing as she went. She couldn't care less.

Their first destination, against Sergeant Varitens's noisy protests, had been the perimeter of the contested zone itself, where Herniatown had once stood. That pulverised area of metallic slag and scorched earth – its walls and ceilings presenting not a single straight line or right angle in their fractured surfaces – had clamoured in her mind with the darkness she'd been seeking, and briefly she'd thought the killer must have died in the inferno. He'd been present, she had no doubt of that. When Herniatown belched itself out of existence he'd been there, at the thick of whatever action had transpired, and she considered the possibility of his death with an uncomfortable thrill of disappointment.

But, no... The trail had reappeared, coal-black, leading away from the ruined zone into the darkness of the western caverns. She led the convoy away from the petty gang squabbles, away from the central settlements with their vestiges of civilisation and their ranting Purgatists, and she resumed the hunt with guilty pleasure.

It had not taken the Preafects long to grasp the reality of their leader's psychic gifts. Mita guessed that had it not been for Cog's silent presence, great machine-hands clenching and unclenching around the autocannon trigger on the tank, their regard for her authority might have been less complete. As it was, they did what she told them *when* she told them, throwing nervous glances towards the giant – and if they did so without the salutes they would have offered their own commanders it was a detail she was happy to forgo. The one remaining irritation was the interminable mumbling of Sergeant Varitens, who insisted on standing beside her, arms crossed, as if keeping her in his sights could keep her (clearly heretical) mutation in check.

She huffed at the off-putting mussitation – a prayer, she guessed – and refocused, fighting the exhaustion that such intense meditation inevitably caused.

The killer's influence wended its way through a knot of twisting alleys – a filigree of black and blue on the very cusp of her psychic sight – and she guided the pilot through with a calm voice, ignoring the hammering of opportunistic bullets on the tank's sides. As the vehicle clambered from the labyrinth onto a rising steppe of detritus, tracks struggling for purchase, an uncomfortable silence settled, leaving her alone with only the sound of the Salamanders' engines.

Strange shapes loomed in the dark, and at first she mistook them for mighty oaks, grown beyond normal scale, their branches rising above, ghostly lights adorning their tips. Only when perspective adjusted itself in her mind that her eyes decoded what they were seeing.

Vast ducts, each a hundred metres across, littered with scaffold and piping, branching in myriad patterns between floor and cavernous ceiling. At odd points on their colossal trunks hellish lights blazed angry red, steam geysering from every rent, and Mita realised with a stab of amazement that she was seeing thermal ducts, siphoning heat from the planet's crust where even the frozen fluctuations of its weather could not hope to diminish it. From below the entire hive drunk the warmth of Equixus, and as the vehicles passed by she found herself humbled, forgetting for an instant the trail she followed.

Varitens's mutterings finally snapped both introspection and temper.

'Sergeant, for the love of the Emperor, would you be *quiet*!'

He glared, helmet clenched between nervous fingers.

'It's come to a bad thing,' he grumbled, 'when a soldier's denied a prayer for his soul.'

'You feel the need to pray?' she scowled, curling a lip. 'You have twenty men with unfeasibly large weapons standing right behind you, sergeant. What's to be afraid of?'

At this his grizzled mouth twitched in a pale imitation of a smile. Even afflicted by terrors of his own, the prospect of highlighting her ignorance was too delicious for him to pass up.

'This here is the Steel Forest, girl,' he said, nodding out into the canopy of tangled pipes and pilot lights.

'You told me you didn't know any names.'

'And I don't – unless they happen to be the sorts of places it's best to avoid.' He turned towards the viewing slot, glaring out into the dark. 'This is where you'll find the Shadowkin. And they don't much like intruders.'

PART TWO: KINGDOM OF FEAR

'Perhaps you believe yourself blameless. Perhaps you have acted, as you claim, in the interests of your people. Perhaps, in that respect, your guilt is negligible.

'But I tell you this: there is strife enough in this galaxy without the ambitions of those who would construct empires of their own. Selfless or not, there is room only for one Emperor in this *Imperium.'*

–Judgement of Madam Inquisitor Trâis Spirrus
at the trial of Grigor 'The Prosperous',
short-lived ruler of the Dactylis system.

ZSO SAHAAL

HIS MIND DRIFTED, detached.

He had not slept in four days, and whilst it was true that the artifices of his enhanced brain and body could maintain alertness almost indefinitely, already the nagging seeds of exhaustion twitched at the back of his mind, threatening his efficacy. In this strange place he had conducted himself with unparalleled caution, never once allowing his vigilance to slip.

This, finally, in the lair of his newfound servants, had changed. Riding a wave of his own authority, surrounded by those who would no more allow him harm than kill themselves, Sahaal at last – mercifully – took the opportunity to rest.

They were named the Shadowkin, and they worshipped him. The fools.

He slipped into the arms of half-sleep with an eagerness he had not expected, and drowned in meditation.

* * *

He had been uncertain, at first. Confronted by a horde of black-shrouded peasants, creeping from the shadows in the wake of Herniatown's purgation, he had nearly slaughtered them without thought, coasting on the fury of what Nikhae had told him.

The Corona *was gone!*

His prize was lost to him, and as he stumbled directionless from the killing fields of Herniatown, these Shadowkin had mistaken him for a warrior of the Emperor.

They had seen pictoslates, perhaps, or illuminations in ancient scriptures. The Emperor had created the Space Marines: that much they knew. He had fashioned their primarchs, modelled their Legions, dispatched them to crusade in his name. They knew little of the intricacies of Imperial history, but they could not question the benevolence of such angelic warriors. A Space Marine was beyond imperfection.

They had never heard of the Horus Heresy. Sahaal wasn't surprised. The churning propaganda machines of the Imperium could hardly countenance the popular exposure of its own flawed past.

In the haze of his trance, Sahaal mused upon revealing the truth to his new acolytes, then discounted the possibility... To learn that half the Emperor's angels had turned to the dark fires of Chaos: to these underhive scum such realities would seem ludicrous. Impossible. *Cruel.*

Sahaal was no more part of the Emperor's vast congregation than were the xenos that infested the galaxy, and it sickened him that the wide-eyed men and women of the Shadowkin should mistake him so easily. It was true that the seductions of Chaos also held little sway over him – he considered such metaphysical corruption a sign of weakness; of lack of focus – but his contempt for the Emperor matched that of any Chaotic anti-zealot nonetheless, and the Shadowkin's mistaken identity was difficult to swallow.

They saw his power armour, his narrow-eyed helm, his wedge-like shoulderguards, his jewelled bolter. They saw the intricate heraldry of his Legion, and whilst they could not hope to recognise it, they understood that such icons had ever been the remit of the Adeptus Astartes. They had watched him single handedly wipe out a nest of their most iniquitous enemies, and any doubts as to his righteousness were immediately expunged.

They saw him, and they saw a Space Marine, and so they saw a reflection of their god.

He had almost killed them for it.

And yet their devotion had warmed him – as mindless as that of a machine – and slowly, with growing momentum, his thoughts turned to another, shrewder path.

Herniatown had burned behind him, Nikhae's words – *'I-it's gone... It's sold!'* – had scorched his mind, and the Shadowkin had fallen to his feet and praised him. Their worship had filled him with pleasure – pleasure borne upon a lie, but pleasure nonetheless – and slowly, hating himself, resisting the bile in his throat, he had said the one thing that could assure their loyalty.

'Ave Imperator.'

They had brought him to their lair, they had worshipped him, they had given him food and sanctuary, and so he slept.

Adrift upon the trance, he remembered Nikhae's screaming face as slice by slice he was skinned alive.

'Where is the package?'

'I told you, Zagrif's blood! It's gone!'

'Gone where?'

'Sold! W-warpspoor and piss! Y-you sh... shit! Sold!'

'Sold to whom? Speak, or I'll take your eyes.'

'No! N-not th–'

'Sold to whom?'

'Slake! The Collective! I swear it, Throne-as-my-witness! Slake!'

'What is this... "Slake"?'

'I don't... n-nuh...'

'Your eyes, Nikhae. Do you need both?'

'S-sweet Terra, a-a middleman! A go-between for upcity merchants! Slake!'

'Where is he, Nikhae? Where did you find him?'

'I didn't, h–'

'Where is he!'

'I don't know! H-he found us! H-he knew the ship would fall from the sky! He told us to be ready! He commissioned us, *warpdammit!'*

'He knew?'

'Yes!'

'He ordered the package by name?'

'Yes!'

'That is not possible.'

'I don't know how, but he kn–'

'You're lying to me.'

He was still screaming when there was no skin left for Sahaal to cut away.

Before he planted the fuelcell that destroyed the Glacier Rats' lair, Sahaal vented his rage upon the meaty husk that had once been Nikhae, expelling his fury on muscle and sinew and bone. It had made quite a mess.

The Corona *was gone. He had a new target.*

And like a dream, in that moment, when he staggered exhausted from Herniatown already planning this new hunt, the solution had delivered itself like a gift from the Four Gods.

The Shadowkin. An army of slaves, bound to him in devotion for the very thing he hated the most.

They would help him find Slake – whoever, *whatever*, he was.

THE TRANCE HAD lasted some four hours, he judged, when his slumbering senses awoke him. Someone was approaching.

The Shadowkin lair clung to the trunk of one of the great stacks that comprised the Steel Forest, jutting from its girth like a fungus, and Sahaal had found its fortification impressive. As the frightened mob had conducted him aboard their iron-pulleyed elevators he had observed their regimented movements, their well maintained weapons, their silent obedience. Their discipline was impressive, their focus commendable and their arsenal – in the midst of such squalor – fearsome indeed.

They were a tribe of zealots, he had quickly learned; puritans that had rejected the wickedness of the hive centuries before, sinking down to the depths of the underhive where they could pursue their veneration unhindered. They saw in their Emperor a divine judge, in whose name iniquity was purged and impurity burned away. Through long decades their worship had intertwined itself with a morbid indulgence: deifying their lord in his aspect as Death – the ultimate leveller – and revelling in the melancholic symbols of mortality.

Bone worshippers. Scalp hunters.

Corpse-bearers.

Further, finding themselves surrounded by filth and hedonism, hemmed in by false worshippers and iniquitous licence, they had elected themselves to a divine mission, reasoning that *they* alone must execute the Emperor's law.

They were pious vigilantes, these quiet warriors, and in them Sahaal saw echoes of his master's youth, stalking the streets of Nostromo Quintus, judging and striking from the shadows.

They reminded him of himself, and were it not for their misplaced reverence he might whole-heartedly have accepted their hospitality, told them the truth, secured their obedience for all the *right* reasons...

But no... No, they were the Emperor's sons and daughters first, and creatures of the night second. He could seek sanctuary amongst them but could never fully lower his guard. His dark beliefs would be anathema to these pious fools, and the irony of the situation was not lost on him: such similar disciplines, such reflected methods, such matching values; but such opposite causes.

So it was that when their priestess scrambled towards Sahaal's mediation platform on her hands and knees, her heart hammering like a drum in his ears, he was awake before she had even opened her mouth.

'Why do you disturb me?' he said, and he smiled inside his helm at the shiver that rattled through her.

'F-forgive me, my lord, I did not intend to discomfort you...'

He dismissed her cowering with a flick of his wrist, tilting his head to regard her closely. 'By what name are you known, child?'

This request seemed to confuse her. Whatever news she'd rushed to divulge, a personal introduction had not been amongst it. 'Chianni, my lord.'

'You are the leader of this band?'

'N... I... I was the second, my lord. B-beneath Condemnitor Kalriian.'

'And where is he?'

Her eyes, if possible, bulged wider still.

'Y-you… you killed him, my lord…'

Sahaal recalled that first simpering figure, approaching from the shadows outside Herniatown, cut down in mid-exultation. He smoothly extended his duplicity: 'He was remiss in his devotions. It was a mercy to cut him down.'

If she doubted the excuse she gave no sign of it. 'A-as you wish it, my lord.'

He pointed a long claw at her heart, enjoying her squirms. 'You shall be the new condemnitor.'

She dipped her head in shivering gratitude, sweat glistening in the dark. 'You honour me, lord, but I–'

'You may leave me. I would continue my meditation.'

For a second she seemed torn, as if her body would love nothing more than to comply, but her brows dipped and she remained where she was, struggling to speak. Sahaal watched her with interest.

'It is… please, lord. The scouts sent up flares. There are intruders abroad. Judge-men from the city.' She cast her eyes upwards towards the distant struts of the hive-bottom. 'Vindictors from above. We… we seek your counsel.'

'What do they want?' Sahaal's voice contrived to indicate that such tedious announcements were beneath his interest.

'I do not know, lord. T-they share our cause – in the main – though their laws are lax in the Emperor's eyes. Is it not said tha–'

'Spare me the lesson. Are they your enemies?'

She swallowed hard and shook her head, eyes bright in the gloom. 'They have never sought our ruin, lord. They would not enter our territory without cause.'

'I see.'

'T-there is something else...'

'Yes?'

'They... they travel with a mutant. A... a giant. The scouts have seen it. It is... *unchained*.' She spoke this last word as if it wounded her to say it, and Sahaal marvelled at the depth of hatred in her voice. Here, even in the filth of the underhive, the Imperium's contempt for all that was 'impure' had found ample representation.

'A mutant?'

'Yes my lord. An abomination in the eyes of the Emperor! I... I have prayed for guidance but–'

'That is unnecessary. *I* am the Emperor's voice here.'

For a moment she looked as though she might cut her own throat. Sahaal found himself gratified by her discomfort.

'My apologies, lord. I did not mean offence...'

'These "vindictors". They are in the employ of the Imperium?'

'Y-yes my lord.'

'And they have no reason to come here?'

'No, my lord.'

The truth sagged into Sahaal's mind.

They are hunting me. They have my trail.

Something akin to nervousness passed through him, then, but seemed mixed perversely with a measure of excitement. After so long, after such care and secrecy, it was almost a pleasure to face enemies openly.

And in a moment of inspiration, slicing into his consciousness like a blade from the heavens, the solution came to him.

'They are corrupt.' he said, standing. Chianni staggered backwards, dwarfed.

'M-my lord?'

'Listen carefully. You will struggle to believe me.'

'I... I will believe what you tell me, my lo–'

'I was sent here at the Emperor's own command, condemnitor. Do you believe that?'

She sunk to her knees as if struck, mouth agape.

'*Ave Imperator*!' she shrieked, overcome.

'Stand, child. We haven't much time.'

She glanced upward with the look of a drunkard.

'I was sent here because this world has fallen from the light of Terra. It is consumed by corruption. From tip to base, only impurity remains.'

'But... but this is...' She gasped for air, like a fish removed from water, and for a brief instant Sahaal found himself pitying her. Her entire universe must be crumbling around her.

'Equixus has fallen to Chaos, child, and there are few of the Emperor's faithful that remain.'

She vomited, clutching at her belly, moaning in horror.

'No...' she whispered, drool sagging from her lips. 'It's not true... it's not true... it's not true...'

'Stand!' Sahaal gripped her collar and yanked her upright like a heap of rags, leaving her tottering in a fugue of terror and misery.

'I don't understand, my lord! T-there was no war! No invasion!'

'You underestimate the ruinous powers. There was no invasion, only *infection*. The taint spreads like disease. The governor is corrupted. His house and barons are lost to the dark. And piece by piece the purity of this hive is sundered.'

'But... but...'

'I was sent to assess the extent of the corruption,' he said, lies pouring so easily from his mouth. 'I was sent to discover if any of the Emperor's faithful remained.'

'We do, lord! *We do*!' she almost sang the words, arms raised above her head, delirious with shock.

'You do,' Sahaal nodded, 'and I have found you. And now... now these false servants of the Emperor, these "vindictors", who make a mockery of all that was pure, have descended to crush us all. We must stop them. Do you understand, condemnitor? The Emperor Himself has spoken! We *must* stop them!'

THE INTRUDERS' VEHICLES were familiar, at least. Coiling their way through the Steel Forest, they made light work of the debrisflows around the ducts' bases: Chimera-class chasses, albeit lacking the artillery mounts and dozer-scoops of their forebears. He had once orchestrated the advances of legions of their kind, savaging the enemy with his Raptor packs whilst the guns of the Chimerae battered their flanks. It seemed somehow ludicrous that he should now find himself opposing such familiar machines, accompanied only by a mob of zealots devoted to his enemy's worship.

This time his master's voice echoed almost whimsically through his memories, and he fought a brief surge of affront in its implied disapproval.

How the mighty are fallen, it said, over and over, like a mantra in his soul.

The intruders rounded the final corner in their approach to the Shadowkin lair and Sahaal returned his mind to the present: there was an ambush to oversee.

Forewarned, the Shadowkin attack was as devastating as any Sahaal had seen. Dressed for war, cloaked in tattered rags of black and red, with bones stitched to collars and stolen knuckles swinging on cords from sleeves, they were a grim sight: wraiths that slunk in the dark, skeletal trophies adorning their brows.

Sahaal waited until the first two vehicles had passed below before giving the signal to attack; a single swipe of his clawed fist, reflections flickering like a galaxy in the half-light.

The first hint of danger, a roiling pulse of electric sound and the shadow-stitching flare of a discharge, came far too late for the vindictors.

That first carefully gauged blast from the Shadowkin's solitary lascannon, positioned at the edge of a high balcony, punched through the trailing vehicle's tracks like a fiery blade, gobbets of molten metal sputtering from the wound. The pilot's attempt to brake was as doomed as the vehicle itself: its track peeled, thrashing at the hull as it sluiced away, whipping back on itself at the last instant to slice the vindictor riding shotgun into two ragged halves.

First blood. Time seemed to stop.

Then the Shadowkin howled, like wolves after a kill.

The tank slipped from its line, wobbled across unstable debris, hit a bank of shapeless scrap and flipped onto its back, trailing oil and dust. The screams from within filtered quickly through its mangled shanks.

And then the lasguns opened fire, the volley of grenades from above rattled down on the stricken convoy, the Shadowkin rappelled from their balconies with a chilling shriek, and the battle of the Steel Forest began.

To their credit, the intruders were swift to react. The remaining vehicles about-turned, tracks shifting in awkward patterns, to circle their stricken fellow. Their passengers tumbled out in short order, using their vehicles as cover and firing thunderous shotguns into the shapeless shadows, shouting terse orders. To Sahaal, watching from above, they seemed like miniature parodies of Space Marines – their glossy carapaces shaped in obvious reflection of the Astartes' power armour, helms open below the nose, solid gauntlets clutching at stocks and mauls. He sneered in contempt and launched himself from his platform's edge, following the whooping Shadowkin towards the ground, jump pack slowing his descent.

A killing ground had quickly formed between the remaining tanks and the gangers slunk forwards with weapons blazing, pinning the vindictors in their places. Already a gaggle of armoured bodies thrashed and moaned in the circle, blood staining the spongy ground, and the remaining lawmen struggled to find return targets. The Shadowkin were more than adept at stealing about the perimeter of the ring like sharks, snapping off shots then melting away. Even the autocannons on the Salamanders' spines seemed useless; hammering their ammunition into the wastes in near disarray, their bright flares dazzling the vindictors further still, rendering the darkness all the more impenetrable.

A frag grenade, dropped almost casually from the gantries above, split apart an exposed Preafect, showering his comrades with whirligig shrapnel and gore. His shriek lasted a fraction of a second, aborted on a froth of viscera and clutching limbs. His comrades hollered and regrouped, more and more of their armoured fellows tumbling from the safety of the Salamanders to confront the threat, and in reply more of the death-masked Shadowkin slipped along black ropes to surround them, lasguns shifting shadows and colours across the distant walls.

Sahaal set himself down at the periphery of the ring and drew his bolter. Rushing into the face of a shotgun salvo would be a folly, but there were... *other* ways. Whooping his hawk-like shriek, kicking himself into the air, he crossed the deadzone in a single bound, glaring down on the besieged vindictors with trigger depressed. Through gunsmoke and airborne ash bolter shells kicked sticky craters in muscle and sinew; encased bodies jerked as shells detonated and helmeted faces craned up to observe this new threat, gliding on darkness overhead.

Somewhere, lost to the rushing of his blood, Sahaal heard a cheer blossom in the gloom. The Shadowkin were saluting their master.

He savoured their awe, and each discharge of his bolter was an offering to his master, each scarlet-splattered scream a guilty intonation to the Chaos Gods that he neither worshipped nor denied. The sight of his victims' wide eyes and pale faces, gaping up as they realised *what* they faced all too late, warmed him to his core, and he shrilled as their bodies dissolved in fire and smoke and blood.

'Ave dominus nox!'

His arc complete, he set down on the opposite boundary and spun in his place, eager for a second pass. His feet had all but left the ground when the lascannon fired its second pulse and the world went white.

A dagger of light punctured the ablative guts of the overturned Salamander, a wound that lanced thick armour and stabbed deep into its fuel reserves. The vehicle seemed to judder and draw a breath, swelling, before detonating in a storm of shattered light.

The metal carcass lifted high on a spout of flame, breaking apart and littering the air, razor fragments blizzarding outwards. At its apex it slouched onto its back like a dying whale, flames running off its scars like water, then crashed – ruined – to the earth.

The Shadowkin roared their approval, weapons brandished high, and the vindictors crawled and bled in the wreckage. Only the hammering of the remaining autocannons swelled the silence, and for every lead gobbet that found a target in the dark – flipping some nameless zealot to his knees with a jet of crimson – a hundred chattered uselessly against the mangled surfaces of the debris flows. Such was the madness of the scene that Sahaal went unnoticed as he clawed his way vertically along a rusted duct, a monstrous lizard adhering to a wall.

He gauged his release with precision, snapping free his claws and tumbling with a cry to land, as elegant as a cat, on the cab of the nearest tank. The pilot's wordless shriek filtered from within, and it was only when Sahaal lunged at the autocannon pintle – severing its plinth and blasting its gunner's head from his shoulders – that the shrill exclamation found words: a rush of curses and prayers. Sahaal leaned inside with a hiss, snipping at the pilot's thrashing arms, spraying the interior with arterial muck.

The shrieks increased in pitch and volume.

Sahaal leapt clear, snagging at an oily overhang and swivelling to watch the vehicle caper out of control, skidding on its axis and ploughing through the diminishing knot of vindictors. Gore-splattered, it rushed into the darkness and quit the battle, dust and waste lifting from its tracks, vanishing to topple to its doom in some forgotten corner. The dismembered pilot's screams dwindled with it into the shadows.

With their cover thus diminished the vindictors were easy prey. The remaining Salamander had tasked itself with knocking out the las-crew that had so decimated its shattered fellow, and its futile tracer sweeps of the balconies above had taken it away from the action on the ground, leaving the Preafects vulnerable.

Sahaal saw the trap an instant too late.

'Stay back!' Sahaal roared to the Shadowkin from his vantage. 'Stay in the shadows! Spare no one! Spare nothing!'

The warning was too late. Flushed by the excitement of victory, led by Condemnitor Chianni, the shrouded warriors rushed forth through the ring of corpse-dotted wreckage to smash against the vindictors.

In the face of a direct assault the Preafects released one final devastating volley before lowering their shotguns, raising instead the power mauls holstered at their sides. There was something of the parade ground in their synchronous movements: thumbing activation runes together, striking combat stances in a perfect circle of glossy armour and fizzling maces. The Shadowkin rebounded from their flanks like bloody waves against a cliff, and every failed swipe of a notched blade or jab with a tarblacked dagger was followed by the precise, deadly swing of an energised club. Sparks burst in bubbles of light, flesh charred and skulls popped. Here a black-robed man staggered clear with a scream, his eyeballs gone; there a young woman limped to escape, the bones of her leg jabbing at ugly angles from her flesh. With no space to put their numbers – or their stealth – to their advantage, the Shadowkin were being massacred. Sahaal found himself swooping to join the frenzy when the lascannon crew fired their third – and final – blast.

This time, perhaps recognising that the remaining Salamander had found its range and was already tilting its autocannon towards them, they eschewed the obvious target presented by the vehicle and tilted their scripture-pocked weapon towards the vindictor ranks; resolving to inflict as much damage as possible before the end.

Had their actions not been undertaken in his name, Sahaal would have derided their sacrifice. A true warrior, he had learned, values his own life at least as much as he values the loss of his enemy's. There was little room in his heart for martyrdom – beyond that, of course, of his dead master.

His betrayed master, who had died for his principles – and so forged a bitter vengeance in his own blood.

His master, whose memory he served.

His master, whose mantle he had inherited…

…and then lost.

At the centre of the killing ground, where the lascannon's discharge slid like an arrow into the earth, the vindictors fell apart at their joints: swallowed in a torus of iridescence that incised bone and sinew like a blade through water. They found themselves blasted up and out on the cusp of a shockwave; meaty slabs parting along torn seams, shredded alive. This was no great pyrotechnic spectacle, no flaming tumult, no smokeless fireball: merely a sooty chrysanthemum of uncontainable energy, blindingly bright, that dismantled its targets like dried leaves before a storm.

As if in reply, the autocannon found its target. The lascannon crew died in fire and lead; tumbling to the earth like rag-dolls, dead of their wounds long before they struck the ground.

A stunned silence settled.

Through the shifting smoke and lapping fires, beyond the charred bodies and shattered armour-plates, now only the single vehicle remained of the convoy. The Shadowkin stared at it with weapons brandished, skeletal trophies on proud display, as if daring it to advance.

And then their warrior-angel, their black/blue lord, their benighted messiah, dropped like a stone from above, plunging bright claws into its ablative sides and rising up its flanks: a hawk taking a dove.

This close, beyond the smoke and dust, Sahaal could finally see what manner of beast manned the autocannon.

It was a giant.

It raised its arms as he slunk near and clenched iron fists, face contorting with a challenge-roar. Sahaal extended his claws and laughed, gratified at the prospect of a worthy opponent. He would enjoy killing this mutant, he decided, this ape-faced freak, and in so doing would secure the loyalty of his xenophobic little slaves forever. He imagined himself surging forwards, claws snickering, blood raining around him.

And then a head appeared at the hatch into the tank's interior: an unarmoured female, as lowly an opponent as he could imagine. She was beneath his attention – *unworthy* – and he returned his focus to the hulk, claws flexing.

'I know what you are,' the woman said, startling him. Her eyes were wide and her skin bleached with fear, but her voice sounded strong and certain; resonating somewhere deep, transcending his ears. 'Go back to the shadows,' she hissed, lips curling. 'Go back to the warp, Night Lord!'

And then a great dagger punctured his mind: an inelegant swipe of immaterial force that took him by surprise and detonated a bomb within his skull, and he slipped from the Salamander's back onto the floor.

Darkness swallowed him up like an old friend – like the mother whose face he could no longer recall – and it was only on the very edge of his consciousness that he could hear the sound of heavy tracks clawing at soft earth and an engine, dwindling away into the distance.

The witch and her pet giant were gone, and as unconsciousness clouded around him he recalled her words with a start.

Go back to the warp, Night Lord!

She knew what he was.

She had recognised his heraldry.

She had spoken his Legion's name.

In that instant, on the cusp of waking reality, galvanised by his own discovery, he reached a decision: secrecy was futile. He would summon his brethren. No matter what had happened to them, no matter what glories and solemnities ten thousand years had inflicted upon them, he would summon them to his side, and he would greet them with the Corona in his possession, so that they would know, without doubt – Zso Sahaal, Captain of the Night Lords Legion, chosen heir of the Primarch Konrad Curze, had returned from his slumber to claim his throne.

Ave Dominus Nox!

MITA ASHYN

He – the great, the holier-than-thou, the Scourge of Namiito Ophidius, Deliverer of the Claviculus Ultimatum, lord high-and-fragging-mighty Inquisitor Ipoqr Kaustus – was waiting.

Mita half expected a red carpet.

That he had deigned to leave the crystal towers of Steepletown and the comfortable decadence of the governor's palace, that he (and his retinue, of course) had swarmed to the unfashionable depths of Cuspseal, was an indication, she reflected, of just how much trouble she was in.

He received her in Commander Orodai's quarters, and where before she had faced him with the retinue circling behind, now they stood arranged around her, glaring as she entered.

It was a little like stepping onto a stage.

She noted without much surprise that Sergeant Varitens was standing to the left of Orodai's desk. Of the nineteen vindictors and two staff-drivers who had failed to return from the Steel Forest, she found it particularly galling that *he* hadn't been amongst them. Doubtless he'd filled Orodai's head with tales of his own heroism and her – Mita's – mistakes, leading his men into a massacre. She could imagine the bureaucratic paper trail that followed: from here all the way up to the inquisitor himself–

Who, she had very little doubt, had lost his temper.

Mita had been back in Cuspseal for ten hours – much of which had been dedicated to a futile attempt to sleep – and with exhaustion clinging to every fibre she was in no mood for yet another dressing down.

'Get it over with,' she said, not waiting to be addressed.

Several of the retinue exchanged glances. She'd be damned if she'd treat them to another dewy-eyed performance of apology and supplication.

'I beg your pardon?' said Kaustus, fingers steepled. His features were once again concealed within his mask, its gloss accentuated by his exquisite gown of red webbing, and Mita met her own reflected gaze and held it, chin jutting proudly.

'The execution, inquisitor,' she said, refusing to be cowed. 'I've failed you twice. I went against your orders. I'm responsible for the deaths of twenty-one of the Emperor's loyal Preafects and I haven't any wish to be kept waiting for summary exe–'

'Sergeant Varitens tells me that you have identified the killer.'

The defiant bite-back she'd been preparing died in her mouth.

'W... what?'

Kaustus leaned forwards. 'He speaks of an armoured warrior, interrogator. He suggests there is a... how did he put it?... A *living blasphemy* at large.'

Something a little like triumph planted tenuous roots in her belly.

'I-is that so, my lord?'

'It is. What do you say to that, interrogator?'

She glanced at Varitens, seeking confirmation of his collusion. The man's eyes seemed fixated on the floor, wide with child-like fascination. Like a sword of Damocles, descending to puncture her scant shred of victory, a long cord of spittle parted company with his lip and spattered to the floor. Mita's heart sunk.

'As you can see,' Kaustus added, interrupting her before she could answer, 'the good sergeant required some... calming. He was almost ranting, the poor beast.'

'He's been drugged?'

Kaustus's eyes glimmered within the narrow slats of his mask.

'Not quite. We thought it best to cleanse his mind – and that of the surviving driver – using a more...' he waved a thoughtful hand, '...*permanent* method.'

Lobotomisation. With such impunity could an inquisitor wipe away a man's thoughts and memories.

'Is that to be my fate, my lord?' she scowled, prideful rebellion sputtering in her belly. 'And Cog's? Our minds stripped away because you refuse to believe the truth?'

For an instant, there was silence.

Then Kaustus moved faster than her eye could follow, and with barely a hiss registering in her ears she found herself spinning in her place, the floor rising to meet her, cheek stinging. When the lights cleared from her eyes she found the inquisitor stood over her and she realised with a thrill that he'd struck her.

So much for the cool, collected Inquisitor Kaustus.

'Your insolence stops here, interrogator,' he said, breathing hard. 'And should I wish it I can command far worse fates than mere lobotomy. This is your last warning.'

'B-but why h–'

'Why have I erased the testimonies of the sergeant and the driver? Use your brain, child! If what they say – if what *you* say – is correct, then the taint is abroad.'

'So you believe me n–'

'I will not tolerate panic and rumour-mongering, is that clear? This is damage limitation, interrogator. Be grateful I consider you capable of keeping secrets.' He returned to his seat, eyes lowered, adding quietly, 'and yes. Yes, I believe you.'

Mita tottered to her feet, dizzied. Such an uncharacteristic performance from the inquisitor had prompted a chorus of astonished thought from the retinue, and Mita struggled to shut out the psionic clamour.

'So,' Kaustus intoned, returning to his brooding position with fingers toying at his pendant. 'Tell me. What manner of corruption draws me so successfully from my Holy Work?' The boredom in his voice was as theatrical as it was palpable. 'A cult of the Dark Powers? Some mutant animal, perhaps? Or some tainted aristocrat, seeking thrills and kills in the underhive?' He folded his arms. 'Speak, child – I would know the agent of this... *distraction*.'

Mita squared her shoulders.

'It is a Traitor Space Marine, my lord.'

Uproar.

The retinue dissolved in a froth of gabbled prayers and startled exchanges – outrage clamouring with denial and anger.

Only Kaustus remained silent, and it was only Mita – who regarded his reaction scrupulously – that noted the tightening of his knuckles and the stiffening of his spine.

His eyes burned into her, betraying nothing.

'Impossible!' It was Commander Orodai who first summoned the ire required to speak out, rising to his feet and stabbing an infuriated finger at the floor. The venom in his voice astonished even Mita.

'I won't listen to this!' the commander stormed, arms waving. 'No warpshit *daemon* ever set foot inside my city, and I won't have some slip of a witch suggesting otherw–'

'It's no daemon!' Mita interrupted, gorge rising. 'It's a *Space Marine*, you fool! One of our own, fallen from the light. It's more cunning than any daemon!'

'This is intolerable…' Orodai turned to Kaustus with his cheeks burning. 'Are we to listen to these heresies all day?' he snarled. 'Silence your brat before I do it myself!'

He drew his pistol.

Mita's heart skipped.

In the mist of her senses the psychic nebula of Orodai's mind turned black and red; an ugly bruise of murderous intent. She staggered away, a warding hand raised. Her eyes tracked the commander's fist with morbid absorption, every centimetre of the gun's slow ascension like a countdown to thick, endless night.

'Have a care, Orodai.'

The voice seemed to come from far away, and it took Mita's revolving senses an eternity to stabilise, to draw her eyes away from the rising gun, and to note the tip of a sword, paused centimetres short of pricking at Orodai's skin.

'It is unwise to issue orders to an inquisitor,' said Kaustus tiredly, 'or to threaten his flock.'

Mita hadn't even seen him draw the blade.

'I... I...' Orodai seemed torn between outrage and self-preservation, anger and terror jockeying on the surface of his thoughts. Mita allowed herself a tiny smirk, enjoying his dilemma.

'One cannot trust the testimony of a *mutant*,' the commander said carefully, tone levelled to be as reasonable as possible. The sword did not waver. 'She's probably in league with whatever "taint" she's uncovered, by the Throne!'

'A grave allegation,' Kaustus said. The blade stayed where it was.

Orodai eyed the inquisitor along the sword's edge, lip curling, and abruptly he seemed to sag, shoulders drooping. 'She'd bring down the wrath of the Inquisition on my world...' he said softly, his voice almost plaintive.

'Aaah...' Kaustus lowered the sword with a chuckle, sliding it into its sheath. 'Suddenly it all becomes clear.' His voice was thick with amusement. 'Your objection has more to do with your fear of *me* than of whatever bogeyman my interrogator has exposed.'

Orodai rallied with the look of man determined to preserve as much dignity as he could, though there was precious little to salvage.

'Your organisation's reputation precedes it,' he snapped, fingers questing for blemishes at his throat. 'I've heard the stories. Worlds virus-bombed on the strength of a single rumour. Whole populations wiped out for fear of one heretic.' His jaw tightened. 'I won't trust the fate of my city to the word of... of...' he glanced across at Mita, searching for some sufficiently derogatory term, settling finally for a derisive: '*that*.'

'Nor,' said Kaustus, enjoying every moment, 'would I.'

And right on cue the retinue chuckled its vicious amusement. Orodai re-holstered his gun, mollified by the shared ridicule of the psyker, the mutant, the wretched interrogator.

Mita bowed her head and thought: *In shared cruelty lies acceptance* – her own lesson, recalled time and time again.

The Emperor loves me. The Emperor loves me. The Emperor loves me.

Bitter comfort.

She acknowledge with a start that she despised them all, every last one.

'So you don't believe me,' she said, doing her best to ignore the laughter.

Kaustus seated himself again and waved an untroubled hand.

'Spare me your damaged pride,' he said. 'I've already told you I believe you. Something is loose in the underhive and it must be brought to heel. There's no question of that.' He fixed her with a pointed look. 'Whatever that "something" might be.'

'My lord! I recognised the traitor's heraldry!' Her voice came almost as a whimper. 'A fanged skull, leather-winged and horned, rampant against a field of lightning.'

Kaustus's casual posture did not change.

'The mark of the Night Lords!' she shouted, furious at his tranquillity. 'I would not mistake it! I've studied the *Insignium Tratoris*! I was zealous in memorising such th–'

'Your schooling is of no consequence, interrogator. If reading ancient texts is the full measure of your wisdom then I suspect your tenure with my retinue shall be very short.'

Another guffaw from the mob, another burning moment of shame and hatred.

'My lord...' her voice was quiet, almost plaintive. 'You must believe me...'

'Child,' Kaustus preened at the sleeves of his robe, voice sceptical, 'if a heretic Marine is indeed at large, perhaps you could account for how it is that you – a mere interrogator – were able to escape him?'

Mita opened her mouth.

And closed it again.

In truth, she had barely been able to believe it herself. She had lashed out at the monster with an impetuous psychic strike, a panicky assault without measure or hope of success. It was as if the Night Lord had been utterly unprepared, not just lacking in psychic defence but unaware that such a thing even existed. His mind had been like that of a child, as if the very last thing he had expected to face was a psyker.

Not the type of vulnerability one identified with the Traitor Legions.

'I... I don't know my lord,' she muttered, beaten, 'but I'm certain of the identifica–'

Kaustus silenced her with a sigh.

'That is beyond the point, interrogator,' he growled, looking away with a dismissive wave. 'We thank you for your report nonetheless. It shall be dealt with.'

She opened her mouth to remonstrate, to make him see sense, to scream and shout and vent her frustration until her throat bled, but Kaustus cut her short with a raised palm and a glare.

'It shall be dealt with,' he repeated. 'But not by you.' He turned to face the retinue, crooking a finger to beckon forth a solitary member. '*Dissimulus.*'

A man, whose name Mita did not know, stepped from the throng and turned to face him, dipping his head. Mita instinctively dipped inside his mind, tasting the surface of his thoughts. Visually he seemed unremarkable; what few features his robe betrayed were average – his age was indeterminate, his hair cut to a medium length, physically neither tall nor short. Little wonder, Mita reflected, that she'd paid so little attention to him: amongst the menagerie of personalities comprising the retinue he was positively mundane.

In the boiling ocean of his mind, however, he was unique.

Never before had Mita encountered such an indistinct *anima*. In a typical personality the fronds and tentacles of outward thought clustered at their roots around a solid core of *ego*; that diamond-hard seed of identity that informed all else, as a bitter stone informs the growth of a peach. Not so here. In the tormented mindscape of this plain man no such centre existed, no nucleus of *'this-is-me'* presented itself, and the one uniformity she could identify was a lust, a desire, a *craving*: though for what she could not say.

She withdrew with less information than she'd held before, and regarded the uninteresting figure with a new sense of caution. What manner of human was unaware even of its own personality, its own gender, its own name?

'Approach, child…' Kaustus said, and the man stepped forwards until he all but touched his master. Kaustus leaned down towards him, and for one surreal instant Mita wondered if the inquisitor planned to kiss him, irrespective of his mask. At the last instant he diverted his face towards the figure's ear and there, looming over like some ancient ogre, he whispered his secret plans.

If the rest of his acolytes felt any jealousy at this preferential treatment, or frustration at being so excluded, even their thoughts failed to betray them. Mita alone struggled with her annoyance, consumed by something that bore all the ugly hallmarks of envy.

She was the interrogator. *She* was the inquisitor's second. *She* had found the enemy, and this was her reward – to be ridiculed and excluded? This was the glory she'd pursued?

And then the nameless man broke away from Kaustus's clinch and was gone, walking from Orodai's office without a backward glance. The inquisitor glanced at his remaining disciples and barked a surly 'dismissed', and Mita imagined that he paused as his eyes passed hers and something dark, some shadow of malice, shifted minutely in the lagoons of his irises.

She left Cuspseal alongside the rest of the retinue, returning to Steepletown with resentment clouding her mind, and with every breath she cursed her master's name for not believing her, for not taking her seriously, for not seeming *troubled*. There was a Chaos Marine loose in the hive, by the Emperor's tears, and he seemed no more bothered than had he found a fly in his drinking grail.

Mita watched him, and brooded and seethed, and did nothing.

THE NEXT MORNING, installed once more in the drab envelope of her meditation cell, she awoke to the knocking of a servitor-herald, pompously dressed in ermine and satin. She received its monotone message half awake, unashamed of her nakedness before a creature so devoid of emotion, and slammed the door just a *little* too loudly as it left.

Kaustus had once more requested her presence.

She prepared to join him with all the usual surges of apprehension and frustration that his beckons always entailed, and spent several flustered minutes considering what to wear. It was as if the turmoil of the previous days had never occurred and she was reduced once more to panicking over how best to secure his respect. She hated herself for such meaningless exactitude as fussily choosing her costume, but was enslaved to it nonetheless.

Cog slept on the floor beside her simple palette, and she stepped over him to rummage in her luggage without even attempting stealth. Having noted her dismal mood, he'd come to her cell the night before with child-like words of comfort, and she'd allowed him to sleep on the floor beside her palette with guilty gratitude – there was *someone* in the galaxy, at least, who liked her. She knew from past experience that nothing short of a blow to the head would wake him from his contented slumber, so she left him to it and got on with the business of dressing. She began by shrugging on a scarlet robe with white and gold filigree at its seams: nothing too ostentatious, but fittingly colourful for the hive's upper tiers. In these decorous corridors and it was the gaudiest and most patterned who went unnoticed, and the drab who attracted the most attention.

Today, attention was something she could do without.

To her great relief the retinue was absent when she reached Kaustus's chambers. He stood amongst a gaggle of macabre servitor-attendants and skull-drones, meticulously fastening his power armour and layering his magnificent robes. Up until the moment that a hovering arcocherub – a baby's corpse riddled with preservative machinery and cogitation engines – settled his mask over his tusked features, he appeared utterly bored by the whole procedure.

Ignored in the doorway, Mita found herself reflecting upon how differently he wore his armour to the fiend that stalked her nightmares, that blue/black monstrosity from the underhive. As an alumnus of the Inquisitorial scholastia she knew more than most about the elaborate biological changes that the warriors of the Adeptus Astartes – the Emperor's Space Marines – underwent. Such things were shrouded in mysticism, and the mere knowledge that each Marine started life as a lowly human marked her as the recipient of privileged secrets. Nonetheless, the specifics of such alterations were beyond her, and she had imagined that, like Kaustus, such warriors wore their armour as she wore a cloak: the fastenings more complex, perhaps, the fabric more arcane, but 'clothing' nonetheless.

And yet the Night Lord had moved like his armour was his skin; unencumbered, his movement recalling liquid in its smooth, roiling reactions.

Compared to that shadowed figure Kaustus's motions abruptly seemed cumbersome, and Mita marvelled to find herself so unimpressed by him where previously she had thought him awesome.

'My lord,' she said, announcing herself. The flock of servitors dispersed quietly, their task complete, and Mita noticed with chagrin that her master too had chosen a scarlet and white ensemble, albeit far grander than her own.

'Interrogator. Good.'

'You sent for me, my lord?'

'I did. I've decided it's safer to keep you where I can see you. I think we shall spend the day together.'

He sounded almost cheery. Mita feigned a smile.

GOVERNOR ZAGRIF SURPRISED Mita by being neither old, corpulent, sinister or pompous. She'd met a small but illustrative number of Imperial commanders on other worlds, and in her experience the post bred one of either melancholia or megalomania. To a psyker, such things were as palpable as girth, height or clothing, and she failed to detect either in Imperial Commander Cinnavar Zagrif.

He was skinny and short, dressed entirely in white. As she and Kaustus approached his straight-backed throne, flanked by bronze combat servitors like toy soldiers, he regarded her with a watery-eyed expression of pleasure. Dwarfed beneath the vast heraldry of a familial tapestry – crossed sword and sceptre upon a dappled ice-field, crested by a crescent moon and a ring of stars – he seemed the very opposite of authoritative. Mita's expectations were utterly confounded: amongst them all the one thing she had failed to anticipate was a softly spoken man of her own age, with an astral presence that was profoundly dull. When his subconscious flickered a brief tendril of lechery towards her it came almost as a relief.

Almost.

'Kaustus!' he exclaimed, rising with an outstretched hand. 'What news from the deepest darkest depths?' He giggled at his own alliteration, like a child reciting a nursery rhyme.

To Mita's astonishment Kaustus returned the handshake.

'Nothing troublesome, Cinnavar.'

Mita almost choked. The governor didn't notice.

'Good, good.' He glanced towards her. 'And who is this? A consort, perhaps?' He nudged Kaustus mischievously. 'I thought better of you!'

Mita held her breath, waiting for the inquisitor to chop the man in two for his insolence. When he merely chuckled and waved the insinuation aside, she was left wondering if it was she, or he, who had gone insane.

'I'm afraid not, Cinnavar. This is my interrogator.'

Mita bowed formally, doing her best to ignore the smog of promiscuity ebbing from the governor's mind. It was one thing to suspect someone of undressing you with their eyes but quite another to share the experience.

'And to what do we owe this pleasure?' The governor rubbed his hands, eyes flitting to meet the inquisitor's. 'Is she here to help us with the lock?'

For an instant – a single horrific moment – Mita *felt* Kaustus's emotion. Where before he had presented a solid ball of impenetrable thought, impossible for her to examine or invade, abruptly his defences fell, and what boiled beneath was *rage*.

But it was only an instant, as sudden as it was intense, and his mind – whatever had caused it to flex so venomously – was once more locked away beneath layers of self control.

'No,' he said.

And was that a blush of guilt swelling on the governor's psyche? Had he said something he shouldn't have? Mita grit her teeth at the uncertainties, the secrets. Something was going on here, something she knew nothing about. What was 'the lock'?

'Fine,' the governor said, struggling to seem dismissive. 'Good, good.'

'I thought the interrogator might appreciate a view of your collection,' Kaustus said, voice tight. 'That is all.'

The governor nodded with the look of a man who has narrowly escaped an unpleasant fate, and gestured towards a set of painted doors to one side. 'B-by all means. Please. By all means.'

Mita found herself regarded by governor and inquisitor alike.

'My lord?' she said.

'Through there,' Kaustus grunted, nodding at the doors.

She pushed them open with a strange sense of foreboding, feeling like some performing animal, and found herself on a narrow bridge, enclosed on all sides by thick plasplex. Even through the ice and settled snow that patterned the tunnel's outer surfaces she could see that the causeway stretched between the hive's central peak – in which the throneroom skulked – and a lesser tower, rising parallel from the shadowed depths. She crossed the abyss with a lurch of nausea, horrified at the vertiginous chasm below her feet, and it was only Kaustus's quiet footsteps at her heel that kept her from crying out, or clinging to the handrail for her life.

The tunnel ended in a second set of doors and, with an impatient nod from her master, she pushed her way through.

And stopped.

In all of the palace – a maze of jewelled stairways and intricately frescoed chapels, cloistered archways hung with tapestries of spun gold and elaborate congresia sporting sculptures of alabaster and onyx – it was difficult to imagine encountering anything that might shatter the atmosphere of perpetual, unyielding opulence. Nonetheless, Mita stepped through the painted doorway and felt her knees weaken.

'The governor has a fondness for curios,' Kaustus muttered, in explanation.

It was like a gallery. A bazaar. A treasure trove. And it was *vast*.

There were windows marking the entire periphery. Tiny reinforced portals, perhaps, but windows nonetheless: a subtle symbol of wealth which implied this one chamber, this circular cavern with its sky-blue dome and pearlescent columns, stretched the *entire* diameter of its tower.

And within it?

She'd never seen such treasures. At close intervals, raised on silver plinths and bordered by bright illuminators, the governor's collection of antiquities and valuables could have easily held her spellbound for weeks. Books, archeotech, pictslates, sculptures, pickled beasts, jewels, antiques... At every angle there stood some priceless rarity, some article of unthinkable value, and Mita's blood raced to see them all. She tottered forwards as if drunk, and extended a hand towards a nearby exhibit – a great emerald containing at its heart the shadowy form of a tiny lizard.

'No touching,' Kaustus chided behind her, like a parent slapping his child's wrists. A gloved finger gestured vaguely upwards, drawing her eye towards the ceiling. Set in a wide ring around the plinth, like spotlights with narrow apertures, a bevy of lasguns glared down upon her, crude servos tracking every movement. At their centre, like some grotesque trophy displayed at the heart of a spider's web, a disembodied human head fixed its baleful eyes – long since replaced by compound optics – upon the tip of her outstretched hand.

'Security servitors.' Kaustus shrugged, voice bored. Mita noted without surprise – and only a small shiver of revulsion – that similar effigies, rotting flesh hanging from slack bones, gazed down upon each and every item in Zagrif's collection.

She pulled back her hand slowly, uncomfortably aware of the machine intelligence above. At some arbitrary point its attention seemed to dwindle, as if no longer judging her a threat, and the lasguns returned to a neutral spread with a soft hiss.

'Effective,' she said, controlling her voice.

'Indeed.'

She turned towards the remainder of the room, her eyes drawn towards an accumulation of spotlights on one side, and a dais higher than any other. She took a step towards it, curious, and stopped.

Something uncoiled in her brain like a great spider, scuttling between uncertainties, and she *knew*.

'He's here...' she whispered, fists clenching, head jerking from left to right, seeking that hunched shape, that midnight form, those burning red eyes.

'What did you say?' Kaustus said, his voice so close to her ear that she jumped.

'H-he's here! The Night Lord! I feel him! He's in *here*!'

And then something sharp tugged against the fabric of her arm, and before she could glimpse down to see what had punctured her skin the lights of the gallery dimmed in her eyes, the sky-blue dome clouded over, and her consciousness spiralled away.

ZSO SAHAAL

Zso Sahaal sat upon a throne of fur and bone, armoured fingers steepled before him, and brooded on past and future.

Tomorrow he would strike. A guildhall, perhaps or some other Administratum stronghold some communicatory centre where the Imperial fools would keep their mutant slaves.

It had been the witch that had given him the idea. Mutants and slaves... Yes.

That was tomorrow. The future. The first step upon a road to redemption.

As for the past, as for that swirl of violence and chaos that had brought him here, to this smog-thick place; as for the madness that left him seated in darkness upon a throne of bone; as for yesterday...

They had carried him.

Following the battle of the Steel Forest the tribe had lifted him from the debris where the witch had struck him down, placed him carefully on a litter, and borne him up to their secret platforms amongst the canopies of the heat vents.

In retrospect the treatment was as galling as it was comforting. True, he found himself amongst a community that would go to any length to keep him from harm... but to be so *manhandled* – and by devotees of the withered Emperor, no less! Sahaal had awoken with a suppressed shiver of disgust at the thought.

But then, his memories were thick with ugliness already.

The witch, the witch... She had struck him to the floor with a single flex of her powers, like a bomb between his eyes, and he shivered that such a slight being should hold such power over him. The witch. The *bitch*. He had not expected to face psykers.

Steeling himself – disgruntled by the need to sink so low – he breathed a reluctant prayer to the Dark Gods. The ruinous powers had always been allies to his cause – enemies of his enemies, but never his friends – and even now, when he needed their patronage, he shivered at the prospect of openly courting their involvement. If the deities of the warp resented his reluctance they gave no sign of it; within instants a dark stirring played at the edge of his senses.

He would not be unprepared for the witch a second time.

Had the Imperium truly fallen so far from its much-vaunted light during his absence? Had the Carrion God truly allowed such deviants to enter his service ungoverned? Sahaal could hardly despise the impurity of mutation – the gods to whom he had just appealed thrived on such things, after all – but it was a needle of hypocrisy that fed his hatred nonetheless. The mutant stood for everything the Imperium reviled – impurity, uncertainty, vulnerability, *corruptibility* – and yet here they were, put to work, devils made useful. Just another sign of the Emperor's weakness. Another symptom of his unsuitability for deification.

How long before these psykers too were made scapegoats, blamed for actions that were both sanctioned and encouraged, just as Sahaal's master had been?

Oh, my master...

Konrad Curze. The Night Haunter. The Shadowed Martyr. Antecedent of the Corona Nox. Sahaal breathed his mentor's names with choked reverence and, as ever, found himself calmed and angered in equal parts.

'We shall repay their insult yet,' he whispered, voice lost to the darkness of his helm.

He returned his thoughts to the witch, flexing his fingers introspectively. She had tasted his thoughts. She could find him again – of that he had no doubt. She had known what he was.

And he, equally, had seen *her* true self.

She had worn it emblazoned on her collar, a thing so inconspicuous he had barely noticed it at the time, and only in the fog of enforced sleep had the symbol come to the fore of his mind: an embroidered 'I', bisected three times by bars of black and silver, with a tiny skull fashioned at the crux of the central bar.

The Inquisition. Hunting him. He had no time for such distractions.

A day had since passed, and the Shadowkin lair within the Steel Forest had been deserted at his command. Centuries of tradition, long decades of territorial security, had perished in the instant it had taken him to shrug and announce: 'We move.' The witch had escaped, and that meant the Inquisition would return. They must leave at once, he knew, and seek refuge in a place better suited to repel attack.

And the Shadowkin, his dismal little allies, had not complained once. Overtly.

And yes, his motives were pure; yes, the move was necessary; yes, the gang would be purged if they did not leave. But still he could hear the mutters in the shadows, he could taste the resentment of his flock, he could feel their worship wane. Condemnitor Chianni had not survived the battle, and with her leadership lost his grip upon his miniature empire had grown tenuous indeed.

He took them into the deep, leaving behind only a gaggle of scouts to watch over their former domain. He led them into those boundless wastelands he had explored in his first days within the hive, into the foetid swampzones where the heat of the planet warmed the air and sulphur bubbled across the pools. In these smog-thick caverns he prowled before them, eschewing the snaking caravans that trekked at his heel and the throng that sang devotional songs to raise their spirits... And also muttered, always muttered, when they thought he could not hear.

There was no place deeper than this.

He brought them to where the hulk of a drilling behemoth pitched like a rusted island from the sludge of an oily ocean, lost to the shadows. He guessed that at one time it had dug these basins and caves, these rustmud caverns, a swarm of humanity building and settling in its wake. And here it had faltered – perhaps blunted by its labours or else merely forgotten, with none caring to settle so deep – and rotted in its own fuel, drowned in the snow that its exertions had melted, with only its massive loins rearing from its caldera like a tombstone.

Here Sahaal had hidden his cache of weapons and ammunition, and here he brought his children, his black-draped tribe, on their exodus from the Steel Forest.

The Shadowkin crossed the thick waters and tried to ignore the silvery fronds that moved in the deep, and settled upon the island without comment. Their lord had won a great victory, he had driven the heretic interlopers from their cherished lands – why then must they leave those lands behind? Why must they come to *this* blighted place?

And in low voices, in muffled hisses that they didn't dare imagine he could hear, they asked: How was he struck down so easily by the witch? Was he not supposedly mighty? Could he not have crushed her with ease?

Sahaal issued two tasks to his tribe, before even they hunted and fed their children. The first was that they dispatch scouts into the shadows, to listen to rumour and collect gossip, and to bring to him the man named Slake. He commanded this without explanation, and those warriors thus selected scattered into the night without question.

His second command was that they build him a throne.

For all that he considered his command above dissent, Sahaal was no fool, and as his tribe worked with bone and rag to fashion a fitting seat for their lord, their prayers seemed muted, their prostrations half-hearted, and their anxious glances of fear betrayed the simmering glut of resentment. Sahaal took it all in and stored it away, but could not bring himself to be troubled. The Night Lords commanded obedience, not affection, and whether these scum liked him or not was irrelevant. They would do what he told them, and that was enough.

They built the throne from the crippled spars of the great digger, sealed in improvised forges, and covered the seat in furs of black and brown. The arms and back they topped with stolen bones and teeth; a skull upon each hand pommel and freshly-taken heads – those of slain vindictors they had brought with them – mounted on spines above the whole. Sahaal found their grim iconography gratifying: they, like his ancient Legion, understood the power of morbidity and the fear that went along with it. That they devoted their gruesome trophies to the glory of the Emperor was the one sour note in an otherwise pleasing practice.

He ascended his throne with no small measure of pride, and as the Shadowkin dispersed to tend to their own needs he lost himself in the memories of glories that had long since passed, never once pausing to consider the dissatisfaction of his people.

ON TSAGUALSA, THE *carrion world, the Legion had raised a palace for its lord.*

He had gathered his captains together, and they came with a fleet of bladed prows and bitter warriors, skulls displayed at belt and shoulder, scriptures crossed through with bloody ink.

Horus was dead. The heresy that had looked ready to rip the bloated Imperium apart had ground to a halt. The Legions that had turned from the Emperor and sided instead with Chaos, that boiling fount of madness and disorder, were scattered; licking their wounds, bemoaning their losses, running for their lives.

Not so the Night Lords!

Alone amongst them all, the Night Haunter's contempt for his father had outdated, and outlasted, the rebellion. The Emperor's favoured son Horus had corrupted the other dark Legions, pouring poison upon their primarchs with insidious whispers and sweet promises, but not so to the Night Haunter. Not to Konrad Curze. He had seen his father for what he was long before. He had chosen Chaos as a tool – as an ally – but was not seduced by it. And when Horus was cut down, when the other Traitor Legions were shattered, when distant Terra was liberated and the Emperor triumphant, had the Night Lords fled? Had they yelped in fear and skulked into the gloom to fight amongst themselves, as had the others?

No. No, not they.

Their primarch unleashed them, he fed them the fear they yearned, and on Tsagualsa he called them to his side, and showed them his palace.

It was built of bodies: still living, fused at broken joint and sliced skin, knotted around coiling vertebrae and dissected sinews.

In the screaming gallery, where a carpet of moaning faces rose in broad steps – writhing spines and clutching fingers shivering along every edge – the Dark Lord received his captains with a bow.

He was naked, but for a cloak of black feathers, and had never been more magnificent. Sahaal and his brothers dropped to their knees and hailed him: their father, their master, their lord, their Dominus Nox.

He regarded each in turn, and to each he nodded once, a feral jolt of recognition, like a wolf regarding its pack. All of them were there: Quissax Kergai, Master of the Armoury, whose scouring of the Launeus forgeworld had crippled the loyalists of the Trigonym sector. Vyridium Silvadi, Lord of the Fleet, who had routed the flotilla of Admiral Ko'uch and bombarded the Ravenguard for five days before they could retreat, unsupported, like the cowards they were. Even Koor Mass, encased now in the sleek shell of a dreadnought, its every surface decorated with flayed skin, had deigned to attend his master's audience.

There was one other who Sahaal noted amongst the menagerie, and he avoided that one's gaze, finding his countenance distasteful. Krieg Acerbus, youngest of the Haunter's captains, incalculably vast and swollen with pendants and gory souvenirs of his works, leant on the shaft of his great poweraxe and smiled with insolemn pleasure at his master's attention.

Sahaal ignored the giant's smirking features and concentrated instead upon his lord, resplendent upon a throne of obsidian and silver.

The Night Haunter paused to gather his thoughts, drawing his feathered cloak around him like a great crow folding its wings – and then he spoke.

He told them of his bitter crusade. He told them of his hate for the traitor-Emperor who had turned upon him without warning or honour; a hate that burned bright and unquenched, but as patient as time itself. He told them that they, his children, his dark warriors, his prefects of fear personified, were each worth a dozen of any loyalist Marine, with 'purity' on their ignorant lips and devotion in their hollow, hypocritical souls.

He told them that they would have their revenge upon the withered god, and they cheered in the shadows of the writhing mausoleum and clashed their gauntlets against their breasts in joy.

And then he drew breath and told them he was going to die, and their joy crumbled like ash.

SAHAAL RETURNED TO the present in the shifting smog of the rustmud swamplands in a bleak mood, his master's morbid promise ringing through his mind. More than ever the need for action, for some palpable sense of gain, burned through his brain. The bitterness of the Night Haunter was a patient force, but *his* fury was far sharper and his discipline far younger. What did all this brooding achieve? What must he do? How must he act?

Seated amongst his tattered rags, Zso Sahaal found himself dizzied by a rush of panic and impatience, surging in his guts, calling him to action, to violence, to *murder*.

It was not a wise time to approach him with a protest.

THERE WERE TWO: young Shadowkin standing close enough to each other to betray their nervousness. They would not have undertaken their quiet rebellion alone, and so like children clutching for the comfort of their parents, they had come together.

The first was a man in his twenties, shaven-headed and tattooed, whose circlet of shattered ribs and bangles of beaded finger bones marked him out as a fine warrior. Where an older man might have leaned upon a staff this youth clutched at a heavy volume of Imperial scripture like a lifeline, as if no harm could befall him so long as he touched its battered surface.

His companion was a woman of similar age, hair dyed purple and blue, swept back from her skull like a teardrop, whose black cloak dangled with stolen scalps, hands crooked around a tall rifle. A sniper, then – another warrior of the tribe.

Two fools, staggering into the presence of their lord to register their dissent, each silently praying that the other would speak first. Sahaal watched them without movement. He knew how to deal with insubordination.

'My lord?' the woman said after a long pause, unsure whether he was awake. 'M-my lord, may we address you?'

Sahaal let the silence roll, enjoying their squirms.

'Master, we seek an audience…' the man said, prostrating himself beside his fellow.

'Speak,' Sahaal voxed finally, enjoying the thrill of horror that passed across their faces.

Again, the woman found her nerve first.

'M-my lord, we… We are unsure of this place. The hunters have found little to eat and the tribe is hungry. W-we…' she faltered, glancing at the man for support.

'We don't understand why you've brought us here,' he said, the accusation firm in his voice. 'We don't understand what you intend for us. Are we to continue our holy purges, or…'

'Or do you have some new task for us?' the woman's voice too grew more confident with each word. 'We… we would understand your wishes.'

An uncomfortable silence settled. Sahaal decided to probe the depths of this dissatisfaction, impressed by their audacity.

'Have I not given command,' he said, 'that the man named Slake be brought to me?'

'Y-yes my lord, but–'

'Have I not given command that the tribe fortify itself?'

'You have, but–'

'Have I not led you when leadership was needed, and commanded you when command was required?'

'You have, my lord.'

He stood and raised the volume of his voxcaster, towering above them.

'Why then, thrice-damned, do you stand before me to question my *orders*?'

'We mean no insult, lord!' It was almost a squeal. 'We only seek to understand! The tribe is uncertain!'

In that instant, with the woman's silent glimpse into the shadows, Sahaal grasped the magnitude of his problem. This pair were not operating alone, he saw, not a protesting minority amongst a whole. No, they were representatives – great warriors elected to present the clan's discontent to its leader.

'Preysight,' Sahaal whispered, and again the lenses of his eyes blazed with magnified acuity, penetrating the shadows. And yes... yes, there they were: the elders and the youngsters, the women and children and warriors of the tribe, all of them gathered to listen beyond the circle of light around the throne, all of them hungry for answers.

His rule was not as secure as he had thought.

He *needed* the tribe.

'What heresy is this?' he roared, brandishing his claws. 'What *filth* is this!'

The two warriors shivered on the floor and he advanced towards them, step by murderous step.

'What pitiful circumstance has brought me to *you*? The whole hive is lost to the dark, the population corrupted by the taint, and *this* is my army? *These* are my loyal crusaders?' He spread his arms and addressed the dark ceiling of the cavern, theatrical even in his rage. 'A tribe of disloyal fools and simpering traitors! A mob who reject the word of the Emperor's chosen because they *do not understand it*!'

He shrieked the words until the cavern shuddered and, oh – it hurt to claim such a link to the withered god, but...

But oh, it was *delicious* to see such terror in their eyes.

'Kneel!' he bellowed, and the young warriors obeyed without thought.

He would kill them, he resolved. He would behead them so the entire gang could watch, and all of them would know the price of disquiet, the consequence of insolence. They would obey him, or face his wrath.

It was an inelegant ultimatum – he knew that as soon as he decided it. He needed the Shadowkin as his allies – the recovery of the Corona depended upon it – and if he must kill nine in every ten to secure the obedience of those that remained, his army would be small indeed.

But there was no other choice, no option but to let fly his rage, to hack off these two heads – and any other that dared question him.

Yes. It was necessary.

And secretly, silently, a dark portion of his mind giggled to itself and said: *Yes, yes, make your excuses... Deny that you cherish the slaughter... Peddle your pretend-honour as much as you like.*

It will do you no good, Night Lord.

You're a monster. And you know *it.*

He raised his claws and felt the silence of expectation: a hundred eyes regarding him from the shadows, a hundred gasps burning in his ears. The condemned warriors moaned low in their throats, and–

And a commotion arose across the still waters, faint lights wending their way towards the distant shore.

It was the scouts Sahaal had left in the Steel Forest, and with his vision sharpened he could see they were carrying a survivor.

It was Condemnitor Chianni, and as the rafts slunk out from the rusted island to return her to her tribe, her fevered moans rose in volume to echo through the swamps.

'H-hail!' she yowled, delirious. 'Hail the Emperor's angel!'

It was like a shaft of light, striking Sahaal in his moment of rage. His thin lips curled in a smile and slowly, banishing that secret voice to the rear of his mind, he sheathed his claws.

Obedience could be secured through loyalty as well as terror. Sahaal's master had understood that.

Condemnitor Chianni was loyal to him. They were loyal to her. It was not a complex manipulation.

'Behold the Emperor's mercy!' Sahaal said, inventing wildly. 'He spares those that are wise, and offers redemption to those who are not.' He waved the condemned warriors away, returning to his throne.

'*Ave Imperator*!' filtered across the waters, Chianni's plaintive cry repeating over and over.

'You should listen to your leader,' Sahaal said to the warriors' retreating backs, repressing a chuckle at his own good fortune. 'She is far wiser than you.'

HER LEG HAD been peppered by shrapnel from the explosion, and her throat crushed by an inelegant swipe of a vindictor's maul. When her bearers reached the foot of his throne she nonetheless insisted upon standing, staggering as best she could to kneel before him.

'My lord,' she croaked, voice forever changed by the bruise across her neck, 'I am gladdened to see you. I feared the worst when I awoke to find the tribe gone.' Her eyes blinked with joyful tears. 'Emperor be praised that they – and you – are safe.'

Sahaal was uncomfortable with such unrestrained warmth, and struggled to find an answer. The condemnitor's return to the Shadowkin had effected an almost miraculous transformation; all their sullenness and suspicion crumbling upon itself, becoming devotion once more. It was as if they had been waiting to have their zeal directed, as if their obeisance was without question but, lacking an interface, had become cold and bitter. None of them had relished facing their demigod master themselves, and only via the mediating presence of their leader could they direct their energies.

By the mere act of worshipping him, Condemnitor Chianni had abruptly become his most vital resource. He breathed a thankful prayer to the spirit of his master for returning her to his side in his moment of need.

'Rest,' he instructed her, accepting her grasping supplications without any outward display of chagrin. 'Restore your strength.'

He raised his voice so that the whole island could hear him, chilling tones like a breath upon the air. 'We must *all* restore our strength,' he announced, pulling the robes of the throne around him once more. 'Tomorrow... tomorrow we strike a blow for the Emperor's glory!'

And this time there was no muttering, no dark exchanges of glances, no uncertainty in the Shadowkin response.

This time they cheered.

MITA ASHYN

She was dreaming, and that was the one comfort she could take: that no matter how awful, how sickening, how wretched, the things she witnessed were only the product of her own mind, and owed nothing to reality.

There was a procession – that was the first detail that came upon her: a train of walking figures dressed in black cloaks, arising from the nothingness of her sleep like specks of oil, consolidating into figures that moved and sung. Leaning upon gnarled canes, they chanted in mantra-like harmony, stepping in time like a slow-motion army.

Her perspective shifted, widening its net, and a hive-shell starport opened up below her; hangars and towers jostling amongst baroque pylons and sweeping launch-pads, where fat shuttles sulked amongst chanting techpriests, blessed and maintained simultaneously. Here the temperature dipped, subject to the frozen whimsy of the storms that raged beyond the opening in the hive's shell. Here, alone in all the city, a hiver could brave the snow and catch a glimpse – cloud-shrouded and as dark as coal, but a glimpse nonetheless – of the sky.

At the end of a broad concourse, where would-be passengers thronged and shouted and complained, grotesque servitor drones dangled from ceiling joists like flies in webs of steel, needle-arms checking documents, uncaring eyes assessing passengers for concealed weapons, signs of disease, or whatever other arbitrary criteria they chose. Those that passed their capricious test hurried through ferrocrete arches towards the shuttles, whilst those that failed backed away in silent horror, split from their loved ones and destitute, all their funds wasted on the price of a single rejected ticket. Such wretches would invariably wind up dead, or else filter their way into the underhive where all the other dispossessed clamoured for warmth. But there could be no protest here, not beneath the gaze of the vindictors who straddled the entry gates and perched within turrets to either side of the concourse, helmed gazes surveying the sullen crowd for the slightest infraction. The dried blood on the ground was silent testament to the extent of their vigilance.

Amongst the crowds the procession of black cloaks marched like a shadow, and Mita's slumbering mind again wafted past, intrigued, wondering at their relevance. Well accustomed to the psychic insanity of prediction trances, with their excesses of colour and sound, to her this dreary vision could hardly be considered noteworthy. She wondered vaguely what it signified and scolded herself for such unfounded superstition. Beyond the realms of the psychic trance a dream was just that – a dream: no more meaningful than a random scattering of images, drawn together in an approximation of narrative.

But still... There was something not right here, in this fantasy vision...

Something that *jarred*...

Mita had arrived upon Equixus as part of the Inquisitorial caravan, and was therefore received at the uppermost of the hive's three starports. So great was the polarity between that tranquil maze of incense-shrouded lounges and this brutal compound that every detail shocked her, every petty act of rejection burned into her mind. Such was the reality of hive life – on every tier, a different world – but she had never witnessed the place laid out below her in the flesh. Why then had her slumbering brain chosen to imagine it, to fabricate its minutae as part of a dream?

The procession of cloaked figures joined the rear of the winding queue.

For a moment Mita had wondered whether she had somehow slipped into the *Furor Arcanum*, studying the strands of future possibility, but no: such visions were fat with fantasy; abstractions that required interpretation rather than humdrum visions such as this.

There was only one other option.

Could it be that her astral self had left its body? Could it be that these visions were neither dream nor fantasy nor future possibility, but presently occurring events? Could it be that she was remotely viewing things as they happened?

Of the four major disciplines practised in the scholastia psykana, she had always considered herself primarily a *precognitor* – observing the whimsy of the warp to determine future events – and had occasionally employed her talents as an *empathitor* – skimming emotion and thought from the minds of those around her. Even in the field of *animus motus* – telekinesis, the most physically draining of all – she had some small natural talent... but in mastering the role of *proculitor*, the remote viewer, she had failed dismally.

It was a discipline that carried its own risks, and was best suited to those without the distraction of other talents: allowing one's astral form to roam free was to expose it to any malevolent force within the warp that paid an interest. Mita had tried it only once, during her first year at the scholastia, and had been informed by the grim-faced adept-tutors that her mind was too ordered, too anxious, too *uptight*, to engender success. The discipline required the ability to un-focus, to relax – but to maintain a careful veneer of security nonetheless.

Could it be that in her present state – slumbering, surfing on an ebb of dreams and fantasies – her mind had allowed itself to relax enough to break free?

And that it was therefore vulnerable to attack?

With anxiety rising, choosing caution over curiosity, she tried to wake.

And could not.

Panic gripped her then, and as if from a great distance she remembered being in Governor Zagrif's gallery of treasures. She remembered the short stab of pain against her arm and slowly, with the certainty growing, she realised what was happening.

She had been drugged.

She had been knocked out like some misbehaving beast, shredding her defences and her disciplines and now – now, when she needed the ability to awake like never before – she found herself trapped, ineffectual; relaxed to the point that she had been plunged into a discipline that she had never been taught to master.

Her warp-gaze had elected to show her something, and she was powerless to decline.

Even as her astral form flexed in agitation the crowds below her began to shriek. The dreamscape haze turned bloody red and the phalanx of parading figures threw back the folds of their black cloaks to expose weapons held against their chests, and opened fire.

This, then, was what her senses had brought her here to see.

It was a massacre.

The attackers concentrated, where they could, upon the vindictor sentries – pressing superior numbers against them before they could respond. Even in the midst of her alarm Mita watched, helpless, as one by one the armoured Preafects toppled from their perches, lasbolts gashing them open, shotguns tumbling from grasping fists.

The crowd had become a living organism, bolting and flexing with a single voice, and at their heart people fell underfoot and were trampled, screams lost to the collective wail of terror.

When finally those few vindictors that remained summoned the presence of mind to return fire their targets proved more elusive than they had anticipated. With their black cloaks removed the aggressors dispersed, just faces amongst the turmoil, snapping off opportunistic rounds before vanishing into the crowd. Inevitably, the enforces chose retaliation above discretion.

Snapping orders across the breadth of the concourse, they turned their shotguns upon the crowd and opened fire indiscriminately. Such was the reality of the Emperor's law: it was better to sacrifice the innocent in pursuit of the guilty than to allow the heretic, the traitor or the abomination to escape.

At that moment, as the roadway grew slick with blood, as the screams of dying women and children saturated Mita's dreaming mind, her psychic senses struck upon a dark suspicion. A taint, almost; an infinitesimal cancer, gnawing at the edge of her perception.

He's here...

She drew back from the spectacle, noting that already a column of vindictors rushed to reinforce their beleaguered fellows, and cast her eye further outwards. This was a dangerous moment. Where before she had raged against the dream now she must immerse herself within it, sinking into its folds, trawling its shadows for her target. As she did so with a shudder the colours around her intensified, the edges of buildings and cables hardened–

And in the warp, a hair's breadth from reality itself, the unctuous wisp of light that was Mita's astral form brightened, like a flare.

At the gate the crowd broke its ranks and swarmed through the checkpoints. Shrieking and fleeing across the concrete beyond, cloaks flapping, the starport descended piece by bloody piece into anarchy. Hundreds had died already, and as Mita shifted her psychic self towards the dark blemish she sought, leaving behind the crackle of gunfire and the shouts of the wounded, she knew that hundreds more would join them.

And she knew, now, that it was all a waste.

The attack was merely a diversion.

SHE FOUND IT – *him* – nearby, drawn to his spectral shadow like a shark to blood.

He had crawled from the depths of the undercity from a fissure at the hive's base, where industrial smog belched upwards in long curtains, and had scaled the plated walls of the lower tiers claw by claw, rising towards the starport's gaping launchfields not from within, but without. Where normally a squad of vindictors could be found, thermal cloaks flapping in the wind, gazing out in ceaseless vigil for just such an incursion, now the beast's route was clear, now the sentries had rushed off to reinforce elsewhere, now his shadow fell across nothing but empty concrete and silent, unattended shuttles.

The Night Lord's entrance to the starport went utterly unnoticed, by all but Mita.

She swept around him with the dreamscape fracturing at her heel, all her tenuous energies gobbled by his presence. Where before she had felt the taint about him like a faint promise, now it was a wound in reality itself; swarming around him and sucking at her mind. He had opened himself to Chaos, she could see, and in consequence there was some strange quality to him in this esoteric reality, some *otherness* that here, in this place of uncertain physicality and warp-borne visions, burned around him like a corona. She felt as though she swam a viscous ocean, and to even approach him took every shred of her effort. He existed at the heart of a great darkness, a blemish in the warp, and she struggled to see him through the fog of his soul. Something was happening to his boundary, some trick of what passed for light. Some sense of motion.

Of *swarming*...

And the voices... Chittering, whispering, giggling tones, on the cusp of hearing. Were they real?

The Raptor dragged behind him a jaegar squad of humans, coated warriors who wasted little effort in attempting to speed his climb, content to allow their lord to take their weight. One by one they joined him at the edge of the platform, casting off ropes and buckles, unlimbering from cases upon their backs long tubes, hollow and undecorated, like the blowpipes of some jungle race.

The voices reached a keening pitch in Mita's mind and the air – the very fabric of this fantasy place – began to boil around the Chaos Marine's form, as if his mere presence were anathema to reality.

He paused. He glanced around himself as if listening to something that only he could hear, and his companions exchanged nervous glances.

'She is here,' he said.

'M-my lord?'

'The witch. She is here. She is *watching*.'

Mita's panic surged. How could he *know*?

In fear and reflex she tried to kick herself free of the dream, but it was too late; she had immersed herself too deeply; the drug continued to grip her blood, and she could not escape into the waking world.

The Night Lord's companions had taken up combat stances, knives and hatchets brandished.

'Where, my lord?' one hissed, voice little more than a whisper. 'What should we do?'

'Fear not,' the monster said, and its voice betrayed its amusement. 'We each have our guardian spirits. It is not wise to eavesdrop on one such as I. As the bitch will discover.'

And then the distortions that boiled around his outline seemed to pulse, and the fabric of the dreamscape ripped, and there, *there*, like splinters of shadow hanging in the sky, the chittering *somethings* of the warp were released.

They clamoured around her. They pressed in, trying to fasten leech-like mouths to her screaming soul, slipping long claws into her mind.

And finally, as the sound of the Night Lord's laughter rushed in to fill her world, as the cost of scrying too deep unfolded its tentacles and teeth around her, the drugs that crippled her body ran their course and she awoke, mercifully, gratefully, with a scream.

SHE WAS IN her cell, she saw immediately. Whatever had happened to her, whoever had drugged her, she'd been returned to her quarters without so much as a bruise. Given that Kaustus was the only one present when unconsciousness had claimed her, it was an uncomfortable possibility that presented itself. Had *he* done this to her?

But why? Why had he called her to the governor's gallery? Why had he instructed her through those doors? And why, Emperor's oath, *why*, would her own master incapacitate her just as she sensed the enemy's presence?

She pushed it from her mind. It was an enigma that would have to wait.

She was dressed and sprinting towards her master's suite within instants, and with every footfall she blotted out the horror of what had happened inside the dream. Her tutors at the scholastia would have been revolted by her foolishness; scrying so close and so unguarded to a creature of Chaos – little wonder she'd fallen prey to the predators of the warp! She should no more hunt sharks by painting herself in fresh blood than she should use her warpsight to spy upon agents of the ruinous powers, and as she berated herself Kaustus's unkind words came back to her with razor-like clarity:

'You lack experience. You are unqualified in the ways of Chaos.'

He'd been right. The bastard.

Still, she lived yet. She'd escaped – though barely. And now she had news for the inquisitor that could not wait.

'My lord!' she howled, bursting past the sentries at his doorway, 'I know where he is! I know where the trai–'

And stopped.

Kaustus was not in his chambers.

A semicircle of amused stares greeted her abrupt silence; the retinue taking its leisure en masse. Priests glanced up from mumbled prayers, scholars raised horned brows from ancient manuscripts, warriors paused in games of dice, and on every hooded face a demeaning smile played.

'Looks like someone finally woke up,' said one.

Mita blanched. 'I... What? What do you mean?'

'The inquisitor said you were taking a break.' A chuckle rolled across the room.

Indignity burst like a ripe boil in Mita's mind.

'I was drugged, warpspit and piss! What do you expect?'

'Yeah... He said you'd been suffering from paranoia, too.'

More titters circulated. Mita took a breath and rose above it.

'Where is he?' she demanded. 'I haven't time for this. It's important.'

'He isn't to be disturbed.'

'Tell me! I *order* you to tell me!'

She knew it was a mistake as soon as she'd said it. The temperature seemed to drop.

'Is that so?' one of them said.

Several figures – blocky shapes with the roiling movements of warriors – slouched to their feet, drawing close with languid menace, lips twisted in scowls.

'I don't think,' one growled, 'that we're in the mood to be taking orders from you.'

'You know I outrank you,' she said, *almost* keeping the quaver from her voice. The largest of the thugs was all but touching her now, and it was only the psychic pall of amusement from the others that prevented her from staggering away. She refused to give them the satisfaction of another humiliation.

'And you know,' the brute grunted, stabbing a finger against her chest, 'that we could snap you like a twig.'

Prodding her, on reflection, was a mistake.

'I won't tolerate this disrespect any more,' she whispered, as much to herself as to the man, and without warning she raised her knee as hard and fast as she could–

–directly into his crotch.

There was a noise not unlike a damp *crunch*.

He went down with a gurgle, and that might have been enough to end the matter, perhaps even to gain her a modicum of esteem from the shrieking fool's comrades – had she been finished with him. She was not.

She knelt on his chest and pushed a hand against his forehead, ignoring his cries. She dispensed with subtlety, plunged a dagger of psychic thought into his moronic brain, and needled about until the information she sought rose to the fore. She swam through simple thoughts, hunted down her target, and left with a vindictive kick.

The warrior died with a gasp.

'He's with the governor, then,' Mita said, examining the information she'd extracted. The retinue stared agog, mouths hanging open.

'Thanks,' she nodded to the smoking corpse. 'Don't get up.'

* * *

KAUSTUS WAS WAITING for her outside the governor's quarters: successfully taking the indignant wind out of her sails. He'd been forewarned of what she'd done – one of the other retinue members calling ahead, clearly – and hers was not the only foul temper.

'Diota Vasquillius,' he hissed, eyes flashing behind his mask, 'has served me for nine years. I once saw him kill a tyranid carnifex on Saliius-Dictai, loading and firing a lascannon without assistance. I've seen him strangle orks with his bare hands. I've seen him kill genest–'

'My lord,' she interrupted, ignoring his bulging eyes. 'I suspect he never faced a *witch* in a bad mood.'

Kaustus glared at her for long seconds.

'Correct,' he said, finally, and again she felt that strange sense of respect, as though the line between impressing and insulting her master was fine indeed.

'I have news,' she said, pressing her advantage. 'I... I have slept. I have seen where the Traitor Marine i–'

'Interrogator, we have discussed this. I assured you it was being dealt with.'

'There was an attack, my lord! U-upon the spaceport! I saw it! It may still be under way!'

Kaustus eyed her suspiciously, absorbing her words.

'An attack?' he said, and for the first time Mita felt that finally he was taking her seriously.

'Yes! I watched it all! Hundreds died!'

Kaustus half turned away, fingers kneading together. He spoke beneath his breath, and Mita struggled to hear. 'The spaceport...' he muttered. 'Why the spaceport?'

'I... I don't know, my lord.'

He turned back to her as if surprised by her presence, and again she felt that there were elements to this maze she did not understand; pieces moving across a mighty chessboard of which she could witness only a fraction. The certainty was rapidly settling upon her that she could trust the testimony of nobody but herself.

'What should we do, my lord?' she hissed, astonished at her master's display of indecision. Never before had she seen him so affected by a sliver of news, let alone one from *her* mouth.

'Do?' he muttered. 'I... W-we should... We...' His voice trailed off, his eyes gazing into nothing.

She stared, astonished and frightened by this new Kaustus.

'My lord?'

And then abruptly he was back, eyes focused, voice hard, and it was as if he had never been away.

'We do nothing,' he growled, turning away, gesturing at the gaudily dressed servitor-doorman to the governor's chambers.

'But–'

'But nothing! How many times must I say it, interrogator? It is being dealt with. I have my own methods.'

The door swung open and Kaustus stepped away.

'But – my lord!' her cry caught him on the threshold, and he turned back to regard her from the corner of his eye. 'What of the vision?' she said. 'What of the attack? I cannot do *nothing*!'

He cocked his head, sighing, then nodded to himself.

'You will see to it that our mutual friend Commander Orodai keeps his nerve. There will be *no action*, do you understand? The attack must go unanswered!'

She glared down the length of his pointed finger, brandished like a gun, and swallowed.

She wanted to shriek: *But why?*

She wanted to grip him by his peacock-lapels and shake him until he gave her the answers she wanted. *Needed.*

She wanted to understand what in the name of Terra's arse he was playing at.

But more than anything she wanted his approval and his respect, so once more she dipped in a bow, swallowed her objections, and said: 'Yes, my lord. The Emperor prevails.'

'Indeed he does, interrogator. Be about your duties.'

The door began to close. Mita pounced upon her one final chance like a famished tiger.

'My lord?'

This time he did not turn back. '*Yes,* interrogator?'

'I… Before, when I was in the gallery, and… and I thought I felt the traitor's presence…?'

'Yes?'

'Was… was I drugged, my lord?'

His pause was a fraction too long.

'Don't be ridiculous,' he said. 'You fainted again. It is a habit you should learn to control.'

He closed the door behind him.

Mita Ashyn was beginning to consider the very real chance that her master was insane.

SHE RETURNED TO Cuspseal with a sense of urgency, vying with confusion for dominance. Accompanied once more by Cog, she tolerated the elevator descent with cracking patience and raced upon her arrival to Orodai's offices, to carry out her master's orders. That she neither understood nor agreed with them was irrelevant. This time, she vowed, passing stammering vindictor clerks and objecting doormen, she would not fail.

Orodai's office was empty.

She was too late.

In the wake of the assault upon the starport, unwilling to endure one more attack upon his Preafectus Vindictaire, and eschewing the assistance of the Inquisition whose presence he was quickly growing to resent, Commander Orodai had mustered as many of his lawmen as he could, had mobilised the precinct's entire complement of armoured vehicles, and had personally led a battle-group a thousand strong into the darkness below Cuspseal.

Mita had failed. Again.

War was coming to the underhive.

ZSO SAHAAL

IN THE FINAL analysis, it had been easier than stealing fruit from a child.

All had gone as planned, and if the diversionary assault upon the starport gates had left a dozen or more Shadowkin dead. If the place had run thick with the blood of civilians and Preafects alike, if the operation had cost him dear in time and effort and anxiety, then these were sacrifices he was pleased to make.

Offerings, even.

He had the support of the Dark Gods, whether he cherished it or not.

Standing there on the edge of the launchpad, he'd felt the witch's scrying eyes like a whisper at the rear of his mind. And, as if in reply, the certainty that the warp stood at his shoulder, regarding his enemy with boundless hunger, had gripped him. It had flexed, swarmed at the forefront of his soul, and *consumed* her.

She would not be eavesdropping on him again.

So, he had the patronage of Chaos itself.

Before his aeons of dormancy, Sahaal's regard for the Ruinous Ones had matched that of his Legion: Chaos was as capricious a force as it was almighty, they understood that, and Konrad Curze had spent too long overcoming insanity and terror to lie so easily in the Dark Gods' bed.

But still, but still... It was an... *intoxicating* sensation, to have guardians so mighty.

So let the casualties be offerings. Let the Shadowkin dead, with all the civilians and vindictors who had perished alongside, bleed upon the altar of Chaos Undivided. Let the hungry gods have their repast of souls, and let *him* return to his tasks unhindered. It was a worthy transaction.

Seated upon his throne, slouched with claws steepled and a blanket of shadows covering his unhelmeted face, he ignored the sounds of mourning throughout the encampment and struggled for calm.

He must be patient. The venom that the Shadowkin had smeared upon their darts was a potent substance, and the... *prizes* would be asleep a while longer.

Patience.

Focus.

The assault had succeeded. The starport had been breached and his ragtag army had allowed him all the time he had required to steal what he had come for. The prizes – *captives*, of a kind – couldn't be allowed to see him, not yet, and so a team of handpicked warriors had accompanied him, blowpipes brandished, to anaesthetise the fools before they could react.

Carrying them down into the dark – two limp shapes, withered and malnourished, slung upon each shoulder – he had felt in his heart like a warrior king, returning to his tribe with the bounties of conquered realms.

And yes, the Shadowkin had rejoiced in his victory. They'd cheered and feasted on what pitiful foods their dreary territory offered, and praised his name for such a daring raid. But as they consigned their dead to the Emperor's grace there was melancholia in their eyes.

So many had not returned.

And maddeningly, infuriatingly, Sahaal found himself *troubled* by their disquiet. Oh, they remained worms – less than worms! – but he confessed that as his reliance upon them grew he was encumbered by the distraction of pride.

This was *his* empire. *His* tribe. And he could not escape their reflected grief.

He wondered, distantly, whether this was how his master had felt. The mighty primarch of the Night Lords Legion had grown to manhood as a feral creature; a solitary hunter in the shadows of Nostromo Quintus; a vigilante without friend or peer. Only when his reign of terror had swollen to infect the entire city, when the law was *his* law and the streets were *his* streets, only then was he given governance of the populace.

Had he, too, resented the responsibility? Had he yearned to rely upon none but himself, to dispense with counsellors and soldiers and assistants? Had it sat heavily upon his heart that even *he* could not rule a world unaided?

And had he learned, by degrees, to value those at his command?

Had it hurt him when they perished?

Draped in shadow, Zso Sahaal brooded upon his throne at the heart of a web of confusions and distractions, and waited with crumbling patience for the two men that he had stolen to awake from their poisoned sleep.

* * *

So it was, with his attention elsewhere, that the burning drive to locate the Corona Nox had relented to a simmering pain in his guts; an unspoken knot of loss that his present concerns had eclipsed.

And so it was that the issue chose that very moment to resurface; interrupting his meditation with shouts, cheers, and song.

The scouts had found Slake.

'He was in Sewersump,' the man said, voice quavering with a soup of pride and nerves. He was young: still a novice, in tribal terms, but sturdily built and confident nonetheless. A find such as this would secure for him unlimited respect, and it was clear even to Sahaal that the youth intended to savour his moment. 'There's a guild there,' he added, 'does nothing but broker sales for kutroach shells.'

The youngster had chosen to address his report – without instruction – to Condemnitor Chianni, seated beside Sahaal with her wounds bandaged and her face austere. Sahaal found the arrangement pleasing: clearly the tribesfolk felt ill at ease directing their words to their angelic demagogue, preferring to use their priestess as an interface. It represented the perfect fusion of devotion and terror, and their fearful glimpses in his direction gratified Sahaal immensely.

'Kutroach?' he hissed, drawing startled glances from the crowd. He supposed that it was easier for them to think of him as some throned idol, so perfect was his stillness. Every time he moved or spoke it was a chilling reminder that their magnificent, terrible lord was as real, and as alive, as they.

Humans, Sahaal was observing, preferred to keep their gods at arms' length.

Thankfully Chianni's reaction was rather less awestruck, and she twisted to face him with hands clasped. He had spun her a vague lie regarding his search for Slake – 'an enemy of the Emperor', as he'd put it – and her willingness to assist in such a holy quest had been amusing to regard.

'Beasts of the underhive,' she explained. 'Beetle creatures with leather wings and bladed tails. Very dangerous. Their husks are perfect for ornaments and bowls, so the guilds often sell them uphive. The other gangs collect shell bounties whenever they can.'

'But not you?'

She seemed briefly affronted. 'Money is the foodstuff of corruption, my lord…'

'Of course,' he rumbled, resisting the urge to roll his eyes. 'Continue.'

Chianni gestured for the scout to go on.

'W-well… I know the guilds sometimes use middlemen, so I thought it would be worth checking…'

Chianni nodded. 'A wise idea.'

The boy beamed. 'I found him speaking with two others, a-another man and a woman. A guilder came over – handfuls of credits, he had – and called out to him. He called him Slake, I'm certain of it.'

Sahaal's fingers tightened on the skull-pommels of his throne.

'You did well,' Chianni told the boy, perhaps noting her master's eagerness. 'Bring him forwards. Our lord would look upon him.'

The morsel that was pushed into the light, bound at its hands and ankles, shrieking like a stuck pig, was not what Sahaal had imagined.

It was a small man – if not genetically stunted then at least abnormal in his build; features prematurely wizened, scalp clinging to a few last scraps of hair. His simple clothes were stained and dirty and his face was marked with fresh bruises: evidence of the scouting party's rough treatment. Most notable however, were the twin sockets set high on his hydrocephalic forehead, one above each eye: ugly irises that extruded long cable-bundle umbilici, dangling to his shoulders like metallic dreadlocks.

He collapsed to the rusted floor with a wail, took one look at the throned giant looming over, and burst into tears.

'Sweet hiveghosts I didn't do anything don't kill me oh God-Emperor please...'

'Silence him,' Chianni said, a fraction before Sahaal. The young scout dropped to his knees and punched the wailing specimen across the face, splitting his lip and speckling the floor with his blood. His cries died abruptly.

'You are Slake?' Chianni asked, glaring.

'N... no! No! Not on my own!'

The scout punched him again, harder this time. 'Lies!' he roared. 'I heard his name!'

'Breggan,' Chianni said. 'Be still.'

The young scout backed away, breathing hard.

'You are Slake,' Chianni repeated – this time a statement. 'You are a go-between for upcity guilders, correct? Answer me!'

'N-no!' he wailed, tears and snot thick on his face. 'Not on my own! Oh sweet Terra, no! Y-you don't understand! Not on my own!'

Sahaal had heard enough. He was out of his throne and hunched over the man like a great lion, seemingly without movement, and the Shadowkin audience cried out and backed away, astonished at his speed.

The man stared up into the twisted visage of Sahaal's helm, and felt the tears freeze on his cheeks.

'...oh...'

'Four days ago,' Sahaal whispered, so quiet that none but the captive could hear his reed-thin voice, 'you purchased from the Glacier Rat scum Nikhae an item. You knew it was coming. You took it from him and paid him. Yes?'

In the face of such icy terror, the man's stammers were frozen away, leaving only a tight, strangled tone.

'Yes. I mean... I don't know. I have a small piece of the memory but...'

Sahaal pressed a claw against the wattles of his neck.

'Explain.'

'Slake! It's... not a person. Not *one* of us.' His eyes rolled, mouth quivering. 'It's a *collective*. A group, you see? The *gestalim* surgery... we took the implant! Separate us, we're just people. But together, all three joined...' He pawed his bound hands at the cables hanging from his skull, broken nails clattering against their sockets. 'Together we are Slake. Th-three people, one *machina*. We share memories. We share intellect! Alone we are *nothing*.'

Sahaal ground his teeth.

'You are servitors?'

'No! No, the servitor is a slave to the *machina*. Together, we *control* it.'

There had been servitors, even in Sahaal's time. Empty minded things: human bodies with machines for brains, controlled and governed by the chattering logic engines inside. Such contrivances left no room for personality or self awareness; rendering a servitor little more than a mobile tech-console. Their lives – such as they were – were a sequence of parameter and stimulus.

Could it be that these three nothings, these human fools with more avarice than sense, had found a way to retain their minds – their ambitions – yet to foster the cold intellect of a servitor nonetheless?

'How is this possible?' Sahaal rasped, bladed claw tight against the man's larynx.

'We paid! We chose it! We found... found a man who could do it!'

'And who,' Sahaal hissed, already guessing the answer, 'was that?'

'Pahvulti! His name is Pahvulti!'

The cognis logi. The information broker. The renegade tech-priest.

The *bastard*.

It was not a name welcome to Sahaal's ears.

He lifted the shrieking captive in one great claw, and carried him out into the shadows away from the tribe, to question him as only he could.

WHEN HE WAS done with the man, who was one piece but not the whole of Slake, Sahaal brought his head before the Shadowkin and held it high, blood snaking in long chords along his arm.

The man had known little, ultimately. Glimmers of memories, snatches of detail that fired recognition in his eyes but could draw nothing new from the fragments of his third of the Slake computer. It was as he said: alone, he was pifitful. A moronic child, a nothing, a *nobody*.

He could recall meetings. He could glimpse, in agonised flashes, the package that Sahaal sought so desperately.

'Was it open?' Sahaal had raged. 'Was it *opened*?'

But that detail was beyond him, as were any others, and the Night Lord had been quick to succumb to the fury that was building inside him with every day; the hungry voices whispering for blood in his mind.

Sahaal took the man's head and left the body to the waters of the swamp, where luminous tendrils dragged it down to the depths.

The scouts were redeployed to find the remaining pieces of the collective. The youngster who had captured the man went unthanked, chastised for his incomplete prize.

It was all Sahaal could do not to tear him to shreds.

Thus it was, with his blood boiling in his veins, his heart hammering in his ears, and the name 'Pahvulti' spinning in a slick of poison and piss through his mind, that two fawning Shadowkin crept forth to tell him that finally the captives he had taken from the starport were awake.

The savage grin on his face left them ashen with terror.

IN A SHACK at the camp's edge – as sturdy and soundproofed a structure as the meagre building materials had allowed – he took delivery of the first hostage. The tribesmen dumped the moaning creature to the floor, faces twisted with disgust. He dismissed them and they left with relief, pausing only to spit at the blind worm on the floor.

Sahaal wondered vaguely how they might react if they knew the truth: that without such astropathic wretches as this their mighty Imperium was a doomed giant, without eyes or ears or mouth.

He stepped towards the figure – shivering and naked in the rustmud – and crooned with an eagerness that he could no longer contain. His rage would not be restrained.

'W-who's there?' the man quailed, withered features crumpling further. His wrists and ankles were bound with sharp cable and his eyes... his eyes had been taken from him long, long ago. The tortured flesh at their edges was puffy with unhealed scars and infection.

'You cannot see me?' Sahaal teased, already knowing the answer.

'I... N-no! My *visem deus*... sweet, Emperor... It's gone!'

Ah yes, Sahaal reflected. *The second sight.* Such men as this did not *need* eyes to see.

Usually.

'What have you done to me?' the voice grew loud, indignation at the theft of its greatest sense puncturing its fear. Sahaal allowed himself an indulgent smile.

'It is lead,' he said, bending to run fingers across the thick strip of bent metal, powder-white, coiled across his furrowed forehead like a circlet. Sahaal flicked it playfully. 'It is anathema to your... gifts, yes? You may no more penetrate it than a hawk may escape its hood.'

'Who are you?' The astopath's voice became a whisper, an awestruck quail that wrestled between curiosity and horror. 'How do you know so much about the gift? I... I am not afraid of you!'

Sahaal's smile broadened.

'I know the astropath's weakness, little man,' he said, 'because at one time an army of your brothers was at my disposal, through choice or not. And as for your fear...' He wet his lips, trembling, 'I think we both know you are lying.'

'The Emperor's faith is strong in my soul! I am without sin! Whatever your aims I shall n–'

'Do you know of Chaos?'

The man's mouth opened and closed, all his bluster stolen from him; a paroxysm of revulsion wracking him. 'I... You dare speak its name? Emperor preserve m–'

'You *shall* know of Chaos. You shall bathe in its fires, my friend. You shall know its voice.'

'Blasphemy! B-blasphemy!' The psyker tried to spit, to summon a gobbet of rebellious spittle on his flexing tongue, but Sahaal was faster. A single talon snickered from its secret sheath, blurred in the air, and was gone.

The man spat out his own tongue on the crest of a shriek.

'Now you will be silent,' Sahaal said, backhanding the creature's cheek until its screams were replaced only by the wet gurgles of oozing blood, 'and you will listen closely. And you will struggle, and writhe, and try to escape, and in your mind you shall hurt harder than you have ever felt pain before, but you cannot switch off your ears, my friend. You cannot help but listen.

'And feel, of course. Always feel.'

And Zso Sahaal began to cut. To draw slivers of flesh from arms and legs. To glide artist's strokes of tip and blade through unresisting skin and muscle. To sever sinews at knee and shoulder, at groin and ankle. To pluck arrowhead wounds across fatty chest meat, to scrape skin layer by layer from the belly's bulge. To drag deep plough-furrows across yielding buttocks and meaty loins.

To cut and cut and cut and cut.

And as he cut he spoke. He spoke across every scream and cough, ignoring inarticulate pleas and wordless prayers.

He spoke of the darkness that haunts youth's fears. Of the horrors that only the imagination of a child may devise. He spoke of bogeymen and spider gods, of scissor-fingered hags and the writhing of snakes. He spoke of faces in the sky and wet-edged lips, like the folds of a great belly, pursing to suck the light from the world.

He spoke of adolescent terror. Of self-harm and religious awakening. Of Imperial dogma crushing the soul, of familial rejection or parental perversion. Of young pain.

There was always reference to pain.

And always the cut, cut, cut.

He spoke of the terrors of adulthood. Of knives in the dark and rape in the light. Of butchers and marauders, of aliens and mutants. He spoke of fires creeping nearer, of quicksand clogging the lungs, of nooses drawing tight. He spoke of death and torture and eyes in the night.

And he cut and he cut and he cut.

He spoke of the warp, and when his victim's larynx burst from the rawness of its screams he spoke of the Ruinous Ones, of the watchers in the void, of the Empyrean swarms. He spoke of prowling madness, of insanity unleashed upon a million worlds, of the Emperor's wounds and the Traitor's joy. He spoke of the Haunter's palace. Of the blood of angels. Of the tentacles in the warp. Of the steel teeth bared in the echoes of eternity.

Of horror and nightmare and terror and venom.

He vented himself. He raged against the astropath's flesh. He diced and cut and ripped. He disjointed and jellified. He lost himself to a haze of red and he spoke of the primal scream, the banshee howl that echoed in the earliest caves of mankind, the feral simplicity of *Fear*.

And the dam broke open, and the walls of the astropath's resistance crumbled, and the chittering in the warp filled his ears and scratched petulant claws against the man's mind, and as the tumult reached its unbearable climax Sahaal reached through the paste of blood and shit and tears and wrenched away the lead circlet upon the man's brow.

For an instant, the astropath's second sight was returned to him.

He saw a bloodslick daemon with black eyes and claws of lightning steel, that leaned close to his shattered senses and hissed: 'I am Zso Sahaal, Talonmaster of the Night Lords, returned from the veil of time to reclaim that which is mine. Seek me, my brothers.'

And then the astropath was beheaded with a single stroke of the monster's claws.

The swarms of the warp, baited close by such psychic terror as they had never before tasted – an intoxicating fillip that pulsed like a beacon across the ethereum – rushed in to frenzy-feast upon the released soul.

And the warp rippled like a disturbed millpond, and in its clash of hues and flavours it was Sahaal's face, Sahaal's voice, Sahaal's mind, that was borne upon the cusp of the astropath's deathshriek.

Borne outwards, towards eternity.

MITA ASHYN

SHE WAS IN Orodai's empty office, wrestling with indecision, when it hit.

It broke across her defences like a tsunami upon a beach, surging above and through her, overwhelming every part of her mind, leaving her drowning and gasping for air.

It was a bloody-red dagger, hooked beneath her ribs and rising, rising, rising.

It was a branding iron, smouldering with red heat, that scorched her not with a word or symbol, but a vision, an image, an *event*.

It was a psychic maelstrom that boiled the very air, undirected and all powerful, sent blasting into the void like the cusp of shockwave; a telepathic *exterminatus* warhead that swelled like a fattening womb, invisible and intangible but terrible nonetheless. Lost at its centre was a scream – a hidden voice of pain and fear (*oh, God-Emperor, such fear!*) – that howled its horrors to the warp even as it was consumed: squabbled over by hungry beasts, divided and shredded before its echoes had even died.

It shivered along her spine, it froze her blood and sent her knees buckling, hands grasping for support, and this despite the unhappy truth: that the deathshriek was but a fraction of the surge: a motive force to propel it outwards, a pilot light upon which far greater, and more dazzling, visions had been hung.

Mita fell to the floor with a gasp and Cog, who had not even been aware of the psychic shockwave, let alone assaulted by its ferocity, was left mumbling his moronic concerns and trying, clumsily, to restrain her flailing limbs.

She bit her lip and bled, and frothed at the corner of her mouth, and in the punctured atria of her psychic mind she suffocated beneath an avalanche of sights and sounds.

'I AM ZSO *Sahaal, Talonmaster of the Night Lords, returned from the veil of time to reclaim that which is mine. Seek me, my brothers.'*

The voice was a foghorn, aching her ears (though it had no true sound), announcing in a blaze of light and a chorus of dark alarms the identity of her enemy. Beyond the mind's eye, in the haze of telepathy, senses became occluded and intangible: sounds became visible, images bore taste and scent, the cold touch of flesh rode a piggyback upon a musical discord. A synaesthetic whirlwind. An arco-mental maze. She stumbled through its corridors and clung to a shred of chattering lightning, holding it fast.

Zso Sahaal. A name.

And his image – an incandescent pictogram, brighter and more terrible than any auspex, sharper than the greatest *sensoria* – was scratched upon the raw flesh of her flayed brain and scarred it forever: like an electoo within her eyelids, impossible to escape, even in sleep.

It was him. The Night Lord. Her enemy.

She recognised him, despite the confusion and the whirligig tumult of conflicting senses. His face was rendered in music and the soft scents of ash and incense, his midnight blue body a medley of bitter flavours, and his claws... his claws were the touch of an artist's brush upon canvas; the gentle caress of a lover's fingers. All this he was, beyond mere vision, but she recognised him nonetheless. The sallow eyes, with pupils so swollen they were black from edge to edge, the furrowed brow, the hollow cheeks; the pallid pate of a hairless skull. All of it encased in ceramite and steel, flexing plates hung with chains and barbs, marked all over with Legion sigils and dark scriptures.

Zso Sahaal. Night Lord.

'Seek me, my brothers,' the voice purred, and Mita found herself dimly aware of the message swarming past her senses, expanding beyond and through her, climbing ever outwards in a growing sphere. It swept through the hive of Equixus like a wall of steam, and then onwards and outwards, clambering into the void, across the gulf of space. Seeking those who cared to listen.

In the hive, the message went all but unnoticed. Like Cog beside her, most hivers remained as oblivious to the unseen maelstrom around them as if they were blind and straining to see. Some shivered, or blinked in a momentary discomfort they didn't understand, and perhaps even paused to wonder at the meaning of it all – before setting their shoulders and berating themselves for such foolishness, and forging on with their small, empty lives.

In their cots, in starports and Administratum offices, guilder nexus-points and tech-monasteries, astropaths cried out and gibbered in their sleep. Identified in their youth as psykers of mediocre talent, such withered man-morsels formed a communications network, serving and sustaining the Imperium that hated them. Where tightbeamed transmissions would take an age to cross the stellar gulf, an astropath could hurl his or her voice into the warp, relaying messages and instructions upon their masters' behalf. All had undergone the Soul Binding ritual – fortifying their defences, melting their eyes, melding their very spirits with that of the Emperor himself – and as such had little to fear from the predations of warp beings. Their susceptibility to such unfocused visions as now plagued Mita was all but negligible, and so in their cloistered cells their reactions were muffled, the preserve of nightmares and troubled thoughts. Their patient minders, who had grown well used to such disturbed slumbering, calmly administered soothing drugs to their unstable charges.

Alone in all the city, Mita convulsed and screamed, utterly exposed.

Even through her fear and pain she burned with outrage at nature of this psychic storm. Her enemy's cunning – and cruelty – was beyond words, and she was as staggered by her revulsion as by the agony of the storm itself.

The Night Lord had known he could not control an astropath. He could not *force* a psyker to dispatch a message on his behalf, nor could he be certain – if he found a willing dispatcher – that the message had been sent at all. Alone and hunted within an unfamiliar city, he could not place his trust in such uncertain, intangible things.

And so he'd found the one way he could be sure his message would be dispatched. The one way that it would blast outwards in all directions, irrespective of the crude directions of a straining astropath.

The bastard. The cruel, warp-damned bastard!

He'd delivered his message in the psyker's moment of death, in the blink of a psychic atrocity, at the heart of a deathscream formed in the moments of a soul's consumption.

The bastard, he fed *the psyker to the warp, and made sure his face and his words were the last things the poor wretch ever knew; like echoes on the cusp of a dying shockwave.*

How far could such a message travel? How deep into the warp would such a horrific end propel the psyker's scream?

And who might be listening, out amongst the stars, for just such a thing?

'*I am Zso Sahaal. Talonmaster of the...*' Over and over again.

Convulsing on the floor of Orodai's office, Mita clamped down hard with all her willpower and shielded herself from the pain, great mental defences rising in her mind like stormshields. And then, undistracted by the horror, she *shifted* her perceptions of the pulsing signal and coiled outwards from its grasp, turning to regard it in a new and disciplined perspective. Released from the pain, recovered from the shock and awe of its first bite, she sorted her cluttered senses together and was rewarded with order.

The warp was a pool of oil, now – at least, that was how her mind had chosen to rationalise it. The astropath's death had struck it hard; concentric ripples bulging outwards from its centre. Drawing close, Mita saw clearly the process the Night Lord had tapped into, and found herself morbidly impressed by its cunning:

with secret fractal symmetry – each tiny component a replica of the whole – every concentric ripple bore along its bow-wave the shadow, the *echo,* of the event that had caused it. And through it, as it faded with each diminishing ring, Mita found herself able to explore, to taste the ghost of the Night Lord's mind where before she was unable even to approach him. It was as if she had been presented with a pictoslate of her enemy: a transcendent snapshot that had dazzled her at first but that now, now that its brightness had faded, now that she was accustomed to its flare, she could use to study his aspect.

And oh, what rage he held in his soul!

There was loss, beneath it all. A wisp of colour haunting the midnight whole, like a deep sea kraken swimming an ocean of rage.

He has lost something. Something he loves. Something he cares for with holy pride.

He has lost it, and it angers him. And he is alone.

With a precision that she struggled to maintain, she peeled back the layers of this echo-enemy – a perfect but fading replica of the Night Lord's mind – and found a forest of emotion, buried deep beneath layers of time and denial, that shocked her.

Ambition.

Uncertainty.

Frustration.

Loneliness.

Suspicion.

Paranoia.

Power.

She drew back from it with an inward gasp, surfacing from the trance and into Cog's burly arms, wrapped around her in a desperate embrace: the one thing his simple mind had presented as a solution to his mistress's distress.

And as she prized herself away and thanked him, and caught her bearings, and wiped the blood from her lip, her mind lingered on what it had found, and pulsed with a shock that she could barely contain.

Staring at the Night Lord's mind – even through the haze of shadow and echo – had been like staring at a mental map of herself.

Outside Orodai's office, pandemonium reigned. Obeying Mita's instruction with empty devotion, Cog carried her through the narrow door and into the antechamber beyond, where the commander's servitor aides sat lifeless at their desks, bereft of orders. Their human counterparts – acolytes and scribes in the employ of the Vindictare, whose taskmasters had deserted them in their march to war – clustered at the chamber's apex, where a rusting civilian worship viewspex glimmered with a broken image; a breathless voice barking terse reports from horn-like speakers. Periodically the crowd cheered, fists punching at the air, and Mita drew close to their swarm with a sinking heart. She could well imagine what they were watching.

'...and onwards into the gulley known as Spit Run, where resistance was overcome with mighty deeds and...'

Propaganda. Damn Orodai for his wounded pride – he'd led the Preafects on a crusade and he'd taken the Hivecasters with him.

Damn, damn, damn.

The acolytes snapped to a guilty attention when they saw her, decorum returning where excitement had ruled. She ignored them and steered Cog towards the screen, his bulk pushing cowls and autoscholars aside like a ship's keel.

'...and just receiving word from the second wing – they're east of here in the Chalkmire territories – that a rebel

stronghold at Brokepoint Town has fallen to the Emperor's warriors with a total loss of life…'

The presenter, who stood at a safe distance from the growing maelstrom of tracer fire and sooty explosions behind him, was clean and elaborately dressed; his unassuming features betraying not a single hint of mechanised augmentation. Mita was hardly surprised: she'd seen broadcasts on other Civilian Worship systems on other populous worlds – joyous reports of the Emperor's victories, lectures in religious dogma, uplifting sermons, vilification of captured criminals and heretics – and in every case the chosen representative of the state embodied pure, unthreatening humanity. Mita had little doubt that beyond the gaze of the servoskull trained upon him, the small man sported a plethora of control articulators, autofocus diaphragms and self-viewing vambrances to broadcast his own image into his retina; but such paraphernalia could hardly be considered photogenic.

'…seem to have routed insurrectionists with – praise his glory – no reported casualties! Truly an example to us all…'

The little man waved an arm grandly at the scene behind him – some unnamed underhive township being bombed to dust by a circle of Preafect tanks. Through the unclear flickers of pixelated flames, if she concentrated hard, Mita could make out the small silhouettes of staggering figures; writhing and dying. Children and women, burned alive.

She wondered, distantly, how many millions of eyes were fixed upon communal hivecasters throughout Equixus. Most worlds practised compulsory viewing: at least an hour of every day spent by each citizen in passive absorption of CW doctrine, and from what Mita had seen of this hive its customs were no less rigorous than elsewhere. She prayed to the Emperor with what small part of her mind remained untarnished by doubt and exhaustion that Inquisitor Kaustus was not amongst this broadcast's audience.

Not that it would stop him from hearing about it, one way or another.

'...a surge of rebels, but in praise to Him-on-the-Throne-of-Earth – Ave Imperator! – heroes of the Preafectus Vindictaire have broken through the barricades to dispatch the filthy heretics...'

Mita clenched her teeth. *Not heretics.* Just people. The worthless and the dispossessed; the ones who fell through the cracks. The ones being slaughtered in the name of revenge.

She could imagine the scene all too clearly. The winding column of Preafect Salamanders, grinding across drifts of waste and rust. Perhaps their intentions were pure, at the start; perhaps they really *did* intend to seek out those responsible for the attack on the starport, to hunt down the villain behind it all. But the underhive was a warren of suspicion and paranoia, and it would not have taken long for the first shots to ring out, for the first angry outlaws to panic at the sight of such a force and lash out.

The Preafects had no idea who was responsible for the massacre at the starport. They had no clue as to the motive or the goal. In the main theirs was a simple role, and at its crux was an elegant assertion: *Resistance implies guilt.*

Orodai had led his warriors into the shadows to hunt and kill a monster. Instead they found themselves conducting genocide – a glorious, wanton, bloody pogrom upon those who had slipped from the light.

Blood ran thick through the streets of the underhive, and though its inhabitants begged the Emperor for mercy, wept his name as they died, screamed in prayer as their families burned – still the slaughter continued; and it was conducted in the name of the same god to which its victims cried out for help.

As she left the room, feeling sick, a servitor twitched at her side and fixed its dead eyes on her face, a telescopic array of circuitry and shattered bone creaking forwards from its shoulder, pushing a miniature hivelink headset towards her.

'A call,' it announced, lugubrious mouth hanging slack around a voicebox embedded upon its long-dead tongue. 'The inquisitor requests y–'

'I'm not here,' Mita said, hurrying past. 'He's missed me.'

She left the chambers with bile in her throat, and tried to ignore the sounds of cheering from the viewspex gather-halls she passed as she went.

PART THREE: EXODUS

'Give me a child to teach with abacus and chalk and I shall give you a scholar.

None but knowledge is his master.

Give me a child to mould with scripture and incense, and I shall give you a priest.

For him divinity alone is worthy.

Give me a child to train with sword and shield, and I shall give you a warrior.

His obedience is as fickle as his courage.

But give me a child to form as I see fit, with dagger and blade, with the blood of strangers upon his hand, and I shall give you a slave who will ask not for food nor wealth nor glory, and remain at your side throughout all his life.

Nothing forges loyalty like guilt and complicit bloodshed.'

–Extract from *Inquis Tiros*

ZSO SAHAAL

THE UNDERHIVE BARED its necrotic breast to the knives that assaulted it, and poured its blood out onto cold stone streets.

The scouts were abroad; creeping in stealthy corners with eyes peeled and curiosity piqued, regarding each act of terror, each fiery calamity, each bloody attack, with insect fascination. And then one by one, slinking though soot-brick wastes, sliding silent feet along rusted ducts where no Preafect could see or hear, they turned back to their deep, dark terrain to make report to their dark lord.

The pogrom had not yet reached the Shadowkin's lair. Ensconced within their frail homes, casting bright eyes at the vaulted roof of their watery island-cavern, they listened as the lightless territories of the underworld tore themselves apart, bone by brittle bone. The pulses of remote explosions – like the roar of avalanches in the night, echoing from peak to peak –

filtered in waves of dislodged dust and shrapnel. The Shadowkin shivered and prayed, and threw stricken glances at their dreadful lord, cloaked upon his throne once more.

Sahaal had not troubled himself to clean his armour. Where once a host of slaves would undress and bathe him – now he was left to fester. He could demand such a service from his tribe, of course, but in truth he did not care for cleanliness in this place. In this anarchy, in the depths of the depression that gripped him, to adopt a feral countenance seemed a fitting response. The tentacles of failure had returned; the bright pincer-teeth of hopelessness. How could he ever know if his ruse with the astropath had succeeded? How would he ever find the Corona now – whether it be through Slake, or Pahvulti, or by chance alone?

How could he ever resume his vengeful crusade?

Such thoughts robbed him of all energy, imbuing his flesh with a brooding indolence. Far easier to sit and burn in self-hatred, to consume his own mind with reproach and guilt, than to stir to activity.

What else, ultimately, could he do?

He was, he knew, terrible to behold. The swirls of decoration on his helm's swept-back crest were speckled now by a frieze of gore. The astropath's fluids coated him head to foot, and where blood had pooled in the gulleys and joints of his armour it clotted to a dirty brown powder, like an iron giant beset by rust.

The scouts came one by one, ferried across the swamp in makeshift barges, flicking away questing tentacles when they crept too close. The rest of the tribe gathered to hear their testimonies from the worlds above, and with every fresh report they murmured and bit their lips. Their concerns were as palpable in their eyes as had they spoken them aloud, and Sahaal regarded them from the shadows of his helm with a shrewd eye.

How far would the Preafects descend their faces asked? How deep would the massacres cut?

Had they not suffered enough beneath their master's frenzied rule?

Guilt upon shame upon failure upon horror. Sahaal couldn't begrudge them their fear.

The scouts spoke of death and blood and horror. Of whole townships ripped to cinder, populations driven before the clubs of riot-mobs, warriors ground beneath tanktracks and booted feet. Of Preafects with electric shields, charging down fleeing townsfolk, breaking heads and snapping bones.

One spoke of a brothel, half collapsed, as its shrieking women were shot down one by one, soot and blood staining naked flesh, whilst they crawled to escape the flames.

One had watched an alliance between rival mobs – a friendship born in shared peril – only for both to fall to the last man and woman; sliced to slivers when vindictors bottled them in and killed and killed until none remained.

One saw a child throw a stone at the Preafect column, and watched the youth's village burn in retribution.

One saw the kutroaches pick the flesh clean from a rioting mob, gassed in their dozens when they turned on the armoured aggressors torching their homes.

One saw blood running as thick as a stream.

And one... one saw the Preafects regroup and confer, and finally – gore-drenched, exhausted, spent – turn back for the hive above.

The Shadowkin shuddered with relief at this last mercy, embracing one another and praising the God-Emperor, and when the final scout had hurried from the circle of firelight before Sahaal's throne he stepped down from his platform and addressed the crowd. The opportunity was too good to ignore.

'You see?' he told them, claws splayed. 'You see now? You see how the hive is corrupted? How the Preafects themselves are hungry for murder and blood? It is the *taint*, I tell you!' A shiver raced across the crowd, like a breeze rippling through withered trees. 'They reach out to crush the innocent, and we alone – *we*, the faithful, the chosen ones – are spared! We alone, in this place that *I led you*.

'You *see* now? *You see*?'

And oh, they praised him so hard that it all but cut through the bleakness, the loss, the aggression, and for one fraction of one moment Zso Sahaal remembered what it had been to be *adored* without fear.

And then he asked the scouts if they brought word of the Slake Collective, and that ancient terror came back into their eyes, and the adoration was buried beneath a dozen layers of fear.

None of them brought news.

The crowd dispersed after that, when long moments of silence had passed, when it was clear finally that the lord's displeasure would not over-boil with violence – and there was hidden relief on their faces as they returned to their homes to hunt and cook.

Silence settled in the swamplands.

Sahaal sat and brooded, and beside him Chianni fidgeted in her chair, casting anguished glimpses in his direction, shivering.

His patience for her unspoken anxiety did not last long.

'You are troubled, sister,' he said, grateful – grudgingly – for the distraction. 'And yet we are spared. Explain.'

She struggled to find the right words, crippled by awe at the closeness of his attention. 'The Preafects, my lord... Their... their anger is so mighty. They must hate you a great deal.'

He sensed the curiosity behind her words and sighed, anticipating yet more ugly lies and false devotions in the Emperor's name. The falsehood that had secured the Shadowkin's loyalty had grown to a yoke around his neck, and his gorge rose at the thought of strengthening it further.

'It has ever been thus,' he said, dismissive. 'The unjust have always despised the righteous. Their loathing for me is no greater than my disgust for them.'

That, at least, was truth. *He* was the righteous one. Was it not their 'glorious' Emperor that had betrayed his master so cruelly? Was it not *they* who worshipped a weakling, a coward, a traitor?

It was not enough to sate Chianni's thirst for answers.

'My lord,' she quailed, fingers curling together. 'How can we hope to... to prevail in the face of such anger?'

'With focus,' he said, and realised as he said it that it was advice for his own sake, as much as hers. 'With conviction in the cause.' He twisted to stare down at her, hearing his master's words echoed across the gulf of time. 'Doubt breeds *fear*, child. And fear is our weapon, not our flaw.'

'But–'

'We strive towards our goals. We strive with every ounce of our flesh, with every bloody tear, every bead of sweat. And though we may fall in the trying, we are undertaking the work of the *righteous*.'

Fine words. Stirring words. He felt a glimmer of fire return to his belly.

'And... our goals, my lord? The goals we must strive to meet...' she glanced up at him, eyes brimming with hunger. 'W-what are they?'

'I have told you. To find the Slake Collective.'

'Y-yes lord...' Again a glance – first up then away, a sliver of eye contact – and this time Sahaal could see a dangerous recklessness, a desire to comprehend *at any cost,* that underpinned her fear. 'W-what I meant was... *why?*'

He considered killing her, briefly.

Should I be angry? his mind mused. *Should I suffer this curiosity – this impetuosity – in a creature so frail as this woman?*

Should I cut her in two?

His claws began, so slowly that he barely even felt it, to slip from their sheaths. He had not consciously triggered them.

But then... but then...

The priestess's importance could not be understated: to lose her would be to risk losing once more the control of his tribe – and that at this most critical of junctures. For all his might and power he was no diplomat; no empathetic figurehead to safeguard the hopes and fears of a population. His was a diplomacy of terror and carnage, not of words and assurances.

He *needed* her.

A demonstration, then?

Some painful reprimand, perhaps, to punish her undue curiosity; to teach her – and through her the tribe – that his plans were his alone; that he would not tolerate the prying of peasants.

Chianni noticed the claws and gasped in the silence, perhaps understanding, too late, her mistake.

Yes. Yes, teach her a lesson. Make her bleed. Just a small cut...

It was a voice that came from somewhere deep in his subconscious, and as he focused on it, he saw that it was the same voice that had pushed forth his claws, the same voice that had overwhelmed him as he slew the astropath, the same voice that had brought red haze down across his vision time and time again since his arrival on this blighted world.

Cut her. Cut her, you fool!

Was he mad, then? Was he succumbing to that same random insanity – a thing of brilliance and bitterness – that had consumed his master?

He had long ago forsaken the trust of any other creature… could he now no longer trust his own mind?

He snarled in the silence of his helmet and drowned the voice in his mind, and retracted his claws with a silky rasp, feeling foolish. The priestess swam before his eyes, pale with incomprehension, and it was with a sensation like relief, like a clear water scouring the filth of his psyche, that he broke the silence, focused upon her question, and spoke.

'Why?… Because through them I may find something that was stolen from me. My *inheritance*.'

'I-inheritance? Something that will help you? Something that will help *us*?'

He smiled, although of course she could not see it.

'Yes. Something that will aid me.'

'A… forgive me, my lord… a *weapon*?'

He settled back upon the throne and wet his lips, and was no longer irked by her questions. It felt good to speak of such things, finally. It felt good to leave the vacuum of solitude – however momentary, however falsely – and remember the glories of his past. What harm could it do? What harm in telling the truth to this eager creature – or at least those parts that would strengthen her loyalty?

What harm in leaving the shadows, for an instant?

'What do you know,' he asked, 'of the primarchs? Of the Emperor's own sons?'

Her bulging eyes were all the answer he needed. He waved away her astonishment and went on.

'There were twenty. Twenty warrior infants, twenty child-gods. Perhaps they were whelped, like human sons. Perhaps he made them, as an artist fashions a masterpiece. Perhaps he simply willed them to life – who knows? What is known is that they were scattered, cast out into the stars like seeds on tilled earth. And in their absence from their father they grew to manhood – each in reflection of the world that had claimed them, each shaped by the people who took them in. The kindness and cruelty of strangers.'

He paused, and in his mind he saw a snow-white baby, rushing through tortured skies, black eyes squinting against clouds and wind, before being swallowed – consumed whole – by the dark.

'There was one who fell further, and deeper, than the rest. He came to a world without daylight, where cruelty abounded above compassion, where the only honour was a precarious thing shared amongst thieves and murderers. This child, this feral thing, was raised by no man. No human kindness ever taught him mercy, no mother ever shushed his sleeping terrors. And alone of all the scattered primarchs, all those lost babes, no one taught him wrong from right. Justice from injustice.

'Oh, the beliefs of the other primarchs varied, of course. What is "wrong", or "right", after all? Points of view. As each child grew their sense of righteousness solidified, their concept of what to punish and what to encourage took form, guided by the morality of their tutors or brothers-at-arms. Ultimately the conclusion they drew, whatever their circumstance, was the same: that "right" was *whatever they said* was right. That "wrong" was *whatever they decided to punish.*

'Just children, priestess, but already gods to be loved and feared.'

Chianni stirred, throwing off her obvious awe to grasp at the loose end left flailing.

'And the feral child? What of him?'

Sahaal smiled again, warmth flourishing in his chest. *Ah, my master...*

'He had no tutors. No one would take him in, so he grew wild and independent. No one would feed him, so he learned to hunt and feed himself. No one would comfort him when he was taken by the nightmares in his sleep, or by the visions that plagued his waking hours, or by the fits that wracked his body – so he grew strong and wily, and overcame the nightmares, and deciphered the visions, and repressed the fits.

'No one would teach him what justice was, and so – like no child had ever done before, and no child has ever done since – he taught himself. He saw callousness and cruelty, and recognised them. He saw strength being abused; productivity and *peace* being surrendered to terror and violence. And do you know what he learned, child?'

'N-no, my lord.'

'He learned that justice *is* strength. He learned that if he wished to overcome the predators that haunted the darkness, he need only become the strongest predator of them all. He learned that if he wished to punish a murderer, it required only that he be a more accomplished killer. He learned that if he wished to bring peace and equality to his world – and *oh,* he wanted that *so much* – he must hunt down those filth that stood in its way and use their weapons against them.

'And he learned that there is only *one* weapon. Stronger than any gun. Sharper than any blade.' Sahaal leaned close to the priestess, her ashen face reflected with bulbous distortion in the crimson windows of his eyes. 'That weapon is *fear*, child.'

She swallowed, eyes not leaving him for an instant.

Sahaal went on, quieter than before, voice no more than a whisper. 'The thugs and the thieves, the rapists and the murderers: they gripped that world tight in their hands because every man and woman was afraid of them. And so the feral warrior became the one thing that would stop them:

'Something that even *they* would learn to fear. He became the Night Haunter.

'He taught them justice through terror. He led that world into peace and efficiency, where before only violence and anarchy had reigned, and he did so unaided, alone in the dark, for the good of them all.

'His name was Konrad Curze, and he was my master.'

He leaned away from the priestess and watched her closely, gauging her response. She struggled, of course – who would not? – but again the curiosity at her core overcame the awe; an addict demanding *more* before even the drug-rush has faded.

'Your master...' she breathed. 'What happened to him?'

'His father found him. The Emperor came to him and embraced him, and they went into the stars to lead the mightiest crusade that ever was.'

'S-so he lives? He lives still?'

A bleak tableau erupted behind Sahaal's eyes: a scene he had revisited in his dreams a million times over, each one cutting him deeper than the last.

A pale face; awaiting the killer. Black eyes – bottomless, pouring with angst – staring from the shadows of the writhing room. Its fleshwalls and limb carpets shift underfoot… and the bitch draws near.

Sahaal had been there. He had seen it, hiding in the shadows like some child at play, honouring his vow with tears upon his cheeks. He would not intervene. He would not stop her. He would watch and nothing more: and it hurt him like a cold fire in his guts that could never be doused.

She steps close, horrified at her surroundings, entranced by the target's naked form.

He has been expecting her. He has foreseen this moment.

She sweeps towards him and is surprised. She has been expecting guards. She has anticipated violence. Instead the Haunter smiles and beckons her close, and he speaks.

Oh, by the dark, his *voice…*

Such words of venom and vengeance he spoke; such heartbroken sentiments.

He smiles throughout, and even as his voice breaks and the tears puncture their inertia and gather in streams along his pallid cheeks, he is welcoming. He is warm. He is calm.

'Death is nothing compared to vindication,' he finishes, sitting forwards on his mighty throne, 'Now do your job and be done with it.'

And her hand rises, and the thing in her grip flickers bile-green, and…

And…

Sahaal stared down at the priestess, blinking through a film of water, and gathered himself.

'No,' he said. 'He is dead. He was betrayed by one who should have loved him.'

The effect of this upon Chianni could hardly have been more devastating. She rocked back in her chair and scrabbled at her face, tears and spittle oozing between fingers, breath catching in her throat.

Sahaal was unsurprised. To him, a veteran of the Horus Heresy, the idea that the gods and angels of the Imperium might be capable of betrayal was nothing new. But to the peasants amongst whom he walked – people like this woman – he was less a living being than a *myth* made solid. Little wonder their minds rebelled against his words. And little wonder the priestess's nausea: it is not often one is told their gods are just as capable of misery, flaw and evil as any other being.

'Restrain yourself,' he said, tiring of her fit. 'You questioned me regarding my master's legacy, not the reason for his death.'

She recovered her dignity by degrees, straightening into her seat and smoothing her tangled hair. 'A-apologies, lord,' she choked, wiping her face. 'I... I had no idea...'

'He is dead,' Sahaal repeated, eager to return to the story; flushed with a gratification at speaking it aloud that he hadn't expected. It was as if the millennia of his dormancy had allowed the pain to fester in his soul, to expand like some poisoned gas, swelling his ribs with pressure he could no longer contain. Merely speaking of it, merely venting his memories, felt like opening a valve in his mind, expelling the venom in a great invisible cloud. 'He is dead and that is an end to it. He had foreseen it, and for that was grateful, for he could prepare himself. He named an heir, he bequeathed his mightiest treasure, and that heir was – *is* – me.'

'T-then this treasure is–?'

'Is the item I seek on this world.' He clenched his jaw, remembering. 'It was stolen from me before I could even claim it.'

The Haunter's head, so placid in its aspect, tumbles to the floor and rolls. There is no blood.

The killer stands thus poised, grisly mission complete, and perhaps she pauses to savour the moment. Perhaps she reflects upon the ease with which it was done.

Or perhaps she has more still to do.

She bends to the body and plucks at its dead limbs. A ring, she steals, and a silver blade worn in a flesh scabbard at its shoulder. And then she turns, hunched low on the writhing floor, seeking something.

And then she straightens, and in her hand she holds it. Dislodged from his person at the moment of death, she finds it and she takes it.

The prize.

The Corona Nox.

In the shadows, Sahaal gapes. His master had not foreseen this.

And then she is gone; as quick as a cobra. And it is then, only then, with grief overcome by sudden anger, with teeth rasping together and hot tears turning to ice on his cheeks, that Sahaal quits his vantage and races in pursuit.

'S-stolen?'

'Yes. By my master's killer. I should have known his enemies would try to take it...'

'H-he is here? That is who you pursue? This Slake – *he* is the one who killed your master?'

'No. No, this happened... many years ago. She is dead now.'

'S-she?'

'The killer. The assassin.'

Chianni had the look of one who was drowning in a sea of surprises, and still had not even sighted the shore.

'Then... my lord, why *here*?'

Sahaal hesitated. In truth the details of the subsequent calamities were still unfocused in his mind, a gamut of colour and light that no amount of mental dissection could unravel. He knew how it began – in fire and blood aboard the assassin's vessel, grappling with claw and fist against the bitch herself, wrestling the Corona from her grasping fingers then fleeing to the *Umbrea Insidior*...

He knew how it ended, crashing through the mists of Equixus, awaking in the vessel's ruptured guts; his prize stolen.

And between? A hundred centuries. Light. Colour. Capering figures of svelte form and slanted eye, with fluted helms and bright jewels, slipping between reality and warp, gathering around him.

The attack.

The flight.

The trap.

The prison.

Eldar.

'It has reached this world along... intricate pathways,' he said, clearing his mind of the jumbled impressions. 'It came to the Glacier Rats, and then to Slake. And from there...' he sighed, a blister of depression breaking apart, overwhelming even the freedom that had come from speaking with such candour, '...from there I do not know where it has gone.'

Chianni stared at him with wide eyes, and all around the silence of the underhive poured into the vacuum his story had left.

HOURS PASSED, AND Sahaal slept, disengaging the cycadian rhythms of his psyche, relaxing the catalapsean node at the centre of his spine that could oscillate so casually between the domes of his brain.

True sleep. And with it, true dreams.

He saw the ice-light of voidfire, capering and self-consuming as the *Umbrea Insidior* closed with the assassin's transport. He saw melta charges flare in the gloom, and Dreadclaw assault craft punch into soft, yielding iron.

He saw the boarding action, and the slaughter. He saw his raptors make a charnel house of the bitch's craft. He saw her eyes, wide and fearful, as he sliced her hand from her wrist – a bright filigree of blood and oil shivering from the rent – and with it reclaimed the Corona Nox. He saw himself lift a claw for the killing blow: bittersweet vengeance for his master's death.

And then...

Screams upon the vox. His sergeant's voice, fat with anger: 'Warpspit! *Eldar*, Talonmaster! Xenogen *scum*!'

They came like a bloody sword from the sky; breaking from dismal walls in light and warpfire, skimming realities like a pebble across water. Limbs wavering, breathless guns coughing discs and coils. Like spiders, hatching on webs of Empyrean.

Aliens.

He saw the witch-lord. The dancing devil, with antlered helm and silver staff, blue-gold armour and feathered gown; a warlock-warrior, frozen in his pathway, sword alive with wyrdfire.

He saw himself breaking free from the maelstrom, leaving the assassin to cower, every shred of his being bent upon the Corona. They wanted it. They had come to claim it, in his moment of triumph.

They would not have it.

He saw himself, alone, returning to the *Umbrea Insidior*. He saw himself shutting out the cries of his brothers. He saw himself aboard his own vessel, fastening his prize in its casket, sealing it against alien hands.

He saw himself tasting, for an instant, triumph.

And then the warp opened its mouth, prised wide by alien hands, and a bubble of *nothing* intumesced around his ship. She shuddered, a protesting behemoth, a terrible beast floundering into sticky tar to sink centimetre by centimetre, shrieking as she drowned.

They pushed her deep into a timeless bubble, those xenogen spellsingers, and locked her from the warp: a water-filled belljar, sealed with hot wax, cast adrift in an ocean.

They could not enter. He could not leave.

He saw himself rage and roar for a full month. He saw his vassals lock themselves away from his wrath. He saw himself succumb to insanity.

And then finally he saw himself tasting bitter acceptance, piece by piece, until he resigned himself from reality, lost all hope of escape, and entered the trance.

HE AWOKE IN the Shadowkin encampment with the flavour of resignation and loss clouding his mind, and found a commotion in progress.

He found Chianni at the water's edge, staring out across the unquiet swamplands, shouting orders and imprecations at the flotilla of boatmen that approached.

She almost choked when he appeared silently behind her, and in the shallows two of the pugs overturned as their pilots glimpsed the apparition on the shore.

'What,' Sahaal hissed, ignoring the fearful splutters from the unctuous waters, 'is the meaning of this?'

They had gathered in their thousands. In makeshift shelters, beneath canvas bivouacs or else simply stretched upon the hard ground, with oily torches sputtering on rusted spars, wagons and litters clustered in protective circles, gang colours fluttering – half-heartedly – side by side, all sense of territory abandoned: the rustmud swamp *teemed*.

Even as he watched, Sahaal could see the human stream thickening. He had chosen his acolytes' realm with care, placing their encampment at the heart of a patchwork morass of bore-holes and smog vents, but now the winding path that led down from above, snaking from the north, appeared impossibly choked: a flow of humanity like sewage, blocking the pipe that carried it. They stepped from shattered girder to fungal plateau, homing on the great drowned drilling rig like pilgrims to a holy place.

Sahaal cast a brief glance to the south, working his jaw. There – set back from the swamp amidst a tangle of igneous formations and massive fungi – he knew there existed a second route from above: a tunnel so tight and twisting that it could accept only a single body at a time. It was his exit, his bolt-hole; his means of a rapid escape if this unfathomable territory was attacked, and he was pleased to see that its secrecy remained intact. He turned back to the refugees, gratified.

They came with heads bowed and wounds unhealed. They came with the dying carried on palettes behind them, with their faces clouded and their eyes filled with tears. Where once gangs had spat upon the face of their enemies, and died in the name of their totem, now they walked side by side, mutually ignored, hostilities redundant in the face of this harsher, more immediate exodus.

They sought out a new totem, now – a new figurehead – and in the pit of his heart an ugly suspicion as to what it was rolled over Sahaal like a breaking storm.

'Who are they?' he asked Chianni, keeping alive the hopes that he might be wrong.

'J-just... just people, my lord. From the underhive. The Preafects have destroyed half the settlements... They've got nowhere e–'

'What do they *want*?'

Chianni bit her lip, perceptive enough to know the answer would not please her master.

'They have heard of you,' she said, voice quiet. 'They think... they think you're a myth, but... But they know the Shadowkin escaped unharmed. They know us as... Holy zealots, my lord. They've feared us for decades – as long as the tribe has been here – but... but now we have strength, and they are weakened. They're angry. They don't know what they did to warrant the Preafects' violence. They're dying. They're *pitiful*. And suddenly they have seen the error of their ways.'

'I did not ask you who they *are*, priestess. I asked *what do they want*?'

He knew the answer already, of course.

Chianni's lip trembled as she spoke.

'Sanctuary, lord. They come seeking sanctuary.'

MITA ASHYN

SHE COULD NOT avoid her master's attempts at contact for long. She left the precinct when the chirruping of advancing servitors – snatching at her attention with hivelink comms clutched in piston knuckles – grew tedious, and her excuses became untenable. She knew she was being childish, but the swarm of uncertainties clouding her mind, coupled with the ghosts of exhaustion gripping her, precluded even the most lacklustre of attempts to represent herself intelligibly. For all that, she could tell sleep was not yet an option, so she took to wandering the bustling streets of Cuspseal like an eidolon, a lost spirit seeking absolution.

Preachers leaned from pulpits, holding loosebound books in claw-like grasps, eyes alive with fire and piety. Around them crowds accreted, and as she passed by Mita tasted the cocktail of their thoughts: the bright ember of the zealot, the tepid mundanity of his flock (*I believe!* their minds cried – but always the shackles of doubt, of shame, of sin, weighed their spirits down); and always amongst the crowds she found incongruous minds: the strict focus of undercover Preafects, the darting intentions of pickpockets and outlaws, the fearful disgust of whores, grudgingly seeking custom. She walked on quickly, troubled to find so little purity, so little virtue, amongst this ocean of thought.

At one intersection a knot of boys had gathered around a militia post, recruiting sergeants barking false promises of glory and adventure. The youths shouted and whistled as she passed, even the crudity of their catcalls unable to break through the cage of her worries.

The question that assailed her was as unanswerable as the universe was vast, and amongst its myriad strands of uncertainty she found herself gathering it together, kneading into one shape; one indigestible issue:

Why?

She paced across a hanging bridge and paused to stare at the heads of executed criminals fixed upon each of its stanchions, their eyes and tongues greedily devoured by jewelled beetles and albino bats. The flocks chattered as she passed, stabbing at her psychic senses with needles of ultrasonic sound, and she moved on with only the most cursory glance towards downtown Cuspseal – the hulking cube of the precinct dominating her view, towering above the mighty underhive chasm into the shadows below.

Why does the inquisitor not act?

Why does he restrain me with one hand and wave me forth with the other?

Why does he request my presence then drug me, then lie that he did not?

Why does his mood shift like a tide, ebbing and rising against all stimulus?

Why does he sit day after day, ensconced within the governor's palace?

His actions had hardly been heroic, and that in the face of his noble reputation. And whether he trusted her or not, she would have assumed the mere *possibility* of a Chaos Marine lurking in the dark would spur him to action. And yet he smiled and sneered, and dismissed the issue, and told her it was being *dealt with*.

Dealt with! By a single acolyte? A single cowled *dissimulus*, whatever that was.

What if his plans fail?

What if his plans... oh, Emperor, forgive me my doubt... what if his plans cannot be trusted?

What if he *cannot be trusted?*

She lurked in the shadows beneath a tanning factory chewing her lip, and watched as servitor-machines – simian monstrosities with arms like grablifters and thick chords of servomuscle tightening across copper pectorals – hefted tall piles of grox carcasses from uphive chutes into the rambling building. The stench of smoke and tar and burning meat made her retch, and she moved on again.

Is there nowhere to think in this damned hive?

Was that the problem, perhaps? Had she forgone the process of exhaustive consideration that the *tutoria* had encouraged? Had she been slack, dumbly clouded by mistrust that had no basis, listening too hard to instincts that had no place in a position of obedience?

Where has this paranoia come from?

She looped back towards the precinct, more troubled than ever, and when a mugger slipped from the moist darkness of an icemelt-drenched alleyway, blade glittering in his hand, she faced him with an almost indecent joy: relieved to shut out the worries for an instant, relaxed by the simple promise of violence.

The man approached with a sneer, knife weaving mesmeric patterns, holding her attention. It would have been a crude feign even had she not been a psyker, and when his partner, hidden behind her, took her obvious distraction as his cue to attack, she spun a carefully gauged kick into his face, his own momentum snapping the bones of his cheek and ripping an ugly tear across his lip.

The psychic feedback of his surprise and pain was deliciously gratifying.

The first attacker waded in with his knife, all hope of surprise lost, and she ducked beneath his first clumsy swipe to plant a balled fist in his stomach, knocking him down with the breath gone from his lungs.

She rolled aside to avoid any desperate slashing and jumped to her feet before he could groggily arise, imagining Kaustus's tusked face in the place of the mugger's, and half turned with an elegant elbow, dropping him back for a second time, thick ruby fluid gushing from his broken eyeball.

She returned to the first attacker, the broken-lipped nobody, a fraction too late, just as he launched a throwing knife at her head, gurgling on the bloody soup sliding into his mouth. Acting without thought she screwed up her mind and released an impetuous, undirected pulse of psychic energy, deflecting the spinning blade with a clash of blue sparks.

The muggers weren't as stupid as they looked. Seeing what manner of victim they'd chosen, yelping the word 'witch!' with youthful terror, they fled into the shadows on a chorus of shrieks and moans. Mita huffed behind them, irritated at the brevity of the workout. She hadn't even broken a sweat.

Instinct.

Instinct had saved her. Then, as now…

She realised with a start that it made little difference. The realisation overcame her like some prophetic epiphany, and reduced all her confusions and anxieties to a simple certainty.

Whether she thought it through or listened to her heart, whether she applied the humourless frugality of logic or the unfounded passion of instinct to her troubles, the result would remain the same:

She did not trust her master as far as she could spit him.

WHEN FINALLY HIS message reached her, upon her return to the precinct, it was a short, prerecorded affair. He stared from a viewspex thick with distortion and white noise, and pointed a gloved finger down the length of the camera optic.

'Stay where you are, interrogator,' he said. 'Allow no other attacks upon the underhive. You understand me? *No more failures.*

'Remain in Cuspseal. I am sending a mutual friend to collect you.'

The image died with a clipped whine, and Mita sat back from the viewspex with a yawn.

She could no longer bring herself to care.

SHE SLEPT POORLY that night.

Orodai and his Preafects had returned from their subterranean predations with grisly armour and savage smiles; satisfied for now that the iron heel of the Preafectus Vindictaire had crushed whatever flames of rebellion still fluttered at the underhive's heart. She tried to quiz the commander personally – had he seen the Night Lord? Had they *killed* the traitor? – but the man's exhausted irritation at her continuing presence had earned her few answers, and only by skimming his mind had she tasted the seed of doubt that lingered there.

They had seen nothing of the shadowed monster. Oh, Orodai told himself that it was irrelevant, that he barely believed it was real anyway, that the aim of the assault had been to prevent any further incursions into *his* territory and to repay the horror of the starport massacre. He even began to believe his own reassurances, but when he ordered Mita out of his office it was with the look of a man who knew he was fooling himself, that his actions had achieved nothing unless perhaps to exacerbate the situation, and that the excesses of the day's violence had all been for nought.

She left him only when he vowed there would be no more attacks, and commandeered a small Preafect dormitory for her and Cog's exclusive use. She snapped at the giant's moronic prattling with more venom than it warranted, and fell into a shallow interrupted slumber to the sound of his suppressed sniffles.

She dreamed of embers – or eyes – burning in the darkness around the edges of her vision. She saw a great shark with blades for fins, cruise through inky water before turning away, rejecting her taste. And then the water was the void, and the spectral currents were eddies in the warp, and a shoal, a school, a pod – a *swarm* – punctured the nothingness; not of fish nor squid but eagles, silver and blue and black, swooping and gambling in the updrafts of nothingness.

A voice said: *'Seek me, my brothers…'*

And out in the dark, where no light could fall, something heard the call. Something paid attention, and listened with a keen ear, then turned and cried into the deeper depths, where some other remote listener waited.

Again and again the cry was repeated, circulated, echoed from ear to mouth to ear, across time and void and warp, until it reached the eagles themselves. One by one they dipped their wings, flexed their steely claws, and raced towards the light.

Towards an island of pearly white. A planet. An icy world, with its face turned from the sun.

Equixus.

She awoke in the small hours of the early morning with the same old uncertainty: how much of a part had the gift played in her nocturnal fantasies? How much was dream, and how much prediction?

She did not sleep again after that.

THE FOLLOWING DAY found her huddled over the steering pillar of an impeller bike, a great plume of ash towering behind her like the tail of a dusty rooster. She had cast off indolence, washed clean her indecision, and decided to *act*.

As she saw it, the distinction between observation and interference ran deep. She had been expressly forbidden from indulging in the latter. Kaustus's message had said nothing of the former.

In every city, and especially in every hive, Mita knew that there was a certain *niche*. Sometimes it was naturally filled. Often it was a position to be squabbled over, traded between those who felt inclined to occupy it. Inevitably there would come to each of these conflicts a natural resolution; a winner. Such characters were cunning. They were ruthless. They were scrupulous. They were *clever*.

She had made her enquiries discreetly, at the start. She had considered Cuspseal from the perspective of a social jigsaw, and had taken pains to direct her interest towards those pieces of a higher calibre – the guildhouse quartermasters, the merchant tsars of the docking quarters, the madams of Whoretown and the recruitment sergeants of the small Fleet Ultima offices adjacent to the precinct. She had thought such characters far more likely to be familiar with the goal of her enquiries than lesser souls.

She needn't have bothered to focus her attention so closely. In the minds of *everyone* she encountered, be they peon or bourgeoisie or authority, the existence of an information broker, a spymaster, a watcher, was as firm as cold rock. That none of them dared speak his name, or to be overseen in the act of betraying his identity, merely confirmed to Mita his monopoly.

His name was irrelevant. His whereabouts were not. She plucked it – ultimately – from the mind of a bounty hunter, drunk and leering, in a saloon on the outskirts of Cuspseal. He seemed to Mita to be a prime source of answers: such mercenary scum as he could be guaranteed to have had dealings with the broker, or at least his associates, at one time or another. She'd plunged her astral tentacles into his unresisting consciousness without thought for his safety, relishing the shouts of dismay from his fellow drinkers. Revulsion and disassociation were reactions to her mutation to which she had grown all too familiar; the ability to terrify was something she had had little chance to enjoy. Until now.

To skim a mind for the vaguest impressions of its inner workings was one thing; to hunt for specific detail was another, far more damaging thing entirely.

She shattered his mind and left his brain haemorrhaging – blood pouring from eyes and nose. Her own objectives outweighed everything now.

(*Is this how Kaustus feels,* she wondered? *This impunity? This endless authority?*)

And so she found herself riding hard, impeller wheels grinding against litterflows and ashdunes, as she made her way towards the broker's home – deep in the teeming habzones of the eastern mezzanines.

Cog rode ahead, his primal instincts and hardwired reactions far superior to her own. When he swerved to avoid some hidden crevice, or jinked his impeller to one side just as other traffic passed – a cavalcade of bikes and trams, scuttling beetlemounts and garish servitor vehicles, dead torsos welded to chasses like fleshy steering columns – she followed suit immediately. Allowing him to lead was a pragmatic deference: on the off-chance that anyone was foolish enough to attempt an ambush, it would be he who absorbed the brunt of the attack.

Practicality, even through affection. The stuff of the Inquisition.

They entered the Warren through a looping series of bridgebacks and checkpoints, where queues of impatient civilians gathered to pass. She kept her identity to herself at such times, slotting the cruciform 'I' pendant of her office into the tiny fleshholster on her shoulder, enduring the sleazy searches of militiamen with uncharacteristic patience. It would not do to broadcast her presence ahead, and if the broker was as adept as his reputation suggested he would know they were coming long before they arrived.

The Warren was a honeycomb of stagnant architecture: hexagonal block after hexagonal block, interlocking in drab material harmonies, facets pressed together for support like stifled teeth in a cogged machine. Here the workers lived; the billion no ones. The antscum. Factory fodder, condemned to lifetimes of drudgery, but thankful to their Emperor for the same. Here the uncomplaining masses awoke, worked, and slept: every day, every year, every century. Termites in a concrete mound, as unique as grains of sand upon an endless island beach.

Cog and Mita swept into a culvert at the base of a particular hab, the memory of its pitted surface and its devotional graffiti no less vivid for being stolen from the bounty hunter's brain. Only on closer inspection was the sham inherent to the construction made plain, and then only through a careful appraisal of tiny details. No clothing dangled on flexing poles from tiny slit-windows. No shadows moved behind blinds and drapes, as they did in surrounding habs. No preachers ranted in fiery oration from the stepped buttresses along each corner, replaced on this edifice by tall human figures: servitors with long shanks and countless eyes, which stood in silent voyeurism of all within their gaze.

It was a statement, of course.

You are being watched.

They left their impeller bikes at the central entrance, and Mita could feel without extending her psychic self the cold intellect regarding them. Through numberless electric eyes, through a myriad of cameras – both hidden and overt – its perpetual interest bored into her from somewhere within.

This, then, was the information broker. And to her senses, which relied upon the whimsy of emotion as a retina relies upon light, his astral presence was a thing of jagged edges and ugly ambitions.

She stepped inside scant seconds behind Cog. It saved her life.

HE HAD USED combat servitors, of course. Clever.

Devoid of emotion, lacking even a basic self awareness which might have betrayed them to her senses, they were as invisible to her astral gaze as any other machine. They dropped from recesses above the door and sprung from concealed pits in the rockcrete of the lobby with only the whine of smooth hydraulics to betray their movement. Four of them: sleek models with gangly parts and chequerboards of surgical scars, ramshackle homunculi with a dangerous, graceful aesthetic. Two racked ungainly weapons from plastic holsters, deformed remnants of human flesh held together by circuit wiring. Autoguns – multibarreled and undecorated – loomed in each cybermetallic paw.

The two others started forwards, bird-jointed legs endowing them with a predatory, hopping gait, like reptiles hybridised with zombie corpses. Each sported a shimmering forceblade in the place of a left wrist – flesh and absorption coils interknitted like brambles – and a three-digit powerfist to the right.

Two to shoot the hell out of any trespasser, and two to get in close and finish them off. Cute.

The autoguns opened fire with a roar and Mita ducked on impulse, acknowledging even as she did so that it was a futile gesture: not a single part of the lead firestorm could find its way to her. Bullets impacted on Cog's broad chest like stones striking the flanks of a tank – punching ragged holes in his robe and plucking messy eruptions of blood and flesh into the air – but appearing only to enrage him further. He stretched wide his tri-jointed arms and roared like a beast, great fists clenching in rage, bullets whining as they ricocheted from steel knuckles. A gobbet of his flesh painted itself across Mita's brow, snapping her awake from the urge to freeze up that had seized her. She dropped to her knees and grabbed for the holster at her waist.

She was an interrogator of the Ordo Xenos, warp-dammit. She wouldn't be bested by a hivetown infomerchant and his metal cronies. She'd come *prepared* for this.

Her boltpistol was loaded and armed before conscious thought even impelled her to seek targets, and she squirreled her way forwards to peer between Cog's legs with the weapon supported in both hands. Through the oscillations of his robe – now tattered and dripping gore – she caught a brief glimpse of the nearest gundrone, wide eyes rolling in metal sockets with whatever vestiges of machismo its human biology retained. She took her time drawing a bead, recalling her training, shutting out every other element of the world, dissolving peripheral threats on a wave of focus, then fired.

The servitor jerked backwards once, then spun at an impact upon its shoulder, then arched backwards with a sudden *snap* as a third shell caught it in the centre of its forehead. The warheads detonated one by one – dancing their victim like a ghastly marionette – until its head burst apart on a cloud of shrapnel and brain flesh.

Towering over her, Cog's living shield was quickly losing its efficacy. His roar grew weaker with every instant, replaced all too often by anguished moans, and the fabric of his robe drizzled moist gore around his feet like a saturated sponge. Doing her best to stay behind him – and to shut out her shame at accepting his unspoken sacrifice – Mita became aware of a blurring shape to her left. The first of the combat servitors closed with an electric rattle, its face a featureless mass of stretched skin, pulled taut around a single fish-eye lens. Its attack was as brutal as it was efficient – a horizontal hack with the crackling blade instants before a vertical swipe with the powerfist – a combination impossible to dodge. She backed away with a wordless howl, aware already that she was as good as dead.

Cog saved her yet again, clawing with an exhausted grunt at the servitor's head and throwing it, knife chopping uselessly at his tree-like arm, across the room, bowling over the remaining gundrone in the process. Mita followed his lead without hesitation, pumping a glut of bolter shells into the knotted machines as they struggled to disentangle, watching with enormous satisfaction as they blew apart with smoke and sparks dancing around them.

The intervention was one effort too great for Cog's wrecked body: mangled to the point of dissolution, eyes thick with a film of blood and tears; his massive legs gave way and he slumped to the ground with a hiss, hands reaching out.

'Didn't... didn't saved Mita,' he burbled, child-like. 'Suh-sorry...'

'Oh, Cog...' she whispered.

And then it was just her, and in a slow motion dream that had no business invading her reality, the second combat servitor hopped gaily from the plumes of smoke and ripped her boltpistol away, crumpling it in its powerfist.

It placed its blade to her neck and chirruped.

'Shit,' she announced.

'I wouldn't go that far, dear,' said a voice, startling her. 'I thought you did rather well, considering. *Het-het-het.*'

The curious tone seemed to come from the servitor itself – or at least from the enamel speaker-mouth hooked above its ragged ear – but its unctuous tones stood incongruous against the machine's vapid mind. Someone speaking from afar, then, using this murderous machine as a mouth.

'You must be the information broker,' she said, feeling ridiculous.

'*Het-het-het*,' the voice sounded positively delirious, its weird laughter grating at her ears. 'Very good, yes, very good! And you must be the inquisitor's witch, yes? Yes? Heard so very much about you, *het-het-het*. Blinded one of my agents earlier, even, poor little lamb.'

'The muggers? That was you?'

'*Het-het-het*. It pays to find out as much as possible about strangers in my city.'

'"Find out"? They tried to murder me!'

'Yes. *Het-het-het*. So I found out you can't be killed by cretins. You see? Thus my metal friends, here.'

The servitor thumped itself on the chest with a hollow clang. Like a puppet, dancing to its master's strings. At its feet, Cog shifted his weight and groaned, watching events through rheumy eyes. Not dead, then. Yet.

'Who are you?' Mita said, the forceblade's charge prickling at the skin of her throat.

'That, my dear, is something you aren't in any position to discover.' The servitor cast an eye – independent of its twin – down to the bleeding giant on the floor. 'Not now that your pet ogryn can't quite find his feet – *het-het-het*.'

Cog stiffened.

A warning bell rang in Mita's mind.

'What... What did you call him?' she said, bracing herself.

'Didn't you hear me? An *ogr*–'

Something blurred before her eyes.

The sounds of metal and flesh being ripped apart went on for a long time, even after Cog stamped on the servitor's voicebox and silenced its curses.

'He doesn't like being called that,' Mita muttered, needlessly.

She went to find the broker.

ZSO SAHAAL

THEY CAME SEEKING sanctuary. The underhive recoiled from its wounds, slinking in the dark like a crippled fox, and where before its people had held the Shadowkin in contempt – fearing their vigilante strikes, deriding their zealotry – now their perceptions were changed. Now they saw strength, fortification, protection.

There was not a single family untouched by the Preafect's pogrom, and without a spoken word, without vocal alliance or official consent, they gathered themselves in meagre packs, as best they could, and they trod the winding path into the depths, to where the snaking road descended no further, and there, on the shores of the rustmud swamps, they stopped.

In the heart of Sahaal's domain.

They came seeking sanctuary, and amongst the hordes of their number they brought with them their former masters, their warriors and outlaws and leaders. Their heroes and their villains.

At the start of the second day following the vindictor attack, when the stream had become a trickle, and then finally cleared, Sahaal stared out from his throne across the sea of seething refugees, tasted their stink upon the air, felt their fear and dispossession and dejection, and smiled his secret smile.

He would use them.

'WHAT DECEPTION IS this?'

'Curse you, Shadowbitch! I'll not stand for–'

'Back off! One more! One more push–!'

Snarls of aggression jittered throughout the Shadowkin encampment; a ring of torches and weapon-gloss glints tightening around twelve strange – and furious – figures. They had come in good faith. Dejected at their flight for sanctuary, ashamed, even, of the exodus from their own territories, they were proud nobles nonetheless. And now, as they stepped from cobbled barges onto the russet-brown island of their former enemies, to find themselves encircled by Shadowkin gunsmen, they reacted with all the outrage of displeased royalty.

'Slit your vile little throats, by the frogspirits–'

'Suggest you lower your *weapons*, Shadowscum–'

And so on.

Condemnitor Chianni directed their corralling with the confidence of one born to lead, and as he watched the unfolding spectacle from the secret places of the island-drill's mouldering carcass, Sahaal reflected gratefully upon her transformation. She had come to him as a stammering under-condemnitor; a witness to her leader's casual slaying by a monstrosity from her nightmares. And now?

Now she was a representative of divinity, no less.

He had ordered her to gather their current guests in the Emperor's name and she had obliged him without complaint. In the unfamiliar waters of politics and diplomacy, she was his most valuable tool.

'Priestess! You get these guns out of my sight or–'

'Angry! Killing soon! Hiveshit Shadowkin blooding!'

The Shadowkin warriors ignored the threats with patience borne of confidence, driving their charges on up the flanks of the rusted heap; towards the dark culvert at its heart where the vast throne of bone and rag – accruing new grisly pennants and morbid trophies with every day – stood empty. Its owner watched the visitors from other, secret vantages, and relished the fear their indignation concealed.

Since their arrival in the Shadowkin territories the swarm of refugees had maintained a fearful distance from the shade-slicked island with its black-ragged denizens and rumours of living horrors. Like mice clamouring at the entrance to a tiger's lair – grateful for its presence but too terrified to approach – they left their protectors well alone, and went about the re-establishment of their feudal structures in new, miniaturised empires; shanty towns and canvas camps pushed against the shores of the swamp. Shadowkin spies watched it all, and through them Sahaal had observed and calculated, and followed their petty dominions with interest.

It was, he supposed, a natural process. In the world above this dismal wasteland, before the Preafects came and changed everything, every aspect of underhive life was governed by the ganghouses. Underworld atristoc-racies, each as assiduous of its heritage and racial purity as the Steepletown nobles themselves. Their number were impossible to determine and their internecine squabbles, schisms and betrayals impossible to chronicle; but what was certain was this: of them all, seven houses had risen to dominate the rest: seven great clan-tribes of warriors and outlaws. And all – bar one – had swallowed pride and territory in the face of the vindictor raids and fled into the silent deeps of the Shadowkin lair. And thus they now stood, trivial empires scattered along the shores of Sahaal's domain.

First were the Quetzai – a brood of nimble warriors whose gaudy suits of colour and feather slipped amongst the refugees of the northern shore: tall totems moving above the raggedy shelters, each bearing a living kutroach with its limbs and fangs removed.

Second, to the east, the towering brutes of the Atla Clan: warriors ritually scarred from head to toe, poisoned quills worn at the tip of each finger, like the paws of great bears. Their guttural commands – demands for food and drink from the dispossessed peoples over whom they had claimed stewardship – resounded across the waters with irritating frequency.

Beyond them, isolated from the refugee swarm where other houses mingled (and terrorised) at will, the quiet albinos of the Pallor Steppes fashioned sturdy teepees and burnt strange herbs, soporific fumes mixing with those of the swamp. Their hunched forms – so frail, in appearance – belied a fierce martial tradition, and Sahaal found himself reminded of the white-skinned people of Nostromo Quintus, his master's ancient home.

To the south the exiled underhivers found themselves beneath the custodianship of the House Magrittha: genderless warriors with long limbs and high-boned faces, tall rifles clutched in elegant hands, uncertain physiques tattooed and naked, displaying their sacred androgyny for all to see.

In the shallows of the southern shores, where the weakest of the refugees had been pushed by the ungentle Brownian motions of the encampment, the shamanic savages of the Frog Princes had established their oleaginous quarters. Convinced that the bloated amphibians of their former territory were reincarnations of Imperial saints – through whom the Emperor could be contacted – their priests dressed in moist skins, eyes bulging with lugubrious scrutiny, demanding tithes from the hivers beneath their rule not of credits nor food, but unpleasant organic curios: hair from the head of a child, an old man's spittle; ingredients for their rituals of worship.

And finally, to the west, the haughty guards of the Sztak Chai Warlord moved amongst the throng, demanding respect and taxation in equal amounts. Their plain robes disguised bodies honed to teak hardness by decades of martial 'meditation', and their dawn exercises had captured Sahaal's attention – and his appreciation – from across the waters.

The seventh noble house, un-represented in all of the rustmud caverns, was the Glacier Rat scum: piratical vermin wiped from the face of the hive in the blink of an eye.

Before the exodus these families, these wolf-pack brotherhoods, had ruled the underhive with a clench of iron and blood: and woe betide the settlement that neglected its taxes, or disrespected its territorial overlords.

And now this.

They found themselves reduced to fragmentary slices of shoreline; divisions of power that encircled the drill island like a moat of shifting lava – creeping and insidious, but ultimately slow and unthreatening. They had lost the respect of the underhive. They had existed for centuries as protection merchants: extorting 'their' peasants for the right to stewardship; and when at last their protection was required, when the armoured fist of the Preafects smashed against the underhive's unprotected belly – they had failed. They had fallen from grace. They had come to Sahaal's tribe with begging bowls outstretched and now – the insolence, the gall! – they were resuming their old ways: formulating petty hierarchies amongst the dispossessed camps, demanding fealty and wealth from those with neither to offer.

Sahaal could not stand for that. There was one authority in this rusting hinterland, and one authority alone. He would *not* be challenged, whether they knew of his existence or not.

And so to each noble family, through scouts that he sent to each camp, he offered an invitation – a communion with the condemnitor of the Shadowkin – and true to form, blustering, face-keeping, puffed with misplaced pride, each was accepted. The head of every house, and his or her finest warrior, summoned to meet with those whose sanctuary they had claimed. That was the deal. That was the *bait.*

They arrived like visiting princes, of course, and now... now they snarled like caged beasts at every ungentle prod of a lasgun muzzle in their ribs, every hand-heel push towards the centre of the island.

How the mighty are fallen...

The Night Haunter's words, ringing in Sahaal's mind.

'–demand to know the *meaning* of this, warp's piss!'

'–be repercussions! The Sztak Chai does not tolerate–'

'–kill! Cut slice-and-dice – *kill* all!'

And then there was a new voice, neither raised nor strained, which cut through the objections like a razor and left jaws gaping.

'Be silent,' it said, from above their heads. 'Be silent and bow to your new lord.'

He dropped from the stain of darkness that covered the cavern's ceiling without a noise; a long-shanked vision of black and blue, devil-red eyes glaring from a pall of shadow, striking the brown earth and straightening, black cloak of feather and rag settling across him like a funeral shroud. To their minds, alive with such terror that they had never before known, he was not real. He could *not* be real. This gangle-limbed beast – this filth-slicked spider – that had broached the walls of nightmare and found form in corporeal flesh. Towering over them, a half-seen ghoul, veiled by darkness and design, his respirator steamed unctuous coils of vapour like a daemon's breath, and as he tilted his head through light-dappled chinks of shadow he flexed his claws from their sheaths, slicing the awe-frozen moment in half.

The visitors came to their senses all at once. Some screamed.

Some tried to run. Some fell to their knees.

They had heard the rumours, perhaps. They had heard that the madmen of the Shadowkin – those zealous fools who had shut themselves away from the rest of the underhive, eschewing contact and wealth, concerned only with their morbid deathcult, dedicated to the Emperor's purity – had a new master. They had shrugged and spat, untroubled by the machinations of that which did not concern them.

They had heard tales, even, of something *new* in the underhive, some dark presence that prowled in the night and killed without compunction. They had heard of mutilations and bloody atrocities; of bodies disjointed and violated, of eyes put out and fingers stolen.

They had heard rumours of terrors and abominations, and dismissed them as idle tales to scare the children.

They were regretting their flippancy now.

'The leaders will approach,' Sahaal said, voice a mere hiss.

None seemed prepared to obey; each 'noble' hiding behind his or her accompanying warrior, faces drawn, mouths agape, refusing still to believe what their eyes were telling them.

Sahaal hissed and gestured at Chianni; a half-flick of his claws that he knew she would translate accordingly. On cue the condemintor waved forwards the Shadowkin warriors, overseeing their rough advance: pulling apart nobles and protectors like clinging lovers, threatening and clubbing when resistance was offered, pushing forwards the gang leaders to stumble, alone and unprotected, in a gaggle at Sahaal's feet.

Six little pigs, quivering in their fat.

'You came to this place,' Sahaal said, gaze sweeping across them, arm gesturing out across the smog of the swamps, 'in terror. You fled before your enemies like *vermin*, and you ran here. Into my arms. To *me*.'

He took a step forwards, light smearing itself a fraction further across his armour.

'You came to me for sanctuary – uninvited, unwanted – but have I turned you away? No. I have tolerated your presence. I have let you slip among the shores of my domain like snakes in tall grass... and how have you repaid my kindness?'

Another step, claws flashing across flickering torchlight, eyes burning. The nobles cringed in their places.

'Have you visited me, to bow? Have you offered fealty, to the Emperor's own warrior? Have you *yielded* to me? *No*. No, you have said nothing. You have waited until you were *called*.'

Another step, and this time the group's cohesion splintered: the frail head of the Pallor House fell onto his knees with a moan, the feathered priestess of the Quetzai fumbled for a weapon at her belt – long since taken by her captors – and the Frog Priest turned his bloated body and tried to flee, eyes spinning, only to be thrust forwards again by the Shadowkin circle.

Sahaal did not pause at the interruption.

'The hive has fallen from the Emperor's light and turned against the Underworld, and like children running for their mother you have expected from the Shadowkin protection, sanctuary, comfort... And at what price? *None*! You have offered me *nothing*!'

His voice echoed across the silent wastes, strong and shrill and terrible.

'I shall tolerate the disrespect no longer. If you are to stay, if you are to plague my territory like wolves, then it shall be at *my* pleasure.'

He leaned down, helmed countenance shedding shadows like oil, eyes burning with ruby fires. 'You are the guests of Holy Warriors,' he hissed, breath steaming, 'and if you are to remain so it is fair that you should share their burden.'

He straightened abruptly, cloaks rippling, and extended his hands towards the group, each fan of razor-light claws snickering away to its secret sheath, leaving only gloved fists.

'Which of you will accept my rule?' he asked. 'Which of you will taste divinity, and join my crusade? Which of you will surrender his house to the Emperor's mercy?'

One by one the nobles swallowed their terror, licked dry lips and forced down the shivering in their limbs, and stepped forwards to kiss the hands of the beast.

'Good,' he said, when they had finished. He glanced up towards the waiting Shadowkin, and the six champions of the ganghouses restrained amongst them, watching events with earnest eyes. They had witnessed their own masters signing away their autonomy, and their expression told Sahaal everything he needed to know:

They would have done exactly the same.

As he returned his gaze to his newest slaves he stole a glance towards Chianni, noting without surprise her expression of unconcealed disdain. She had spent all her life despising the underhive's other gangs, punishing their iniquity when the Emperor's will allowed, protecting her tribe from their predations when it did not. It was a mark of her utter obedience to Sahaal that, as he claimed their strength as his own, she did not raise her voice in protest.

He had a pleasing surprise for her, yet.

'Do you know,' he said, glowering at the nobles, 'of lions?'

They stared, bewildered.

'Great predators of ancient Terra,' he explained, 'pack beasts – loyal to their clan, and obedient. Always obedient to their strongest member.' He paused, enjoying the drama of the moment despite himself. 'And when a new leader arose, a blooded-claw ready to assume command, his first action was always the same.

'He could not tolerate disloyalty. He could not risk challenge to his authority. He could not spare any remnant of the old regime, the old *order*.

'Do you know what he did, little nobles?'

Their eyes were wide. Their lips trembled. Perhaps some knew what was coming.

'He killed all the cubs.'

Sahaal beheaded the six nobles with two strokes of his claws.

The champions of the gang houses, who had witnessed the transferral of power and could no more deny it to their brothers and sisters than they could rail against it, were returned to their petty empires with a single message, to spread amongst the dispossessed masses of the underhive.

You belong to the Shadowkin now. Prepare for war.

'C-CONDEMNITOR?'

'Why do you disturb our lord's sacred slumber?'

Voices flourished on the cusp of Sahaal's hearing; pricking at his sleeping mind like an itch, drawing him up from the depths of his dreams to an intangible, half-awake plateau.

'S-something's happened, condemnitor!' a man quailed, directing his stammerings, Sahaal assumed, to Chianni – seated as ever beside him. 'We... we thought that... that h-*he*... w-would wish to know...'

They can't even speak my name...

'Explain,' Chianni grunted, sounding unimpressed.

'It's the prisoner. From the starport...'

'The warp-seer?'

'Y-yes.'

Sahaal was fully awake in a second. He rose to his feet and jabbed a finger towards the cowering man, prostrated before the throne.

'What is it? What's happened to the prisoner?'

'S-sweet Emperor!'

'Tell me!'

'We... we think he's dying, lord!'

BOUND IN CHAINS at his wrists and legs, the second astropath – a prisoner in a squalid Shadowkin hut since his capture – drooled a thick paste of spittle and bile from his mouth, tongue snagging against his teeth, running red with his own blood. At irregular intervals his body stiffened as if electrified, each narrow-corded muscle standing out from his emaciated frame, withered face crumpled in wordless agony.

He had soiled himself, and coupled with the strands of drying blood and vomit that pooled around him, streaking his pigeon chest, his cell stank like a madhouse; an impression his shrieks did little to dispel.

Like his dead comrade before him he wore across his brow a twisted strip of lead, and it was to this that Sahaal's attention immediately flew. It glowed red hot, faint clouds of steam boiling above it, scorching the man's flesh like a cattle brand.

'My lord!' Chianni cried out from his side, horrified by what, to her, must seem some cruel form of witchcraft.

If only she knew...

'Get out,' Sahaal ordered, waving her and the cowering messenger away, ignoring the flash-flicker of disappointment that crossed her features. 'Now.'

He closed the door – such as it was – behind them, listening carefully at its corrugated frame, enhanced senses outstretched, to ensure neither were eavesdropping.

And then he turned back to the writhing astropath, rolling and moaning, shattering his own teeth at the strength of his gnashing, and bent down close to watch.

And yes, there it was... at the edge of his perception; a grating presence... whispering... promising, teasing, cursing...

The warp swarms, gathering around, scratching with immaterial claws, fighting to break through the lead shield.

'Someone,' Sahaal said, wiping a tender finger across the man's sweaty brow, 'is trying to say hello.'

Working with an abruptness that drew a strangled gasp from the psyker, he hooked a talon beneath the metal coronet and snipped it away, exposing the man's singed forehead. Opening the way.

He did not need psychic senses to know what happened next. It was like an indescribable sound – some ultrasonic pitch that went unheard, but *felt* nonetheless – dwindling away to nothing. It was like a pressure being released, like a faucet opening in the sky to pour away all the psychic waste, all the vile shit that clamoured beyond perception. And the waste pipe, the reservoir into which it all flushed clear, was the psyker's head.

He jerked upright, like a meat puppet, body moving in strange unbalanced steps that were not its own. Blood poured from his mouth. The warp beasts tore at his soul, a frenzied feast beyond the veil of reality.

Sahaal backed away, heart racing. Had it worked? Had someone heard his call? Had the predators of the empyrean stretched out their shapeless tongues at the arisal of a beacon? A message, trying to get through?

The psyker's head twisted around, muscles manipulated by a mind that was not his own, until he faced Sahaal, empty eye sockets glaring into him.

And then he spoke – falteringly at first, like a marionette guided by an inexpert hand – but with growing confidence, and clear intention.

'W-we... we... we are c-coming... fuh... for you...'

Sahaal dropped to his knees, overcome.

'B-brothers?'

'We are coming for you, Talonmaster. Prepare the way. *Ave dominus nox.*'

'*A-ave!*'

The psyker's head exploded like a bursting bubble, scattering fragments of skull and shredded brain across his cell, and in some distant dimension his soul sobbed as the swarms fought for their feast.

Sahaal removed his helm and, unashamed, wept with joy.

THE NEXT DAY Shadowkin scouts moved amongst the refugee camps with a message, gathering crowds at every junction, filling the air with shouts and protests.

In every part of the shanty town the message was the same.

Go now into the hive, they read, parchment sheets held in trembling hands. *Rise now in the corrupted world above us, and gather for your new masters your tithe.*

The Emperor's Angel is among us, friends, and he taxes not our wealth, nor our food, nor our blood. He demands payment in justice.

Every able man, every able woman. Each shall present to the Emperor's Angel the head of a sinner, or else themselves be branded so – and culled accordingly.

Those below the age of fifteen years are exempted. They shall be overseen by the Shadowkin in their parents' absence.

You have two days.

There was outrage, at first. Outrage and horror and disbelief. But the story of the nobles' executions had circulated, the uncertain presence of some terrible Holy Thing lurking upon the island had gathered weight with each retelling, and beyond the outrage and the horror, above all else, there was *terror.*

The Shadowkin were strong where all other tribes had been crippled. The reprisals for failure were no idle threat. The refugees could not flee. They could not hide. They could not desert their children.

It did not take long for small groups – faces set, teeth clenched, fists curled around blunt-edged machetes and crude blades – to set off on the long, tortuous trek into the hive itself.

Equixus faced a bloody night.

MITA ASHYN

WHEN SHE WAS finished with the *cognis mercator* – the information broker she'd risked so much to find – Mita returned to Cuspseal feeling uncomfortably pleased with herself. She hadn't broken the rules her master had imposed, hadn't prosecuted her own attack against the nightmare lurking in the underhive, hadn't sanctioned such an attack from any other source, and certainly hadn't interfered with the inquisitor's own plans. Whatever they were.

All she had secured was an element of... insurance. Kaustus need never know.

At the secondary tiercluster, alongside the Arbites precinct, she paused to lead Cog into a hospice of the Order Panacear. The giant had fared well despite his wounds, stalwart physiology seemingly impervious to the pain his injuries looked likely to cause.

Or perhaps, Mita reflected cruelly, he was simply too stupid to know when he should have been dead.

Either way, she found herself quietly affected by his plight. His defence of her safety had been selfless, his loyalty utterly beyond reproach, and in some emotive corner of her mind she found herself sharing his pain, empathic senses indulging her shame with masochistic relish.

It could not be ignored, of course, that Cog's loyalty to *her* was a far purer, more successful thing than her loyalty to her master. Had Cog ever questioned her orders? Had he ever doubted her, or mistrusted her, or sought to disobey? Of course not.

And look where it got him...

He was a mess. Great ragged holes bled freely all across him; the vast musculature beneath revealed in all its grisly glory. One of his cheeks was ripped – a vacant chasm that exposed gums and molars to the very back of his mouth, leaving a tortured flap of flesh trailing from his jawline. His eyes were bloodshot and swollen, his knuckles grazed of almost all their skin, and his long arms punctured with more holes than a cratered asteroid. Even the sisters of the Order, fluttering from bed to bed in cassocks and starched wimples, with a quiet prayer and a dispensoria of arcane drugs for every occasion, did not seem overly optimistic at his chances of recovery.

After, that is, Mita had bullied them into accepting 'the abomination' as a patient. The authority of the Inquisition remained unsullied in some quarters at least.

She left her loyal giant in their care for a scant hour, returning to the precinct to change her clothes and steal a short moment's soothing meditation, before returning to oversee his care. She walked between the Preafect fortress and the hospice with an irrepressible spring in her stride, satisfied that whatever the movements of the *thing* prowling the shadows below her feet, whatever clandestine actions it undertook, she would be fully aware of it.

And then she stepped into Cog's cramped healing cell and recalled, with a jolt, Kaustus's words.

'I am sending a mutual friend to collect you.'

There was someone waiting for her.

HE WAS THE sort of man, Mita had decided during the tedious minutes that followed, whose petty affection for authority had come to dominate every part of his persona, to the extent that any story, any piece of unshared information, was delivered with trembling relish. *I know something you don't,* his gimlet eyes said, *and I'll take my damned time in telling you.*

'It was on the seventh tier that we found them,' he expounded, waving an arm for emphasis. A small fleck of froth had gathered in the corner of his mouth as he talked – an unpleasant detail that Mita found herself unable to ignore. 'Wretched creatures. Totally disorganised, of course – their kind always are. So pitifully earnest.'

He locked his lips around the tip of the hookah he wore in a strap against his chest, dislodging the bead of spittle, and drew bubbles through the bulb at its base.

...buglbuglbuglbugl...

'Mmm.'

He breathed out cherry-scented smoke, lips curled in a feline smile; a set of onyx-black false teeth twinkling like a starry void within. Mita repressed the temptation to apply a fist to their gloomy surface.

'We killed them all, of course,' he droned, 'bar the leader. We thought you might appreciate an interrogation. *Heh.* When you're ready.'

He was a priest – or at least that's what he called himself. His obvious self-adoration was hardly in keeping with the selflessness that came with devotion, and were it not for the winged aquila burned above his right eye he would look no different to any other member of Kaustus's retinue. She wondered why the inquisitor had chosen him as his errand boy.

'Tauists,' he blurted, red smog spilling from his nostrils like some ghastly dragon. 'Got hold of a tau propaganda vidslug – we're looking into how. Heretical hogwash. "*Greater good*" this, "*mutual benefit*" that. And the idiots believe it – can you image? No place in the Emperor's light for fools like that.'

Mita kneaded her temples, exhausted and headachey. That Kaustus had dispatched this man to fetch her – to rein her in – was obvious, and that he had thus far occupied his time with meandering anecdotes and tales of inconsequence was not helping her mood. She might as well have been talking to the inquisitor himself.

Her patience for her master's obliqueness was rapidly reaching its end.

...buglbuglbuglbugl...

And to make matters worse, it was becoming increasingly difficult to imagine a more irritating sound than the hookah's incessant watery mussitation.

'Why,' she asked, diplomatic to the end, 'are you telling me all this?'

He scowled at her over the ridge of Cog's chest – rising and falling with the shallow sleep into which he had slipped – as if affronted by her ignorance. His mind told a different story; an unsubtle blend of smug superiority and false piety. He was enjoying himself, talking down to his supposed superior like a parent patronises a child.

'Because,' he sniffed, 'last time I checked you were an interrogator of the Ordo Xenos, and – *hah* – an affiliate of the team that conducted the raid. I thought you'd appreciate the successes of your comrades.'

'Oh, spare me,' she snapped, patience expiring. 'We're on the Eastern Fringes, you fool. The chances are there are Tauist cells on every warpdamned tier. You didn't come all the way from Steepletown to boast about shooting up a bunch of bored idealists.' She crossed her arms and slumped, inwardly annoyed at the ease with which her temper had broken.

The priest's thought patterns changed with frightening speed. Cold, boundless distaste flooded her senses. Briefly, she wished Cog was still awake.

'That sounds an awful lot like rebel sympathy,' he hissed, every word a barb. 'You should have a care, interrogator...'

'I seem to be managing fine so far.'

'That is a matter of some... debate, amongst our lord's disciples.'

I'll bet it is, she snarled internally. *Last time I saw the obtuse bastards I killed one of them.*

She kept the sentiment to herself, this time.

An uncomfortable silence settled, broken only by the incessant thought-destroying *buglbuglbugl,* and as she drummed her fingers against the edge of Cog's sleeping pallet a sliver of enquiry arose in her mind. She knew she should repress it, should control her insolence in the presence of this ghastly little man – who would, of course, relay this encounter word-for-word to the inquisitor – but her curiosity was engorged and, as ever in its implacable face, her objections were bulldozed as if insubstantial.

'Tell me, father,' she said, raising an ironic eyebrow. 'During this... *heroic*... attack...'

He met her gaze undaunted, her sarcasm wasted. 'What of it?'

'What part did the inquisitor play?'

The priest narrowed his eyes. 'Why do you ask?'

'Indulge me.'

The man worked his jaw, fingers tapping at the pipe's stem. 'He led from afar.'

'He wasn't there?'

'His duties with the governor absented him. He planned the raid beforehand and judged that it didn't require his personal attention. What is your point?'

'And his absence didn't trouble you?'

He glared, mind fizzing with disgust. 'Why should it?'

But deep down, beneath layers of obedience and dogma, through thick walls of blinkered devotion and preconception, Mita could taste it: like a ghost of a flavour, playing across the man's mind.

Uncertainty.

She had touched a nerve.

Kaustus brought us to this world to uncover xenophile cells, to purge the heretics who had placed the word of the alien above the light of the Emperor. That's why we're here, *warpdammit.*

And finally he has the opportunity to perform his sacred duty, to maintain the mantle of heroism he's been so keen to foster – and he sends his thugs in his stead?

It makes no sense.

What are you doing up there, Kaustus? Sneaking about with Zagrif, as thick as thieves, prowling through treasure-galleries and ancient archives?

What are you up to, you bastard?

'No reason,' she said. 'No reason at all.'

The priest grunted, unconvinced, and Mita smirked; that tiny particle of uncertainty in his mind feeding her distrust; her conviction that all was not well.

'You don't like me very much, do you?' she smiled, confidence renewed, deliberately provocative.

The priest raised his eyebrows. 'I'm hardly alone in that respect.'

'Is that a fact?'

'Oh yes.' Another smile, ghostlit by crimson smog – black teeth making her squirm. 'The inquisitor... struggled, when seeking a messenger willing to find you.'

'But *you* overcame your personal dislike in the name of the Emperor? Poor, burning little martyr.'

'Such hostility, interrogator. It does not become you.'

Her jaw tightened, fists clenching.

'Let me show you what *becomes* me,' she snarled, half standing.

The man seemed infuriatingly unperturbed by the threat, drawing puffy clouds of rosy smoke from his pipe, its *buglbuglbuglbugl* grinding further against her nerves. When finally he spoke he glared from beneath heavy-lidded eyes, making no attempt to disguise his contempt.

'The inquisitor is displeased.' he said, sausage-fingers caressing the pipe's mouthpiece. 'Furious, you might say.'

Mita's mouth was opening before she could stop herself. 'Now there's a surprise.'

The man made a show of shaking his head, eyes rolling in their lidded orbits. Red vapours coiled around the edge of his cassock.

'He had hoped your... resentment... your sarcasm... might be tempered by your time away from the retinue.' The spittle gathered again beside his mouth, like froth on a toxic shore. 'It seems not.'

She threw a pointed glare at the door. 'Is that it?' she demanded, impatient. 'Is that the message? Don't let me keep you.'

'Oh, there's more. Much more.'

...buglbuglbuglbugl...

'Could you stop that?'

'Stop…?'

'The smoking. It's annoying.'

He leered.

'The inquisitor has requested that I put to you a question. A very simple question.'

'Yes?'

'He requests your counsel. He asks… "What would you do?"'

Mita frowned. The ground had been swept from beneath her.

'What?'

'You heard me. The situation, as it stands. Rumours of xenophilia in the hive, a bogeyman stalking the underworld. In our lord's place, interrogator, *what would you do?*'

'Is this a test?'

'You know very well that it is.'

Her mind raced.

Passivity or aggression. Submission or challenge.

Every time she had tried to toe the inquisitor's line, every time she had kept her head down, played by his rules, obeyed him without question, she had found herself marginalised, disrespected, held in contempt for some imagined weakness. And every time the fires of rebellion had coiled in her stomach, every time she'd dared to challenge Kaustus's lead directly, to stand up to his bullish ways, she'd engendered a curious sort of respect from him. Was that the way?

Do I swallow my pride and lie – 'I would have done exactly as he has done'? Or do I remain true to my heart? True to my instincts?

There was no contest.

'I would divert all my attention towards the threat in the underhive,' she said, flatly. 'I would prioritise the possibility of a Chaotic incursion far above the existence of xenophile cells. I would commission every force at my disposal – the Preafects, the retinue, the warpdamned militia, if need be – to find and utterly crush the monster in the shadows.' She nodded, as if reassuring herself. 'That is what I would do, priest, in the inquisitor's place.'

The man pursed his lips, the hookah forgotten.

'I see,' he said, presently. 'That is... a shame.'

'A shame? I don't unders–'

Abrupt anger blossomed across the priest's mind, shocking her questing senses, his face clouding like a thunderstruck sky.

'How many times?' he barked, black teeth flashing like oil. 'Understanding is not a requirement! The inquisitor demands obedience – that is all! No questions. No warp's-piss assumptions. And *no initiative*.'

'But you asked what I would do! How can I answer without initiative?'

'*Ha*.' He settled into his chair, a cruel grin curling his face. 'Indeed, yes. Perhaps you are not entirely stupid.'

'I... What? How dare y–'

'I asked you a question, interrogator. There is only one correct answer.'

'What answer, damn you?'

The priest steepled his fingers. 'That you are *not* in the inquisitor's place, and not privy to the information at his disposal, and therefore unable to judge. The only correct answer, interrogator, is that it is an unanswerable question.'

'That's ridiculous! Riddles and warpshit tricks!'

'What is ridiculous,' he hissed, coldness filling his gaze, 'is for a chit of a witch to think she knows everything. There are forces beyond your sight, girl! There are details which only the inquisitor may know. The retinue understands that. Do we assume that we may overrule his judgement without knowing all the facts? Are we so colossally arrogant? No! No, that is a position occupied by you alone.'

She blustered, trying to muster an indignant reply – but his words had cut, and he knew it.

He's right. Emperor's blood, he's right!

The priest leaned forwards, acrid breath washing across her, as if to rub astringent into an already gaping wound. 'The inquisitor hopes you would have learned, during your time alone. There is *always* more than meets the eye.'

As if to demonstrate he lifted the hookah pipe in one withered hand, thumb caressing the beads of silver filigree at its root.

A blade snapped from its tip like a launching missile; a concealed stiletto spine lurching to a halt and juddering, lancing the air.

'What are you d–' Mita stammered, reactions made sluggish by the priest's accusing words, warning bells chiming slowly – *too slow!* – in her mind. But even as the threat flourished across her senses a glut of self assurance steeled her muscles. He was just an old man, armed only with a blade.

A voice deep in her subconscious snarled in the shadows. *Rip him to shreds!*

And then lethargically – like a viewspex display crippled by faulty lightcells, rendering its sanctified image in glacial slow motion – the priest reached out not for her, but for Cog.

'Oh, God-Emperor, no…'

The blade punched into the meat of the giant's throat with a wet thump.

Bracing himself, black teeth bared, the priest sliced outwards, cutting through jugular and windpipe, opening a fleshy crevice in Cog's neck. To Mita's horror he awoke for an instant, and the burst of innocent bewilderment, the flash of contact with her own eyes – questioning, pleading, trusting – would haunt her for as long as she lived.

Time returned to normal with the hot spray of released blood against her face, a geyser of scalding magma, patterning walls and ceiling. She cried out, senses tumbling, thrashing to escape from the sticky eruption.

'Your loyalty should be to your inquisitor alone,' the priest hissed into the dying warrior's ear, harsh voice thick with triumph, eyes flicking up to glower at Mita through the crimson drizzle. 'Not *this* creature.'

Cog died with a gurgle.

Something snapped behind Mita's eyes.

'No!' she screamed, psychic claws boiling outwards, all self-control gone, slash-stabbing into the ether to shred the priest's thoughts like paper. Red venom covered her vision, rage slipped between her defences like sand pouring through fingers, and she reached out for his brain like a hungry wolf, relishing the terror on his face.

And then corded muscles closed around her shoulders, a gauntleted hand swatted at the back of her head, and the retinue of Inquisitor Ipoqr Kaustus ripped through the connecting wall of the next cell in a riot of dust and fabric, hollering prayers and warcries, shouting for her blood.

She should have known better.

Of *course* the inquisitor would send backup.

Of *course* he wouldn't leave it to a withered priest.

She'd failed his test. She should have known that wouldn't be the end of it.

As power swords flickered in the dust and guidance optics shimmered from hooded binox headsets, Mita realised it was probably the last oversight she would ever make.

A BLUE-METAL blade burned itself across her vision, its wielder shouting wordlessly as his stroke descended. Somewhere nearby the sisters of the Order Panacear were screaming, the hooded figures of the retinue pushing past them, ignoring their protests, boiling from the shattered wall hollering curses and orders: all of them impressions of a chaotic environment that swirled into Mita's overloaded senses.

She ducked beneath the swordstroke and spun inside the acolyte's guard, elbowing him in the guts then driving the heel of her hand into his nose as he stumbled, feeling it crackle and puncture his brain somewhere within. A razor-stab of premonition – a frozen image of scorching contrails streaking towards her, like toothy-mouthed maggots – caught behind her eyes, and without conscious thought she seized the tumbling corpse beneath its shoulders and pulled it upright.

Bolter fire exploded across her senses, true to the premonition: throbbing at the air and dazzling her with its phosphor bright muzzleflash. The corpse shuddered beneath her grip, clotted lumps of fat and bloodpaste tumbling forwards like a waterfall, shedding its weight – and its shielding – with every moment. The force of each percussive blow forced her backwards, legs straining, crumpling into a ball.

She was being caged. Overborne. *Destroyed.*

And whilst the gunservitor pinned her down, kept her sprawled against her grisly cover, she could guarantee that the rest of the Inquistor's loyal warriors had split, sneaking along adjacent corridors, surrounding her like wolves around a lamb.

Get up.

That dangerous voice again, whispering its incautious counsel into her heart.

Get up, fool! You're better than this!

The servitor paused to reload – whispering columns of metal sliding a fresh clip into place, smooth actuators ejecting its predecessor on a tide of gunsmoke. Mita seized the opportunity to assess her surroundings, gaze flashing left and right as her head crept above the mangled body's charred shoulder.

Don't die here, Mita. Don't die on the floor.

You're better than this!

Everywhere was smoke; a thick blanket of bittersweet stench that itched at her eyes and clouded her nostrils. The servitor stood foresquare in the doorway; hunched back rising from heavy unjointed legs, head a sunken battery of optics and twitching sensoria that dangled, like a vulture's beak, between and below the line of its shoulders. Beyond it the veiled shapes of the retinue capered in the adjacent room, every action underwritten by the dull tone of a cognis logi, assessing tactics and possibilities aloud. Nearer still, cringing in a corner beside the bloodslicked bed with his robe dishevelled and a strangled prayer on his breath, was the priest.

The split-second of eye-contact was all it took Mita to acknowledge he hadn't intended on finding himself trapped in a room with her.

Footsteps echoed through thin walls at her back; other warriors, taking up position, preparing to close the iron claw around her.

You're better than this!

The voice was right.

The bolterfire resumed, and now with every impact and subsequent detonation the corpse that covered her unravelled more, hammering at her legs, driving the breath from her body, hurting her.

Concentrate.

The priest. Remember the priest!

She closed herself down. She wiped away the world from her senses. She rose up from her body and slid like a harpoon into the priest's head. He tried to resist, for all the good it did him.

Down, down, down... Through layers of character and bubble-slick tiers of memory, past instincts and dreams, sliding between secret desires and repressed rages like a rip-blade, aimed at a heart. She closed astral fingers around that slumbering pearl, that black beacon of uncertainty and disloyalty she had felt before. A tiny seed, perhaps, the faintest of rebellious sentiments, but fully formed nonetheless. She pricked at his neuroses, swelled his paranoia with an artist's hand, and suddenly – like breaking an egg – she cracked it open and *released* it.

In his mind, clenching upon itself, protesting at the invader within its bounds, every certainty the priest had ever felt collapsed beneath him. Every faith, every trust, every loyalty: all of them dissolved, turning inwards, burning at his soul.

He could trust nothing.

He could tolerate no one.

The world was against him.

The instinct, of course, was to flee.

He leapt upright with a startled shriek, hookah clattering free of its straps and shattering at his feet. His charge propelled him out from his corner, robes fluttering, and into the path of the servitor. He crashed into its hulking frame even as he crossed the stream of its firestorm; bolter shells shredded him, picking clean his bones. His frail form was gone within instants, reduced to jelly and bonepowder, but it was enough.

Mita arose behind the wailing man from her moist cover with a shriek, hand closing around the discarded powersword as she moved, gliding to one side and lunging with all her might.

Even as the servitor's field of fire cleared, the unexpected obstacle blasted to wet fragments as quickly as it had arisen, a cautionary algorithm chattered against its engine-brain. It was nowhere near fast enough.

Mita cleaved the massive beast in two with a single stroke, punched through the shocked crowd of non-combatant retainers still lurking beyond the door, and was gone.

As she sprinted through the clamouring wastes of Cuspseal, breath catching in her throat, muscles aching, clothes slick with Cog's blood; a single word swam in her thoughts like a leviathan, rising from some twilight realm, absorbing every iota of her mind.

Outlaw.

SHE WENT INTO the shadow.

ZSO SAHAAL

TWO DAYS SEEPED by as if captured in amber, struggling against viscous time to claw their way free; to taste liberation for one endless, impossible moment. Sahaal counted each second with truculent impatience, fingers drumming at the arms of his throne, mind adrift with possibilities, plans, frustrations.

Still no word of the Corona.

Two days in the shadow, in the foglight of the rust-mud caverns. Two days of torpid nothing, with only the flickering of firelight to indicate life; like the hive-ghosts themselves, gathered where the nightmares became flesh, swirling about their new king.

Sahaal stared across the water and viewed his domain, and nodded his quiet pleasure. In the north, against the edge of the lapping waters, a tall mound was taking shape, rising up like some swollen stalagmite to challenge the cavern ceiling. The rushing figures at its base had no inkling of his scrutiny, and when – as he had now taken to doing with spiralling frequency – he quit his tattered seat to scuttle across the beams and stanchions of the swamplands, play-stalking the Shadowkin and their refugee guests without their knowledge, still his presence remained secret. He burned with the desire to act, but had no outlet for his energy.

He was everywhere and nowhere. Free to roam, cursed to wait.

He did not need the *preysight* of his helm, nor the nocturnal vision that was his birthright, to know what the growing mound was built from. Two days, he had given them. After that they would be his.

His master would be proud of him.

In moments of indulgence, when he slipped beneath the waters of meditation, he fancied that he could see Konrad Curze's face. In glittering hazes of pallor and shape, he fancied he could visit the Night Haunter, could speak with him as he had once done, could seek comfort and counsel in his master's voice.

It was all an illusion. The primarch was gone forever; his legacy was all that remained.

In life Konrad Curze had been a tortured soul. Plagued by the wildness of his childhood, haunted by visions of his own demise, he struggled with every fibre of his being to earn the respect and admiration of his brothers, and – above all else – to prove himself worthy of his father's affection. In adulthood as in youth he struck from the shadows, he waged war with fear and steel in the Emperor's name, and he raised his own sons, his Night Lords, with a martial pride unmatched in all the galaxy.

There was little glory in his aspect, if truth be known.

Where other primarchs wrestled for heroic deeds and the favour of their God-Emperor, Sahaal's master pursued only results. He would never be as charismatic as Lion El'Johnson, as articulate as Roboute Guilliman, as demagogic as Horus the Favoured... but he could be strong. He could shatter any enemy. He could be pragmatic. He could be *terrifying*.

In a universe of terror he robbed the Emperor's enemies of their horrific mantle. He overcame savagery by outstripping it. He purged the brutal by outdoing their brutality. He sacrificed what scant charm he had and took up the crown of scapegoat – the foulest of the primarchs, the dirtiest of fighters, the Emperor's own devil – so that none, *none*, would stand before him.

Rebels surrendered at the mere suggestion of his intervention. Raiders fled with his name upon their lips, swords unbloodied. Those that were feared were made to fear *him*. Those that were hated were made to hate *him*.

Obedience through terror.

He had never been human, but like all the primarchs there lurked in some deep corner of his luminous heart a flavour – a bitter taste – of humanity.

Konrad Curze sacrificed it. He wiped tears of insanity from snowy cheeks and cast his warmth to the wolves, and he did it in the Emperor's name. He lost everything.

He became what he had always been destined to; what the galaxy demanded he become; what the Emperor himself sanctioned, moulded, *needed*: He became a loyal monster.

And when he turned to his father for succour, for affection, for the merest *glimmer* of gratitude–

–he received only contempt.

Sahaal surfaced from his musings to find that his grip had splintered the arm of his throne to dust, long shards of bone and iron cutting his hand. He'd bitten his tongue without realising it, and his mouth was filled with the metal tang of his own blood.

Contempt.

That was the Night Haunter's legacy. The contempt of a betrayed son for his father.

And the need for revenge.

Oh, how the mighty are fallen.

'I vow it...' he whispered, unheard. 'Master, I vow it to you. We shall be mighty yet.

'We shall make him pay for what he did.'

THE HEAP GREW massive. From humble beginnings – a cluster, a clutch – it swelled upwards: layer upon layer, compacted together, shovelled one upon the next in imitation of the hive itself.

The stench, by the second day's end, when the camps teemed with life once more and Sahaal slipped across the swamps in secret to view the results of their labours, was an almost physical force.

Men and women, old and young; mouths wide, a rheumy film coating dead eyes. Tongues limp. Flies scuttling and tasting slack skin. From a heap to a hillock, and thence to a mountain; blood spattered, bruised, cold.

A multitude of dead heads glared upwards in mute accusation, and Sahaal met their gaze with a tiny smile.

Most had been taken messily. In distant alleys, he guessed, in maze-like habsprawls and secret places – necks severed with untidy force. Machetes and domestic knives, swinging and bludgeoning; notched daggers and antique blades. The damage to some spoke of sawing, of blow after blow, of hacking without precision through gristle and vertebrae. Of struggles in darkened places; of hands clutching and pushing; straining to defend.

'How many failed to return?' Sahaal murmured, flicking a gesture towards his condemnitor. She alone had joined him before the pile – flickering torches aggravating their shadows.

'Not many,' Chianni said, her voice low. 'The ones who refused to partake were soon... harvested, by those who did not.' Sahaal had at first mistaken her hush for revulsion, but no... no, the Shadowkin were adequately familiar with the tokens of mortality. Her quiet was instead a thing of awe and devotion, centred about the monument before her. 'We think perhaps sixty are unaccounted. Whether they've fled or been captured we don't know.'

'We have their children?'

'Of course.'

He turned to face her, unhelmeted eyes glistening. 'Then you know what to do.'

She nodded. Sahaal was impressed: even the notion of infanticide could not perturb her. Not she: the favourite of a Space Marine.

Yes, it had been wise to confide in her.

Sahaal turned back to his prize and cleared his mind, appreciating its majesty anew; a cone of scattered shapes, an altar to terror.

It was a harvest worthy of the Blood God himself: a mountain of gristle and gore, of gap-toothed grins and severed spines, befitting the brass throne of Khorne.

Not that Sahaal would ever offer it as such. No, these stolen skulls would be gifted to no deity, pledged to no metaphysical spirit.

There was, after all, no God of Fear.

'To the memory of the Night Haunter...' he whispered.

It had been a masterful plan, he knew, to dispatch the refugees on such a ghastly errand. At its most base level it had secured their loyalty: they became complicit to his crusade, bloody-handed allies whether they liked it or not. Few had relished the prospect of murder – fewer still had achieved it with precision and clean conscience – but now… now, with their morbid tithe paid and the faces of their victims haunting their nightmares, now their minds were his to mould.

He had tasked them with targeting sinners – the iniquitous, the mercenary, the impure – and they had made their solemn way into the hive, dispersing like a cloud of flies along elevator shafts and unknown duct crawls, to do that very thing. The hivers were fools if they thought the Cuspseal floor-rents were the only way up from the underhive, and the refugees had scattered across the city in defiance of the their so-called 'containment'. From the lowest to the highest tiers, in every shadowed recess and crowded street: a cry, a shout, the wet retort of metal finding flesh, and then only pumping blood and sprinting feet.

Had each and every victim been a sinner? Was every last head the fitting trophy of a slain delinquent who deserved his fate? No.

Of course not – no more so than *any* being may be considered guilty for the raft of petty evils for which, every day, every human was accountable. Here were the heads of the innocent mixed with the stolen skulls of scum, but he'd wager that each murderer would now *convince* his or herself, for the sake of their conscience, that their victim had been an abomination worthy of execution. That their brutality had been undertaken in the name of the Emperor. That no matter what violence they had committed, what horror they had seen, it was all excusable as part of their new lord's Holy Campaign.

Sahaal *owned* them all, now. Truly, the human mind was a wonderful thing.

But more important still, in the act of chaining themselves to his will, this horde of vigilantes, these thousand-strong killers, had injured the hive more than he could ever hope to have achieved alone.

The number of lives taken was irrelevant. Alongside the city's millions this mountain of skulls was a tawdry fraction, and yet... and yet in every level, in every township and city, the fear would be felt. He knew it, as a cognitor knows numbers and a poet knows words.

Let the Civilian Worship Channel deny it. Let the Preafects shake their heads and ring their bells, and claim that all is well. The more it was refuted, the more the rumours would spread. A wave of murders – insidious, motiveless, random. A slinking tide of death.

In a single disparate swoop, more punishing than any spectacle, more invidious than any gaudy massacre that could claim a million lives, fear would blossom on a tsunami of rumour and suspicion. He could well imagine the whispers, the frightened glances, the questions raised in every home.

Who is responsible? What do they want?

What had the victims done to incur such wrath?

The hive would become a restrained place. Doors would lock. Neighbours would cast troubled glances across cramped habways and avoid conversation. Families would huddle in the dark and whisper of ghouls in the night.

Kill a thousand men and they will hate you.

His master's voice, slipping upon runnels of ghostly memory.

Kill a million men and they will queue to face you. But kill a single man and they will see monsters and devils in every shadow. Kill a dozen men and they will scream and wail in the night, and they shall feel not hatred, but fear.

Sahaal nodded, pleased.

He had taken the first step. His brothers were coming for him, and he would be damned for a weakling and a fool if he was unready.

'Summon the captains,' he said to Chianni – and for an instant he fancied that he was back upon Tsagualsa, commanding his raptors, directing the Night Lords with the focus they required.

'Of course, my lord,' Chianni trilled, shattering the illusion. 'In respect of what?'

Sahaal grunted, eyeing the skulls with half a smile.

'In respect of *war*, condemnitor. What else?'

ANOTHER MOMENT'S INTROSPECTION, as he paused for his warriors to gather; another slip back in time: once more to the great halls of the *Vastitas Victris* and the Night Lords fleet; once more to the side of his master, black-feathered and veiled, leaning upon the Vulture Lectern to address the brothers. Such reminiscing gripped Sahaal more and more often, and at times the vividity of the visions scared him – so convincing was their colour, so remarkable their detail. At times he feared he was going mad.

But always he relished the opportunity to revisit his master's lifetime, and with each occurrence he immersed himself further in the words, treating each as a message intended for him alone. His master's legacy lay with him now. He must be true to the primarch's teachings.

'To kill an enemy, strike you in three places.'

That was how the lecture began; initiates and veterans side by side – Marine and Raptor and Scout and Terminator – each an equal in their lord's eyes, each dwelling upon every word with fevered concentration.

'Strike you at his hands, and he shall not cut you.

'Strike you at his heart, and his life shall wane.

'Strike you at his mind, and his courage shall fail; his faith shall leave him; his defeat is assured.'

Sahaal's enemy was the hive. He gave thanks to his master's ghost and, when finally his captains scurried to join him, he sent six squads to remove the city's fingers, one by one.

Surface to air batteries. Orbital defences. Overwhelmed by sudden coordinated attacks, sabotaged beyond the point of rapid reconstruction. *Strike you at his hands, and he shall not cut you.*

Four groups he sent outwards into the edges of the underhive, where the pulsing hearts of the city stood and rumbled.

Power stations. Geothermal vents. Great melta charges and jury-rigged bombs tightened against churning pumps, depriving the hive of its power and heat. *Strike you at his heart, and his life shall wane.*

And the mind... The onslaught upon the city's mind, he led himself.

HE HAD EXPECTED militiamen, or perhaps PDF regiments; skulking and morose in the xanthic lights at the compound's entrance, passing bacsticks and hipflasks to fend off the cold. As it was, he was not alone in acknowledging the supreme importance of propaganda, and it would not be so easy to gain entry. Clearly he had underestimated the vindictors' commander.

The city's population was jumpy – the murders had seen to that – and with citizens locking themselves away in their habs, mumbling prayers to keep the monsters away from their doors, Sahaal's small warband had little trouble reaching its destination undiscovered: sneaking through secret streets, forgotten shafts, desolate tramways. At the midtier intersection his scouts had indicated, they pulled themselves from a disused duct and prowled towards the industrial arcade that was their destination; only to find no fewer than six Preafects ringing its heavy gates.

Glutted by the success of their stealth, Sahaal cursed himself for not anticipating that their goal would be better guarded. The Shadowkin melted into the adjacent alleyways, awaiting his command. He sized-up the enemy with a practiced eye.

Two *dervishi*, heavy carapace armour marked with red stripes, hefted actuator-stabilised lascannons at either edge, with a quartet of shotguns – no less dangerous for their lighter armament – prowling between. In the wake of the attack upon the starport, clearly, the Preafects were taking no chances.

Sahaal grinned despite himself. He had spent too long on his throne, too long brooding and sulking in the gloom, to be dispirited by the odds. It felt good to be active again.

He took them from above, ululating as he dropped into their midst. The first *dervishi* he had cleaved apart before the squad was even aware of his presence, and before they could gather their instincts and round their weapons he'd stepped through the bloodspray to find a second victim; punching claws through glossy visor and skull alike, twisting through meat and bone. A shotgun pulsed to his left, a panicky blast that barely scratched him, and even as he dislodged the shattered face from his claws he was raising his bolter with his free hand, planting a round in the assailant's face and ducking beneath his thrashing grasp like a ghost; a blue and bronze streak, too fast to follow. By the time the shell detonated in the muffled confines of the dead man's helmet, far behind him, Sahaal had closed with the remaining men. The hiss of a charging lascannon pricked at his senses and he bounded across the shotgunners with a precise burst of his jump pack – snatching at their heads with his talons and dragging them behind him, flinging them with a final shriek – diced by the blades that released them – at the remaining *dervishi*. The lascannon discharged into their tumbling bodies and vaporised itself – and much of its wielder – in an orb of incandescence, scattering ash and fluid.

Sahaal settled beside the glowing debris and applied his claws to what few scraps of flesh remained, disappointed to find nothing left to kill.

The attack had lasted no more than five seconds.

'We move,' Sahaal announced, beckoning the awestruck Shadowkin from their cover, tearing at the gate with his claws.

The legend above the portal, smouldering now where the lascannon had singed it, mottled with the slurping remnants of the squad that had been intended to protect it from invasion, read:

CIVILIAN WORSHIP BROADCAST STATION

Sahaal smiled as his miniature army slipped within, the echoes of his master's advice warming him.

'*...Strike you at his mind, and his courage shall fail; his faith shall leave him; his defeat is assured...*'

ONCE WITHIN, THE task he had taken upon himself took little time to complete.

It went without saying that the tech-priests made poor targets for his attentions. In his need for technical expertise they might have served him well, but he knew from bitter experience that such devoted – and inhuman – stalwarts were difficult to persuade. With time he could have broken their minds and forced them to do his bidding – there was little doubt of that – but time was the one resource he was without.

Instead he slew them all, gathered together where the priests made their daily broadcasts, and with his Shadowkin holding weapons in clammy palms against their backs, he forced the legion of acolytes, retainers and novitiates to watch. Stripped of their masters, unguarded by the surgical/mechanical paraphernalia that kept the Omnissiah's brood faithful and unafraid, these youths were quick to accede to his demands. And after decades of conducting their masters' orders, of undertaking every tedious duty, every minor maintenance, they were more than adept at complying.

From entry to completion, it took no longer than twenty minutes. The consoles were blessed – clumsily, falteringly – by the captive novices, the servitors chattered with relayed orders and data packages, the bunched cables that led from studio to chapel, to sanctification-nodes and then upwards to all parts of the hive, crackled to life.

Sahaal killed the unwilling partisans who had helped him – quickly and disinterestedly – and rushed to review the security. Twenty minutes was a worthy time: but more than enough for the vindictors to gather.

Perhaps the guards at the doorway, cut down like vermin in his first assault, had missed a scheduled vox report. Perhaps a routine patrol had chanced upon the devastation at the broadcast-station's gates. The truth hardly mattered – only the situation: leaning from a narrow window he could clearly see the armoured figures below, slipping from cover to cover, releasing thick red smoke to cover their advance. From elsewhere in the building Sahaal's Shadowkin traded opportunistic shots with the attackers, bright laserbolts flicking from windows into the smokepall; hellguns rattling without any great effect, spattering the façade with lead.

'Preysight,' he murmured, more interested than concerned. His enhanced gaze stripped away layers of ruby smog, confirming what he'd suspected. The rattle of gunfire was a distraction – and a crude one – for the phalanx of heavily armoured *dervishi* assembling in the cover of the shattered gates: an assault squad, preparing to enter. Clearly the ministorum had little patience for protracted gunbattles. They wanted their station back. *Quickly*.

Sahaal shrugged to himself, sight returning to normal. As he dragged himself onto the rocky ledge of the window he wondered vaguely whether the Shadowkin – spread throughout the building by now, straining beneath the weight of weapons and grenades – had secretly suspected they were never intended to escape alive. Certainly it would take a fool to think he could run the bottleneck gauntlet of the main gates as they now were. Had they known? Had they followed his lead (through loyalty or terror) anyway?

He told himself with a sigh that he didn't care one way or another, that such worms were fit only for sacrifice, and as he poised himself against the edge of the ledge he almost managed to convince himself. Another tiny twinge of guilt, of shared pain, pricked at him, and he struggled to shake it off.

There was no escape from this building, he knew, unless one happened to have the gift of flight.

He launched himself into the smoke, unseen by friend or foe, and as he bounded across the abyss towards the safety of the shadow beyond, he hoped that his tribesmen would sell their lives dearly, and commended them to a peaceful grave.

The sounds of gunfire echoed at his back for a long time.

IT WAS AS he returned to the safety of the underhive, pushing through cobweb-choked kilometres of inter-wall ducting, slipping between steel bulkheads like a ghost within a recess, that it happened. He hopped from a tall plateau of coolant bulbs, macerated by rust and time, onto the scorched remains of a factorial chimney, long since stunted, when the noise arose from the gloom; an unctuous retort that sent shivers of recognition – and rage – up and down his spine.

'*Het-het-het…*' it went, rising on dryair thermals, scattering flocks of white bats. '*Het-het-het.*'

It was Phavulti, the cognis mercator. He sat and leant against a dripping oilvent, exuding every impression of sedate relaxation, and waved gaily as Sahaal inched from the blackness of the tunnel ceiling. Whatever damage Sahaal had done to him before was long gone, replaced without thought for elegance by mechanical contrivances. It had become more difficult still to detect where, if at all, human flesh remained.

'See you, up there, *het-het-het*. Been waiting for you. Heard about the attack on the CW… Walls have ears, yes. Thought you'd probably come this way. What kept you?'

Sahaal backed into the shadows, teeth grating.

What to do? What to do?

He was, ultimately, a warrior. He understood conflict. He *breathed* guerrilla war and terrorism. In such simple pursuits there was little complexity, little uncertainty. It was a thing of victory and defeat: he that was strongest, he that was cleverest, he that was *most terrible*, would win.

He was also a lord. He was used to obedience. He had grown accustomed to swimming an ocean of terror; to being feared and worshipped by those around him. That was as it should be.

But Pahvulti's familiarity; his infuriating laughter, his intractable inability to feel fear: these were things that Sahaal could neither understand nor tackle.

As ever in such instants, instinct took over.

'Scum!' he roared, quitting the shadows like a bolt of darkness, claws rasping from their sheaths mid-flight. He thumped into the robed man like a meteor, shredding cable and sinew, and whooped aloud, gyrating on streamers of superheated air, twisting for another strike.

Pahvulti stood and stared at him – both his arms torn away – and shook his head.

'Dear, dear, dear,' he grinned. *'Déjà vu. Het-het-het.'*

There was little point in prolonging the attack, after that. Sahaal felt himself deflate: how could one terrorise a fool intent only upon ridicule? He set down in the gloom near to the smiling creature, restraining himself as best he could, and crossed his arms.

It didn't work. Patience was not a virtue that could contend with his rage.

He took an abrupt step forwards, headbutted the information broker with the deathmask-crest of his helm, dropped an armoured knee onto the fool's chest, and pressed his claws against what little flesh remained of the man's neck.

'Look at me, worm,' he hissed. 'Look at me as I kill you.'

'Het-het-het. Why would you want to do *that,* by Terra's teats?'

'You've insulted my honour. You've played games with forces beyond your comprehension.' He leaned down, so close that the curling vapours of his rebreather wafted around the broker's mechanised face. He would not tolerate this disrespect any longer. The fool had nothing to offer. 'I shall eat your heart, broker, if you have such a thing. Your skull shall adorn my throne.'

'No, no... Not Pahvulti. Not when he's been sent for such a task.'

Sahaal paused. 'What task?'

For the first time the broker's face clouded – losing its contemptible grin. For the first time, Sahaal fancied, the man was taking him seriously. 'I was sent as a spy,' he said, optics chattering in the place of his cheeks, 'by a witch of the Inquisition.'

Warning bells shrieked in Sahaal's mind.

Kill him! Kill him!

'The Inquisition? You admit to it freely? What madness is this?'

'*Het-het-het.* She thinks to make a fool of me, friend. She thinks to threaten and cajole, to have me tell tales. I have chosen to confound her.'

'Oh?'

'I have chosen to help you instead.'

'Help?' Sahaal forced a bitter laugh. 'How could *you* help me?'

Still the man gave no indication of being put off, lips twitching apart. 'Knowledge,' he said, simply. 'Nothing is beyond Pahvulti. Nothing escapes him. He sees all...'

Riddles and delays. Kill the worm. Be on your way.

But...

But if he sees all...

Sahaal wet his lips, an uncomfortable thought swimming into focus.

'Such as?'

'Places, people... Names... I know you understand, Marine. I know there's a name you want to hear.'

He's lying. He's crawling to save his life. Kill him!

But…

But what if…

'What name?'

'Slake. Little collective Slake. Hiding from you. Cowering in the dark. *Het-het-het.*'

Sahaal's blood ran white hot.

'You… you know where he is? Tell me!' He pushed a claw through the man's chest, snapping through layers of rubber and steel as it went; an irritable, truculent gesture – venting his spleen. It had little effect.

'Not he. *They*. Of course I know. I *built* them. *Het-het-het.*'

'Tell me! Tell me where they are or I'll rip you to shreds!'

'No, no… Not Pahvulti. Not when he knows so much.'

'What do you think you know, fool?'

'I know what you're doing, yes. I know who you're doing it with. Where your little empire festers; I know. I've seen it. Eyes everywhere. *Het-het-het.*' He blinked, a languid affair, like a crocodile nictitating its eyes. 'I know what you *are*.'

Sahaal rocked back on his haunches. 'And what am I, little worm?'

'*Het-het-het.* Traitor Marine. Child of the Rebellion. Ally to the Great Betrayer. *Night Lord.*' He grinned. 'Recognised your markings the instant I saw you.'

Sahaal forced down the surprise in his belly. He had not expected this. 'And?'

'And I've been listening to rumours. Gossip in the dark.'

'What gossip? Confound your tongue!'

'A holy warrior – that's what you're calling yourself, yes? Your little tribe, you've told them – *het-het-het* – you've told them you're here to *deliver* them. You've told them you're a lovely little candle, a rose of purity in the darkness of corruption. That your brothers are coming to help you. Yes? I hear such things, such lies... You told them, didn't you? You told them you must prepare for your brothers. Yes? That *is* what you've said, isn't it?'

'What of it?'

He knows so much!

'We both know it's a lie, Night Lord. We both know they're not coming to save the hive. *Het-het-het.* Quite the opposite...'

'You threaten to expose my falsehoods? Is that it? Is that your best threat?'

'No threat, Night Lord. Only confirmation of my suspicions.'

'Then what do you want? Why should I spare you? Tell me!'

'Slake. You should spare me for Slake.'

'Tell me where he is.' Sahaal struggled with the words. 'I'll spare you. I'll vow it.'

I'll kill him! I'll cut his face from his skull!

'*Het-het-het.* No, no... last time... last time I helped you, what was the price?'

'There was no price! I spared your life. That is all!'

'Yes. No price. First one is always free, I told you. This time... this time Pahvulti's expenses are far greater.'

For the first time in his life Sahaal found himself speechless.

'Y... you...' he stammered, oceans of rage and astonishment pummelling against his restraint. 'You don't get to... to make *demands* of me, worm! You're nothing! I'm the Talonmaster! I'm the chosen of the Haunter! I'll cut you into a thousand p–'

'You will do nothing. Not if you want Slake.'

And that was the crux.

The Corona was everything. The Corona was mightier than his esteem, mightier than his rage, mightier than his pride.

Through Slake, it would be his.

And through Pahvulti, he could find Slake.

Kill him! Rip him to shreds! Slice him apart!

Still angry; those inner voices, but growing fainter: swallowed by the cold sludge of his pragmatism. That Chaotic part of his soul, tainted indelibly by the invitation of the Dark Gods' patronisation, raged and stormed ever one, but slowly, struggling with each word, he blotted out its tumult and swallowed his pride.

'What… What is your price, broker?'

'*Power,* Night Lord. The witch will go without the reports she expects me to make. I shall give you Slake. Your brothers will come, the city will fall. Who will reign in their wake?'

He smiled, steely teeth sparkling.

'Me. Pahvulti will reign.'

MITA ASHYN

MITA AWOKE TO the sound of screaming. She was on her feet and poised for combat before even her dreams had receded, and she stood in addled bewilderment for long seconds, blinking in the light, before reality distinguished itself from fantasy.

God-Emperor, it's freezing...

The invidious cold of Equixus had been invading the hive in disparate tiers for days: thermal conditioners sputtering and falling silent, power flickering and dying in random quadrants. Such interruptions were, of course, temporary, but as teams of techpriests and armies of acolytes roved from switchboard to grid-centre, chanting and blessing, diverting power from here, there, *anywhere*, still the tremulous vagaries of heating ducts and silent fans couldn't hold the frost at bay. Mita wondered what the power failures signified and who was responsible. She felt she could take a pretty good guess.

She shivered, not entirely from the cold, and peered around.

The alleyway where she'd slept was unchanged: filthy walls covered with oil and rust. No snarling vindictors loomed over her with power mauls flaring, no hive-mobs threw bottles and swore in the gloom, and no fiery purgatists poked at her raggedy form with barbed rods, hollering imprecations and zealous damnation. For two days she'd lived thus: a streetsleeper, an outlaw – freezing by night, starving by day. She'd exchanged the gaudy threads of her Inquisitorial robes for thick rags, and had cut her hair short and ragged, guided only by the reflection in a sump-puddle. There were more than enough agents of hostility against vagrants, without encouraging recognition at the hands of Kaustus's agents. Given the fierceness of the environment and the apathy of its population, she supposed it was little wonder that she hadn't thus far encountered a single other vagabond. Such unfortunates had two choices: to descend into the bosom of the underhive where their status allowed acceptance – but not affection – or to die.

She guessed it was a tough decision.

For her part, she had no intention of doing either. Homeless she may be, hunted by the Emperor's own Inquisition, but she at least had a *purpose*. She at least had straws to clutch. She had the information broker...

None of which was especially relevant to the fact that someone, nearby, had screamed. It was hardly an exceptional thing: the Cuspseal environs could hardly be equated with the anarchy of the underhive, but it was still a society far from utopian. Muggings, murders, rapes; such were the lifeblood of the hive's darker quarters, and given the strange events of recent days – the beheadings that had thrown the streets into such fearful discord - a cry in the night was just another background sonata.

But the scream that had awoken her had not been alone. A chorus of voices had called out together - and continued in their distress. She hurried from her concealment, pulling her cloak tight against the cold, and gauged the sound's location.

That, perhaps, was the one remaining distinction between Mita Ashyn and any other Cuspseal transient: anyone else would have run *from* the sounds of terror.

She headed directly for them.

It was a gather-hall. Such low-rise huts - frequently domed, often decorated with holy tableaux (inevitably of such poor quality that saint X was indistinguishable from Ecclesiarch Y) and devotional graffiti - were a common sight throughout the hive: bulging chambers squeezed into opportunistic gaps like rubber igloos. In their gloomy little bellies, packed with row upon row of uncomfortable plasteen pews and staffed - in the more uptown districts - by a quivering maintenance servitor, the local populace flocked to digest their daily dose of Citizen Worship broadcasting. Such places were never empty and rarely quiet, disparate factory shifts staggered to allow a fraction of the locality to visit, each in turn. From these communal *indoctria* arose the sounds of wavering hymns, chanted chatechistic responses, cheers and exclamations at the fiery words of whatever dogmatist was picked out in the crackling haze of the viewspex screen.

And now, it would seem, screams.

Mita hurried inside, prepared for a fight, and stopped dead in her tracks. It was not the audience that snagged at her attention, rocking back as they were in their seats; some covering their eyes, others clutching at one another like infants seeking comfort, but rather the focus of their horrified gazes: the great viewspex screen, hanging on optic cables and bundles of datawire like a great luminous spider, wreathed in the incense of devotional thuribles suspended around it.

Picked out in its flickering light was a cardinal – *the* cardinal, she guessed, who fronted whichever rousing show was scheduled for this early hour – and he had been crucified.

Set against a dark background, the broadcast optics zoomed upon his meaty frame: stripped naked, beaten across face and chest, cut in a multitude of places by small, razor incisions. He had been lifted bodily upon a weird rig – a thing of draped umbilici and sinister outcrops, multifaceted lenses glaring from its trunk like the boles of a plastic tree – which Mita recognised as a photoseer: a camera servitor similar, no doubt, to that which had filmed this grisly tableau. Held against the tall machine, arms splayed, legs bound together, the priest had been stapled down. Up and down each arm, punched through the fleshy crutch betwixt fibia and tibia, through shoulders and collar-sections, through the fat of his thighs and the tense elastic of his heels; a dozen or more ugly, rusty pins had been driven.

At the foot of the unmoving photoseer, now bright with his blood, other bodies lay heaped: black robed and augmented, long-nailed hands and servo *manipuli* arms clutching emptily at awkward angles. Tech-priests, Mita guessed – devoted servants of the Emperor in his aspect as the Machine God. Every last one beheaded.

The cardinal was still alive, somehow. The slow suffocation of the spread eagle had given him a deathly grey pallor, and even were it not for the gag pushed hard between his jaws she doubted he would have been able to scream – but still he eyed the lens of the photoseer, throat wobbling to whatever pleas he was trying to vocalise.

Worse yet, sucking at her vision as if alive and hungry, writhing in some hellish geography of the eye, was the single word that had been cut into the Cardinal's chest, scrawled in incision and blood.

'Excommunicate.'

Mita felt her knees weaken. Little wonder the crowd's distress.

The image zoomed towards the hateful word, pinpricks of bloody sweat thrown into sharp detail on the viewscreen, and just as the audience felt sure the horrors were over, a voice began to speak.

It tore at Mita's soul like a hungry wraith. She knew it. She recognised it.

The Night Lord.

'Behold,' it whispered, not so much spoken as insinuated upon the air, like the breath of the wind given form, 'the price of false zeal.'

The audience gasped and gibbered amongst itself, trading prayers.

'A corrupt little cardinal, I found – fat with the wealth of his flock, soiled by gluttony and decadence. It was a mercy to spill his blood.'

Someone in the audience vomited. Nobody looked around, all eyes wide, brimming with tears of terror. The sheer force of their anxiety pushed at Mita's senses, threatening to overwhelm her.

'It was a mercy to hear his screams.'

The image jumped abruptly. Still pushed to its highest magnification, the photoseer swept its gaze to the side: a blur of nonsensical shapes, flitting one across the next. Formless dark and flickering light gave way to panoramas of blue and bronze, of red-tainted confusion and glossy tones; all of it chipped and hardened by harsh shadows. It found its target in a flash of nauseous focus and – with an instant's pause for swirling minds to decipher what they were seeing – the crowd erupted anew.

Devil-red slits, burning from a field of shadow, swept up and backwards in arrowhead slants, tickled by a wreath of misted breath.

Eyes.

'So shall perish all who have fallen from the light,' their owner hissed. 'The Emperor's gaze has fallen upon this world–' (shrieks and fainting amidst the audience) '–and he has found it wanting. Corruption is all he sees. A city of iniquity and injustice, ruled by the weak and the selfish.'

The image began to loosen, pulling away from those eyes, smouldering with malice. Whatever form held them remained indistinct, bathed in shadow, hinted only in flashes of blue and bronze; in hulking dimensions that fooled the eye and mauled the senses.

'You have seen the deaths amongst you. The sinners cut down. I took their heads to clean their corruption. They are the first among many. They will not be the last.

'Repent, sinners. Fear your Emperor's wrath. Fear his angel of vengeance.'

At its widest angle, the viewspex was a poor interface for the horror of its subject. This shape, this unseen *thing,* leaned from the lightless void, eyes afire, breath steaming. Spines and chains caught at flickering firelight; half-seen allusion to its size and shape. Neither were obvious: it was a *presence* first and a solid being second; an ethereal devil; a graceful silhouette. The audience clothed its faceless hulk with whatever nightmare-flesh their minds conjured, and all along they suspected that whatever terrors their imaginations supplied, the reality was sure to be far, far worse.

It hissed at the photoseer, and claws like bolts of lightning snapped into view from nowhere. Shrieks rang out in the cramped gather-hall.

'Judgement is coming,' the beast said. 'Do not resist it.'

And then the broadcast ended, and the fizzing snow-storm of white noise was all that lit the gloomy cavern.

There was a moment of silence.

'He's lying!' Mita cried, heart pounding. 'He's lying! He wants us to fear him! He's no child of the Emperor!'

She might as well have tried to whisper in the face of a hurricane. No one was listening to her.

They were too busy screaming.

IT WAS THE same all across the city. Wherever she went, wandering unseen – as only the vagrant can truly be – the sobbing and screams rang out in the dark. In the frantic colours of the klubzones, in the smoggy wastes where the factories clamoured with downmarket habs, in every street and every stairway: unbridled horror. Whispers. Rumours.

The Citizen Worship broadcasts were resumed quickly; control of the station clearly regained. The stammering denials and assurances – 'All is well, all is well' – did little to quell the storm. Indeed each authority that attempted placation and denied the corruption of the hive merely fed the dissent, branding themselves as partisans to the iniquity by attempting to conceal its existence. Only a sliver of the teeming masses had been present to see the broadcast, but it hardly mattered. The mouth-to-ear machine worked its cogs to nothingness as the story was told and retold, mutating and growing with each hour.

Chapels groaned with bodies: crying out for forgiveness, demanding mercy from unprepared priests, themselves shaken to the core of their faith by the threat of divine justice. On streets the purgatists found themselves outdone by the sudden zeal of those seeking absolution; wailing and gnashing, striking themselves with thorny canes until every tramway and stairwell was moist with the blood of flagellants.

But most... most of the hive did not resort to such excesses. Most slunk home with faces pale, deserting the factories in their droves, locking doors and bolting shutters, whispering fearful reassurances to sobbing infants and telling spouses over and over, 'I love you, I love you...'

Just in case.

The Emperor's angel was abroad, and in his path all sin would burn, all unrighteousness would bleed itself dry, all mercy would be denied.

And not a single thing that Mita said could convince the city otherwise. The Night Lord had outmanoeuvred her.

Where is your 'It is being dealt with' now, Kaustus?

Skulking in the gloom of a frightened city, she realised with her heart sinking that the time had come to deploy the one ace she still held. She found a secluded spot in the dark beneath the struts of a mezzanine stairwell, and sat with her legs crossed, clearing her mind.

This was going to hurt.

WHEN SHE HAD visited the information broker, days before, when his servitors had come so close to finishing her and Cog, she had watched it dawn upon him with amusing slowness that all the arrogant bluster in the world would do him little good.

She plucked his secrets from his mind.

She'd found him enmeshed at the heart of a great room/machine, cursing the destruction of his cybernetic warriors. Like a fat spider in its web, the cords of his data-empire snaked from every corner; a morass of *sensoria* consoles, *augaria* readouts, clattering logic engines, auspex monitors, fluttering dials and bank upon bank of viewspex screens: meeting in a knot, a tangle, a halo of rubber and metal, at his head. From here he controlled photo-optics, cameras, servitors and communicators hive-wide. From here he intercepted transmissions, he eavesdropped like some digital god, he watched a thousand transactions in a thousand places, and he stored it all away like a bee, hoarding its honey.

He had thought himself implacable. He had tamed a Space Marine, by the hiveghosts, how could a mere woman hope to hold any sway over *him*?

In his world of computations and logic, of bitter numbers and black/white divisions, of strength and weakness, there was of course one parameter he could never hope to calculate: the realm of the psyker.

And yes, he may have spent his life severing his ties with humanity, rebuilding his body time and time again, augmenting and reshaping his mind like a sculptor working clay – but he could not escape from the raw biology of his brain. It was an emotive organ, and if his media were metal and mathematics, then Mita's were thoughts themselves.

She had slid into his consciousness before his smugness could even take flight, and he had been powerless to stop her. He'd told her everything: who he was, how he had been created, the extents of his empire. He'd told her about his meeting with the Space Marine, about the creature's quest for the Glacier Rats, about the ongoing hunt – spreading rumours across the entire underhive – for the Slake collective: always in pursuit of some unknown package. He had bared his steely soul before the scalpel of her astral self, until she'd had him exactly where she'd wanted him.

She'd threatened him with the one thing that was guaranteed to scare him – informing his former masters at the Adeptus Mechanicus of his existence and whereabouts, reminding him that it wasn't too late to undergo the *puritens* lobotomy a second time – and he had capitulated like the unctuous little worm he so clearly was.

He would find the Night Lord, she'd insisted. He would report every movement – every orkspoor *word* – back to her. She arranged times and places, and then she let him go.

He would betray her, of course. It was inevitable – that was just the sort of mind he had. She imagined he would wriggle his way into the Night Lord's debt, seeking protection and power from the beast she had sent him to spy upon. It was of little consequence. She had taken... *other* precautions.

The *tutoria* of the Scholastia Psykana called the procedure *inculcati*. It involved depositing a fragment – a *parsus* – of one's own astral self, like a souvenir, within the subconscious of another human. Once detached, the psyker could form a brief link with their target – location and distance notwithstanding – and ride, like some insidious piggyback signal, upon their very senses. It was a poor alternative to remote viewing at the best of times, but – given her difficulty with that discipline, and the Night Lord's guardian *warpthings* – that was no longer an option.

The *inculcati* was difficult. It was painful. And it allowed only one chance.

When she'd pushed her way inside Pahvulti's mind, revolted at his cold ambition, acknowledging the probability of his betrayal from the start, she had screwed up her courage, braced herself, and cut away a piece of her soul, pushing it down into the efficient columns of his brain. If she could no longer spy on the Night Lord herself, she'd decided, she'd send this fool on her behalf: to stare through his eyes and hear through his ears.

Which, seated beneath the mezzanine, sweat pricking her brow, moaning with effort and agony as if on some secret childbirth, she did.

—AND HIS EXTERNAL *temperature at 30.4°C: the result, no doubt, of coolants within his armour. His throne is built of rusted iron and bone, decorated in feathers, and stands at 3.1 metres from base to tip.*

Pahvulti's clipped thoughts, spiralling around her like a river. She fixed her fingers into the rush and concentrated, overwhelmed by alien impressions and thoughts. To see through Pavhulti's eyes was to be immersed in a sensory ocean, ridged by tsunamis of detail and analysis.

At a depth of 1.5km below ice-level, the rock is warm. He is the lord of the underhive – undisputed – and I am at his left. To his right sits his condemnitor. I recognise her from my surveillance locus as Avisette Chianni. She is one of the Shadowkin.

I have no arms.

I have seen two hundred and six Shadowkin since I came to this place. I have seen many more refugees.

Each carries a weapon. He has built an army.

Far above, seated in the boiling heart of the trance, Mita was staggered. The *inculcati* link was not strong – remaining sapient in the deluge of another being's thoughts was far harder than she had imagined, and the conflicting inputs of Pahvulti's body with her own had all but severed the connection at its start – but still she was overwhelmed by the broker's secret admiration for the domain the Night Lord had built.

One point two metres above me, to my right, He says: 'Bring them forwards.'

I have given him Slake. All is well.

The scouts – three of them, all men, though one is an albino of the Pallor House – push their prize forwards. No doubt the Night Lord is mixing the resources at his control, forging links between those who serve him voluntarily, and those who have discovered themselves dominated. It is a salient tactic: There is no shortage of loyalty in this place.

The scouts found the collective in the safehouse I revealed. The Slake members seem bewildered at the heart of the Shadowkin camp: there are two remaining, and with a third of their efficiency compromised their situation confuses them. They are rendered children; summoned before an elder. When the male stumbles his companion falters with him: linked to his temple by a cord of copper umbilicus.

The woman was once Sicca Yissen; aspiring heiress to the Yissen Guildhouse. The man, at one time, was Apolus Jaque, illegitimate child of the Rogue Trader Corleoni. And their missing member was Kuloch Sven-Dow, whose putsch of the WestHab trading consortium failed so spectacularly.

I know their names because I created them. They came to me, disgraced by guild and gold, each hungry for a second chance. They needed an edge above their competitors, and so I created the gestalim. I fused their memories together, I gave them the power of the cognitor but preserved their personalities. They have existed for three years, four months and sixteen days. In that time they have become junkies.

Information-narcotics. Middlemen desired and sought-after all over the hive, but indebted only to me.

Until today I have patronised their custom with paternal pride. I have allowed them autonomy (at the price only of their loyalty) and even hidden them, in this time of peril. I have been like a father to them.

And now the Night Lord has demanded them, and I have provided.

Poor, poor little Slake.

Something lands in the mud at their feet, cast down from above and behind me. It is a skull, polished clean; shining sockets above each eye trailing useless cables like antennae.

Kuloch Sven-Dow. Rest in peace, fool.

The Slake collective is reunited in a tangle of scrabbling grasps and piteous groans. Its living members need no prompt; they jack into the dead skull like starving slaves presented with a meal, lolling and mewling in pleasure at the surge of data.

The collective is reunited, and whatever childish anxiety they had suffered is eclipsed in an instant. When the initial rush has passed they face the Night Lord with disinterested eyes and say:

'You are going to kill us, then?'

They speak together, perfectly in harmony. It is an amusing effect.

If their straightforwardness is of consternation to my new master, he does not show it.

'I will,' he says. 'But there are a thousand deaths at my disposal. Some are slower than others. You understand'

The collective trades glances. I know they are discussing within the confines of their secret union, unheard voices crackling back and forth. They display no outward signs of fear.

'We accept,' they say. 'It will be painless?'

The Night Lord shrugs. 'It will be fast.'

They were a fine creation, the gestalim. I shall be disappointed to see them gone, but we are all of us made slaves in the Night Lord's presence, and to accept his dominion is the clearest, easiest path.

'There was a package,' he hisses, and I fancy that one pont three seconds into his pause there comes a quiet sigh, unheard by all but me, and I wonder what thoughts circulate in his mind. 'You commissioned the Glacier Rats to steal it.'

'We did.'

'How did you know it was coming?'

'Our buyer anticipated its arrival. He employed us as middlemen. We would locate and hire agents to retrieve the item. Their fee, as was ours, was generous.'

He hisses behind me. He is eager.

'Where is the package now? Was it opened? Was the seal broken?'

'It was not opened by us. It has been delivered to the customer.'

In the throne, the monster leans forwards. He deploys his most pertinent query like a pict-gambler presenting an ace of cups.

'Who,' he said, unable to disguise the hunger in his voice, 'is the customer?'

In the world above, through pain and sweat, Mita cleared her consciousness and focused, struggling to hold the *inculcati* connection. This, her senses told her, was a critical moment.

The *package...*

Something stolen from the *Umbrea Insidior.*

Something worth a thousand deaths to pursue.

The package was at the crux of it all.

She pushed further into Pahvulti's consciousness, straining to hear.

'We do not know,' the collective says.

There is no hiss from the Night Lord, no explosion of temper and carnage. I wonder, perhaps, if he has come to anticipate disappointment.

'We have only a location,' Slake continues, harmonious voice unwavering. 'A meeting place and a signal code, to summon the customer's agents. They come to collect, and to make payment.'

'And where,' the Night Lord says, voice a whisper, 'is that?'

'The Macharius Gate! The Macharius Gate!'

A cowled scribe – who had made a spirited attempt at tackling her legs – received a heel in his face for his troubles. She sprinted on, past bemused acolytes and oblivious servitors, shouting as she went.

'Orodai! Orodai, you bastard! The Macharius Gate!'

The Cuspseal Preafect-precinct was busy, even for the insanity that passed as the norm in these parts. She leapt over a scrum of off-duty *Dervishi* – too slow to intercept her – and pounded up alabaster stairs to the next level.

'Orodai! *Orodai!*'

Obstruction to her hurtling progress was certainly growing now. She'd bolted past the fat desk sergeant at the precinct's entrance with a discourteous ripple of psychic energy – not enough to kill, but plenty to leave him sagging and corpulent in his chair. By now alarms would be ringing in higher levels, squads would be closing like black-glossed claws upon her hellish advance, and perhaps someone, some unctuous little aide, was informing Orodai that a madwoman was indulging in a laughable attempt to deliver an unsanctioned message. She just hoped the news pricked his curiosity.

Nothing's ever easy.

'Orodai! The Macharius Gate! Damn your eyes, man! Can you hear me? The Macharius Gate!'

A young Preafect went down behind her, an elbow catching him squarely in the face. His partner – an older vindictor with a well-polished punctiliousness about him – decided to forgo the non-lethal approach and raised his shotgun. She blasted him with a messy crackle of astral energy and resisted the urge to grab for his gun as she passed. Being armed was a sure way to get oneself shot.

At the penultimate level, leaving behind her a scattered trail of bewildered aides and psychically-battered Preafects, whichever security-servitor was coordinating the 'emergency' presented the result of its labours: a ten-strong block of Preafects, fully armoured, which let rip with a salvo of shotgun fire in the tight confines of the stairwell at the very instant she rounded the corner. It was only the premonitionary flicker of imminent obliteration that flashed through her secret senses that compelled her to skid to a halt, leaping back in the direction she'd come, and even that wasn't quite fast enough. A thick wall of leadshot snagged at the edge of her shoulder as she vanished, spinning her in her place and dropping her to the floor, crying out.

Hot blood warmed her arm.

Heavy footsteps clumped down towards the corner and she mustered what little energy she still had to prepare another psychic strike. But then shouted commands and the heavy clanking of armoured bodies rose up the stairwell from below, the first of many vindictors pounced around the corner with gun bared, and she realised with a particularly foul curse that she was utterly outnumbered.

'Macharius Gate…' she mumbled, unable to think of anything else to say, as the first of several dozen shotgun muzzles nudged against her skin. 'Macharius Gate, you bastards…'

'What about the Macharius Gate?' a voice said, from above. She felt a flutter of recognition at the dry tones, and looked up with the first stirrings of hope. The Preafects inched aside to allow a plainly dressed figure past.

'Orodai!' she exclaimed.

'*Commander* Orodai,' he corrected, expression none-too-impressed to see her. 'What are you doing here, girl?'

'Delivering vital information on behalf of the Inquisition.'

He sighed.

'Miss Ashyn, the last I heard was that you had been ejected from that body for gross insubordination. Your former colleagues visited me. They were very keen to impress upon me what to do if you were found.'

I'll bet they were, the bastards.

One of the Preafects racked his shotgun, pointedly.

'Commander,' she hissed, heart throbbing so hard she could barely hear her own voice. 'You know as well as I do that Kaustus is making a mistake.'

'Have a care, girl. An outlaw is hardly in the position to disparage an inquisitor.'

'For the Emperor's sake, Orodai! The inquisitor's a fool! A warp-damned *fop* more troubled by the governor's treasures than the danger in this hive!'

Orodai glared at her, working his jaw.

Which way will you go, you efficient little bastard?

Slowly, eyes narrowed, Orodai reached into his belt and lifted his pistol, training it upon Mita's head. Her heart fell.

'Dismissed,' he barked to the Preafects. 'I can handle this whelp.'

The vindictors vanished without complaint. Orodai waited until they had all gone, until the echoes of their clattering strides had faded, before re-holstering the pistol.

Mita frowned. 'I... I don't understand...'

'It does not do to discuss politics in public, girl. Walls have ears.'

'I... I...'

'I'm assuming you've come to me for a reason. I'm no more a fan of the Inquisitorial bastard than you, but then the enemy of my enemy is not necessarily my friend. Particularly when she's a warp-piss witch who lost a squad of my best men.'

Mita suffered the chide with good grace, refusing to rise.

'I know where you can find him.'

'Who?'

'You know who. The Night Lord. The Chaos Marine. The beast that's made a mess of your pretty little city.'

He shook his head. 'Still you insist upon *that* notio–'

Her mouth fell open. 'How can you doubt it?' she stormed, outraged. 'You *must* have seen the hijacked broadcast!'

'I did. All I saw was a pair of red eyes.'

'Don't be a fool! Why deny it to yourself? There's a warp-damned Traitor Marine loose in *your* city, Orodai, and I can tell you where it is! Are you so thick-skulled that you'll refuse to hear it?'

He sighed, and when he spoke his voice was calmer, quieter: thick with exhausted frustration.

'Child, whether the creature is real or not is irrelevant. All we know is that someone – *something* – has formed an army in the underhive.' He raised an eyebrow at her stunned expression and half-smiled. 'The Inquisition isn't the only body that has its spies, girl. So you see, you really have nothing to offer me. We already *know* where your... "beast" resides, whatever it is. But to attack it in its own lair would be fo–'

'Not there.'

'What?'

She allowed a smile to curl her lips, the throbbing of her bloody shoulder rescinding to nothing.

'He's leaving his lair,' she said. 'He has an appointment. The Macharius Gate, Orodai. That's where we slay the dragon.'

PART FOUR:
COMMUNION

'I should like to know who it was that first said "Know thine Enemy." It has always struck me as the sentiment of an unrepentant heretic.'

–Last recorded words of Commissar Jai'm Baelstus, hours before his death at the hands of rebel insurgents (later postulated to have been concealed within his own Command Unit.)

ZSO SAHAAL

THE MACHARIUS GATE was a place of unlikely amalgamations: where the trappings of the rich punctured the realm of the poor; a jewelled knife sinking through tumorous flesh.

Pressed against the inner shell of the hive at its southernmost point, rising and falling no further than a single tier, it was, to the city's aristocracy, a means of escape. Oh, there were starports elsewhere in the hive, and other doors leading to the frozen exterior pocked its rim like airholes; but such outlets were the remit of peasants and workers – inelegant drawbridges and sphincter-portals leading to loading bays and vehicle silos. They were rarely used: who, after all, would *choose* to venture into the frozen wastes?

But the Macharius Gate – that was a more civilised affair. Slipping into its cambered ceiling, descending in the shadow of the colossal snowgate doors, a tangle of stairwells and plungeshafts tumbled from above, thick with ancient elevators and gearlifters. A single broad illuminator, affixed to the ceiling by a steel cord, smeared its unkind luminosity across all below, flickering with whatever tenuous energy fed it. Here the aristocrats could slip down from their distant pinnacles, unburdened by the unpleasant need to mingle with lesser populations as their descent progressed.

To each noble house its own shaft, and to each the opportunity to travel secretly to this seedy place, as desire dictated. Here the opulence of Steepletown collided with the filth of the first tier: tapestry-hung reception booths mouldering; elegant brass instrumentation pilfered and sold on down the years, leaving now a hotchpotch of exquisite craftsmanship and improvised squalor. Staffed only by a squad of militia auxiliaries – fat part-timers recruited from the local habs who lolled uncomfortably, unshaven faces incongruous with the bright uniforms they'd been given to wear – the gateroom could hardly be considered impregnable. Perhaps, bored and pampered in their spires, the nobles who frequented this peculiar place enjoyed the fact of its relative unsafety? Perhaps they thought it exhilarating?

More likely, they knew that no attacker was stupid enough to try gaining access to the upper hive without the call-codes to which each elevator responded; the sheaf of access papers required to placate the militia elite who patrolled Steepletown, and a sizeable army to rely-upon when things went sour.

The Equixus aristocrats had little to worry about.

The nobles descended here to hunt, primarily. To snort and guffaw amongst themselves, to engender upon their privileged, empty little lives a measure of excitement. They slipped out through the massive snowgates to the vehicle bay beyond, crooning their inflated machismo. They wore heated mouldsuits to shield them from the weather, drove vast juggerkraft loaded with fine wines and sweetmeats, carried decorous weapons of such high calibre that the rare yokkrothi bears they tracked (or, rather, their servitors tracked) would literally vaporise in the unlikely event of a direct hit; and still they somehow managed to slap one another across the back and pronounce themselves brave, manly citizens. Sahaal took one look at it and felt himself angered. This bloated pretend-bravery, this decadent waste of space: it was everything he had come to despise about the Imperium.

Vast. Gaudy. Overconfident.

Spiritually empty.

See how the mighty are fallen…

He would change all of that.

The Slake collective had been true to its word. On bundles of parchment its members had scrawled maps to reach this place: descriptions of its interior, directions upon which elevator to approach, what runecodes to enter into its ancient control panel. It would summon their customers' representatives, they assured him. It would lead him to the ones who had purchased his stolen prize.

He'd left them alive, for now: chained to a jagged wall down in the guts of the rustmud caverns. They would receive their swift deaths, as promised, when – *if* – their assurances were borne out.

The militiamen guarding the gateroom did not pose too great a struggle. Sahaal killed all six without a single shot fired, and waved his ragtag troops past their shattered bodies with a jerk of his bloody claws. As ever, it felt dangerously good to kill again.

He had brought with him a colourful menagerie of warriors – at least one from each subjugated ganghouse, a selection whose eclecticism he owed entirely to Chianni. Still recovering from her wounds, she'd been unable to join his expedition herself; but her advice had been more than pertinent:

Avoid infighting. Avoid favouritism. Take warriors from each tribe. Show them equal respect, and equal contempt. Make them partisan to your struggles, and to one another. Temper their resentment with inclusion and glory.

And it had worked. Such was their awe for the beast that roved ahead of them, such was their terror of the sleek devil that drew them on through shadow and shade, that their mutual loathing was forgotten. Former enemies became allies in fear and devotion: they were gangers no longer. They were Children of the Night.

She was quite the devious diplomat, his condemnitor.

He'd also brought with him the cognis mercator. Pahvulti: the cringing little bastard. Sahaal had conspicuously refused to trust the grinning creature, despite his successful delivery of the Slake collective, and to leave him alone amongst the Shadowkin was not something he cared to countenance. The man knew too much.

That the armless figure – stumbling with a *'het-het-het'* and an endless barrage of useless chatter – had enraged Sahaal was a given. That he had gloated and sneered where he should have bowed and offered obeisance had not helped his case. That Sahaal had vowed again and again that he would repay the cackling worm's insolence with death should have sealed his fate…

And yet…

And yet his information had proved flawless. He had helped plan the ongoing attacks upon the hive:

its fingers and its heart, in accordance with the Night Haunter's lessons. Pahvulti's knowledge of the city was unmatched, and when ordering his warriors to strike at power stations, orbital armaments, PDF armouries and geotherm ducts, Sahaal had found Pahvulti's input frequently useful. He was a resource that should not be squandered too quickly.

But, more so, the man's hunger for power – as crude as it was – allowed Sahaal at least a measure of dominance over him. The gift of rulership, if and when his brother Night Lords arrived, would be *Sahaal's* to confer. Pahvulti was no longer in control of their union. Now it was Sahaal who had something the broker wanted; and that was a situation he was keen to enjoy.

And... Yes... yes, he must admit it to himself...

Keeping the bastard alive gave Sahaal something to look forward to.

Within the gateroom, when his mob had entered and swept the place for security and surveillance devices, Sahaal found himself quietly disappointed. The elevator door to which the instructions directed him was an inferior thing: plain and unadorned where others sported intricate frescoes and colourful records of their owner's exploits. Naturally such pomposity revolted Sahaal, but in some strange way he felt that anything connected to the Corona Nox – even the warpshit who had stolen it – should represent a level of... superiority compared to all around it. Amongst a society of princes, he felt as though he'd been mugged by a beggar. It angered him, without him fully being able to explain way.

These days, the anger needed little excuse to arise. The voices rustled and hissed in his mind, tentacles of Chaotic warpstuff playing across his soul, plucking and needling it to ever greater peaks of savagery. For the hundredth time he drew a breath and calmed himself, seeking in vain the focus that his master had always preached.

He entered Slake's code with a steady hand – gratified at the apparent efficiency of the unfussy console – and stepped back to wait.

Behind him the ranks of warriors shifted in their places. A brute of the Atla Clan scratched at his quilled scalp with a moronic grunt, and behind him a pair of androgynous gunners of House Magrittha exchanged glances through heavy lashes.

The warband was edgy. Sahaal wondered vaguely whether it was the result of the situation, or their proximity to him.

He hoped it was the latter.

'My lord?' asked one, an impressive female of the Sztak Chai whose chain-glaive was as tall as Sahaal himself. 'Has it worked?'

He ignored the interruption and glowered at the console. A small brass dial shifted slowly, inching from one side to the other.

153, it read. The label at the head of the dial was marked, simply: *TIER*.

It took a little over one minute to reach *152*.

The Macharius Gate was, of course, on Tier 1.

'This may take a while,' Sahaal sighed.

The warriors silently took up positions at the gateroom's entrance, perhaps detecting the impatience in their lord's vox-distorted voice, thankful for the opportunity to stay out of his way. Pahvulti slumped into a corner, crossing his knees and chattering quietly to himself.

With the hunger for violence gnawing at his mind, Sahaal anticipated the wait for his quarry's arrival as if preparing to be tortured. In some quiet sliver of his soul he recognised that this burgeoning fury was a far from useful state of mind, but it lingered nonetheless: as if a fire had been stoked inside him which no amount of dousing could extinguish.

Resolving instead to contain the blaze – to let it burn slow and steady, without fiery impulse or crackling explosion – he knelt at the elevator's dull entrance and emptied his mind, pushing himself deep into a trance.

He was so *close*. He could *feel* it...

He could afford to wait a while longer.

His past called him back, and he slipped into a dream with a sigh.

ON TSAGUALSA, FROM *the shifting flesh of the Screaming Gallery, the Night Haunter called forth his captains and rose to address them...*

The Heresy was ended. The other Traitors had fled. Chaos owned them, now.

Not so the Night Lords. Unseducable, their hate. Incorruptible, their focus. In their hearts Chaos could find little fuel to ignite its insidious fires.

Their hearts burned already, *with hate and injury; with the need for vengeance.*

Konrad Curze, the Night Haunter, gathered his captains as a father gathers his sons, and he filled them with pride and joy in the Bitter Crusade they would undertake in his name. They chanted his name and praised his wisdom, and he accepted their devotion with a melancholy smile.

And then he told them that he was soon to die, and everything crumbled to dust.

Sahaal was there. He saw it all.

And as the captains raged and boiled, as outrage bred denial, he watched his lord with a sad eye and knew it was true.

The Night Haunter would die – not because he would be powerless to overcome his attacker; not because he would be slain like some common foe–

–but because in death he would find vindication, of sorts. And, perhaps, peace.

The Night Haunter silenced his captains with a word, and told them that he would select an heir. He told them that he would take from among them a son to lead in his stead.

Sahaal had felt, at that instant, the first stirrings of an unquenchable ambition. He gazed from face to face of his brother captains, and wondered if they shared his hunger. If they wanted what he wanted.

Not power.

Not blood.

Revenge.

Most avoided his stare. Most remained flushed with sadness and rage at the news of their master's death. Most crumbled from his regard – from his concerns – like salt before a torrent of blood.

Only one met Sahaal's eye. Only one gloated with flushed cheeks and teeth brandished; pale lips ringed with tribal scars; bright eyes unrepentant for the aspirations worn within them: a brazen lust for the offered position that he did nothing to conceal.

Krieg Acerbus. The giant. The Head-taker. The Axemaster.

The Brute.

Konrad Curze closed black-glazed eyes and opened his mouth, and the name on his lips was Zso Sahaal.

SOMETHING RUMBLED AT the edge of Sahaal's perceptions; dredging his mind from its reminiscence and pulling him back into the light. He quit the trance as if casting off a cloak, his master's voice echoing in his ears, and was troubled to discover the meditation had done little to cure his nascent rage. The vision of Acerbus, in particular, had merely stoked the fires higher.

There had been little love lost between Battle-brothers Zso and Krieg.

The elevator was on the verge of arrival. The dial on the console read *TIER: 3*, and Sahaal calculated quickly that something in the region of two and a half hours had elapsed since his meditation – and the carriage's descent – had begun. As the capsule neared the end of its journey – its diagonal progress hampered by the changing gradient of the hive's walls – the shaft into which it was delivered began to rumble, protesting at the vertical stresses placed upon it.

One by one Sahaal's accompanying warriors slipped from their places at the gateroom entrance, sensing the arrival of their target. They gathered at the elevator's doors, racking weapons with a professional disinterest that did nothing to hide their curiosity, training loaded muzzles upon the unadorned surface of the heavy portal.

'Stay to the side,' Sahaal commanded, unsheathing his claws with a rasp. 'And kill nothing. I want prisoners.'

The warriors edged aside, clearing the space before the elevator. If the sight that greeted whoever was within was a posse of scowling outlaws and deephive gangers with more guns than sense, Sahaal was confident their first act upon opening the doors would be to immediately close them again.

He turned to face Pahvulti – still seated in the corner, watching with eyes and optics narrowed – and crooked a finger to beckon him over. His uncertain expression filled Sahaal's heart with infantile joy.

He knows I don't need him any more, he thought. *He knows he's expendable.*

'You stand in front of the doors,' he said, looming over the broker. 'You greet them. You draw them out. You draw them out so we can take them. Understand?'

Pahvulti nodded, mute. There was little else he could do.

Sahaal slipped into the darkness beside the elevator doors where his warriors lurked, and slowed his breathing, fighting the anxiety.

So close... so close.

Out of his view, around the corner of the shaft's terminus, the doors opened. Sahaal watched Pahvulti's face assiduously, trying to ascertain what manner of person – or people – was within by gauging his responses. It did him little good: Pahvulti's face was a mass of twitches and arcane mechanical movements,none of them obviously connected to his emotions.

A cautious voice ebbed from within the elevator.

'You aren't Slake...' it said. 'Who are you? Where did you get the codes?'

Something cold and metal racked out of sight. Sahaal could hear the heartbeat of his warriors accelerating. Whoever was within the elevator had a weapon.

'Friend of Slake's,' Pahvulti said, nodding and scraping. '*Het-het-het*, yes, yes... Friend.'

'You've got no arms.'

'Yes, *het-het-het*. No arms, no guns. No need to be alarmed.'

'What do want, raggedy man? Answer me!'

'Slake, yes? Sent me to discuss more... acquisitions.'

'Don't be ridiculous. We've got what we wanted. The three-headed freak has nothing else to offer us. You hear me?'

Footsteps clattered against the floor. Whoever occupied the lift – still beyond Sahaal's vision – was marching forwards to confront Pahvulti up close.

Several things happened at once.

At the edge of Sahaal's sight, creeping past the corner of the elevator, he caught his first glimpse of the man he had come to seize. It was an official of some sort: colourfully robed, holding a small pistol in his manicured grip. A major-domo, Sahaal guessed: a personal servant of whichever noble house owned the elevator. A slave of whichever bastard had purchased the Corona Nox.

Sahaal leaped from his concealment with a shriek to freeze the fires of hell: a banshee-wail that stunned the wizened figure as if electrified. Panicking, the fool's finger tightened on the trigger of his pistol, and at the heart of the thunder-peal that followed Pahvulti's head burst like a bubble, metallic waste and brain-flesh detonating outwards. Sahaal eclipsed the death from his mind and reached out talons to snatch the major-domo up, to lift him on plumes of air away from this ugly little chamber–

The light spilling in from the doorway – the entrance his warriors had left unattended in their rush to confront the elevator – was blotted out, and the thud of marching feet filled the world.

The Preafects had arrived. A *lot* of Preafects.

They were led by the witch.

THE FIRST SHOTGUN salvo decimated Sahaal's warriors lurking to the left of the elevator. Flesh left bone like jelly, pulverised beyond recognition. Thick slabs of paste scrawled themselves across rusted walls: powdered bone and strangled cries lost to the air. Hands clutched at nothing and were shredded, faces dissolved beneath an expanding cloud of lead shot, screams died in lacerated throats and warding arms, held across faces in primal protection, detonated like ripe fruit.

The echoes of the blast circled the gateroom like a captive bat.

In the course of a single second the Night Lord had lost half of his troops. The feathered headdress of a Quetzai clansman, still affixed to the ruptured clumps of scalp and hair of its former owner, slapped across his shoulder with a moist report. He ignored it and surged onwards, stretching out for the major-domo. Nothing else mattered.

The vindictors poured into the room like a tide of black-coated crabs, perfectly in step; ranks punctuated by the red stripes of an occasional heavy-weapons *dervishi*, or the unhelmeted snarl of a shouting sergeant. And the *noise*... the noise shook the room to its foundations and left dust curling from its distant ceiling. Armour clashing together, feet pounding the terracrete in robotic unison, voices raised in a sonorous chant:

'Lex Imperator... Lex Imperator... Lex Imperator...'

It was like an army. Even from the midst of his memories, dredged from the days of the Great Crusade, when glittering hosts without number swept across alien plains, Sahaal could not recall seeing its like. Perfectly precise movements. Every man dressed alike. Black. Shining. Hundreds upon hundreds of them, spilling into the room like oil from a drum.

A perverse part of his soul was gratified. *All this, just for me...*

Somewhere behind it all, through the tight spaces of the gateroom entrance – immovably blocked by the onrushing troops – a trio of Salamander tanks lurked. Command stations, Sahaal guessed, leading from the rear. Cowards.

He tried in vain to find the witch again; he had seen her enter at the forefront, dressed in rags, but had lost her amidst the swarm. She, at least, had dared to face him. He would enjoy ripping her to shreds.

Somewhere beyond his focused vision he registered a retort like the splintering of a thousand trees. Shotguns being racked, gloved arms pumping fresh shells into place.

The second salvo, en route; all conducted with machine efficiency. There was no cunning trap here, no subtle advance and flanking manoeuvre. Sahaal and his warriors were outnumbered twenty times over: bottled in a dead end, engulfed by a wall of black gloss carapace that seeped forwards like tar.

There was no hope of victory. No hope of defeating them. No hope of escape.

Not on the ground, at any rate.

And then he was upon the shrieking major-domo, wrapping gracile limbs around the man's midriff, locking claws together like the teeth of two gears. He spun as he went, turning his back towards the vindictors, shielding his prize from their pernicious attentions and kicking off; jump pack flaring behind him, delivering him into the air.

For an instant he considered leaping for the open elevator, riding its slow carriage up to the domain of whatever pompous noble had stolen his treasure. But before he could even twist towards it, dipping his rising body to bank left–

BOOM.

The second salvo. Right on time.

The blast swept the world from beneath him like a tidal wave of lead. His launch skewed, his legs flared with pain and jinked out to one side, spinning him backwards even as his feet left the ground. The ancient armour held its cohesion – its spirit moaning in the static of his vox – but where his greaves met his thighguards the metal storm peppered his joints and found his flesh. He shut out the pain, clearing his mind, and put his faith in the larriman coagulators haunting his blood. Unconcerned by the wounds he concentrated on restoring his trajectory – twisting with a furious roar – before his disastrous launch could deliver him into a wall or, worse, the floor: a greasy smear of flesh and armour. The jump pack protested at his ungentle contortions, the spirit that fused it to his true armour hissing deep in his psyche like a part of his own body. Its spiralling ascent smoothed, lifting him now at a shallow angle, fizzling and spitting as it went. It wasn't enough. The great snowgates, locked tight, loomed massively before him.

Mustering an effort that sent adrenaline bursting in his brain, cursing the weight of his captive, he rolled onto his front and banked hard, streaking across the heads of the astonished Preafects, silencing the major-domo's shrieks with a deft backhand across the man's face. With balance regained and agility restored, he whooped aloud and resought the elevator. It was too late: the black ranks had closed across it like a lead shield, and he dipped down in fury to rake a single claw across the Preafects' heads, shattering helmets and cleaving skulls like a ploughshare through their midst.

More blasts followed in his wake – no longer disciplined salvoes but panicky, opportunistic shots – thumping at the air like flak charges. But Sahaal was too fast: streaking across vindictor helmets like a ground-hugging missile, every careless discharge had little effect other than to scatter lead shot amongst the shooter's comrades.

In the blink of an eye the implacable advance collapsed. There was something in their midst, now:

something that moved faster than they could see; something that shrieked like a child and lashed out with bright claws, cutting and hewing. Something that could dance between raindrops.

Somewhere behind Sahaal the pounding of a hell-gun joined the acoustic maelstrom, reverberating like a drum between the breathless gasps of lasguns. His remaining warriors, he guessed, cornered in their tiny alcove, fighting for their lives.

Let them die. Let them take as many of the faceless fools as they can. Let them sell their lives for me.

The prospect was strangely invigorating.

He ripped a *dervishi*'s head from its body with a casual sideswipe, bringing up his legs to claw at another man's face as he did so. A fist caught the edge of his helm and he laughed at the futility of the attacker's blow, lost in a vicious world of madness and blood. He turned and crouched, igniting the jump pack with a spoken command, chuckling at the screams of agony from behind him as its blue-fire backwash incinerated a knot of scrambling vindictors, pushing him high into the air.

This! This is life! To kill and rejoice!

Immortal! Superhuman! Scion of the Haunter!

Feel their fear! Taste their terror!

It was... intoxicating.

And then something vast and black, like a great fist reaching out to seize him, slipped up into the air and bulged. He moved on instinct, swooping with the avian grace that was the gift of the Raptor, and dodged the unfurling veil with scant centimetres to spare.

Net-cannons.

He had not anticipated this. In the air he was immortal – or, at least, *felt* immortal. These swarming maggots sought to bring him down, to earthbind him: to tangle his claws and crush his life.

The giddying rush of sublime power crumbled beneath humility and anxiety. He'd been swept up in his own magnificence. How could he have been so foolish? How could he have allowed himself such arrogance as to believe he could overcome this... this *sea* of enemies?

It was the rage, he knew. That ugly voice in his head. That cold wisp of savagery, fooling him, making him reckless and unbalanced.

What had the Night Haunter said? Something... something about a flaw...

'It festers in our blood... It makes us fools, my heir... Do you know what it is?'

Focus, Sahaal! Focus!

Somewhere in the shadows the hellgun stuttered and fell silent, the last of his colourful warriors torn from their concealment by a vengeful plume of lascannon fire.

Cursing himself, vigilant for the next unfolding net to come billowing up towards him, he ululated and spiralled higher, feeling his hopes crumbling around him, claws sinking into malleable iron. Upside down, he scuttled across the jumbled beams and awkward buttresses of the ceiling, the major-domo still clutched to his chest. Shotgun blasts raked his back; ineffectual at this distance, stones cast against a mountainside. But there was little respite here: even now he could imagine the *dervishi* tilting lascannons towards him, bracing themselves against ferocious recoil.

Quelling the panic in his heart, he raced across the inverted topography of the ceiling like a fleeing spider, darting into every crevice; every lightless nook in his search for safety. Flashlights snapped to life beneath him, dazzling him like the wash of a miniature supernova. Horror coiled into his mind: a whirlwind of loss and shame. He was exposed; he was defeated. To a creature of the dark, such as he, the light was an acid envelope, scouring not only his eyes but his confidence, his dreams, his courage. Deprived of the shadows, stripped bare of his armour of darkness, he felt as frail as any human worm, and he clung there to the ceiling like a roosting bat, waiting to be picked-off.

A failure.

'We shall not rest. We shall not flee. We shall not succumb.'

His master's voice. Dredged from memories, again. Circling in his mind, now as always.

'No relief until the insult is repaid. No satisfaction until the traitor-Emperor is dead. No rest until the galaxy cries aloud with one voice, one shriek, one howl of terror:

'Ave Dominus Nox!'

Sahaal threw back his head, cursed the doubts that had even *dared* to enter his mind, and shrieked with the hate that had sustained him for one hundred centuries.

Let him die! Let him be torn to shreds! But let him die with fire in his heart and blood on his claws.

He reached out to the single massive illuminator, dangling like an anchor from a cord at his side, and he sliced apart the steel cable with a contemptuous flick.

The rig tumbled earthwards. He would teach these human scum the meaning of fear.

'Death to the False Emperor!' he roared, drawing his bolter. *'Ave Dominus Nox!'*

And he dropped down in the wake of the illuminator, clung to the major-domo with every last shred of his strength, and smiled a feral smile.

MITA ASHYN

THE FIRST THAT Mita knew of any danger, the first that *any* of the vindictor party knew, was a sound like the planet splitting itself open: rumbling from its guts to its skin.

The illuminator landed amidst the Preafects like an asteroid, splintering the rock floor and engulfing a section of the black-clad ranks in fire and shrapnel. Twenty men died in an instant, and like all those around her Mita surged outwards on the crest of a wave: a tide of broken metal and whirligig sparks. At its heart a sooty fireball rolled and blackened, tumbling upwards into a tall plume of black smoke, plucked-through by rushing figures and shouting voices.

And from the gulf above them, before they could regroup, before their dazzled senses could recover, throaty shots rang out through the shrill whoop of an airborne howl. Mita recognised the roar of a bolter: barking over and over, muzzleflash flickering on high.

Picked out in the haloes of the vindictors' flashlights, burning like phosphor in the sudden storm, the plummeting Night Lord rushed towards them – a thing of midnight skies and lightning bolts; able somehow to exude an impression of shadowed malevolence despite the brightness around it.

Its shriek cut the air keener than any knife.

Bolter shells struck each flashlight dead in its centre: unerring accuracy from a creature moving so fast. Angry eruptions shuffled shadows and shrapnel into the air, warheads blasting each torch to shredded metal, slicing exposed skin all around.

And then there was only darkness.

Total. Complete.

Endless night.

But not silent. The shrieks of the Night Lord became the whole world: a sonic vista of frozen screams and blood-chilling yelps. Others rose to join it – the moans of terrified vindictors; the shouts of confused and panicky men, corralled together with fingers on guns; the pained grunts of those who imagined themselves slashed, ripped and torn by the unseen monster...

It was chaos.

Here a Preafect would cry out: the sharp tug of an impact against shoulder or thigh preceding a hot burst of fluid, a slow swell of creeping pain, and then the piece-by-piece revulsion as the amputated limb failed to respond. Most never even felt the cut.

Here a sergeant's head thumped into the ruck like a moist bomb, parted from its body on the other side of the room, deposited from above by the unseen devil.

Here a gun hand was abruptly missing; here a slice of armour and skin was peeled back and gone in an instant; here a man hollered as his scalp was taken and his eyes filled with his own blood. Here a man tripped on his own guts.

Here a man tried to shout, and found his jaw and tongue ripped away.

Mita felt it all closing around her; a dizzying kaleidoscope.

The Night Lord was everywhere all at once: circling above, swooping to cut and kill with delighted impunity. He dipped down here and there; he sliced and he slashed and he shrieked. Blood splattered like rain; warm drizzle without direction or colour.

In the blackness, every shape was a threat, every voice a scream.

The rational core of Mita's brain understood all too well what was happening. The beast was not indulging in genocide, nor establishing a massacre. The odds were against it, and yet it had refuted the threat, stared it down, and turned it on its head.

It had coaxed forth panic from disciplined minds, and like a dam bursting its banks; like a stampede that could not be contained, those same minds turned in upon themselves, cut away any bonds of comradeship that they felt to those around them, and devolved, in an instant, into self-concerned, self-protecting, self-trusting beasts. They became molecules at the heart of a storm: packed together, chafing to be free, and yet repelling every other particle – be it friend or foe.

Shotguns rang out in the dark. Randomly fired, aimed at nothing but the night. They were killing one another.

There were too many of them, Mita understood with a jolt. Mustered from the precincts of Cuspseal and its surrounding cities alike, the vindictor force had been presented with simple orders: enter the gateroom. Kill anything that moves. Allow nothing to escape.

They had followed the commands with commendable efficiency, but in his haste to destroy the monster haunting his city Orodai had overlooked a simple factor. He had poured his ranks into the narrow chamber like sand filling a grail: piling through the narrow doorway, packing tightly together as they assumed firing positions. It was true that their quarry could never hope to escape this sea of aggressors, but the realisation that was rapidly stealing over each and every Preafect, marooned in a world of lightless fear, pushed forwards from the rear even as they turned and forged back towards the entrance, was that they were as incapable of exit as was their prey.

They were stuck inside their own trap, with a maddened devil.

It was not a pleasing revelation.

Their panic all but overcame Mita, then. Wallowing in its emotive backlash, blasting through her empathic senses like a flamer's kiss, guzzled by the completeness of the dark, the crowd's disharmony scorched her mind: left her shivering and afraid. She fell to her knees, pushed aside and trampled by the rushing figures, and all but lost control, bile rising in her throat. And always above it, like the ghost of a flavour, circling at the apex of the cloud of fear and terror that it had generated, the mind of the Night Lord tingled against her senses.

She would not approach it. She would not try to delve inside it, not now that she knew what manner of force protected its astral presence. Not since the creature's warp-guardians had come so close to overwhelming her before...

But even so, even without the benefit of careful scrutiny, even without the need to look close, to push inside and explore, she could sense the shape of that ancient, awful psyche, and oh... oh, God-Emperor... once more... just as it had been before:

It was like looking into a mirror.

The doubt... the power... the suspicion...

She surfaced from her horror at the sound of a firm voice; tentacles of psychic thought discovering an authoritative mind: a sergeant, she guessed, hollering orders from nearby.

'Binox!' he growled. 'Night vision! All men! Put on your Throne-damned binox, Vandire's piss!'

It was like a beacon. Like a tiny shaft of light in an endless wasteland. That one sliver of order punctured the panic-spell the Night Lord had cast, and all around it the shouting Preafects paused in their directionless flight and took stock, drew breath, fumbled for their goggles.

Mita made a mental node to find out the sergeant's name. If ever she escaped from this killing-room alive she'd be sure to commend the man to Orodai.

She fumbled around her until she found an armoured body, sticky with blood. Whether cut down by the Night Lord or blown apart by friendly fire, it didn't matter: the Preafect was dead. She scrabbled at its belt until her questing fingers found a binox strap, and pulled the blocky device over her eyes.

The world opened up in lurid shades of green and grey.

'Regroup, damn you!' the sergeant roared, and she swivelled to face him as if snatching for a lifeline; a solitary mote of warmth in a place of endless winter. He was nothing, she supposed – just one man amongst hundreds – but already she could see a circle of calmness spreading around him; vindictors pulling on night vision goggles, gazing around to see what damage they had done.

'Arm your weapons!' he cried, swept up on the flames of his own leadership. 'Shoot the Throne-damned shit! Shoot to ki–'

His head left his body.

Mita felt herself groan: a primal shock of horror and understanding; anticipating already what this would mean.

A pulse of blood jack-knifed over the tumbling corpse; a blur of *something* crossed overhead, blades outstretched. Something blue and black and bronze, which knew all too well who to target.

It screamed. It screamed just like a baby.

The panic returned harder than ever. Somewhere outside, in the faint light burning through the gate-room entrance, Orodai was shouting instructions from the back of his Salamander. It could do no good, now. Not from out there. Not so far from the boiling heart of this awful, inky place. The one voice of reason was gone; cut down with contemptuous ease by the unseen *thing*.

So easy to imagine horrors in the dark...

So easy to forget they faced a single foe. A single *mortal* foe...

And that, of course, was how the Night Lord worked. He dissolved his enemies in terror. He let them forget that he could bleed and die. He let them fill the darkness with their own demons, and when he shrieked on high it was like the voice of death itself; riding out to claim them for its own.

They had bottled a devil in a dead end. They had sprung their trap and thought themselves clever: and then the devil had showed them how wrong they were. It had made the dead end its own territory; it had dragged them into its own world – a world of darkness where it, and it alone, ruled – and now it would kill them one by one, at its leisure. Mita could no more pacify the frightened Preafects – lost to all reason – than she could push back the sea. They were all going to die.

She saw it, perfectly clear, in black and white.

The Night Lord would kill every last one.

And the only way to spare them all, to spare *herself*...

Think, Mita, think!

...was to give it what it wanted.

Her goggled eyes fell upon the colossal snowgates; twin blocks of tempered steel and iron – ten metres high – rising with the shallow camber of the room.

What does it want?

Escape.

THE PRESS OF bodies was too great. She'd struggled as valiantly as she could, keeping her head low, pushing through jostling Preafects like a rat between the legs of elephants. At every accidental contact there were rebuttals and curses – *'It's the beast! Sweet Emperor, the beast is here!'* – which inevitably drew the unkind attention of hacking power mauls, slash-stabbing blades and carelessly discharged shotguns. It was thanks only to the utter completeness of the dark that most attacks were carried wide, and to her precognitive senses that she had thus far been forewarned of any imminent weapons-fire.

But no longer. Abruptly the crush was too great; the herd of panicking men was packed together too tight for her to wriggle through, and each was too busy shouting and cowering to listen to the woman in their midst.

'Binox, you fools!' she'd been shouting, all along. 'Put your damned binox on!'

For all the good it would do, she might as well have addressed her advice to the Emperor himself. *Useless*!

Did... did I just think that?

Again, she wondered at the Night Lord's ability to sow discord. A death here, a death there; utter darkness and a medley of horrific shrieks: these, it would seem, were the ingredients of his domination. These simple things, able to turn hardened veterans of street law into cringing whelps. Able to leave her thoughtlessly questioning her own god...

It was, she admitted awkwardly, impressively effective.

None of which offered her much assistance in the task of reaching her goal. A shotgun stock blurred out of the soupy green image of her binox and she ducked it with a curse, amazed – besides anything else – that its owner could be so colossally stupid as to think such a flimsy attack could hurt the Night Lord, even if she *had* been it.

Another push, another repelling jab. This was getting her nowhere. She was so damned *close!*

A spray of warmth patterned her cheek, blood scattered from on high, and another shriek rang out nearby: the beast striking again, like an eagle dipping its talons below the surface of an unquiet lagoon, plucking out some thrashing silvery thing with a cry. Even with the goggles she couldn't see her foe clearly; only a blur, an indistinct *something,* trailing carnage as it leapt away, claws glittering.

The psychic glut hanging above the crowd reached agonising saturation behind her eyes: an intensity of confusion and dread that, impossible to block out, all but destroyed her. She felt her knees weaken and for an instant was sure she would fall. Staggering, she wondered how long she'd last beneath the booted feet of the stampeding Preafects.

And then the one remaining course of action arose in her mind. She could not reach the snowgate controls –

she could barely stand upright, by the Throne! – and like a drowning soul clinging to a rope she grabbed at the idea and did not let go.

The *animus motus*. Telekinesis.

Very definitely *not* her forte.

Like all sanctioned psykers trained by the Scholastia Psykana, her psychic gifts could be shaped and hardened, manifesting themselves as physical forces – albeit clumsily – like opportunistic swings of club and fist. It was a gift borne in the heat of the moment; an impetuous force with which to strike-out like a hammer when danger threatened; or to turn aside a blow before it could fall. Using it as a precision instrument, calculatingly reaching out to change the world, was something at which she had never excelled.

It drained her energy like a bleeding wound.

A good psyker knows his limits, her tutors had smugly informed her. *This is yours.*

Well, warp take them! There was nothing else for it.

Agitated, shocked at her own sudden disrespect for her revered masters, she drew a deep breath and steadied herself, clenching her fists. She tried to be calm, to reach out from the cold centre of her soul, focusing all her will upon the snowgate lever… but of course that was the wrong tactic. She needed not calm, but rage: sudden and impulsive – and to plan for such a thing was to immediately negate it.

Sweat beads pricked at her forehead.

Off to one side, as if in another world, a stumbling vindictor shoved her from his path, the blow of his elbow barely puncturing the psychic realm she was trying to cross. Her body collapsed to the floor, unpiloted, but she paid it no heed: lashing, striking, ripping out with immaterial fists at the gate lever again and again.

Nothing happened.

And then something cried out in the dark, and on the crest of a premonition she swivelled her head up into the inky abyss and saw it; the Night Lord, dropping its shoulders, lifting its grasping boots like an eagle's claws, and swooping.

It had seen her.

It was coming for her.

Directly.

Eyes blazing.

Filling her world.

Shrieking like a dying child.

She was going to die.

And then *there* was the energy she needed, *there* was the adrenaline and fear and mingled rage, and *there* was the crackling fist of her psychic self, taking form, locking around the lever like a snapping maw, pulling with all its strength. Pulling so hard she felt her eyes fill with blood. Pulling so hard her ears popped and her heart roared in protest. Pulling so hard she thought her bones would shatter. She thought her veins would explode.

The lever turned.

The doors awoke like slumbering gods, shedding the layer of dust and ice scrawled across their inner surface, grinding open like the gates to some forbidden paradise. An arctic wind cut between them, flurrying snow boiling into the cavern in tumbling waves, and with it came a modicum of light: a ghostly spillage from the outer shell of the hive itself – wan and incomplete, scarcely a true light at all, but enough to determine shapes. Enough to distinguish friend from enemy.

The vindictors paused mid-riot. Maul blows went undelivered. Fingers eased from triggers. Doused in feeble luminosity, able at last to settle their frayed nerves and seek a modicum of calmness, the Preafect chaos ground to a slow, uncomfortable halt.

And above Mita's exhausted body, eyes blazing in the half-light, the Night Lord changed direction with seconds to spare; a bone-jarring jink from the vertical to the horizontal, the robe-tails of the man it had captured fluttering behind it. It whooped once – as if in farewell – and was swallowed by the ice-spume of the gates; splitting the snowy night with claws outstretched.

There were bodies everywhere. Most were dead of shotgun wounds.

And Mita Ashyn, who had spared the lives of those who remained, whose mind had been all but wiped away by the demands of the *animus motus*, sagged to the floor and felt as if she'd died. She considered whispering a prayer of thanks to the Emperor. It was the sort of thing she'd be expected to do.

But then... the Emperor hadn't saved her. She'd saved herself.

Just like always.

A flash of familiarity circulated through her, and she recalled the reflective shape of the Night Lord's psyche. Such doubt, such solitude. He had nothing but his principles to sustain him, nothing but himself to rely upon. Just like her.

A young Preafect approached, carefully crouching beside each body that littered the floor, checking for injuries, calling out for medics wherever he found life. He reached Mita's huddled form and squatted on his haunches, squinting at the rag-coated bundle that his eyes could scarcely make out.

'You okay? You injured?' he said; voice soft with youth.

'I c-could use some help standing,' Mita stammered, all her energy spent.

The man backed away abruptly as if stung, recognising her face. Orodai had hardly been recalcitrant when it came to letting his men know whose testimony had lead them on this mission.

The Preafect continued his way along the heap of injured and dead as if she didn't exist, and it was only on the very cusp of her hearing that she heard him spit into the shadows, whispering beneath his breath.

'Witch.'

It was the last straw.

I just saved your life, you contemptible little shit.

Squatting on the floor of the Macharius Gateroom, bleeding from her ears and her nose, watching the crowds thin and the medics come and go, Mita Ashyn had something of a crisis of faith.

SHE SAT FOR a long time and considered her place within events. In the main, the uncertainties that troubled her – exacerbated, no doubt, by exhaustion – revolved around a single query:

Why?

Why did she do it? Why had she struggled so hard, since those long-forgotten days when the blackships stole her from her family, to serve this bloated Imperium? Why had she toiled on behalf of these ignorant bastards, these bigoted fools who feared her and hated her and called her an abomination? Why had she bled and cried, why had she poured effort and energy into protecting the glory of an empire that... that had no place for her?

Had she been used? Had she been enslaved by those who sought only her destruction – a tame little witch that they could wield like a weapon until she ceased to be needed, and then snuff her out?

Why had she never felt these uncertainties before?

That, at least, was a question she could answer:

Because you've never found a partisan before.

Because you've never tasted such bitterness in another creature's soul, and it makes you question your own.

Because the Night Lord feels exactly the same.

She tried to shut out the whispers, the cruel inklings that spoke with her own voice, that stoked the fires of her paranoia, but they would not be silenced. They spread to overwhelm her, and in a panic she turned to the one glowing fragment of her soul which they could not penetrate: her faith.

In its glow, all her doubts were excised. By its light the whispering voices were silenced.

Had she been used? Had she been cruelly manipulated?

No, of course not. She fought not in the name of these people, but in the name of the Emperor! *He* did not hate her. Was it not through him that her powers were granted? Was it not through him that the future could be navigated; imparted through his tarot and the *furor arcanum* like seeds of prophecy?

He did not despise her. He would not use her so.

And yes, his agents were a teeming mass, contradictory and contemptible. Let them hate her, if they must. Let them pursue their own agendas, let them lock their horns together and schism like splintering ice. Let the Inquisition cast her out, let Orodai's black-suited worms despise her, let the whole of the universe rail against her if they must.

The Emperor loved her. She was certain.

Mollified, she rose to her feet. The vindictors had erected several small illuminator-tripods to allow the medics to work, and by their pale light she glanced around the room, sickened by the carnage. She wondered vaguely what to do next. Certainly her usefulness as a combatant had expired – she could barely stand, let alone fight – and at any rate the Night Lord was long gone. There would be no hope of catching it now.

Should she report, then, to Orodai? No doubt he would blame her for this calamity, and the curses of hateful men was something she could happily do without. No, she'd stay clear of Orodai, for now. He had more than enough to be getting along with.

Besides, there was one final strand to this vast, tangled investigation that remained un-plucked. One remaining clue to be pursued.

The package. That was why the Night Lord had come here in the first place. That was why he had entered the hive. That was why he had faced the Glacier Rats, captured Slake, ventured here to this blood-splattered room. All to retrieve the package that had been stolen from him.

So what was it? What item could possibly encourage a beast such as he to wreak such havoc in a hostile place? And who could have stolen it from him?

Mita pursued answers in the only way that she could. She stumbled into the open elevator from which the major-domo had been abducted, kicked aside a dissected limb from the door runnels, and watched the doors close before her.

As the elevator rumbled to life, she wondered whether the Night Lord had learned from his captive the identity of his target. She imagined its blue-black form slinking back to its lair, demanding answers from the cringing major-domo, hissing and spitting. Would it be that simple, she wondered? Would he find his thief quickly?

She guessed not. Commander Orodai was not stupid enough to commit all his resources to a single engagement.

The Night Lord would find little sanctuary in his lair.

ZSO SAHAAL

AND THEN, LIKE the end of a beautiful dream, everything fell apart.

SAHAAL RETURNED TO his domain along dark and secret paths, slipping once more into the underhive through the abyssal rent in the earth that had first granted him entry. He'd been concerned, as he raced to cross the snowy expanse outside the Macharius gate, that his unconscious captive might freeze before he could even be interrogated. He needn't have worried: beneath the man's thick cloak he proved to be a porcine specimen, a healthy layer of fat providing adequate insulation from the cold. Just another decadent blob from a decadent world. Sahaal would enjoy getting answers out of this man.

He'd slipped down through the empty underhive like an eidolon, ghosting through settlements that had been decimated days before by the Preafect pogrom.

He sneaked through deserted villages and empty nomad-trains, musing upon their former inhabitants. All had either died or descended to join his army.

His Empire.

The mere thought of it cheered him; exorcising the insult of the gateroom ambush from his mind. His army. His children – ready to rise up at his command and wreak havoc wherever he desired.

Somewhere, in the quiet shadows at the rear of his mind, he reminded himself that they existed only to die. He would throw them into the jaws of their enemies to bring anarchy and madness to this fearful city, and in the crippled wake of their sacrifice his brothers of the Night Lords Legion would arrive to find their path open, their advance uncontested. But these were stifled thoughts, buried at the base of a mind revelling in its dominion. He admitted to himself that the very idea of sacrificing his children troubled him, filling him with an uncertain chagrin that he couldn't explain.

Could it be... could it be that he grew *fond* of them? Could it be that the mantle of overlord had settled upon his shoulders and grown comfortable? Could it be that he was seduced by the devotion and worship of his tribe?

Or was it simply that he enjoyed the power their worship bequeathed, and loathed the prospect of surrendering it?

Was this how the Night Haunter had felt – protectorate of the peoples of Nostromo Quintus; a dark lord who brought them peace and efficiency through fear? Had he loved the blind, empty worms beneath his command? Had it broken his heart to leave them behind him, when the Emperor came and claimed him as his own son?

Sahaal analysed his thoughts and, yes... yes, he was *proud* of his children; a paternal regard for their glories that flushed him with warmth and shame in equal measure. Already they had achieved so much more than he could have dreamed.

'Strike you at his hands, and he shall not cut you.

'Strike you at his heart, and his life shall wane.'

The hands had been wrenched from their wrists: silos of surface-to-air lance arrays that his strongest Shadowkin captains had led ragtag bands to cripple. Pocking the hive like kroothair quills, it would have taken an eternity to destroy them all, but the Shadowkin had done well. Those batteries that remained would exist in fear: their crews awaiting the arrival of whatever unseen attackers had razed the others. Desertions would be rife.

The heart... the heart had been easy. Unprotected and unwatched, the mighty vents that drew heat from the blazing heart of Equixus, feeding the city with warmth and power, were easy targets. Over the past few days, at Pahvulti's direction, they had been breached deep in the underhive – makeshift bombs strapped to metal diaphragms, thick plumes of magma and shimmering air scorching from every fractured edge. Whole tiers had fallen to darkness and cold. And now crops would wither and die as hydroponics *coleria* froze. The militias would find themselves quelling riots, distributing blankets, sharing out meagre rations, pacifying crowds. When the sword fell and the skies burned with Night Lords' vessels, they would be simple prey.

The city was far from crippled – Sahaal was too much a realist to believe that – but it *was* injured and bleeding, and in the face of such wounds the infection of fear was never far behind. When the blow came, when the city faced its darkest moment, how many of its stalwart defenders would stand in the Night Lords' way, with their morale sapped and their stomachs empty?

Not many, Sahaal guessed.

And it was all thanks to his armies. All thanks to the Shadowkin and their refugee comrades, blind little mice, who obeyed his command to assuage the guilt of the blood on their hands. He was their champion. The lord of the oppressed. The master of the dispossessed, who had taken their simmering resentment of the hive above and wielded it like a flaming sword.

He returned to the rustmud caverns by the winding, hidden entrance to the south. He would re-enter his domain quietly, he had resolved, silently, and once there he would torture the slumbering fool gripped beneath his arm to find – finally! – the identity of the one that had stolen the Corona Nox.

He returned to his territory with pride and triumph in his stomach, and he paused at the cusp of the tunnel's exit to survey his domain.

His mouth fell open.

The swamps were burning.

THE TANKS.

He had wondered to himself, as he soared above the vindictor crowds in the Macharius gateroom, weaving his fearful spell like an artist at work, why his enemies had committed infantry alone to his destruction. A pragmatic commander would have blasted entry into the room and bombarded him to paste with shell and mortar, grinding him to dust beneath the wheels of armoured vehicles.

He should have guessed the true reason. The vindictor commander was no fool. Whilst the hive festered and moaned with terror, whispering of nightmares in the dark, imagining him – blue-shanked and bronze coated, blood-spattered and burning with Chaotic fires – at the heart of every new disturbance that rocked the city, the Preafects' salient leader had understood that the *real* threat arose not from a single Night Lord, but from the army he had constructed.

Sahaal almost admired the man. He had seen through the terror-glamour, and reacted to it with a cold efficiency that matched Sahaal's own.

The tanks had come to the rustmud caverns whilst he was absent. They had come with cannons and howitzers, and as he stared out across the churning fires and darting figures that had once been his domain, he knew he was too late. It was over.

A voxcaster voice from each vehicle's spine declared, over and over:

'The Night Lord is dead... You are not our enemies... Disperse to your homes... Resistance shall be crushed... The Night Lord is dead...'

Sahaal's empire was crumbling beneath him.

They had driven a wedge into the refugee encampment, lighting fires across rag rooftops and straw walls as they went. A great phalanx of Salamanders and Chimeras bulldozed all that stood before them, crewmen standing brazenly on each one, glossy armour lit devilishly in the flames of the burning terrain. Despite the destruction the vindictors had been careful to discriminate amongst their enemies: assiduously avoiding the temptation to open fire upon the shrieking, fleeing sections of the crowd.

'The Night Lord is dead... We are here to liberate you from your slavery... The Night Lord is dead...'

It was a masterful piece of duplicity. Arranged against the combined strength of the Shadowkin and the refugees, the Preafects knew that they had little hope of victory. But with words alone they could divide their enemies: appealing to the refugees' self-preservation, shattering the bonds of terror that Sahaal had spent so long cultivating.

They fled in their hundreds, past the ravaging tanks and up, up by the long northern road, back into their empty dwellings in the undercity above. Like insects casting off their cocoons they threw off the shackles of alliance that Sahaal had forced upon them; they washed clean their hands of the murders each had committed; they ran into the dark with a prayer of forgiveness and a backward glance, and then they were gone.

The Shadowkin themselves received no such mercy. They had courted the daemon as their own master. No excuses of slavery could stain their lips.

The tanks gathered at the banks of the burning swamp, and one by one their mighty cannons angled, like knights tilting lances, towards the rusted island-drill. The tribesmen knew what was coming, perhaps, and swarmed from their dwellings with empty warcries and holy condemnations, lined across the beaches with guns blasting ineffectually at the distant tanks, calling down damnation and the Emperor's wrath upon their unclean enemies.

Ironic, Sahaal mused, that a tribe so devout could be so defiled. It was not the Preafects who had betrayed their Emperor, after all...

Should he act? Should he attempt to intervene? Would it do any good?

The cannons opened fire; great pounding slabs of sound that echoed about the caverns like the laughter of giants. And like geysers of metal and smoke, like a field of angry mushrooms of bloody-red fire that snarled and blackened as they capered upwards, the island was swallowed whole.

The Shadowkin died like vermin, and as his kingdom was toppled before his eyes Sahaal found himself sinking to his knees, overcome; wracked by such powerful emotions that he couldn't define where horror became grief, where loss became madness, and where insanity became rage.

He stood abruptly, body rising in a single movement, discarding the captive major-domo at his feet, forgotten.

Rage. Yes... He could focus on rage.

He knew where he was with rage.

His claws sprung from their sheaths with a relish he could barely contain, and he threw back his head and screamed: a primal shriek that burned away every thought, that stripped clean his body and his mind of everything but pure, unpolluted, uncontainable fury.

He would kill them all for what they had done to his people. He would rip apart the tanks with his bare hands, he would rise on thermals of death and glory, and show these pitiful humans what it was to cross the Talonmaster! He would–

Would–

It was too much. His brain was not meant for this. His mind had not been shaped to deal with a slumber of a hundred centuries; to withstand the barrage of loss and uncertainty that he had encountered; to feel compassion for the creatures beneath his dominion.

Kill! the voices shrieked. *Burn the world! Kill them all!*

He was a thing of war. He was a weapon of terror, to be aimed and released. He had never intended to be so lost from his brothers, to grow so isolated from the path of the Night Haunter. He had never been intended to be so subject to human emotion.

He was weak.

He was going insane. And he knew it.

Hidden at the mouth of the secret tunnel, bathed in the shadows of shifting firelight, Zso Sahaal's mind convulsed with the alien sensations – confusion, loss, uncertainty, loneliness – that it could never hope to withstand. His empire had been taken from him, his grip upon sanity had crumbled with it, and he spiralled away into a great darkness without end.

He fell to floor like some contemptible, shellshocked little human – a total breakdown without escape – and unconsciousness devoured him whole.

ON TSAGUALSA, THE *Night Haunter spoke his name, and selected him above all others as his heir. How had he felt, in that frozen moment? How had his selection ignited his mind?*

He felt... unsurprised. He felt as though he had always expected it.

He was the Talonmaster. He was his master's truest son. It was natural.

The brute Acerbus left without comment.

On Tsagualsa the Night Haunter dismissed his remaining captains, and to his throne he led Zso Sahaal.

'Yours, one day. One day soon.'

And he had told Sahaal how it would happen, how he had seen it: burned upon his dreams like a cruel pantomime, played out over and over every night. An assassin of the Callidus shrine would come for him, slinking in the dark, creeping across the writhing galleries of the living palace with her heart hammering in her ears, her fists clenched tight.

There would be no opposition. No attempts to stand in her way. She must be allowed through to enact the final grisly scene.

The Night Haunter, baleful eyes shining, lipless mouth trembling, turned to Sahaal then and made him vow it. Arms interlocked, eyes meeting in shadowed pools.

There would be no intervention. The assassin would fulfil her role.

She would play out her part in the endless comedy.

Sahaal vowed it, and hated himself.

And the Night Haunter, Konrad Curze, his master, made him vow to watch it all. To stare from the shadows to see it happen. He made him vow it on the sacred hatred of the Legion, on the insult that must be repaid, and Sahaal could no more break his oath than he could kill his lord himself.

He would watch his master die. And when the she-bitch was gone – her bloody task complete – he would step from his vantage and lift from his master's corpse the Corona Nox. He would take it for himself. He would show it as his symbol of office, and he would lead the Night Lords ever onwards.

He vowed it.

He would lead them as his master had done, with boundless hate and endless patience. He would unite them in crusade upon the Traitor Emperor, and all would be well.

And his master turned to him and asked him if he knew, if he understood, what it was that made the Night Lords weak. What was the flaw that crippled their hearts?

Sahaal did not know, so Konrad Curze sat and smiled, and told him.

It had something to do with power. It had something to do with rage. It had something to do with the fear that the Legion grasped, the terror they used as a weapon to destroy their foes.

Fear must be a means to an end, he said. It must be used as an instrument in pursuit of a goal, whether it be obedience or peace or genocide. Just as the Night Haunter had been used as his father's ugly tool, so too must the Legion use fear.

But to sow terror without cause; to horrify without goal – that way lay corruption. The fear ceased to be a means to an end and became an end in itself: seeking dominance over others; seeking to terrify them into submission for the simple fact of their obeisance. Seeking carnage and fear with spite and pleasure.

That way lay megalomania.

That way lay the seduction of power, and it was the flaw in the blood of every Night Lord. It was the flaw he had spent his life struggling to defeat, bearing in its womb madness and venom, begetting the fits that had plagued his waking hours; taunting him with visions of his own end.

That way lay Chaos.

'It festers in our blood... It makes us fools, my heir...'

The Night Haunter would not allow his Legion to succumb so easily to the whispers of the Dark Gods. Chaos had served him well as an ally – as a deadly fire to be hurled at his enemies – but he would not countenance its digestion of his Legion.

Their leader must be strong. Not in arm or in courage – that was the remit of those like Krieg Acerbus – fine warriors, mighty heroes: but too burdened by pleasure at their dark acts to lead. Too joyous in their work. Too hungry for supremacy.

He had asked Sahaal if he had understood, therefore, why he alone had been chosen; and Sahaal had lied with a nod.

The Night Haunter said he had chosen Sahaal as his heir because his strength lay in that holiest of disciplines, that mightiest of fields:

Focus.

He would not waver from the Haunter's vision. A vision of a united Legion. A vision of focused hatred. A vision of blue-black ships assaulting Terra itself. A vision of Night Lord claws closing upon the withered neck of the Traitor Emperor.

Vengeance for the ultimate treachery. Vengeance for a Father's betrayal of his own son.

And then, peace. Efficiency and peace through obedience. The Imperium would prosper beneath nocturnal skies.

All in the Night Haunter's name.

That was the goal. That was the focus.

All this Konrad Curze imparted, and Sahaal left him with a storm of vows clouding his mind, awaiting the coming of the assassin with baited breath.

SAHAAL AWOKE TO the crisp bark of gunfire, the acrid stink of ozone, and the unexpected prickle of cold air against his face.

Someone had removed his helmet.

A metallic chime peeled-out in the darkness nearby – *a knife being dropped?* – and with it came the sluggish retort of a body, toppling to its knees and then collapsing to the ground.

Someone with a knife, shot dead.

A voice gibbered in the dark. 'He was about... oh, God-Emperor... he was about to cut your throat, my lord.'

Sahaal opened his eyes and levered himself upright, muscles bunched and ready for combat, and the figure that stood over him with earnest concern written across every centimetre of her face took him by surprise. It was Condemnitor Chianni.

Beyond her, like the plateau of hell, the swamps surged and boiled and flamed. The tanks were stationary now; their crews clambering from pintle nests and embarkation ramps to poke at the dead bodies with power mauls and blades, checking for signs of life. On the distant northern shore, through a haze of smog and sulphur, the tail end of the fleeing refugees slipped around the pathway's corner and up, to begin the long climb to the safety of the underhive. There was nothing left for them here.

Sahaal blinked, his mind drawing itself sluggishly back to comprehension.

The memory of his master had absolved him of insanity. He had awoken refreshed; untroubled by the tentacles of corruption, released from chains that he had not even known existed. He understood now that he had been on the verge of succumbing to the seductions his master had warned him of, all those centuries ago. He had been tempted by the trappings of power. He had discovered within himself a love for Empire-building, an unconstructive regard for the plebeians he had ruled.

He had lost his focus. He had pursued only his own aggrandisement.

Chaos, whispering in his ear.

He realised with sudden clarity that it had been there all along. Since he awoke in the *Umbrea Insidior*: a voice in his mind, counselling him in rage and fury and power.

Well, he was free of it now. His master's words had cleansed him from beyond the veil of time and death. He had lost the patronage of Chaos, he had lost the swarming warp-things that buzzed and tickled his mind, and he felt more alive than he had since his arrival.

Ave Dominus Nox!

He breathed his gratitude without sound, overcome by the strength of the Night Haunter's wisdom.

No longer for him the weakness of rulership. No longer the enjoyment of devotion. No longer did he crave the worship of his underlings, or the obeisance of those who thought him holy.

He had rediscovered his focus. The Corona Nox would be his, and damn his crumbled Empire for the sham that it was!

He returned his mind to reality, making sense of his surroundings. Somewhere out across the fiery territory, the body-checking Preafects stumbled ever closer.

He looked up at Chianni and blinked, confused.

'You should be dead,' he said, aiming a wavering finger.

'I... I heard you, lord.' She bit her lip, throwing a glance over her shoulder at the vindictors, prodding and kicking at charred bodies.

'Heard me?'

'Y-yes... I was on the far shore, overseeing the returning strike-groups. When the tanks came I...' Her head dipped, ears reddening. 'I confess that I thought you lost to us. They said you'd been killed. My lord, I was... oh, forgive me, I was *fleeing*.' She tumbled forwards with a sob and locked trembling fingers around his clawed feet, prostrating herself. 'I have dishonoured, you! Forgive m–'

He waved the rant away, impatient. 'Never mind that! What happened?'

'I...oh, Terra's blood, I heard your cry. A shriek of hate from the south.'

He remembered. He remembered the rage and the fury; the last insidious surge of Chaos, frying his mind, claiming him for its own, before the breakdown occurred and his tortured brain rolled over upon itself.

'The others thought I was mad,' Chianni burbled. 'They said I was hearing what I wanted to hear, but... I couldn't just run! Not without checking.'

'So you came?'

'Y-yes. And just in time, lord.' Her face contorted with anger. 'The... the warpfilth had your helmet off. He had a knife, lord. I didn't know if you were alive or dead, b-but...' Her voice tailed off; Sahaal could see she was in shock, face pale. She stabbed a pointed finger to one side, gesturing for his attention.

A dreadful suspicion arose in his reeling mind.

He followed her gesture and settled his eyes upon the figure sprawled at his side, a smoking laswound singeing the colourful fabric of its robes; the shield-like designs woven across its surface now stained by blood and grime. The body's podgy hands clutched – even in death – for the discarded dagger it had dropped.

The major-domo. He had awoken whilst Sahaal slept. He had prised off the Night Lord's helmet with clumsy twists of his blade, and then he had drawn back his hand to slice the monster's exposed skin.

And then Chianni had shot him.

'No!' Sahaal roared, adrenaline burning his brain, raising him to his feet, spinning him towards Chianni. He snatched her up in one gauntleted fist with a feral snarl, ready to sink his claws through her face, red fires burning in his guts. 'You killed him!' he cried. 'You killed him, warp take you!'

'L-lord! lord, he was going to kill you!'

'I needed him! I needed the name of his master! You killed him!'

The claws of his free hand ripped forth, light motes scattering across them. He pulled them back from Chianni's shrieking face, preparing to punch through her wide eyes and shred her pitiful brain, exploding bone and gore across the burning swamplands. No matter that she had acted in his interests. No matter that she had spared his life.

The Corona Nox. That was all that mattered. And *she* had taken it from him once more!

'I know his master!' she screamed, eyes rolling, spittle flecking her lips. 'I know his master!'

Sahaal paused, eyes narrowing. He wondered how he must look without his helm, how his sallow countenance must horrify her; and indeed her bugging stare roved across his face with disgusted fascination.

Look upon your so-called 'angel', little human…

'You lie,' he hissed, unimpressed. 'You lie to save your life.'

'No! No, look at him! Look at the robes!'

'What of them?'

'The crest! The coat of arms!'

'Explain!'

'My lord… it's the heraldry of the hive itself! The Noble House Zagrif! This man was in the employ of the governor!'

MITA ASHYN

THE ELEVATOR SEEMED to ascend forever. Mita settled herself into a corner, cross-legged with her back pressed against the bronzed interior. It could hardly be likened to the comfort of her old meditation cell on Safaur-Inquis, nor even to the ascetic simplicity of the chamber the governor had granted her here on Equixus, but she was too exhausted to crave the comfort of fine things. The ability merely to sit, to close her eyes, to not spend her life glancing over her shoulder; that was enough.

As the minutes dragged on and a modicum of her energy returned, she found her mind wandering, rising on wings of thought, and a strange sense of prescient *pressure* – like a slowly building mass of water filling the spaces of her head – came over her. She recognised it, of course. It was the preamble to the *furor arcanum*: her senses' crude way of letting her know that a prophesying trance was forthcoming, should she choose to indulge it.

At first she resisted, choosing to take the time to settle her mind, to restore her strength, to prepare herself for whatever tests and feats awaited her at the apex of the elevator shaft. But the uncertainties that clouded her thoughts could not be so easily placated; her exhaustion had become a curious *constant* that required no salving nor assuagement; and how could she prepare herself for the unknown? Indeed, only by accepting the visions that the trance offered could she have any hope of anticipating what lay before her.

She surrendered to the pressure with a quiet sigh, closing her eyes and clearing her mind, and the visions of future madness poured into the cavity of her skull like a plague descending upon unwary heads.

FIRST, THERE IS... *altitude.*

The same old vision, then. Just as before. Always the same.

Coldness assails her, and though she is unsure whether she is truly a part of this vision at all, or simply watching events from some remote 'beyond', she feels nonetheless that she is naked: that ice is forming on her skin, and hot vapour arises from her mouth with every breath.

To every side the world is an abyss. She stands on a monolith of metal, a great cactus-spire that threatens to cast her off, to send her tumbling along its steepening flanks with whichever tawdry zephyr seizes her. She cries out, afraid, nauseous, although she has seen all of this before.

This is the fourth time she has witnessed this vision.

And then there seems to be something in the clouds before her; some unseen presence that breaks the squalling ice, that shifts like a shadow upon a pearl, drawing near.

And just like before, she knows what it is.

It is herself. Held aloft by a beast of smoke and shadow. Dressed in rags, hair cut and unkempt – and in some distant part of herself she recognises changes that have already been wrought, and realises that this scene, this awful tableau created before her, must be almost upon her.

But there is more to occur yet.

Her reflection's arm is gone. She bleeds like an endless river. She tries to see the monster that holds her up and it is indistinct… but already she knows what it is.

The Night Lord carries her into the squalling snow on wings of darkness and smoke, and it seems to her that for an instant there are shapes below it – bright-knuckled beasts that reach out with claw and tentacle to snare him – but he is too fast. He is too agile.

He is gone, and her doppelganger with him, and Mita is left to tumble from her impossible vantage down into the dark, where hate and anger boils around her. She has seen all of this too. She has experienced all of this before.

Except…

Except this time the trance-vision is different. This time there is no hag. No fat-bellied witch tumbling down on contrails of blood and fire, and she thinks to herself:

That was the indicator of another event, then; something that has already occurred…

The Night Lord's arrival. The hag was his vessel. Her bloated belly ruptured and spilled-out the prize that he had come to claim. That is the way of the furor arcanum: *half truths and twisted versions of reality.*

This time is different. This time Mita's fall from on high is interrupted. This time she is caught in mid-air, buoyed up by a steely eagle, lifted in its wake like a leaf in the pull of an engine. This time she is there to witness the endgame.

The eagle returns her to the peak of the metal mountain. It circles and swoops, and fixes beady eyes upon the turrets of the city's crown, where it has business to attend. It can sense something it wants inside. It tilts wings of jetair and fuel towards the monolith, and races down to shatter its beak across the steely surface.

And then the horizon is no longer dark. The endless night is on fire.

And the sky fills, from edge to edge, with the shrieks of hawks and the blood of the ignorant.

MITA AWOKE IN the elevator with a gasp, thick bile pooling in her mouth. She spat and choked, clutching at her belly.

The *pater donum* descended on her like a pleasant breeze; a cloying luxury that tweaked inside every muscle and every bone. Her tutors had taught her to relish it; to enjoy the one luxury her curse/gift would ever bestow upon her. But not so now: seated and nauseous within the cramped elevator, the *pater donum* could give her no comfort.

She slipped into a faint with inexpressible relief, and in her mind the screaming hawks that lit the sky plunged deeper and deeper into the surface of her dreams, plucking flesh and sinew clear with each swoop.

They flocked above her. They flocked above the world.

Her last conscious thought, before sleep claimed her, was:

They are coming. They are coming for us all...

SHE AWOKE WITH no idea how long she had slept. A brief instant of claustrophobic panic gripped her – what if the elevator was sealed? Paused in some doorless cavern? Never to reopen! – but, no, the gentle rumble of its guidance machinery continued apace. Judging by its pitch – almost totally vertical where previously it had skewed along increasing diagonals – she was approaching the apex of the city.

It was a thought that gave her pause. As an outlaw, it occurred to her that travelling to the peak of the hive – where even the stealthiest of intruders couldn't hope to set foot without discovery – hardly smacked of intelligence.

But what else could she do? Lurk in the shadows of Cuspseal forever, growing more hungry and more cold, more confused by the conflicting thoughts that assailed her? Spend her life running from the Inquisition, slipping down into the dark of the underhive like so many dispossessed nobodies before?

Spend her life wondering...?

Of course not. Passivity was not in her character.

There were two mysteries that gripped her above all others, and as she settled in her corner, feeling the ponderous machinery of the elevator grinding higher and higher, she happened to cast her eyes upwards seeking some indicator of its progress, and found herself agog. The twin riddles slid together; mixing like accreting puddles of icemelt, becoming a single unified issue, and all at the single glimpse of what was embossed above the door...

The first uncertainty concerned the package, the stolen prize, the Corona Nox. What was it? Why did it matter so much to the Night Lord? Was it truly at the zenith of this grinding shaft that it could be found?

The second confusion was older, an enigma that seemed to have settled upon her bones like a layer of dust, too thick to ever remove. She felt as though she'd been gnawing at it her whole life, drenched in the suspicion and paranoia that was integral to it:

What are you up to, Kaustus?

Two queries. Two struggles, separate but equally as chaotic within her thoughts.

And suddenly they were one. Her eyes fell upon the bronze plaque above the elevator's sealed doors, and everything fell into place.

It showed a shield. A carefully scrawled coat of arms that sucked at her gaze like some awful abyss. She'd seen it before.

A sword crossing a sceptre, set upon a field of snow, surmounted by a sickle-moon and a halo of stars. The heraldry of the Noble House Zagrif.

This was the governor's personal elevator.

So...

Think, Mita! Work it through!

So the Glacier Rats stole something from the *Umbrea Insidior...*

They did so at the request of the Slake collective...

Who had... had...

'Oh, sweet Emperor...'

Who had been commissioned by the agents of the governor himself.

The audacity of the plot astonished her, sent her reeling. Snippets of sound and sight rushed across her mind, making her wince. She'd been so foolish! Why had she not realised before?

'And to what do we owe this pleasure?' the governor had asked, when Kaustus brought her before him. *'Is she here to help us with the lock?'*

She remembered thinking at the time: *what lock*?

She should have remembered! She should have seen!

And then, glimpsed through Pahvulti's eyes, the Night Lord rasping his venom at the cringing Slake collective:

'Where is the package now? Was it opened? Was the seal broken?'

'It was not opened by us. It has been delivered to the customer.'

Oh, she'd been so stupid!

Two enigmas, one solution!

This was what Kaustus had been doing! *This* was why he had sent his retinue to quell the xenophile cells, rather than attending himself. *This* was what had kept him, day after day, sealed in the governor's company, dismissing every other thing.

Kaustus had the Corona Nox.

THE DOORS OPENED some two and a half hours after they had first closed, and they did so upon an occupant ready for anything. She had had plenty of time to dwell upon the epiphany that had snared her. Plenty of time to allow disbelief and denial to seep across her senses, replaced ultimately by a deep, abiding fury.

She'd been right. Her master had been lying to her – to everyone – all along. He'd known the Night Lord was real. He'd known, somehow, that the *Umbrea Insidior* would come to Equixus. He'd been waiting with eager hands to take delivery of the Traitor Marine's greatest prize.

Why then had he resisted killing the beast? Why had he risked its wrath; its gradual attempts to reclaim what was rightfully its? Why had he done everything in his power to *protect* the monster?

She'd realised with gathering gloom that her epiphany had simply birthed a new generation of questions, and at the core of her simmering anger the fundamental issue remained ironclad and unaltered:

What are you up to, Kaustus? What are you doing, you bastard?

And so she stepped from the elevator with a laspistol in one hand and her senses on full alert, anticipating attack or flight. What greeted her eyes – and her psychic senses – was therefore far from expected.

There was no one waiting for her.

The elevator had delivered her into the heart of the governor's gallery. Treasures without count extended into the gloom on every side; plinths bathed in hard light bearing jewelled gewgaws and priceless archeotech. And just as her alertness settled and she began to relax, once more the terror consumed her, the overwhelming certainty rushed across her:

The Night Lord was here. He was nearby. He was *close*!

She stumbled forwards with the pitiful gun primed, feeling ridiculous and naked. The certainty of the creature's presence – a stormcloud at the forefront of her astral senses, lapping froth-slick pollution against her psionic self – was undeniable: the beast's mindscape a unique image that she could have recognised anywhere, at any time.

He is here! Emperor preserve me, he's here!

And yet... Between each gallery plinth there lurked only an open space. The shadows of the room's perimeter concealed nothing but walls and windows, and for the first time she could remember Mita found herself questioning her senses. She spun and ducked, straining her eyes and ears, all to no avail.

She was so sure! So utterly convinced that her foe was present... and yet, nothing. She followed the pulse of his psychic presence like a bloodhound tracking a scent, and she moved between each exhibit with exaggerated care, all too aware of the servitor eyes tracking her movements from the ceiling, long-barrelled weapons inert as long as she kept her distance.

And then there it was.

It occupied the tallest plinth at the torus-room's natural epicentre, surrounded by a wall of blazing illuminators. Even had her senses not directed her to it she guessed it would have drawn her eye like the brightest star in the sky, by reason of its setup and positioning alone. Most peculiar of all, only it, amongst all the wonders of the governor's collection, had no judicious servitor to watch over it.

It was a box. A dull, uninteresting crate, shining with the oily lustre of adamantium. Across its surface ugly runes and obscene scriptures were daubed in red and white, and at its front – spread across the inverse of its hinge in the shape of a snarling skull, borne aloft on great red wings – was a cryptoseal. It was unopened; the beads of its interlocking plates remained meshed together, unprimed by the one word, the one cryptic phrase/code, that would send pins snapping into place in the tiny logic engine within, grinding upon ancient gears and unlocking the whole.

It radiated thought. It oozed malice. It exuded a palpable sense of presence that... yes, she was sure... that mimicked *life* itself.

She realised with a start that this was the prize. This was the item that had been stolen from the Traitor Marine, and the ocean of sentience that burned from within was so akin to the Night Lord's own mind that it had fooled her. This close up she could detect the tiniest of differences, the ugly inconsistencies that should have told her, long before: she had not sensed the presence of her foe. She had sensed his greatest possession, his dearest treasure; a mystical *something* that burned with an astral presence all of its own.

The Corona Nox.

'You begin to understand why I drugged you, perhaps?'

Kaustus's voice.

He was directly behind her.

He'd been watching. Of course.

Damn him! Damn him to the jaws of the warp!

'What do y–'

'I had to be sure I had the correct item. The thieves who stole it were hardly trustworthy, and whilst I could rely upon the governor's... *interest* in all things rare and valuable, even he lacked the resource to determine the item's true ownership. I knew that you would sense the beast's presence if I had the right package.'

Confusion gripped her. Had the duplicity truly gone so deep? Had he used her so mercilessly?

'This is... oh, God-Emperor, I don't under–'

'Naturally I couldn't let you get too close to the item. I'd already decided you were better off out the way. A microdart in your arm, child. It was the easiest thing.'

Stall for time, Mita. Draw him off guard. Keep him busy. Then shoot the warpshit bastard right in the face.

'I almost died! In my dreams... I... I couldn't get back to my body an–'

'Yes, yes. Very interesting.' Scorn dripped from his voice. 'Now put the gun down, interrogator. Kick it away.'

So much for stalling for time. She struggled to find a tone of rebellion in her voice but it was stifled, crushed down by the sense of defeat that gripped her.

'I'm not your interrogator any more.'

'Ha. Very true. The gun. *Now*.'

She bent to do as he said, and as she placed the pistol against the floor she reached out with her mind, probing for weaknesses. But no, Kaustus's brain was as impregnable as ever, protected by whatever mental techniques the ordo had bequeathed upon him. If he was accompanied by anyone else they failed to register in her psychic senses. There was nothing else she could do but comply.

She skittered the gun away into the shadows with one foot, and turned slowly to face her treacherous master.

He had stepped from the frescoed doorway linking the governor's throne room to the gallery, and stood flanked by six gun servitors: praetorian monstrosities with bodies moulded in polished bronze, bulging with stylised representations of human musculature, faceless heads swarming with sensory ganglia. In each iron-fused hand a weapon was hefted, and Mita found herself staring into the barrels of bolters, meltaguns and flamers alike. It was an impressive show of strength, but – psychically speaking – utterly blank.

'All this for me?' she mumbled, dazed.

'Ha, no.' Kaustus fiddled with a tusk, scowling. 'We were expecting someone taller. It seems he was delayed. I believe we have you to thank for that.'

'W-what do y… oh…'

And piece by piece, like a jigsaw completing itself, the fragments of enigma came together.

The Night Lord would have ascended in the elevator himself had he not been attacked in the Macharius Gateroom. He would be standing here instead of her, gazing down upon the prize he had spent so long seeking, had it not been for her actions.

Kaustus and his gunmachines had not been waiting for her. They'd been waiting for the Night Lord.

They'd *always* been waiting for him.

Kaustus had kept the Night Lord alive, despite all of her efforts. He'd left a trail of rumours and information, like blood in the water – from Glacier Rat to Slake to governor – to be followed piece by piece; a torturous progression of clues and hints for the beast to pursue. It would lead him here. To this place. To this gallery.

To this stolen item.

'You're waiting for him to open it for you, aren't you?' she whispered, dizzied by the scale of the scheme, the complexity of the lie in which she'd become embroiled. 'You stole it from him, but... but you couldn't open it. You had to wait for him. You had to keep him alive. You had to make him think he was gaining ground, coming for you, all by himself. You wanted him to walk into a trap.'

'Very good,' Kaustus smirked. 'And all without even reading my mind.' He held up his hands as if waving, displaying the thick blood that coated them. 'Which is why the governor couldn't join us, by the way. I couldn't have you performing any... mischief... on the little maggot's brain, could I?'

She peered through into the glassy bridge in which Kaustus had been waiting, and sure enough her eyes fells upon a small, crumpled shape; blood ebbing from its expensive robes. Kaustus shrugged. 'He was very understanding about the whole thing, come the end.'

Nausea boiled through Mita. Bile rose in her throat, and she swallowed back on it with bitter tears in her eyes.

Such duplicity! Such convoluted manipulation!

'Why?' she snarled, lips trembling, face burning. 'Why do all this? You had the power to stop the beast! You had the means to kill it! What could be so important that you've allowed a... an *abomination* the freedom of the hive?'

For a second the inquisitor seemed uncertain. For a fraction of an instant his face clouded, his brows dipped, and his eyes roved from left to right – as if he were somehow unsure where he was. For an instant his emotions and thoughts uncoiled from his mind, and Mita tasted the childish bewilderment that was an oil-slick through their midst.

'I...' he whispered, lost.

And then his features hardened, the gimlet-glimmer returned to his gaze, and his jaw clenched with an unpleasant rasp. He waved the servitors forwards, and without vocal command two wrapped sinuous arms around her, ignoring her strangled protests and dragging her out of the endless gallery, onto the vertiginous bridge where Kaustus and they had been waiting. The inquisitor followed behind, closing the doors at his back.

'You want to know why?' he smiled, hand reaching inside his robes.

She nodded slowly, mind awash.

His hand reappeared, holding within its grasp a jewelled lasptisol, and he aimed it carefully at her head. She tensed herself, the world dropping away from her.

'That's a question you can enjoy from within the grave,' he hissed, leering.

And then–

The steel eagle, rising up from the base of the metal mountain, tilting its wing towards the highest peak and racing forwards, snapping with beak and claw, to retrieve what belonged to it.

A sudden flicker of premonition, a recalled burst from the *furor arcanum* she'd endured within the elevator.

'Oh... oh, no...' she muttered, forgetting the gun, forgetting the inquisitor's glaring eyes.

The Night Lord was coming.

ZSO SAHAAL

THE SHUTTLE STRUCK the tower like the sky itself collapsing.

The cockpit crumpled like paper. Brass-edged dials exploded, cable-strewn consoles twisting as their mountings buckled behind them. Limbless servitors and vapid cogitators screamed with what scant vestiges of human surprise remained, ripped apart as conflicting forces crushed them beneath the machines they were created to control. Copper wires whiplashed through bulging spheres of broken glass, sparks infusing the air like miniature galaxies.

For all its smallness, for all its obvious frailty, the craft was built along the same predictable lines as so many other Imperial vessels: a tapered barge with a hammerhead rear and a beak-like prow. Its aquiline hull tore a crevice in the fabric of the hive peak, spewing flame and superheated fuel, burying itself like a dart into flesh.

The universe roared. Everything shook.

In the midsection, behind the flattened ruin of the bridge, Sahaal eased himself from a reinforced bench and checked himself over. Smoke was venting into the crumpled chamber and somewhere an alarm whooped endlessly, but he could find no serious damage to his person. As anticipated, the hardened prow had punched through the hive's armour like a bullet, compacting its forward segments and sparing its aft from damage. Even Chianni, strapped into place beside him, had suffered only scratches and bruises. She appeared to Sahaal unconscious: concussed, no doubt, by the violence of the collision.

The pilot was dead, there could be no doubt of that. What little remained solid of his body hung from between a pair of sealed bulkheads, driven together like the prongs of forceps; a fly beneath a swat. A thin patina of what had once been his flesh decorated the truncated bridge segments, and Sahaal was put in mind of the juice of a crushed fruit, trickling from sealed spaces.

Sahaal shrugged, untroubled by the man's death. He had served his purpose.

It had been Chianni's idea. With the Preafects otherwise engaged in tearing the Shadowkin territory apart, the starport that Sahaal had already invaded once proved deliciously simple to penetrate again. There were few pilgrims travelling now – the lockdown that had gripped the hive had seen to that – and he'd cut through the nominal security at the gateway like a beast possessed. Focused utterly upon the scheme Chianni had tentatively proposed, when the carnage was done he'd looked down to find himself made slick by the blood he'd spilled; a scattered ring of massacred Preafects and servitor bodies patterning the icy launchpad terracrete.

Focused rage. That was the key. Inglorious, he lost himself in carnage in the pursuit of his goal.

Only one shuttle had been ready to depart. They'd boarded it stealthily and followed the curses of its pilot to the cockpit; homing on his mutterings as he berated the indecipherable alarms squawking across the inter-port vox, confused by an inability to contact the orbiting trader he'd been commissioned to join.

'Like there's no warpshit thing *up* there…' he'd hissed to his servitor crew, even as Sahaal's claws pricked the skin of his neck.

He'd required little persuasion to play along. Chianni did the talking. Sahaal found himself too consumed by the burning urge to act to even articulate his words; sliding claws across the puny man's flesh to embellish every threat his condemnitor spouted, using her voice as the perfect counterpoint to his slicing art.

The knife had become a purer medium than mere language.

Let the edge of a blade be his stylus.

Let him cut and cut and cut forever.

Patience… his thoughts had counselled. *You know who has it now. You know where it is.*

Not long to wait…

They had risen through smoke and gloom, and then the battering flurries of ice that smothered the whole of the planet. Engines whining, turbulence rattling at its flanks, the craft had seemed infinitely fragile; an insect at the mercy of a tempest. Sahaal had loomed in the comforting shadows of the bridge, watching the trembling pilot with unhelmeted eyes narrowed, suspicious for any double-cross. Even when Chianni wrenched the steering column from his quivering hands to tilt the vessel towards the broad slope of the tallest peak, the man didn't realise the nature of the journey he'd been forced to undertake.

'There,' she announced with a nod, pointing towards a secondary tower that rose parallel to the central spire, connected at its apex by a narrow glass bridge. 'That's the palace treasury.'

'How do you know?' Sahaal hissed, fingers kneading together eagerly. There could be no mistakes. No oversights.

She'd seemed to bristle, as if annoyed that he still was unable to trust her. 'His collection's famous,' she said. 'Ask anyone in the hive.'

Sahaal had glanced at the pilot, cringing uselessly to one side. If the man had felt at all inclined to disagree he'd hidden it well, and thus convinced Sahaal had nodded his approval at the condemnitor.

'Do it,' he'd said.

Chianni had locked the steering column in position and pushed the pilot back into his seat. The revelation of what was to occur had stolen over the man in crippling increments, and even when the hivewall loomed like some steely god in the viewing port, even when the febrile light of the clouded sky was extinguished by the city's bulk, even when the impact was scant seconds away, still the pilot could not summon a scream.

Sahaal thought it a pity. Nothing soothed his adrenaline like a wail of terror.

He'd ridden out the impact without injury and now, as smoke belched from ruined machines and light poured through countless rents in the vessel's shattered sides, he lifted himself to his feet and brandished his claws.

He could feel it.

He could feel the Corona Nox, like a beacon lighting his senses.

Oh, my master... I can feel it! It is so close!

He remembered how it had been to awake upon the *Umbrea Insidior*, that rage-borne half-awareness, slaughtering thieves across the ruined vessel's shanks like a wolf; aware only that *it had been taken*. For aeons he had sat dormant at the heart of the warp, imprisoned within the cage that the hated eldar had constructed around him, and in all that time the presence of the Corona had given him strength. He had come to feel it as if it were a part of him; a strange connection that seared his psyche and drew a cord between his soul and the item itself. Weeks ago, when it was stolen, he had awoken in the certain knowledge that it was gone; as if a sound that he had heard his whole life – but never noticed – had suddenly fallen silent.

And now...?

In another ruined vessel, clambering once more through crippled decks, hungry once more for bloodshed and justice; now he could feel it again.

Now he was *close*.

He left Chianni where she lay – forgotten, beneath his attention – and raced to retrieve it.

At the craft's outer shell a strange process of segueing had occurred: the chasm-wound inflicted upon the hive seeming to knot with the craft that had caused it. In all directions torn sheet metal was bent and buckled; molten steel glistened and solidified in weird formations; cables and hiveducts twisted around hull sensoria like the tentacles of anemones, and everywhere the first gatherings of snow, probing hungrily at the city's injury, was scattered across the devastation. Illuminators flickered and failed, or else burned brightly with whatever electrical surges the crash had precipitated.

Picking his stealthy way through smoky chambers, Sahaal found it hard to say where the shuttle ended and the hive began. He stepped from a torn bulkhead imaging the outer hull of the shuttle to be nearby, only to find himself confronted by soot-charred tapestries and gold leaf pillars. As if infected somehow by a blemish of crudity, the palace gathered its splendour to itself and sulked, disgusted at the invasive entry. Sahaal scuttled across shattered flagstones and crumpled mosaics, following the pull of his heart; the strange magnetism of the Corona. The shuttle had buried itself across three levels of the tower, and at the head of the furrow it had ploughed into the structure Sahaal could stare into each separate room as if in cross-section, amused at the contrast between mangled entry-wound and untouched opulence.

There was little doubt where he would find his prize. The uppermost of the three exposed interiors was a storage chamber; gloomily lit and utterly ruined. The charred bodies of dormant servitors leaned from recharge booths and gagged on singed tongues, dead eyes lolling in sockets. The second level was a private chamber: gaudily decorated and flamboyantly furnished. A regal bed occupied the centre of the devastated zone, pairs of winged cherubim-drones clinging to its canopy like bats. Evidently a spout of fuel had doused the suite's interior, and now every exquisite tapestry was a blackened sheet, every gold-leaf insignia was a puddle of shimmering slag, every luxurious carpet smouldered like a burning forest.

But the third level, the endless gallery of tedious exhibits and pompous wealth; clipped by the craft's entry – the corner of its ceiling neatly dissected to allow him entry – *that* was a different affair. From amongst its endless parades of useless treasures the

Corona whispered to him, reached out to caress his spirit, promising him all that he had ever dreamed. He slipped into the room's cavernous belly like a lizard: scuttling along a wall, pausing every few moments with reptile precision to cock his head; listening, watching.

Was he disappointed, he reflected, that the thief was not present? Had he hoped, in his secret heart – still burning with the blue-tinged flame of unfocused insult – to catch the culprit red-handed? Had he yearned to bathe in the bastard's blood?

No... No, he could see inside himself now. The mutterings of Chaos were gone. He was stronger than that. Whatever damage his pride had suffered was irrelevant.

The Corona was his.

He found it at the room's centre, placed on a plinth like some common *librium* artefact, and his twin hearts felt as if they might burst with joy.

The package was unopened. The skeletal emblem of his Legion – the winged skull – remained sealed, its cryptic secrets unexposed. He reached out trembling hands and, as if fearing the prize might be a dream – a cruel hologram trick – settled them upon the box's shell, testing its solidity.

He sighed, awash with relief. He twisted the fresco pattern *here* and *here*, then placed fingers at the skull's eyes and tapped twice.

'*Ultio*,' he said, eyes closed. '*Ultio et timor*.'

Vengeance and fear.

Something inside the package chattered. A mechanical clatter shuddered through it, pins meshing together like a shark's teeth, vocal recognition engines awaking, and with the slowness that came from a hundred centuries' inertia tiny diaphragms opened within the skull's eyes, flooding them with red light.

The seal broke.

The box opened.

And Zso Sahaal, Talonmaster, heir to the throne of the Night Lords Legion – the chosen of Konrad Curze – lifted from its dust-dry innards the Corona Nox.

It was a crown, of sorts. A black circlet of mercurial metal, polished and undecorated, burning with an eerie non-light. To either side of its tapered ring there rose tall horns, needle-straight and jagged-edged, like twin sabre-blades dipped in oil.

But most stunning of all, beyond the simple elegance and curious captivation of the thing, set into the crown's frontispiece and suspended upon the wearer's forehead on a platinum mounting, stood a jewel.

A perfect teardrop of ruby-red, its face was uncut by diamond facets or inelegant designs. Smooth and unblemished, it had about it the look of an organic creation; as if not cut from the earth but grown; planted and fostered to glorious life in some secret crystal garden. And despite the dismal lighting of the gallery, despite the shadow cast by Sahaal's colossal body, it *burned*. It burned with an inner light. It burned with a radiance that was unconfined by sight alone, that broke the boundaries of luminosity, that flooded out the visual spectrum and dazzled Sahaal without even passing his eyes.

There was something other than the merely *material* about the jewel, and it bathed Sahaal in such peace, in such confidence and assurance, that the shivering of his limbs ceased, the perpetual furrow of his brow smoothed away, and he blinked a tear of serenity from his midnight eyes.

'*Ave Dominus Nox*,' he whispered, fingers caressing the circlet edge, lifting the horned crown above him, pulling it down towards his own skull.

He was divorced from reality, in that timeless instant. In a dream world of endless calm, the crown descended towards its rightful owner.

He would lead his brothers in their master's name. He would tear from the skies of Terra itself, shrieking with an eagle's cry. He would repay the insult. He would cut the Emperor's shrivelled throat, and paint the withered god's blood across the walls of his defiled palace.

He would have his revenge upon the Traitor Father.

He would be the Lord of the Night.

And then a shot rang out in the gloom, and the fantasy collapsed beneath the weight of dismal reality, and he glanced down from the perfect 'o' of black metal and into the hungry barrels of weapons.

Six gun servitors. Bolters. Meltas. Flamers.

At their centre, a man. From his slack lips arose tall tusks, and his eyes glimmered with secret humour. Power-armoured and massive, but moving with the stultified discomfort of one without augmentation.

No Space Marine, this, merely a *copy*. An impostor. The cruciform 'I' at his collar was all that Sahaal needed to see.

'Inquisitor,' he spat.

'The name's Kaustus,' the man grinned, mocking. 'At your service.'

The men held a small gun against the head of a smaller figure; a raggedy shape with unkempt hair and frightened eyes, whose struggles to escape the tusked fool halted the instant her stare met Sahaal's. He recognised her. Twice before he had met her, and both times she had sought his destruction.

The witch.

Confusion gripped him, momentarily. The psyker-bitch was his enemy – he had no doubt of that. Why then was she the captive of the Inquisition? Was there more than one faction at play within this elaborate game?

Is the enemy of my enemy not my friend?

The uncertainty did not last. Basking in the silent assurances offered by the Corona, it was difficult to feel anything but utter poise, utter confidence, utter superiority.

'Put the artefact down,' the inquisitor said, gripping the witch around the neck with his spare arm and turning the pistol towards Sahaal. 'Put it down and step away.'

It was, of course, a laughable suggestion. Sahaal sneered and bunched his fists, readying himself for anything. 'Never,' he snarled.

The inquisitor shrugged, infuriatingly calm. 'As you wish.'

The servitors moved with frightening speed.

Four sprinted clear of the pack, racing along the room's perimeter – bronze blurs with pistoning legs and eerily static arms, optic-pucked faces twisting to regard Sahaal even as they left him behind. Their very movements spoke volumes of their efficiency and cost: smooth and regulated, flexing with a controlled gait so unlike the staggering lurches of lesser models. Not mere cadaver-machines, these, but prime human bodies, sealed within metal sleeves, blessed with empty vapidity and unimaginable strength. Sahaal assumed they were working to surround him, rushing along the outer edges of the cavern in a flanking manoeuvre. It wasn't a prospect he could afford to dwell upon: the two remaining attackers dropped into firing stances, stabilising limbs hinging from the rear of their knees, weapons auto-racking at mechanical command.

They opened fire, and the world became noise and light.

They were fast, these toy soldiers. Quick to find their range and quicker to draw a bead.

But Sahaal was faster.

The hunter would not tolerate being hunted.

He swept into the air with a whoop, jump pack flaring, dismissing the tumult of detonating bolter shells and pearlescent tongues of flamerfire behind him. He must be focused.

They were fast and strong and accurate, but for all that they were as efficient only as the weapons they used against him; just as his measure could be taken by the tools of his own retaliation. He could not use fear against machines.

He *could* use blades.

He was the Talonmaster, warp take them! He was the first of the Raptors!

These zombie warriors didn't know the meaning of *fast*!

A melta stream glittered across his shoulder, too slow to follow the graceful plunge he initiated. At his back the governor's exhibition chamber became a warzone, exhibits blown apart, melta streams turning ablative walls to mercurial slag. Ice and snow flurried in, confusing the senses of the motion-detecting security drones, and within seconds the entire chamber was alive with lasfire and muzzleflash, weapons throbbing at the air like percussion.

Sahaal twisted and barrel-rolled, slipping with avian grace through palls of smog and ice. He dropped to his feet behind the pair of servitors and diced the first with a casual swipe of his claws, relishing the collapse of its unarmoured skull and the spume of long-dead blood that followed. The second rotated at its waist like a spinning top, legs remaining inert, but even as its flamer belched a jet of incandescence Sahaal was slipping to the floor, rising inside its guard like a wraith, lifting it up with his claws deep inside its chest. Its own weight sliced it in two, and its weapons clattered, dead, to the floor.

For an instant Sahaal considered grabbing one, to draw the bolter at his waist, but quickly rejected the notion. With one hand he must protect the Corona; to sacrifice the blades of the other in favour of something so base as a projectile weapon was unthinkable.

The reverie did not last long. Safely ensconced within their distant positions, the four remaining servitors seized the opportunity to open fire, leaning from cover behind priceless tomes and antediluvian fossils, walls of lead and fire and sound pounding and intercepting. Sahaal bunched his legs and pounced onwards, his prize clutched close to his chest.

It was clear to Sahaal that he had walked into a trap: the slow realisation that the inquisitor had been controlling his movements from afar, awaiting the moment that the Corona's casket was opened before making his play, was stealing over him by degrees. If that was true – a horrific prospect! – then surely the tusked fiend wouldn't risk harming the prize whose capture he had spent so long engineering? Surely that would be an illogical step?

Apparently logic was not a concept with which the inquisitor was familiar.

Whatever simple parameters the servitors were obeying, protecting the Corona from harm was not among them. Bolterfire raked across Sahaal's airborne body, chipping lumps of ceramite from his shouldguards and destabilising his bounding strides. Sparks scrawled vicious patterns across his chest and legs, toppling him out of control and sending him crashing to the ground, unique masterpieces and specimen jars shattering around him. The glutinous wash of a flamer rippled past him like a river, sending him rolling from its path with smoke lifting from singed plates. Even finding cover was a near impossibility: every priceless gewgaw that he ducked behind was attended by its own immobile servitor drone, hanging from the ceiling in mute vigilance, and the slash-stabs of lasfire from above had already punctured his armour along its joints, slicing his face in jagged streaks. He kept moving, strafing as he went, hopping into the air wherever he felt it possible, only to be forced back to the ground by a deadly crossfire from his assailants.

Beneath other circumstances, his storming senses reassured him, the servitors' inflexibility would be their downfall. For all their firepower, for all their strength and speed, they were little more than clockwork toys: obeying simple directives without recourse (or opportunity) to innovate. Their simplicity made them predictable, and had he been willing to wade through their fire to draw close, Sahaal's victory would be assured. But he couldn't risk harming the Corona, and inflexible or not their logic engines had directed them into a horribly efficient pattern: a four-way killing zone that left him with no path of concealment, no hope of escape.

He was reduced to a hunted beast, scurrying to flee from its pursuers, knowing already that they closed upon it from all sides. A melta-burn dissolved the elephantine skull he'd ducked beneath – a steaming lance of superheated air that ripped a hole in his shoulder-guard and ate at the flesh beneath, vaporising muscle and blood. He cried out and dragged himself clear, shutting the pain from his focus and drawing his arm back to its furthest stretch, preventing tightness when his superhuman blood sealed the wound.

Superhuman or not, he was being taken apart.

And then, like a ghost picking its way between realities, stumbling through smoke and fire, there came the solution. Small, vulnerable; tattered and torn, but moving ever onwards, reaching out towards him.

Chianni.

She had left the ruined shuttle to find him.

The servitors' simple minds did not even acknowledge her as a threat. Beyond their commands, without mention in the aggressive engines that drove their desiccated brains, they ignored her as if she was hardly there at all.

Sahaal's instincts rebelled at the idea that seized him, so tainted by a lifetime of suspicion and paranoia that the very notion of trusting someone repelled him. But he persisted; silencing his internal objections with a stubborn snarl.

There was no other way.

In Chianni he had found a slave that he could trust. An acolyte who had never deserted him. A priestess so mindlessly obedient that she had braved fear and fire, limping through a warzone, just to be by her lord's side.

He had gone to pains to make her complicit to his secrets. Let her repay the sentiment now.

With her, the Corona Nox would be safe, at least until he had slaughtered these upstart machines and regained his freedom.

'M-my lord?' she warbled, face pale, as he roared from the fragments of his cover through smoke and gunfire, bolter shells rippling the ground at his heels, and thrust the crown deep into her grasp, barely slowing.

'Run!' he roared. 'Get clear, damn you! Let no one take it from you! *Run*!'

And then she was behind him and he found himself unburdened, and with a shriek of such terrible joy that the hairs at the nape of his neck shivered and stood on end, he brandished his second claws and turned in the air.

He would stride through all the bolterfire in the galaxy, now. He would swim an ocean of flames. He would streak through melta-stream skies to reach the scum that had dared to face him, and when it was over he would put out the inquisitor's eyes one by one, and wear them as trophies upon his belt.

Unburdened by his master's sacred legacy, he could do *anything*!

He could–

The servitors' guns fell silent.

The world seemed to draw breath.

Sahaal dropped to the floor and hissed, wafting smoke and flickering tongues of fire obscuring his senses. The wound on his shoulder had sealed itself fully, but beneath layers of conditioning and focus he could feel the pain of it shrouding his senses, drawing his mind into the dangerous eddies of shock. He shook his head to clear the numbness, eyes roving into the corners of the smog-bound chamber.

The servitors were gone, sprinting back towards their inquisitor-master as if their task were complete, optics twitching to follow him as they vanished into the pall.

A cold suspicion gripped him, like the ice even now sending frozen fingers throughout the gallery chamber, and he turned in his place with it gnawing at his belly.

Chianni.

She should be running. She should be clear of the room, sprinting the Corona to safety.

She was not.

Panic gripped him, cold beads of sweat prickled at the skin of his pale temples. The condemnitor stood exactly where he had left her, the obsidian crown clutched in her pale hands, unblinking eyes fixed upon him through the shifting smoke.

'Run!' he roared, twin hearts throbbing in his ears. '*Run*!'

Time slowed.

The inquisitor stepped from the smoke and placed a fond hand on Chianni's shoulder, smiling. Sahaal's mind did a backflip.

'Thank you, *dissimulus*,' the inquisitor said, lifting the Corona Nox from her unresisting grasp. 'That will be all.'

She nodded, eyes vacant. 'Very good, my lord.' Her voice changed even as she spoke, deepening to a throaty bass, and before Sahaal's horrified eyes her skin writhed like a clenching muscle, swarming across bone and cartilage like molten rubber, dipping away in cheeks and eye sockets: *changing*.

When she spoke next her voice was that of a man; matching the unremarkable – but clearly *male* – features of her... his... *its* face. 'And my ration, my lord?'

Inquisitor Kaustus nodded, meeting Sahaal's eyes with a smug wink. He dipped a hand into the folds of his robes and produced a leather case, passing it to the newly transformed male at his side.

'Polymorphine,' he explained, smirking. 'You just can't trust an addict, eh, Night Lord?'

Sahaal's world fell away beneath his feet.

The battle in the Steel Forest. She'd been wounded – no... no, she'd *died*. She had died and this *thing*, this morphic obscenity, had staggered down into the rust-mud caverns to take her place.

Another betrayal. Another reason never to trust a soul.

He had nothing. He could rely upon no one.

All that was left to him was the *rage*. His master's genetic gift: focused by pain and insanity.

The *dissimulus* hurried from the room with its polymorphine fix clutched to its breast, and in its wake Sahaal pointed a claw at Kaustus's heart, eyes smouldering with the hatred of centuries.

'You die,' he said, and he kicked off from the ground; jump pack screaming at his back. And then everything changed.

Even as the distance between him and his target fell away, even as he imagined the inquisitor's smug face torn apart beneath his claws, even as the prize that had been snatched and regained and snatched again was within his grasp, light distorted the world.

The air opened up. Perspective struggled to translate what human eyes could never hope to comprehend, dimensions writhing upon each other, and in a rush of stale air and the bitter tang of ozone a blazing doorway crept open into reality.

Still Sahaal bounded onwards, claws outstretched, the ground blurring beneath him.

Figures danced from the swirling portal. Lithe forms of fluted limb and gaudy colour, tall helms and plumes of hair blurring at the speed of thought. And amongst them there came a robed prince, a runic demigod, antlers ablaze with electric fire, staff of office humming with uncontainable power.

Sahaal recognised him from his dreams.

The warlock...

The staff flared across every spectrum, crackling gaussfire enveloped him, psychic horror guzzled him whole, and as he fell to the floor with blood in his eyes,

Sahaal's final thought was: *They have come to finish what they started one hundred centuries before.*

They have come to take what they could not take then.

Xenogen scum!

The eldar have come for the Corona Nox!

And as Inquisitor Kaustus turned to their shimmering leader with an ebullient bow, holding the crown like some royal offering, needles of doubt and horror punctured Sahaal's brain, seizing his muscles and crippling his rage.

He crashed to the ground insensible, and knew no more.

MITA ASHYN

It was all happening too fast.

The inquisitor's admission of guilt, the arrival of the Night Lord, the unveiling of the Corona Nox. Held at the point of a gun by her former master, pushed and shoved like some dismal piece of meat, Mita had seen it all.

Something had changed about the nightmare Marine. The sight of him no longer filled her with unspeakable dread; his mere presence no longer wrapped cords of corruption and filth around her heart. No longer was he protected by chittering underlings; invisible and malevolent. No longer did the warpspawn of the Dark Gods gather around his soul like flies around a light: a living armour that she could never hope to penetrate.

Had he, she wondered, somehow escaped the predations of Chaos? Had he somehow cleansed himself of the taint that had threatened to smother him?

Was he now, like her, simply another pawn in this obscene game of manipulation and conquest?

Whatever the reason for his abrupt purification, its effect was pronounced: where previously her psychic senses could no more approach and delve into his spirit than she could swallow hot coals, now she had found herself free to explore. Now she could see his true self.

It was almost too much for her to bear.

It was a thing of such sadness, such loneliness, such suspicion and guilt and paranoia, that it almost tore her heart apart.

Pain, rage, ambition, sorrow. Distrust. Isolation. Bitterness.

His mind was like a reflection of hers, magnified a billion times.

She'd felt his brief victory – a surge of joy – at reclaiming the Corona. She'd spiralled with him into despair as the victory crumbled. She'd shared his pain as the servitors tore him to shreds, piece by piece, and she'd risen like a float upon the crest of his triumph as he entrusted the crown to his aide...

The aide, whose mind she had recognised. A swirling psyche without centre; without certainty or solidity of ego. She had seen that mind once before.

The unveiling of the *dissimulus* had come as no surprise to Mita, although she shared the Night Lord's horror from within his coiling spirit.

And then she shared his revulsion and his awe at what had followed.

The eldar came in a storm of warp-forces so focused, so potent, that Mita slipped to her knees and bled from her ears. Kaustus had left her beneath the guard of his four gun servitors – toys, no doubt, of the murdered governor – and even as she stumbled at the astral crescendo dizzying her senses their guns remained focused intractably upon her head. She didn't care. They were a side-show; an insignificant concern when placed beside what was now unveiling across the smoke and devastation of the room.

Kaustus, you bastard. You made a deal with the devil...

As part of the Ordo Xenos, Mita knew more than most of the alien scourge that was the eldar. Ancient and technologically superior; that their bodies were ostensibly similar to humans' was the one aspect of their race that could be considered familiar. They thought differently. They moved differently. They lived lives of carefully partitioned vocation: monkish existences devoted utterly to a single pathway.

Humanity travelled in the warp like trees casting seeds arbitrarily into the wind; placing trust in providence, guided only by the most rudimentary of navigatory processes. To humanity the warp was an untameable ocean, in which only the foolhardy dared to swim.

The eldar had built roads across it.

They grew old at the speed of stars. They fought like ghosts. Where the teeming masses of the Imperium struggled with crude senses and ugly language, the eldar burned bright with thought: a level of astral awareness and psionic capability that reduced Mita's talents to those of a child. She was a beast compared to them: a primitive fool, barely able to remember to breathe.

She was a baby in the presence of demigods, and at the quiet rear of her mind where the awe at the aliens' arrival had not yet penetrated, where she did not share the pain and rage inculcating the Night Lord's thoughts, she wondered:

Is this how other humans think of me?

It this why they hate me so?

Privileged knowledge or not, the eldar were as great a mystery to Mita as they were to any other human. In her studies in the Librium Xenos on Safaur Inquis the testimony of countless inquisitors was the same: the eldar seemed to act without motive – random and abstract – playing out some ineffable game according to alien rules that only they comprehended. All that was known was this:

Their grasp upon the future, upon the vortex of chance and event that was borne on the warp like froth on a sickened ocean, was unrivalled.

Kaustus had known somehow that the Corona Nox would arrive on Equixus.

It had been foreseen...

He'd been in league with the xenos from the beginning...

There seemed to be eight of them, although it was difficult to say with any certainty; they moved like liquid light, capering and bounding, never still. She thought she could make out weapons clutched in their long limbs, flat-headed catapults like the fruits of an exotic tree. They slipped from their portal – an entrance, she guessed, to their famed 'webway' of tunnels and paths that circumnavigated the warp itself – like a knot of frail decorations swept upon the wind: armour of blue and yellow laced by a billion engravings, a myriad of serpentine runes and glowing sigils. And at their head, burning Mita's psychic gaze like a phosphor lamp, their leader.

He dealt with the striking Night Lord with a single swipe of his staff, wyrd lights flaring between its glaive-pommel and the robed creature's antlered helm. Watching it all, probing the Night Lord's astral self at the moment of his defeat, she felt his collapse as though struck herself.

Somewhere, in another world, the eldar gathered around Inquisitor Kaustus. Somewhere, impossibly distant, the tusked man stretched out his hands towards the warlock, the Corona Nox held firm in his grasp. Somewhere the antlered xeno reached out to receive it.

Mita regarded it all as if it were a dream, spiralling away from her at the moment of awakening, and it was only as blackness closed in upon her that she came to understand what had happened.

She had been inside the Night Lord's mind when the eldar lashed out. The Traitor Marine had been knocked down, his senses overwhelmed, his certainties pulverised. He'd been crippled by the strength of the warlock's attack, and as he crashed to the floor and lay still, as his mind shut down and entered a troubled, enforced slumber–

–Mita's mind was dragged down with it.

SHE FOUND HERSELF *immersed within a world unlike any she had seen before. Purple skies raged like bruises; tormented clouds swirling and gathering together – defying the logic of what little breeze there seemed to be. Faces leered from their gaseous topography: half-seen grotesqueries that Mita neither recognised nor cared to see fully.*

The ground itself seemed little more solid: a porous sheet of sand and rock that, against all sense, felt spongy to the touch. A charge filled the air, a greasy static that clicked in the ends of her ragged hair and oppressed her skull, like a coming storm.

Nothing seemed real, here. Distant mountain peaks wavered like uncertain mirages; wobbling in their foothill roots; vanishing and reappearing at the whim of…

Who?

For a fearful instant Mita wondered if she had somehow travelled to a world of daemon world. She had heard of such places: confused realms where physics held little sway, where every aspect of every molecule was inseparable from the stuff of Chaos itself. Such worlds were the dreaded rumour of the Inquisition, and as Mita stumbled across fractured landscapes, negotiating ethereal gorges and sudden rivers that oozed from nowhere, the fear that she had somehow been transported to one lay heavy in her mind.

But, no... No, this was no Chaotic realm. The more she observed its howling skies and its weird tides of light and dark; the more she studied the scenes that shimmered in the surfaces of puddles and the images borne on the crest of rocks; the more she sent feelers from her own mind tasting at the sand itself, the more she came to realise where she was. She recognised its flavour.

As if to double check, she paused and stared at her hand; concentrating, altering her perceptions, working hard to focus her psychic self.

'Sword,' she said.

A bright sabre appeared in her palm. She nodded, unsurprised, and walked on, casting the blade away. It vanished before it landed.

She found the Night Lord, as she had known she would, at the peak of a plateau, ringed by a cauldron of rocky outcrops, set upon a cross of stone. Chains bound his arms to the rock, snaking between his ankles and his wrists, pinioning him like a butterfly upon a page. His armour and helm were gone. His claws had been taken from him.

For the first time, unconcealed by shadow or night, unmoving and unresisting, she saw him clearly. His skin was so pale as to be almost translucent, revealing along arms and legs every blue vein, every inner augmentation, every limpet-like crater where some ancient injury had marked his flesh. Across his shoulders and chest the skin was concealed, hidden behind an exterior layer of black plating that, in places, dipped beneath his flesh, intermingling with muscle cords and bony outcrops.

She had never seen so many scars in her life.

Most remarkable was his face. She had expected a countenance of malevolence. Of unrestrained and unrepentant evil. She had expected snarls and burning embers for eyes; a daemonic visage that brandished its corruption openly, like a festering wound.

Instead she found herself meeting the gaze of a troubled child. Oh, his face was that of a man – sallow and gaunt, perhaps, twisted by too many years of frowns and rages – but his eyes were an infant's. Impossibly old, and yet so full of bewilderment. They were the eyes of a youth that had never been allowed to grow old, that had been plucked from its humanity at an early age and never since allowed to return.

'Where is this?' the crucified man said, and if he retained any sense of trauma from the madness of the gallery room, or the rage that had gripped him at the moment the eldar warlock had attacked, he gave no sign of it. He seemed to Mita to be in shock; his voice monotone, his eyes unblinking.

He was a pathetic thing, she thought, spread-eagled before her.

'This is your mind,' she replied, unable to bring herself to hate him. 'A dream, if you like. You're trapped here.'

'And you?'

She shrugged. 'I don't know. Perhaps I'm trapped too.'

He considered this. For all the surrealism of the situation, for all the horror of finding oneself crucified and stripped of their armour, he seemed remarkably calm.

'The eldar did this?' he asked.

'In a way, yes… They made you do it to yourself.'

He nodded as if unsurprised. 'Yes. Yes, they've done it before. Though not to my mind.'

Mita frowned. 'Oh?'

A distant look stole the Night Lord's gaze. 'At the start,' he said. 'The assassin killed my master. She took the prize, s-so I followed. You see? I took it back from her, but the eldar came.'

'The prize? You mean the Corona Nox?'

'The Corona, yes... Yes, they tried to steal it, but I prevailed. I would not let them have it, witch, you understand? So they tricked me. They trapped me. My ship. All of us, deep in the warp.'

'What is the Corona Nox?' Mita asked, giving voice to the question that had tormented her so long.

For the first time since she entered this weird realm, his face creased in a frown, eyes dipping to meet hers. He looked as if her ignorance wounded him, deep within. 'You don't know?'

She shrugged. 'It... it looked like a crown.'

'Ha! Just a crown?' He shook his head, black eyes flashing. 'No, little witch, it's more than that. Fashioned by the Night Haunter himself, forged from the adamantium core of Nostromo, his birthworld. He wore it through all his life, and when he would have screamed with insanity and terror, it calmed him. When he would have listened to the whispers of the warp, it deafened him. When he burned with vengeance for the injuries his father wrought upon him, then it tasted his anger and stored it away. It's all that remains of my master, witch. Imbued with his divine essence, sealed with a perfect bloodstone. It is no mere crown.

'It is the captaincy of the Night Lords. He bequeathed it to me on the day he was murdered.'

Understanding came to Mita piece by piece, and with it came disbelief.

'But... but that's... Konrad Curze was killed millennia ago...'

His frown deepened. 'Ten *millennia. One hundred centuries. I have been imprisoned a long time.'*

And she knew as soon as she heard it that he spoke the truth. She sagged to her knees, astonished, overwhelmed by the ancientness of the creature before her.

He had been hating for aeons.

She knew she ought to destroy him, this atavistic relic of the Great Heresy. He was, after all, vulnerable before her. Naked; defenceless. Here, in this realm of psychic material, trapped within his own brain as if sealed inside-out, here she could crush him like a worm. In her mind's eye she imagined a weapon forming within her hand, and sure enough a cold weight sagged into existence, gathering solidity.

But his eyes...

So lonely. So wounded.

'Who are you?' he said, derailing her thoughts. 'Who do you serve?'

She swallowed and hid the gun behind her back, diverting her dangerous thoughts towards his question, relieved at the distraction. 'I am Mita Ashyn. Interrogator of the Divine Emperor's Holy Inquisition.'

'You serve this... this Kaustus? The one who has stolen my inheritance?'

'Yes. No... I did. Once. Not any more'

'He rejected you, yes? Cast you aside.'

'It's not that simple, I–'

'It's always that simple.' He looked away. 'For the likes of us, at least.'

'What do you mean?'

'You know what I mean, little witch. Little mutant. Little abomination.'

She shook her head, forcing herself to calm, clearing her mind. 'You won't anger me, traitor,' she said.

The Night Lord tried to shrug, chains tightening across shoulders and arms, and returned his eyes to her face. 'I don't seek your anger,' he said, voice calm. 'Only your understanding. I ask you again: who do you serve?'

'I told you. I serve the Imperium.'

'But they hate you.'

'The Emperor does not! Ave Imperator! *The Emperor loves all who give him praise!'*

'Ha. You believe that, do you?'

The words formed in her head as if automatic: of course she believed it! Of course the Emperor loved her! And yet even in the confines of her mind, unspoken aloud, such dogma sounded empty, thoughtless, the recitals of a simpleton who knew no better.

Frustrated, angered by her inner turmoil, she raised the gun and aimed at the Night Lord's heart.

'I don't have to listen to you, traitor,' she said.

The quaver in her voice was impossible to conceal.

And oh, oh warpspit and piss, she did *need to listen to it. She* did *need to hear what the beast had to say.*

Why? Why did she feel so obliged?

A self-appointed test of her faith, perhaps?

Or perhaps just the comfort of knowing she was not alone in feeling such doubts…

The crucified beast gave no sign of fear at the gun's wavering attention.

'So,' he nodded, brows arching, 'you have the love of one being, out of countless billions? And that is enough?'

'More than enough! You'd understand if you hadn't turned from His light.'

He smiled, genuine warmth appearing on frozen features. 'And can there be an Emperor, without an Empire*?'*

'No, but–'

'No. They are intertwined. One billion billion souls despise you. A single soul – so you say – loves you. You don't think this a bitter ratio?'

'Without the Emperor's love there is nothing. Vacuus Imperator diligo illic est nusquam.*'*

She was reduced to parroting lessons of her youth, and the Night Lord's slow smile told her that he knew it.

'I used to think the same,' he said, as if conceding a generous point. Then: 'Once.'

She racked the gun meaningfully, trying to find a reserve of conviction in her voice.

'Spare me your attempts at corruption. My faith is stronger than steel.'

He leaned down from his tall perch, eyes brimming with earnest curiosity. 'Why do you fight me,' he asked, 'when we are the same?'

'I'm nothing like you!'

A petulant rage gripped her then, the last vestiges of her tattered pride spreading wings of outrage at the very suggestion of her likeness to that... that devil*... and before she could stop herself she'd squeezed the trigger of the apparated weapon.*

The shot struck the crucified figure in his side, tearing a strange slash of flesh clear, to boil off into the sky, dissolving as it went; and in this curious inner-realm what flowed from the rent was not blood, but light.

He gave no sign of pain.

'Of course you are,' he hissed, and any trace of shock was gone now; any sense of childish bewilderment was lost. Now his eyes glimmered with guile. 'You are the unclean filth that serves in His name. You are the hated one. They fear you, and they loathe you, but still they use you...'

'No, no...'

'Yes. They use you up until you cease to be useful, you understand? And what then, little witch? You think they will thank *you?'*

'It's... you're wrong... it's not like that...'

'The only difference between us, girl, is that where you still wear your yoke of slavery, my master broke me free!'

Mita almost roared, sudden venom choking her mind, clearing the clouds of doubt that the Night Lord had sowed. 'Free?' she snarled. 'You got your freedom by turning to Chaos! You got your salvation from Heresy, warp take you! That's not freedom – that's insanity!'

Such calmness in his face. Such ancient sadness.

'You're wrong, child. We were never slaves to the Dark Powers. We fought beneath a banner of hate, not of corruption.'

'Hate? What did you *have to hate? You fell from grace by choice, traitor, you were not pushed!'*

For the first time real, honest emotion ignited behind his eyes. This was not a part of some elaborate game of words, she understood suddenly. This sentiment boiled from his guts and infected the air before him like a cloud of locusts; as heavy with conviction as it was with contempt.

'Hate for the accursed Emperor. Hate for your withered god.'

'I'll kill you! Speak one more word of this filth and I'll–'

'You ask what I hate? I hate a creature that speaks of pride and honour, that fosters the love of his sons, that smiles and scrapes at every obedient act, and then turns like a diseased dog and stabs his own child in the spine!'

'Shut up! Shut up, damn you!'

'I hate a being so sick, *so certain of his own brilliance, so twisted by the call of glory, that he repays the greatest sacrifice of all with* betrayal!'

Mita seized at the flapping cords of the Night Lord's voice, struggling to pull herself free of the confusion gripping her.

'Sacrifice? Your master sacrificed nothing but his soul!'

The Night Lord's eyes bored into her.

'He sacrificed his humanity, child.'

And suddenly his voice was so melancholic, so deep and so calm, so bloated by sadness, that Mita found all her rage dissolved. The gun faltered in her grip and she lowered it, tears in her eyes.

'W-what?'

'He became a monster. He formed us, his Night Lords, in his own image: to spread terror and hate, to forge obedience through fear. He rescinded whatever purity he had, he cast off the humanity that was never intended for him... he risked insanity and damnation, and all to bring order *to his father's Imperium.'*

'He sacrificed his soul to the dark, and–'

'You aren't listening. You weren't there. *I tell you, little witch: he sacrificed his soul at the Emperor's behest. He became the tame monster the Imperium needed. And how was he repaid? He was reined in. He was humiliated before his brothers. And then? The assassin's kiss.'*

'He went too far! The histories do not lie! The excesses of the Night Lords are famed thr–'

'Excesses? We obeyed every order! We did what was asked of us! Listen to me, child! The "excesses" of the Night Haunter were sanctioned!*'*

'No...' her mind rebelled at the suggestion, lights flashing before her eyes. 'No, no, no... the Emperor would never countenance th–'

'He needed order, where only savagery could bring it. He sent in the Night Lords, and we gave him the order he yearned. And then he made us his scapegoats. He cried with false outrage, and the Imperium cried with him.'

'You're wrong, you're wrong, you're wrong...'

'My master craved nothing but pride from his father. And all that he ever received was scorn. Little wonder he threw-in his lot with the Heretic rabble. Little wonder he marched to war beside them, sensing that they might weaken his father's grip. He was wrong.'

'...no no no no no...'

'Look at me, child. Look at me!*'*

Mita's head snapped up at the command, the empty mumblings falling away from her mouth. It was all too much to take; too much to absorb. Too much for a single mind to contain.

'My master was killed by an assassin. You know this, yes?'

She dredged details from long-gone lessons, struggling to recall histories that had seemed so unreal, so mired in the soup of myth.

'Y-yes… yes, she was sent to kill the fiend w-when the Heresy was over… The other Legions fled in… in disarray. Not the Night Lords. The High Lords of Terra, they… they thought if Curze was slain the Legion would dissolve…'

'Half truths. Half truths and lies.'

'I… I don't understand…'

'Do you know what the Night Haunter's final words to me were? Do you know what he said, as he seated himself and awaited the assassin?'

'N-n–'

'He said "See how the mighty are fallen."'

'W-why?'

'Because he had finally realised what nobody else had ever seen. That his father, his glorious Emperor, his Divine Creator, was just as vicious, just as terrible, just as merciless, as the Night Lords themselves. See how the mighty are fallen. See how divinity lowers itself to dispose of the monster it created.'

One final pulse of rebellion – alone and drowning in a sea of doubt – struggled to be heard in Mita's heart. 'L-lowers itself? By sending an assassin? After all that Konrad Curze had done? After the horrors of the Heresy? What else could the Emperor have done?'

For an instant the doubt seemed to retract. For an instant she felt she'd somehow scored a point; landed a blow.

The Night Lord remained resolutely unphased.

'What else? Nothing, to be sure – if, as you say, the killer was sent to avenge the terrors of the Horus Heresy.' He leaned forwards again, as far as his chains would allow, and his black eyes were pools of oil, sucking her soul down into their lightless depths. 'But, child, the assassin that killed the Night Haunter was not the first to seek him out.'

'W-what?'

'She was the last of a long line. A line that he had evaded at every stroke. A line whose endless attempts had exhausted him beyond his desire to retaliate. He had endured enough, do you understand? He was the hunter! He was the first, and the mightiest! He ruled the shadows! He reigned in the Dark! And then his father rescinded his sanction, and at the end of the Great Crusade, before the Heresy had even begun, he was brought before his lord and his brothers, humiliated, and held to account. Did he betray the Emperor's honour, then? Did he excuse his actions by telling the truth? By revealing to his kin their father's duplicity? No. Loyalty gripped him still, and he endured his father's derision with boundless humility.'

'I remember the tales...' Ancient texts swam through Mita's memories, the echoing spaces of dusty libraries vivid in her mind. 'He attacked his brother-primarch, Rogal Dorn. Where was his loyalty then, Night Lord?'

'Dorn's pomposity infuriated him. Was it not enough that he had toed his father's line, without the chiding of ignorant fools? Of course his temper snapped. Whose would not have?'

Mita opened her mouth, a suitably acidic reply prepared, but stalled herself. There was little acid left in her, and that which remained was certainly not directed at the melancholy creature suspended above.

'What happened?' she breathed.

'My master was confined to his quarters. He sought time to meditate, to confer amongst his honour guard.'

'And?'

'And the conference was interrupted by a black-suited devil. An assassin, child. You understand me? Sent to kill the Night Haunter. Sent to silence his outbursts. Who else could have sent him? Who else but your holy, righteous Emperor? And, witch, remember: this was long before Horus unveiled his treachery and turned from the light.'

'That's... that's impossible...'

'The attack was foiled and my master flew into a rage. Finally he recognised the truth of his father's so-called "justice". He fled from the conference to gather his strength, to consider his movements, to fume at the insult of the attempted murder.

'It was the first of many. Before, during and after the Heresy. On Tsagualsa the Night Haunter stopped running. He built a palace that he knew would be his mausoleum, and he awaited the bitch that would take his head and steal his crown.

'So you see, child, the Haunter was not killed for his part in the Heresy. He was not killed to halt excesses or unsanctioned behaviour. No... no, he was killed by a father who thought nothing *of using him. Of twisting him into a hated monstrosity. Of demanding atrocities and horrors from him to scare his enemies into submission. Of taking from him everything that was pure, everything that was human, and then repaying the sacrifice with betrayal.*

'So tell me this, little witch. Do you still believe you aren't being used? Do you still think you'll find some... some reward in death for your loyal service? Do you still think the hatred of the masses is irrelevant?

'Do you still think your Emperor loves you, girl?'

If she'd had a stomach, if this incorporeal realm had taken form and replaced her astral self with a physical body, she knew she would be vomiting blood at the disgust that gripped her. Disbelief battled certainty; the doubts spiralled and flocked to dominate her whole soul, and like an island sinking beneath the sea, like a ship that had been considered impregnable splintering apart and slipping down into cold and lightless depths, every shred of faith that Mita Ashyn had ever felt in the Emperor of mankind crumbled to dust.

She peered through her tears, raised the gun, and fired.

The chains that bound the Night Lord to his crucifix splintered and unravelled.

Zso Sahaal smiled a savage smile, and tore free of the prison inside his own mind, to reclaim what was his.

PART FIVE: DOMINUS NOX

'We are coming for you!'

–Battle cry of the Night Lords Legion
(*Excommunicate Tratoris*)

ZSO SAHAAL

It was not a gentle awakening.

He arose from the mire of sleep – that psychic trap that the warlock had constructed around him – with red rage in his eyes and every muscle tightening together. He felt the cords stand out on his neck. He felt the knuckles of his hands strain against the flat blades of his claws, brandished before him like a bevy of swords. He felt the talons of his feet – autoreactive pinions studding the periphery of each boot – scratching at the metallic floor on which he'd awoken, pushing him upwards.

All without conscious thought. All at the whim of his fury alone.

He felt the rush of boiling air as his jump pack swooned to life, and the dizzying acceleration as he left the ground.

He felt the soup of hormonal insanity that was his armour's chem-boost deploying into his flesh like a liquid sigh, and for the first time he did not struggle against it. For the first time he welcomed its unsubtle burst; he drew its burning promises into his blood as if accepting a second layer of armour, and he opened his mouth and screamed like a flaming banshee.

There was alien blood patterning his claws before his mind had fully thrown off the shackles of slumber.

They had not expected his revival, that much was clear. He was upon them like a lion before even they, blessed with lightning reactions and impossible grace, could react. The first he clove in two with contemptuous ease, turning away and rolling as he touched down from a shallow swoop, tumbling onto his injured shoulder and springing upright. A second startled xenogen appeared before him, fumbling for its weapon, and he tore through its frail chestplate as he rose. The tips of his claws slipped so far through eldar meat that they cracked the inner orbs of the alien's eye-slits, like branches growing from within. He shook the body away and leapt onwards, luminous fluids drizzling clear.

Somewhere in the crucible of his peripheral senses he registered the tusked inquisitor, standing agog with the Corona clutched in his gloved fingers, and he diverted his aerial leap towards the astonished figure, forgoing the urge to rampage out of control. Beyond, in the decorous shadows of the doorway from the glassy bridge, he could see the witch rise groggily to her feet, held helpless in the ring of vigilant servitors. Inwardly Sahaal spared a curious thought for how long had passed since he was first knocked unconscious. His communion with the young psyker seemed to have lasted a lifetime, whilst in reality scant seconds had passed.

The warlock had not yet placed his elegant fingers upon the horned crown.

Nor shall he!

No sooner had the defiant thought arisen than the antlered fiend itself swept into his path, staff crooked. Sahaal bunched his muscles, preparing to dip aside, to dodge the blast of astral fire the creature was doubtless summoning, when a wall of pain unlike any he had felt before caromed into and through him.

Striking with unerring accuracy, satisfied that its target was otherwise engaged with its warlock master, one of the capering xenos had fired its catapult unnoticed; a spinning shuriken slipping deep into the heart of the grievous wound upon his shoulder, unhindered by armour.

It all but severed his arm.

Howling, struggling to shut out the agony, feeling numbness gripping the dead limb, Sahaal's flight-arc stalled and he twisted in the air, his remaining arm gripping uselessly at nothingness. Thus crippled, slipping towards a ruinous impact, he was ill prepared for the warlock's shrewd intervention.

Lightning engulfed him for the second time. A thick strand of gauss power burst from the creature's blade-tipped staff, needling its way past flesh and bone, sinking dog-toothed jaws into the pulp of his mind. As before, it tweaked at his doubts. It blossomed beneath fields of uncertainty and sadness and urged him to yield, to withdraw, to lock himself away within his own psyche.

It bid him spiral away into blackness.

It stroked at his mind and soothed him, coaxing him to surrender.

Not this time, warpspawn.

This time he was forewarned. This time his mind was not so easily overturned, his vulnerable uncertainties were buried away, and his muscles could no more be overridden than his bitterness could be neutralised.

Above all he was in the grip of a rage of such purity, such strength, that the warlock's machinations could do nothing to deter it.

This time all the psychic tampering in the world could not stop him. He was a juggernaut of phosphorous hate, and he would not be denied his fill of slaughter.

He descended like a swooping hawk, ineffectual psionic incandescence crackling like a halo around him, and punched his remaining claws through the alien's antlered helm with a whoop. Blood and bone scattered like shrapnel, and through its splattered clouds his momentum carried him and his victim's limp body down to the ground, smearing the creature's fluids across his face and his armour.

The remaining eldar reacted as if electrified. They spoke not a word, exchanged not a glance, and fired not a single shot: turning as one and rushing – *blurring* – towards the bright vortex from which they had issued. It swallowed them and dissolved; a pinprick of suspended flame that dwindled and died in their wake.

Sahaal dropped to his knees and shook the warlock's body free from his claws, exhaustion finally overwhelming him. He felt as if he'd spent an eternity struggling; as if he couldn't remember a time without pain and violence. The wound at his shoulder continued to bleed, coagulation impaired by the sliver of alien metal embedded deep within, and every movement sent daggers throughout his body.

He could see already he would never use the arm again.

And then slowly, eyes rolling in their sockets with planetary patience, he lifted his gaze to find the thief. The villain. The Lord Inquisitor Ipoqr Kaustus.

'Servitors!' the tusked man yelped, backing away, his arms wrapped around the Corona like a child clutching at its favoured toy. 'Protect me! Protect me!'

Across the room the bronze machine-men tilted heads to regard their controller, and swivelled jointed limbs towards him. The witch stood dumfounded as they stalked away from her, released abruptly from their attention.

'Kill it!' Kaustus shrieked, stabbing a finger towards Sahaal. 'Keep it away from me!' He staggered through the machines' midst, racing for the doorway beyond them and freedom, taking the Corona Nox with him.

Sahaal sighed. He should have known it wouldn't be so easy.

Once more, like the bitter twist at the end of a sick joke, he watched his sacred prize dwindling into the distance.

The servitors closed in. It seemed he was not yet finished with the day's violence.

And then the hive shook. From base to tip it shuddered; it creaked and groaned as ancient metals strained, and into its colossal walls there thumped massive, fiery ruinous craters.

It seemed as if volcanoes had opened across the city's flanks. The sky blazed with tumbling fire, every face in every part of the hive tilted up to stare in wonder at the quaking ceiling, and in a ruined chamber near the peak of the central palace a crippled Space Marine of the Night Lords Legion smiled a bloody smile, rose to his feet, and faced the machine aggressors closing upon him with his vigour abruptly renewed.

'They're here,' he hissed, to no one but himself. 'They're here!'

MITA ASHYN

MITA CAROMED INTO Inquisitor Kaustus like a vengeful meteor.

She couldn't say exactly what she was thinking. For days her mind had seemed to be a warzone: torn apart, artillery-blasted and entrenched, a ravaged land with its sovereignty contested. If the analogy was valid, then the Night Lord's revelations had been cyclonic warheads; *exterminatus* missiles to cleanse her tortured thoughts of any rational structure.

If once her mind was a warzone, now it was a wasteland.

The Emperor had betrayed his own son, and in so doing had shown himself capable of breathtaking duplicity. How could she go on now, turning the other cheek at every hateful comment, every declamatory 'abomination!' or 'mutant!' hurled at her in the street, no longer safe in the knowledge that the Emperor loved her?

How could she go on with the suspicion that she was being used: a tame little monster, manipulated and abused, only to be cast aside when no longer desired?

The answer, of course, was that she could not. What, then, was left for her?

Nothing. Nothing obvious.

A wasteland.

And now she found herself released from the gun-point attentions of the governor's servitors, alone in an unfamiliar place, unbalanced by crippling quakes that struck the hive and shivered every centimetre of its enormity; and amongst it all there was only a single detail to which she could cling.

Kaustus.

Kaustus, you bastard.

This is all your fault!

He tried to flee past her, the Corona held to his chest in trembling fingers; and the fact that he ignored her, that his eyes barely dipped towards her, simply enraged her further. She was beneath his regard, clearly: a creature so ineffectual that he barely paused as she stepped into his path and, with a feral shriek, launched herself at him.

She might as well have attempted to tackle a stampeding grox.

Rebounding from his power armour with a thump and a sharp crackle – a rib, she guessed, blinking through sudden pain – she had a brief glimpse of the Night Lord through the smoke and ice, spinning and swooping amongst the servitors. In that blurring tableau he seemed to her to be a dervish; a god of blade and flight, dancing between gunfire and slashing at the unresisting metal of his foes.

She wondered if he would come to her assistance if she cried out.

She wondered if she would accept his help if he offered it.

The hive groaned again, dust and smog loosened from the ceiling as titanic forces shook it, and in his haste to flee Kaustus stumbled. Mita seized the opportunity without thinking, screwing up every last vestige of her inner strength, drawing deep on reserves that she barely knew existed, and lashed out with a pulse of psychic force.

She could not invade the inquisitor's mind. That wouldn't stop her from crushing his body.

The force of her own attack astonished her. The inquisitor was blasted from his feet as if struck by a grenade, shredded chaff from his robes scattered upon the air. The Corona slipped from his grasp and skittered across the floor, skidding in eldar blood. Beneath the torn gauze of Kaustus's cloak Mita could see that the very plates of his armour had been splintered; great cracks scuttling across chest and thighs as if struck by an invisible hammer.

Is this what I've been repressing? she wondered, dazzled. *Is this what my faith has been denying me?*

Unfettered by ritual and prayer, unblinkered by needless devotions, the truth was as radiant as the warp itself.

The Emperor does not give me my power. My tutors lied! It is my own!

She was on Kaustus in a flash, straddling his wide chest and beating knuckles across his nose. It snapped with an unpleasant crackle, so she punched it again, and again, venting the maelstrom of frustration and resentment that had been building in her soul for weeks.

'Bastard...' she hissed between blows, catching her breath. '...warp damned empty-skulled bastard!'

He recovered faster than she'd anticipated. Stunned or not, bleeding from a dozen rents, he was still an inquisitor. He still wore armour designed for the angels of the Adeptus Astartes. She should have known he wouldn't stay down so easily.

'Fool girl!' he roared, throwing her off. 'Where is it? Where *is* it?' He dragged himself upright and cast angry eyes across the floor, hunting the Corona Nox. Spotting its oily ring, already gathering a frosty patina, he lunged for it with a cry of triumph, once more forgetting the psyker that had brought him down.

Mita was ready for him. She knew exactly what to do.

One final effort. One final catching of her breath, one final reach down into her soul, clutching for dregs of power. One final attempt at the *Animus Motus*.

The Corona moved, edging away from the inquisitor's grasping fingers.

'Warp take you!' he raged, scrabbling after it. 'Give it to me!'

Another centimetre... another centimetre...

Klunk.

The crown jolted to a halt at the foot of an exhibit plinth; shadowed beneath whatever priceless relic – a leather-bound book, blasted apart in the earlier crossfire – occupied it.

'Ha!' Kaustus roared, locking fingers around its glossy frame. 'Mine!'

Mita smiled, muscles burning with endless fatigue. 'Not yours, you stupid bastard.'

And the security servitor that hung from the vaulted ceiling above the singed plinth blinked its metal eyes, ratcheted its slave-linked weapons towards the intruder it sensed below, and opened fire.

Kaustus fell apart like rotten meat.

Smoke lifted. Mita stared at the shredded morsel that remained of her master with confused feelings; triumph struggling against shame. Somewhere, out in the smoke and fire, the Night Lord shrieked and another servitor collapsed to the ground, torn apart. Mita barely heard it.

Kaustus was still alive. Just.

'C... clever...' he smiled, blood slipping in frothing streamers from his mouth, patterning his tusks like scarlet totems. He winced, pain consuming his ruined form. 'Clever trick...'

She nodded, frowning. Something strange had happened to the inquisitor's mind, like a cloud passing from before the sun, and abruptly she found herself able to feel it, able to skim its surface emotions – pain, mostly – just as she could anyone else.

Abruptly she understood.

'The eldar,' she whispered, thunderstruck. 'They've been controlling you from the beginning...'

'Y...yes. C-came to me before I recruited you. Did things... *hkk*... things to my brain. Th-the voices... oh God-Emperor...'

'Why? Warpdammit, Kaustus – *why*?'

'H...*hah*... Who knows? S-sometimes... sometimes the control faltered. Sometimes I could think clearly... *nnk*... hear their whispers... It meant nothing...'

She remembered the moments of uncertainty, the troubling instants in which his mind had seemed to convulse; briefly visible to her psychic senses.

She'd feared for his sanity. If only she'd known the truth.

He'd been a puppet, struggling to cut his own strings.

'That's why you let me live...' she said, understanding flourishing. Another blast rocked the hive, tremors slipping through ice and steel. She ignored it: it was all background noise, irrelevant. 'That's why you never had me executed.'

He struggled to speak, blood puddling beneath him. 'I th-thought... I thought I could overcome it... The voices – Emperor preserve me – I... I thought I could resist. I-I was wrong. But sometimes... *nn*... sometimes I could... could fool them. I made them think you would be a help. I... I recruited you. They wanted me to kill you b-but... But I knew... I knew you'd be the one... to set me free...'

The light went out of his eyes. The Corona fell from his hand and rolled, slick with blood, wobbling as it tumbled, and she lifted it as it passed her, blinking tears from her eyes.

Such a simple thing. Such a little thing.

And then the world went white, and the gallery room pitched like a sinking ship, and the wall beside her was torn away like paper, crumpled in hands of razor steel.

Ice swarmed in through the rent, and with it came a wave of such agony that she screamed and screamed until her throat was raw.

Pain filled the universe. A shrieking like a million banshees drowned her senses, and clouds – *worlds* – of darkness stormed into the air. The warp lazed into reality like a descending blade, and every light that had ever existed was snuffed, every happiness was shredded, every quiet joy and instant of ecstasy was swallowed up and burned away.

A giant stood at the threshold of the shredded wall. It folded wings of tattered leather; wings that slipped between material and ether as if on fire, venting smoke and ash. It moved on legs of incorporeality; it bled across the spaces of the cavern like an echo of a figure.

It was not real.

It was more than real.

It was Chaos given form.

And through psychic torture that blinded her, through the shrieking of warp-beasts that exploded her ears, through coils of darkness that snared her soul and promised damnation to all who felt their touch, she saw the Night Lord Zso Sahaal stagger from the smoke and frost, arm hanging limp, face bleeding from a dozen cuts, and stare up at the vision of terror incarnate that had defiled reality with its presence.

'It's been a long time, Acerbus,' he growled. 'I barely recognise you.'

ZSO SAHAAL

He was too late.

He knew it the instant his ancient brother insinuated himself upon the chamber, like an infection taking root. There was no place for focus, here. No hope of reclaiming his master's legacy. No hope of inflicting order and control upon a creature so utterly lost to Chaos.

The daemon prince that had once been Krieg Acerbus paused, shadows shifting despite its stillness, and eyes that had once been human glared down upon Sahaal and narrowed.

'You're smaller than I remember...' it said, amused. Its voice was a thing of mingled screams and the echoes of tortured souls, harmonised and directed. It bypassed sound and arrived fully formed, like a migraine, in the centre of Sahaal's brain.

He fought the urge to vomit. The creature radiated despair as a fire emits heat, and he felt it coil through his senses, churning his confidence to paste, reducing every triumph he had ever enjoyed to failure.

That the creature was Krieg Acerbus was beyond doubt. He was changed almost beyond belief, but still there remained about him some essence of self; some expression of his eyes, perhaps, that betrayed his identity. He had always seemed monstrous to Sahaal: now his outward appearance had merely altered to reflect its inward counterpart.

He had grown massive. Where once there had been armour now there was iron flesh; living warpstuff that writhed and tightened, swarming with wicked runes. He was no longer a thing of corporeality; that much was clear. In every dimension he ghosted and hardened, then faded to smoke, as if uncomfortable with solidity: burning with immaterial energies that flared not with light, but with dark. Smouldering emissions poured from his long limbs like steam from a smithy, tentacles of shadow bulged from his spine, and when he moved, when he unfurled the shadows that crooked upon his shoulders like a vulture's wings, it was as if the existence of light itself was forgotten. It was as if perpetual night had arisen, and morning would never arrive.

At the tips of arms so long they plucked at the floor, claws glittered and spat sparks: forged not from flesh nor metal, but from the raw stuff of darkness itself.

They made the air bleed.

'Where,' Sahaal said, pushing down the stifling failure, denying it for a sweet second longer, bolstering himself with foundationless courage, 'is my Legion?'

The beast crooked its pale face, sneered through lipless jaws, and aimed a smoking talon at the rent in the wall.

Sahaal approached the torn metal like a cripple; limping from more wounds than he could count, wincing at every movement, his dead arm hanging by a nerveless thread at his side.

The skies of Equixus were on fire.

An orbital bombardment had been the first step. Great glittering teardrops of incandescence flared below the clouds, hurtling down at impossible speeds to inflict ruinous tears across the city's surface. Those few defences untouched by the Shadowkin attacks were picked clear one by one, gouged from the surface like tumours, and with each impact shredded metal churned up and out, the hive wobbled as if shaken to its core, and thousands upon thousands died.

The Raptors followed the bombardment, and in the face of their dizzying descents Sahaal's hopes were crushed further. These were not the agile warriors whose kind he had created. These were not the assault squads he had formed and trained an aeon ago; spreading amongst the other Legions as their successes became legend. These were not the Raptors he knew.

They came like daemon vultures, chainswords snarling, pistols flaring in the snow-choked sky. They whooped and cackled and shrieked, and their twisted armour shimmered with unholy light, like an ember's dying glow. Ghastly deathmasks patterned ancient helmets, crooked forwards in beak-like snarls and aquiline grimaces. They flocked above the hive like carrion birds, gathering for a feast, and when they dived together the sky was filled with their ululations and the hissing of whatever unnatural forces buoyed them up. They were a plague, Sahaal thought, and as they vanished one by one inside the wounds of the hive's surface he slipped to his knees, his mind rebelling against what it witnessed.

And then the warriors themselves: a rain of drop pods and assault craft that vomited from the heaving stormclouds, smashing against the city's shell like hammers pounding anvils. In lightning-flash tableaux and the stolen flare of detonating munitions Sahaal could glimpse the ranks of his so-called brothers as they fell upon the crowds within.

Blue and bronze whirlwinds. Without grace or poise. Frenzied. Out of control.

Utterly Chaotic.

The Night Lords descended upon Equixus like a bloody rain, and the screams of the population drowned out even the howling of the perpetual ice storm.

Oh, my master... What have they done?

What have they become?

The failure was a firebrand, slipping into his eyes. It was a tidal wave; the bow-blast of a supernova, rolling and boiling to devour him whole. It settled on his shoulders like the weight of the galaxy itself, and he felt every bone in his body splinter to dust, every blood vessel burst, every atom of every part of him split and die.

He was too late.

He wondered if he'd already known, deep within himself. Perhaps he had *always* known; since awaking in the ruptured belly of the *Umbrea Insidior*. Too long had passed. Too many centuries had glided by, bereft of his influence and leadership. His master had chosen him as his heir to bring focus to a Legion in peril; to unite a body that threatened to tear itself apart; to offer some measure of temperance against the whispering seductions of power and rage. He had been selected as the Legion's deliverance from corruption, and he had not been present to fulfil his vows.

One hundred centuries – unguided, unprotected – was more than long enough to succumb.

The Daemonlord Acerbus hissed behind him, delighted by the carnage enacted below. Howls rose like smoke: the shrieks of dying men, the moans of tortured women, the tears of youths.

'This is without purpose…' Sahaal whispered, gazing down into the flames. 'Where is the sense in this? Have you no worthier targets than women and children?'

'Every target is worthy,' the Daemonlord breathed; waves of despair carrying his voice. 'And the purpose…? Little Talonmaster, do you not remember our master's lessons? The purpose is fear. It is *always* fear.'

Sahaal turned to face the abomination, tears in his eyes, and above him it drew sensuous claws across its incorporeal chest, eyes closed, face upturned, as if savouring a fine scent.

'Do you taste it?' it whispered. 'Do you taste the terror of this world? It is… *mm*… it is intoxicating…'

Sahaal felt disgust engulf him.

'You *dare* to lecture me on the Night Haunter's lessons?' he snarled, anger gripping him, breaking through the shame and failure like a hatching beast. 'You *dare*, when you've fallen so far from his wisdom? Fear is the weapon, fool, not the goal!'

The devil crooned, maw spreading in delight.

'Ah… Righteous little Sahaal. How I have missed you…'

'Look at you! Look at what you've become! You've spat in the face of his legacy. Have you no shame?'

'Our master's legacy lives, little Sahaal.' The beast brandished a fist, clenching claws together. 'Through me, it *prospers*.'

Sahaal's bolter was in his hand before he had even considered drawing it.

'You are not fit to call yourself a Night Lord,' he said, and squeezed the trigger.

The *Mordax Tenebrae* spat shells like a hateful dragon. With every blast he saw his master's haunted features, heard his soothing words. With every shell he whispered his master's name.

And then the smoke cleared, and he saw that he'd barely scratched the monster's skin. Through boiling frost clouds and shifting shadows its eyes burned, and before Sahaal had even registered movement its great paw slipped from the smog and swatted him like a fly. His armour cracked.

He crossed the room on his back.

'You,' Acerbus said, pouncing across him at a speed inconceivable in a creature so massive, holding him down with invisible cords of warpstuff and poking with child-like interest at the wound on his shoulder, 'should have more respect for your lord.'

His whole body burned. Each vicious slash-stab, each playing prod of the daemon's claws, was a universe of agony compressed upon his brain.

Acerbus ate his fear and crooned to himself.

'You'll never be my lord!' Sahaal stormed, reserves of rage spilling through the cracked edges of his soul. 'The Haunter chose me! *I* was the heir to the Corona Nox!'

'Little Sahaal. Little Sahaal…' the beast shook its head, smoke oozing from burning eyes. 'So foolish… You were never its heir. You were merely its keeper.'

'Spare me your lies, scum! Let me up! Fight me!'

'*Ha*… Have you never considered, little Sahaal, that Konrad Curze intended all of this?'

'How dare you speak his n–'

'He had seen his own death. He had tasted the future. You know that. It plagued him all his life.'

'W... What of it?'

'Do you truly believe, foolish little Sahaal, that he had not foreseen your disappearance? Do you truly believe he did not know you would be lost to this galaxy for ten thousand years? Have you never asked yourself why he would allow such a thing?'

'I... I...'

Lights bulged before his eyes. His world quivered around him.

It couldn't be true. The Haunter had never foreseen it!

Acerbus's voice was a poisoned needle, pumping toxins into his brain. 'Of course he knew,' it hissed. 'He understood his own soul better than anyone. He understood the division in his heart. He understood the choices before him.'

'But he chose me... he chose me!'

'He chose *me*, Sahaal. He knew that he was two men. One was... just and righteous–' the daemon spat the words, disgusted '–whilst the other... *mm*... the other had felt the kiss of Chaos all its life. One thrived on focus. The other *ate fear*.'

'And he chose the first, damn you! He spurned Chaos! He chose me!'

'No.' The claws scooped at the flesh of his shoulder, igniting every nerve in his body. The voice was relentless, crumbling every bastion of his resistance. 'He fooled himself. He was divided, but the dark side was strongest. He had foreseen the fate of the Corona, so he bequeathed it to you. He set you to chase after it like some vapid dog, doomed to an era of sleep. He sent you away, so your... *ha*... your worthy witterings could not obscure his vision. His vision of a Legion that sowed fear in his name. A Legion to eat the terror of the Imperium. He knew you would never accept such a thing. He knew you had to be removed.' The beast leaned down, so close that its fanged maw all but touched Sahaal's cheek. Hot breath washed over him.

'He condemned you to your prison, little Sahaal. He *exiled you.*'

'No! You're lying! If that were true he would have simply killed me!'

'And leave the Corona unguarded? Leave his killer to steal it? Use your sense, Sahaal.'

'But he told me everything! The... the sanctioned genocides! The Emperor's betrayal! The assassin before the Heresy!'

'Lies. The whispers of his Chaotic side, pouring poison in the ear of his virtuous self. Perhaps... *hah*... perhaps he even believed it himself.'

Sahaal's brain collapsed upon itself. This would not stand. He could not allow himself an instant's doubt. He could not permit the suggestion – the *suspicion* – that Acerbus spoke the truth. To do otherwise would be to make a lie of everything he had ever believed, and everything he had struggled to achieve.

The Daemonlord was wrong. That was all there was to it.

'You're lying, warpshit!' he snarled, spitting in the creature's face. 'The Corona is mine! He gave it to me!'

'Ah... ah yes, the Corona. I have been without it long enough. I think I should like to have it now.' The creature dug claws further into Sahaal's wound, twisting with a vicious grin. 'Where is it?'

A voice spoke from nearby.

'It's right here, you bastard.'

It was the witch. Little Mita Ashyn, the woman who had set Sahaal free. She stood with blood pouring from her eyes, legs shaking at the tumult of psychic revulsion pouring from the monster, the Corona brandished before her like a halo of darkness. She looked on the verge of insanity and death, and were it not for a single detail, a single redeeming facet, Sahaal might have cursed her for all of eternity, for presenting the prize to the Daemonlord.

In her spare hand she held a melta gun – prised, no doubt, from the dead fingers of a broken servitor.

She smiled.

The melta-stream hit Acerbus full in the chest, and he barrelled away from it as if struck by a rogue meteor. The indistinct tentacles that held Sahaal down whipped away, tangled amongst the devastation of the tumbling beast. It roared so hard that the hive seemed to shake, flexing and mewling at a wound on its front; as if a great scoop had been plucked from its flesh. Raw warpstuff – liquid gore that glimmered and dissolved even as it touched the air – geysered from the crater, becoming smoke and ether before even hitting the ground.

Sahaal was on his feet and sprinting before the beast's collapse was complete. He had no energy to speak of, his mind was a wreckage without hope of salvage, and every truth he had every believed had been stolen from him. In all the world, in all the brutal realities of the galaxy, one thing alone held any meaning.

'The Corona!' he roared, leaping towards the witch. 'Give me the Corona!'

Acerbus was faster.

Like a striking crow, like shadow-wreathed lightning, he was on her, swatting Sahaal aside with a deft flick of his midnight claws and pinioning her to the floor, great tendrils of smoke and shadow tightening around her arms and ankles, wings opening like a canopy of perpetual night. The melta gun crumpled in his grip.

She screamed and screamed and never stopped.

The Daemonlord leaned close to her face, running a broad tongue across her cheek. 'Mm...' he mewled, intoxicated. 'Her fear is... *exquisite*...'

Sahaal leapt at his brother with a wordless howl, stabbing out with claws outstretched, hacking through semi-real pseudopods of smoke and dark. The Daemonlord spun to face him, spined shoulders glittering in constellations of darkness, amused at the crippled warrior's truculent attack.

Claw met claw like the peeling of razor bells, and for long instants the pair slashed and stabbed, parrying blows that would split a man in two. Sahaal found himself dancing between bloody-tipped blurs, leaping above vengeful thrusts and spinning through blows like hail, never more than a moment ahead of his foe's attacks.

Acerbus was playing with him.

Let him.

Sahaal changed tack with a feral growl. Twisting his body, wincing as wounds reopened and ribs crackled at unpleasant contortions, he slipped away from the savage blades and pounced towards Mita. Blows landed on his back, gashing him open, flooding his senses with fire and fear, but none of it mattered. Only the Corona.

He cut the witch free of the boiling limbs that held her and dragged her to her feet, gore pouring from his wrecked body. Holding her tight against his shoulder with his one useful arm, he staggered with her towards the great rent in the wall and stared out at the shifting tempests of Equixus. Ice bathed him: a frozen baptism to cleanse his tormented mind. Somewhere behind him the Daemonlord realised what was happening; howling at the thought of his prey's escape. Sahaal bunched his legs; final reserves of energy pushing him out into the void.

Let the storm swallow him. Let the ice enfold him.

Let the darkness claim him as its own.

He had the witch. The witch had the Corona. Nothing else mattered.

And then the daemon oozed from the smoke at his back with a roar, fire spouting from hate-filled eyes, and snatched at the witch's arm.

The limb parted from its shoulder with a wrench and a sticky slurp.

The Corona Nox tumbled from slack fingers and spun, tilting and flipping over, catching the firelight of a dying world in a single glorious reflection–

–and then it was gone: tumbling end over end into the smoke and the fire and the ice, dwindling away along the sides of the hive until darkness swallowed it.

The witch screamed, blood pulsing from the open wound. The Daemon Prince Krieg Acerbus roared so loud that the windows of the gallery room burst, like droplets falling from a fountain.

And Zso Sahaal, the Talonmaster, heir to the throne of the Night Lords Legion, pushed himself out into the void – his jump pack flaring in the endless dark, the witch howling from her perch upon his ruined shoulder – and chased his legacy down into the abyss.

He would not give up.

The Corona Nox would be his.

He would bring the vengeance of the Night Haunter upon the heads of those that stood in his way.

One day he would kill Krieg Acerbus. He would lead his Legion once more.

One day he would descend from the skies of Holy Terra, and set his claws upon the bulwarks of the Palace itself.

One day, in the name of his master, he would have his revenge upon the Traitor Emperor.

Ave Dominus Nox!

EPILOGUE

Rec: Congresium Xenos
Dis: Inq. Palinus
Conduit Path: Tarith–
Maneus–
Pirras–
J'ho
Ref: INQ5#23-33
Sub: Disappearance/Kaustus

INCIDENT AT EQUIXUS

My lords,

I have set foot upon Equixus, and I believe it is a memory that shall haunt me until my death.

You will recall that I was dispatched some weeks ago to investigate the disappearance of Inquisitor Ipoqr Kaustus.

At the point of my departure he had failed to engage the ordo in routine report for three consecutive years. Whilst hardly an exceptional hiatus, given the clandestine nature of his work, this was considered uncharacteristic. Kaustus's record indicates a level of assidiousness in such matters that rendered his silence troubling and, in the name of our blessed organisation, I set out to follow his trail in earnest.

My lords, I shall not burden you with the oblique course upon which the subject had meandered. Of most relevance are surely his final movements: a brief (and indeed unofficial) visitation aboard the Pervigilium Oculus, *and an even more contrite stay at the Inquisitorial fortress-world Safaur-Inquis (also unrecorded). His rendezvous with the former, as chance would dictate, coincided with its commission by Munitorum officials as a sanctioned surveillance craft, tasked with maintaining a discreet watch over the eldar craftworld 'Iyanden'. His presence on Safaur Inquis is less opaque, although it is known that he recruited a new interrogator – a woman named Ashyn – during his visit.*

From there the trail takes the erstwhile inquisitor to the hive-world Equixus, and here my investigation bore fruit. It is impossible to state with any certainty why Kaustus and his retinue travelled here (although, given the high incidence of Tauist cells amongst worlds in this region, perhaps we may speculate?), but we can be very clear on a single point:

Equixus is where Inquisitor Kaustus died.

Approximately one month before my arrival upon this world, the Night Lords Chaos Marine Legion descended upon the planet – for reasons of their own – and in the course of a single day brought unimaginable carnage to its people. I have spent two weeks with my retinue in the anarchic wasteland that remains, witnessing the deaths of hundreds from exposure and hunger, attempting in vain to uncover some reason for the Traitors' attack. I have found none.

My lords, the sheer enormity of the slaughter at Equixus would seem to draw a veil across the investigation. Certainly Kaustus did not leave the planet – my Magos Biologis identified what little remained of his body from gene-records shortly before our departure – and it is tempting to think of that, therefore, as the end to the whole affair.

There is, however, a single troubling enigma that continues to allude my logic:

Telemetry from the aforemention Pervigilium Oculus *indicates that a sizeable flotilla of renegade vessels – notably including the* Vastitas Victris *(long suspected of harbouring the Night Lords' highest commanders) – was gathering near to the Iyanden craftworld at the time of Kaustus's visit. Cogitator matrices had indicated a 93.2% probability that the Chaos fleet planned to attack the craftworld itself.*

The assault never occurred: for whatever reason the Night Lords diverted their attentions towards Equixus, sparing the eldar from harm.

It would be remiss of me to suggest that Kaustus in some way precipitated the genocide upon Equixus. The Night Lords have a reputation for impulsive, arbitrary movements, and it is indeed unlikely – even if he were involved somehow – that the presence of a single inquisitor would have swayed their plans. Nonetheless, it is a curious coincidence that Kaustus was present in each locale that the renegades selected for their muster: a coincidence that is ultimately of benefit to nobody except the eldar.

Did they have a hand in this? Had they somehow anticipated an attack upon their fragile craftworld, from some distant point in the past, and sought – somehow – to divert it elsewhere? My lords, it is unlikely we shall ever know.

Kaustus is dead. Equixus has become a morgue. There is nothing else to say.

In Service to the Holy Emperor of Man,

Inquisitor Palinus, Ordo Xenos

Addendum:

MY LORDS, FORGIVE *this brief postscript. I was on the verge of dispatching the above report when I encountered a further, tantalising, nugget of information.*

Two days' travel from the Equixus system is the colony world Baih'Rus. As we passed by, preparing to enter the warp, my crew exchanged routine recognition codes with the long-obsolete clipper that comprises the entirety of that worlds' orbital security. Upon receipt of Inquisitorial codes the clipper's captain indicated surprise, questioning aloud why there should be such a strong Inquisitorial presence in the region. Perplexed, I demanded to know what he meant.

It transpires that a week ago another vessel passed near Baih'Rus: a small shuttlecraft formerly registered to the merchant starport on Equixus. When hailed the pilot – a woman – produced Inquisitorial recognition codes only slightly inferior to my own. As is his habit, the captain of the clipper ordered his sanctioned astropath to conduct a 'headcount', a psychic sweep to indicate crew numbers. This command was duly obeyed.

Shortly before dying ('screaming and bleeding like someone took a piss in his brain,' as the captain so delicately put it), the astropath indicated the presence of two souls aboard – one male, one female.

Whether relevant to the disappearance of Kaustus or not, or whether merely a part of a greater picture than I am presently unable to determine, I felt it wise to bring this curious incident to your attention. It seems that whatever truly occurred upon Equixus, solutions to its mysteries shall continue to elude us a while longer.

–Palinus

ABOUT THE AUTHOR

Simon Spurrier has been writing since an early age, successfully having his work published first in the form of comics and latterly in prose fiction. Since earning a degree in Film Production and a bursary to attend the inaugural Screenwriting class of the National Academy of Writing, he has become a frequent contributor to titles such as *2000AD*, the *Warhammer Comic* and the *Megazine*. His prose work includes several short stories for *Inferno!* magazine and, to date, three novels. *Lord of the Night* is his second Black Library novel.

Read till you Bleed

Do you have them all?

1 Trollslayer – William King
2 First & Only – Dan Abnett
3 Skavenslayer – William King
4 Into the Maelstrom – Ed. Marc Gascoigne & Andy Jones
5 Daemonslayer – William King
6 Eye of Terror – Barrington J Bayley
7 Space Wolf – William King
8 Realm of Chaos – Ed. Marc Gascoigne & Andy Jones
9 Ghostmaker – Dan Abnett
10 Hammers of Ulric – Dan Abnett, Nik Vincent & James Wallis
11 Ragnar's Claw – William King
12 Status: Deadzone – Ed. Marc Gascoigne & Andy Jones

13 Dragonslayer – William King
14 The Wine of Dreams – Brian Craig
15 Necropolis – Dan Abnett
16 13th Legion – Gav Thorpe
17 Dark Imperium – Ed. Marc Gascoigne & Andy Jones
18 Beastslayer – William King
19 Gilead's Blood – Abnett & Vincent
20 Pawns of Chaos – Brian Craig
21 Xenos – Dan Abnett
22 Lords of Valour – Ed. Marc Gascoigne & Christian Dunn
23 Execution Hour – Gordon Rennie
24 Honour Guard – Dan Abnett
25 Vampireslayer – William King
26 Kill Team – Gav Thorpe
27 Drachenfels – Jack Yeovil
28 Deathwing – Ed. David Pringle & Neil Jones
29 Zavant – Gordon Rennie
30 Malleus – Dan Abnett
31 Konrad – David Ferring
32 Nightbringer – Graham McNeill
33 Genevieve Undead – Jack Yeovil
34 Grey Hunter – William King
35 Shadowbreed – David Ferring
36 Words of Blood – Ed. Marc Gascoigne & Christian Dunn
37 Zaragoz – Brian Craig
38 The Guns of Tanith – Dan Abnett
39 Warblade – David Ferring
40 Farseer – William King
41 Beasts in Velvet – Jack Yeovil
42 Hereticus – Dan Abnett
43 The Laughter of Dark Gods – Ed. David Pringle
44 Plague Daemon – Brian Craig
45 Storm of Iron – Graham McNeill
46 The Claws of Chaos – Gav Thorpe
47 Draco – Ian Watson
48 Silver Nails – Jack Yeovil
49 Soul Drinker – Ben Counter
50 Harlequin – Ian Watson
51 Storm Warriors – Brian Craig
52 Straight Silver – Dan Abnett
53 Star of Erengrad – Neil McIntosh
54 Chaos Child – Ian Watson
55 The Dead & the Damned – Jonathan Green
56 Shadow Point – Gordon Rennie
57 Blood Money – C L Werner

WWW.BLACKLIBRARY.COM

58 Angels of Darkness – Gav Thorpe
59 Mark of Damnation – James Wallis
60 Warriors of Ultramar – Graham McNeill
61 Riders of the Dead – Dan Abnett
62 Daemon World – Ben Counter
63 Giantslayer – William King
64 Crucible of War – Ed. Marc Gascoigne & Christian Dunn
65 Honour of the Grave – Robin D Laws
66 Crossfire – Matthew Farrer
67 Blood & Steel – C L Werner
68 Crusade for Armageddon – Jonathan Green
69 Way of the Dead – Ed. Marc Gascoigne & Christian Dunn
70 Sabbat Martyr – Dan Abnett

71 Taint of Evil – Neil McIntosh
72 Fire Warrior – Simon Spurrier
73 The Blades of Chaos – Gav Thorpe
74 Gotrek and Felix Omnibus 1 – William King
75 Gaunt's Ghosts: The Founding – Dan Abnett
76 Wolfblade – William King
77 Mark of Heresy – James Wallis
78 For the Emperor – Sandy Mitchell
79 The Ambassador – Graham McNeill
80 The Bleeding Chalice – Ben Counter
81 Caves of Ice – Sandy Mitchell
82 Witch Hunter – C L Werner
83 Ravenor – Dan Abnett

84 Magestorm – Jonathan Green
85 Annihilation Squad – Gav Thorpe
86 Ursun's Teeth – Graham McNeill
87 What Price Victory – Ed. Marc Gascoigne & Christian Dunn
88 The Burning Shore – Robert Earl
89 Grey Knights – Ben Counter
90 Swords of the Empire – Ed. Marc Gascoigne & Christian Dunn
91 Double Eagle – Dan Abnett
92 Sacred Flesh – Robin D Laws
93 Legacy – Matthew Farrer
94 Iron Hands – Jonathan Green
95 The Inquisition War – Ian Watson
96 Blood of the Dragon – C L Werner
97 Traitor General – Dan Abnett
98 The Heart of Chaos – Gav Thorpe
99 Dead Sky, Black Sun – Graham McNeill
100 Wild Kingdoms – Robert Earl
101 Gotrek & Felix Omnibus 2 – William King
102 Gaunt's Ghosts: The Saint – Dan Abnett
103 Dawn of War – CS Goto
104 Forged in Battle – Justin Hunter
105 Blood Angels: Deus Encarmine – James Swallow
106 Eisenhorn – Dan Abnett
107 Valnir's Bane – Nathan Long
108 Lord of the Night – Simon Spurrier
109 Necromancer – Jonathan Green